6/15

LOVERS & FIGHTERS, STARSHIPS & DRAGONS

LOVERS & FIGHTERS, STARSHIPS & DRAGONS
Twelve Science Fiction Stories

by Tom Purdom

In-house editor: Darrell Schweitzer

Fantastic Books
1380 East 17 Street, Suite 2233
Brooklyn, New York 11230
www.FantasticBooks.biz

ISBN 10: 1-61720-943-0
ISBN 13: 978-1-61720-943-7

First Edition

For Sara,
for all the circling years

Table of Contents

INTRODUCTION

"When people live on the shores of unexplored seas," Tom Purdom once wrote, "they make up stories about the marvels and monsters that may be hidden on mysterious islands and unknown continents. Modern humans live, in effect, on the edge of two seas: the galaxy and the future. Science fiction writers spin stories about those two seas in the same way the Greeks told stories about islands in the Mediterranean and Shakespeare wrote about the wizards and spirits who inhabited an island in the Atlantic. Their work arises from an impulse that's been part of our makeup since we first started sitting around campfires."

It is tempting, when writing about Tom Purdom, to dwell upon his longevity as a writer. He made his first two sales in 1957, after all, and as of this writing, coming on sixty years later, he's still going strong. But that accomplishment, pleasant though it is, pales beside the fact that the stories he is writing today and the ideas that drive them are fresh and original. The sad truth is that writers tend to stale with age, to repeat themselves and to recycle ideas that the passing decades have rendered all too familiar. Not so Purdom. The impulse to tell stories remains the same as it ever was, but his are written not by the firelight of the past but by the quiet glow of a computer screen filled with the latest developments in science and technology.

The very best example of this is the first story in this book, "Fossil Games," a tale of posthumans whose intelligence is so highly enhanced that in conversation they'll switch between machine-generated and music-based languages in order to convey nuances of mood and yet so outclassed by their contemporaries that they must flee Earth in search of a sanctuary for inferior minds. It is a cascade of brilliant ideas worthy of Greg Egan or Stephen Baxter at their best. On my first reading, I could all but hear the plates of my skull creaking as my brain swelled with the effort of following his characters' thinking. Yet the writing is smooth and the narrative flows naturally from beginning to end. It is a genuine *tour de force* and a terrific introduction to the pleasures of Purdom's fiction.

This story also incorporates several of Purdom's signature intellectual themes. The most striking of which is his ongoing portrayal of future societies that are gentler and more humane than our own. The very worst of the people he portrays here are far better than we are today. So when conflict breaks out, it is genuinely shocking, even though the form it takes is as nothing compared to what we ourselves are capable of. As technology makes us wealthier and more comfortable, Purdom suggests, we will increasingly have the luxury of being good.

Which is not to say that he expects the painful aspects of the human condition to go away. As witness "Canary Land," Purdom's meditation on the immigrant experience. George Sparr is a brilliant geneticist, but not quite good enough to find employment on Earth. But when he migrates to the Moon in search of a new start, he finds he has only traded one trap for another. Encumbered with a pidgin-level understanding of Techno-Mandarin, the only work he can find is a minimum wage job playing classical music—an easily programmed skill—for uninterested restaurant-goers. And then things get worse.

This might be a good place to mention that Purdom is a music critic, and as such, much beloved in the Philadelphia classical music scene. Music is recurrent in his fiction, sometimes as a subject but often simply as one of the things civilized people do.

Purdom's stories follow the classic science fiction form: a dramatic situation created by technological change which could well happen in the future, embodied in the lives of those people most movingly affected by that change. So it's no coincidence that the recurrent themes of his fiction are those actions in which human beings are most commonly involved. Including, as this collection's title implies, love and war.

"Haggle Chips" and "The Path of the Transgressor" are not love stories, though they superficially resemble the form, but science fictional explorations of the nature of love. Both involve imprinting techniques whose effects are very much like—but not identical to—the workings of love. The questions raised in the first story are, by my reading anyway, resoundingly answered in the second. To say more would be to give away too much. But it's strange to reflect on how rare such explorations are in science fiction. And it's to Tom Purdom's credit how often he returns to this question.

Of Purdom's interest in military tactics and military culture, however, much more can be said. "Dragon Drill" is set in an only-slightly mythologized Eighteenth Century, at a moment when the world turns decisively away from fantasy and superstition and toward science and reason. When a creature out of dreams and chaos threatens the common good, it must be countered by the very latest in technology: military drill. This is a marvelous whimsy, rigorously researched and worked out. But pay attention to the critiques of the Hapsburg princess: Purdom's stories are never about only *one* thing.

Purdom, the son of a submariner, grew up in a Navy family, and this colors his military fiction, which is not so much about war as about the people caught up in it. He has also had a lifelong interest in war gaming, which in "Sheltering" allows him to explore the relationship between real and imagined warfare. "Legacies," however, is specifically about military professionals and their families. It is a careful exploration not only of how they think but of why they must do so in that particular way in order to be effective.

And the interaction between Medical Captain Dorothy Min and her father is perfect.

"The Mists of Time," which closes out this book, is made up of two interwoven tales of conflict. One is the story of a young British Navy officer engaged in fighting the slave trade, very much in the tradition of C.S. Forester and Patrick O'Brien. The other is an intellectual struggle between two future observers over how best to interpret that officer's actions. Is he engaged in a noble cause—or simply out for prize money? It is a question that can only be answered by someone who understands the military mind.

This failure of people outside of a particular sub-culture to understand its values and reasoning is also central to "Research Project." In the frame story Jinny, a bright young student, is researching an assigned paper. Her project is based on an historical event, the fleeting contact with alien colonizers desirous of settling in the Solar System. In the core story Postri-Dem, the alien scholar-negotiator, and his human counterpart, Dr. Orlando Mazzeri, strive to achieve common understanding for their peoples though a furious exchange of information, all the while hoping to prevent a disastrous clash of civilizations.

There are many pleasures to be found here, including the speculations on the alternative evolution of intelligence from swamp-dwelling herbivores and the creation of an alien psychology based on that past. But to me the greatest pleasure was finding out why it was important to tell the story through the eyes of a bookish young lady.

I have seen reviews of "Bonding With Morry" stating that it's about an old man learning to bond with his service robot. But that would be banal, and Purdom is never banal. Rather, the old man's fight is to retain his clear understanding of the difference between people and appliances. This does, however, raise the opportunity to point out that Purdom's treatment of people is as meticulously thought through as his treatment of technology. The small battles that Morry fights against those whose sentimentality renders them blind to the human beings standing before them might seem pointless in the face of his impending death. But they are what make him a person worth respecting.

In "Sepoy," the Tucfra Hegemony has seized control of the Earth in order to save it from destruction—while at the same time enriching themselves by skimming off the top fifteen percent of its GDP. Jason Jardanel, crippled from childhood by a lingering bioweapon disease, is approached by a recruiter for the tucfra, who need human employees—the equivalent of the Indian sepoys who fought for their British conquerors—to run the world for them. She offers him the ultimate incentive, a new and healthy body, in exchange for becoming that most despised of human beings—a collaborator.

The rest of the story, like so much of Purdom's work, is the acting-out of a moral situation where neither side has the advantage of being entirely in the right.

"A Response From EST17" is another of Purdom's most inventive stories. A probe the size of a soccer ball, containing the electronic avatars of its human sponsors, arrives at an extrasolar planet to discover both intelligent life and a competing probe. Beginning with machines that could be mistaken for viruses, they start building an observation post. But though their behavior toward the aliens is inherently ethical, "microwar" breaks out between the two probes. The newly discovered civilization, however, knows more about the observers than they suspect. Worse, the aliens have a horrifying past and terrifying intentions.

Tom Purdom is an advocate of Frederik Pohl's description of good science fiction being stories about "interesting people doing interesting things in an interesting future"—to which he adds a fourth quality, that the author should have an interesting point of view.

By all four standards, Purdom's work comes up aces.

It perhaps says more about me than about Purdom that I love best the stories that have the highest idea content. But however you order them and whichever you prefer, there's not a clunker in the lot. This is a book I have been yearning for, along with many more of Purdom's fans, for a long time. It is a scattering of island-stories to be found somewhere in the future, elsewhere in the galaxy. It is a delight to read.

There will, I profoundly hope, be more.

Enjoy.

—Michael Swanwick

To me, a science fiction story is primarily a story about people coping with some development that could take place in the future. There are other kinds of science fiction but I think of that as the core of the genre. Sometimes, of course, they have to cope with several developments simultaneously....

FOSSIL GAMES

Morgan's mother and father had given him a state-of-the-art inheritance. It was only state-of-the-art-2117 but they had seen where the world was going. They had mortgaged twenty percent of their future income so they could order a package that included all the genetic enhancements Morgan's chromosomes could absorb, along with two full decades of postnatal development programs. Morgan was in his fifties when his father committed suicide. By that time his father could barely communicate with half the people he encountered in his day to day business activities.

Morgan's mother survived by working as a low-level freelance prostitute. The medical technology that was state-of-the-art-2157 could eliminate all the relevant physical effects of aging and a hidden computer link could guide her responses. For half an hour—as long as no one demanded anything too unusual—she could give her younger customers the illusion they were interacting with someone who was their intellectual and psychological equal. Morgan tried to help her, but there wasn't much he could do. He had already decided he couldn't survive in a Solar System in which half the human population had been born with brains, glands, and nervous systems that were state-of-the-art-2150 and later. He had blocked his mother's situation out of his memory and lived at subsistence level for almost three decades. Every yen, franc, and yuri he could scrape together had been shoved into the safest investments his management program could locate. Then he had taken all his hard won capital and bought two hundred shares in an asteroid habitat a group of developers had outfitted with fusion reactors, plasma drives, solar sails, and anything else that might make a small island move at nine percent the speed of light. And he and three thousand other "uncompetitive", "under-enhanced" humans had crept away from the Solar System. And set off to explore the galaxy.

Morgan had lived through three lengthy pairings back in the Solar System. Six years after the *Island of Adventure* had begun its slow drift away from the sun, he established a fourth pairing with a woman he had met through the ship's information system. The ship's designers had endowed it with attractive common spaces, complete with parks and cafes, but most of the passengers seemed to prefer electronic socialization during the first years of the voyage. Biographies and lists of interests were filed with the system. Pseudonyms and electronic personalities proliferated. Morgan thought of old stories in which prisoners had communicated by tapping on the walls of their cells.

Savela Insdotter was eleven years younger than Morgan but she was a fully committed member of the EruLabi communion. She used pharmaceutical mental enhancers, but she used them sparingly. Morgan consumed all the mental enhancers his system could accommodate, so his functional intelligence was actually somewhat higher than hers in certain areas.

The foundation of the EruLabi ethos was a revolt against genetic enhancement. In the view of the EruLabi "mentors", the endless quest for intellectual and physical improvement was a folly. Life was supposed to be lived for its own sake, the EruLabi texts declared. Every moment was a gift that should be treasured for the pleasure it brought, not an episode in a quest for mental and physical perfection. The simplest pleasures—touches, languor, the textures of bodies pressed together—were, to the EruLabi, some of the most profound experiences life had to offer.

One of the most important texts in the EruLabi rituals was the words, in ancient Greek, that the Eudoran king had spoken to Odysseus: *Dear to us ever are the banquet and the harp and the dance and the warm bath and changes of raiment and love and sleep.*

The *Island of Adventure* had pointed itself at 82 Eridani—a Sol-type star twenty-one light years from the Solar System. 82 Eridani was an obvious candidate for a life-bearing planet. A fly-by probe had been launched at 82 Eridani in 2085—one hundred and eighteen years before Morgan and his fellow emigrants had left their home system. In 2304—

just after they had celebrated the first century of their departure—the *Island of Adventure* intercepted a message the probe was sending back to the Solar System.

It was the beginning of several years of gloomy debate. The probe had found planets. But none of them looked any more interesting than the cratered rocks and giant iceballs mankind had perused in the Solar System.

The third planet from the sun could have been another Earth. It was closer to its sun than Earth was but it could have supported life if it had been the right size. Unfortunately, the planet's mass was only thirty-eight percent the mass of Earth.

Theorists had calculated that a planet needed a mass about forty percent the mass of Earth if it was going to develop an oxygen-rich atmosphere and hold it indefinitely. The third planet was apparently just a little too small. The images transmitted by the probe were drearily familiar—a rocky, airless desert, some grandiose canyons and volcanoes, and the usual assortment of craters, dunes, and minor geological features.

The *Island of Adventure* had set out for 82 Eridani because 82E was a star of the same mass and spectral type as Sol. The second choice had been another star in the same constellation. Rho Eridani was a double star 21.3 light years from the Solar System. The two stars in the Rho system orbited each other at a promising distance—seven light hours. With that much separation between them, the theoreticians agreed, both stars could have planets.

When you looked at the sky from the Solar System, Rho was a few degrees to the left of 82 Eridani. The *Island of Adventure* was a massive, underpowered rock but it could make a small midcourse correction if its inhabitants wanted to expend some extra reaction mass.

The strongest opposition to the course change came from the oldest human on the ship. Madame Dawne was so old she had actually been born on Earth. All the other people on board had been born (created, in most cases) in the habitats the human race had scattered across the Solar System.

The *Island of Adventure* had been the first ship to embark for 82 Eridani. Thirty-two years after it had left the Solar System, a ship called *Green Voyager* had pointed its rocky bow at Rho. The texts of its transmissions had indicated the oldest passengers on the *Green Voyager* were two decades younger than the youngest passengers on the *Island of Adventure.*

If the passengers on the *Island of Adventure* approved the course change, they would arrive at Rho about the same time the *Green Voyager* arrived there. They would find themselves sharing the same star system with humans who were, on average, three or four decades younger than they were. Madame Dawne would be confronted with brains and bodies that had been designed a full century after she had received her own biological equipment.

Morgan was not a politician by temperament but he was fascinated by any activity that combined conflict with intellectual effort. When his pairing with Savela Insdotter had finally come to an end, he had isolated himself in his apartment and spent a decade and a half studying the literature on the dynamics of small communities. The knowledge he had absorbed would probably look prehistoric to the people now living in the Solar System. It had been stored in the databanks pre-2203. But it provided him with techniques that should produce the predicted results when they were applied to people who had reached adulthood several decades before 2200.

The *Island of Adventure* was managed, for all practical purposes, by its information system. A loosely organized committee monitored the system but there was no real government. The humans on board were passengers, the information system was the crew, and the communal issues that came up usually involved minor housekeeping procedures.

Now that a real issue had arisen, Morgan's fellow passengers drifted into a system of continuous polling—a system that had been the commonest form of political democracy when they had left the Solar System. Advocates talked and lobbied. Arguments flowed through the electronic symposiums and the face-to-face social networks. Individuals registered their opinions—openly or anonymously—when they decided they were willing to commit themselves. At any moment you could call up the appropriate screen and see how the count looked.

The most vociferous support for the course change came from eight individuals. For most of the three thousand fifty-seven people who lived in the ship's apartments, the message from the probe was a minor development. The ship was their home—In the same way a hollowed out asteroid in the Solar System could have been their home. The fact that their habitat would occasionally visit another star system added spice to the centuries that lay ahead, but it wasn't their primary interest in life. The Eight, on the other hand, seemed to feel they would be sentencing themselves to decades of futility if they agreed to visit a lifeless star system.

Morgan set up a content analysis program and had it monitor the traffic flowing through the public information system. Eighteen months after the message from the probe had triggered off the debate, he put a two-axis graph on the screen and examined a pair of curves.

Morgan's pairing with Savela Insdotter had lasted over sixty years and they had remained friendly after they had unpaired. He showed her the graph as soon as he had run it through some extra checks. The curve that charted the Eight's activities rose and fell in conjunction with the curve that measured Madame Dawne's participation in the debate. When Madame Dawne's activity level reached a peak, the Eight subsided into silence. They would stop agitating for their cause, the entire discussion would calm down, and Madame Dawne would return to the extreme privacy she had maintained from the beginning of the voyage. Then, when Madame Dawne hadn't been heard from for several tendays, the Eight would suddenly renew their campaign.

"I believe they're supporting the change to a new destination merely because they wish to disturb Madame Dawne," Morgan said. "I've created personality profiles based on their known histories and public statements. The profiles indicate my conjecture is correct."

Savela presented him with a shrug and a delicate, upward movement of her head. Morgan had spoken to her in Tych—an ultra-precise language that was primarily used in written communication. Savela was responding in an emotion-oriented language called VA13—a language that made extensive use of carefully rehearsed gestures and facial expressions.

No one, as far as Morgan knew, had ever spoken VA12 or VA14. The language had been labeled VA13 when it had been developed in a communications laboratory on Phobos, and the label had stuck.

"Madame Dawne is a laughable figure," Savela said.

"I recognize that. But the Eight are creating a serious division in our communal life. We might have reached a consensus by now if they hadn't restimulated the debate every time it seemed to be concluding. Madame Dawne is one of the eleven wealthiest individuals on the ship. What would happen to us if she decided she had to impose her will by force?"

"Do you really feel that's a serious possibility, Morgan?"

The linguists who had developed VA13 had been interested in the emotional content of music. The speaker's tone patterns and rhythms were just as critical as the verbal text. Savela's word choices were polite and innocuous, but her rhythms communicated something else—a mixture of affection and amusement that would have seemed contemptuous if she and Morgan hadn't shared a pairing that had lasted six decades.

To Morgan, Madame Dawne was pathetic, not comic. She spent most of her days, as far as anyone could tell, in the electronic dream worlds she constructed in her apartment. No one on the ship had seen her true face. When she appeared on someone's screens, her electronic personae were impressively unimaginative. She usually imaged herself as a tall woman, with close cropped red hair, dressed in the flamboyant boots-and-baggy-shirts style that North Americans had adapted during the third decade of the 21st Century—the body type and clothing mode that had been fashionable when she had been in her natural prime.

Morgan had put a wargame template on his information system and had it explore some of the things Madame Dawne could do. Savela might smile at the thought that a limited, under developed personality like Madame Dawne might undertake something dangerous. The wargame program had come up with seventy-four weapon systems a wealthy individual could develop with the aid of the information in the databanks. Half the systems were straightforward modifications of the devices that dug out apartment spaces and extracted mineral resources from the rocky exterior of the ship. Most of the others involved an offensive use of the self-replicating machines that handled most of the passengers' daily needs.

Madame Dawne couldn't have designed any of the machines the wargame program had suggested. She probably didn't even know the ship could place them at her disposal. Did she realize she could ask a wargame program for advice? Morgan didn't know.

Morgan's political studies had included an exhaustive module in applied personality profiling. He could recite from memory the numbers that described the kind of person who could become a successful small-community politician. He hadn't been surprised when his profiling program had told him he scored below average on most of the critical personality characteristics. He had made several attempts to enter the course change controversy and the results would have evoked I-told-you-so head shakes from the technicians who had developed the profiling program. The program had been almost cruelly accurate when it had informed him he had a low tolerance for disagreement. He could have given it fifty examples of his tendency to become hot tempered and defensive when he attracted the attention of aggressive debaters. For the last few months, he had been avoiding the public symposiums and feeding private suggestions to people who could turn his ideas into effective attempts at persuasion. Now he fleshed out the profiles he had been storing in his databanks and started recruiting a six member political team.

Morgan couldn't proselytize prospects and debate verbal brawlers, but he had discovered he could do something that was just as effective: he could win the cooperation of the people who could. Some of the people he approached even *enjoyed* accosting their fellow citizens and lobbying them on political issues. They couldn't always follow Morgan's logic but they considered that a minor problem. They were extroverted, achievement-oriented personalities and Morgan gave them suggestions that worked. If he told them a visit to X made good sense at this moment, and a visit to Y would be a waste of time, they approached both prospects the first couple of times he made a recommendation, and followed his advice after that.

Most of the political strategies Morgan had studied could be fitted into three categories: you could be *combative and confrontational*, you could *market*, or you could explore the subtleties of *the indirect approach*. Temperamentally, Morgan was a marketer who liked to use the indirect approach. Once he had his political organization going, he ran another analysis of the profiles in his databanks and organized a Terraforming Committee. Five engineering-oriented personalities sat down with a carefully selected political personality and began looking at the possibility some of the planets of 82 Eridani could be transformed into livable environments. Eight months after Morgan had established the committee, the first simulated planetary environment took its place in the public databanks. Interested individuals could soar across a planetary landscape that included blue skies, towering forests, and creatures selected from three of Earth's geologic eras and two of its mythological cycles.

It took almost five years, but Morgan's efforts succeeded. An overwhelming consensus emerged. The ship would stay on course.

Unfortunately, the Eight still seemed to enjoy baiting Madame Dawne. By this time, however, Morgan had constructed detailed profiles of every personality in the octet.

The most vulnerable was a woman named Miniruta Coboloji. Miniruta's primary motivation, according to the profile program, was an intense need for affiliation.

Morgan had known his pairing with Savela Insdotter would end sooner or later. Everything had to end sooner or later. The surprise had been the identity of the man who had succeeded him.

Morgan had assumed Savela would grow tired of his skeptical, creedless outlook and pair with someone who shared her beliefs. Instead, her next partner had been Ari Sun-Dalt—the outspoken champion of a communion that had been founded on the belief that every member of the human race was involved in a cosmic epic: the struggle of matter to become conscious.

Life was not an accident, the advocates of Ari's worldview asserted. It was the purpose of the universe. The idea that dominated Ari's life was the Doctrine of the Cosmic Enterprise—the belief that the great goal of the cosmos was the unlimited expansion of Consciousness.

Ari had been adding organic and electronic enhancements to his brain ever since he had been in his thirties. The skin on the top of his skull concealed an array that included every chip and cell cluster his nervous system would accept. His head was at least twenty-five percent longer, top to bottom, than a standard male head. If something could increase his intelligence or heighten his consciousness, Ari believed it would be immoral not to install it.

"We can always use recruits," Ari said. "But I must tell you, my friend, I feel there's something cynical about your scheming."

Morgan shrugged. "If I'm right, Miniruta will be ten times more contented than she is now. And the ship will be serener."

They were both speaking Jor—an everyday language, with a rigidly standardized vocabulary, which had roots in 21st century French. Morgan had told Ari he had detected signs that Miniruta would be interested in joining his communion, and Ari had immediately understood Morgan was trying to remove Miniruta from the Eight. Ari could be surprisingly sophisticated intellectually. Most people with strong belief systems didn't like to think about the psychological needs people satisfied when they joined philosophical movements.

Miniruta joined Ari's communion a year after Ari set out to convert her. She lost interest in the Eight as soon as she acquired a new affiliation—just as Morgan's profiles had predicted she would. Morgan had been preparing plans for three other members of the group but Miniruta's withdrawal produced an unexpected dividend. Two of the male members drifted away a few tendays after Miniruta proclaimed her new allegiance. Their departure apparently disrupted the dynamics of the entire clique. Nine tendays after their defection, Morgan could detect no indications the Eight had ever existed.

On the outside of the ship, in an area where the terrain still retained most of the asteroid's original contours, there was a structure that resembled a squat slab with four circular antennas mounted at its corners. The slab itself was a comfortable, two story building, with a swimming pool, recreation facilities, and six apartments that included fully equipped communication rooms.

The structure was the communications module that received messages from the Solar System and the other ships currently creeping through interstellar space. It was totally isolated from the ship's electronic systems. The messages it picked up could only be examined by someone who was actually sitting in one of the apartments. You couldn't transfer a message from the module to the ship's databanks. You couldn't even carry a recording into the ship.

The module had been isolated from the rest of the ship in response to a very real threat: the possibility someone in the Solar System would transmit a message that would sabotage the ship's information system. There were eight billion people living in the Solar System. When you were dealing with a population that size, you had to assume it contained thousands of individuals who felt the starships were legitimate targets for lethal pranks.

Morgan had been spending regular periods in the communications module since the first years of the voyage. During the first decades, the messages he had examined had become increasingly strange. The population in the Solar System had been evolving at a rate that compressed kilocenturies of natural evolution into decades of engineered modification. The messages that had disturbed him the most had been composed in the languages he had learned in his childhood. The words were familiar but the meaning of the messages kept slipping away from him.

Morgan could understand that the terraforming of Mars, Venus, and Mercury might have been speeded up and complexified by a factor of ten. He could even grasp that some of the electronically interlinked communal personalities in the Solar System might include several million individual personalities. But did he really understand the messages that seemed to imply millions of people had expanded their personal *physiologies* into complexes that encompassed entire asteroids?

The messages included videos that should have eliminated most of his confusion. Somehow he always turned away from the screen feeling there was something he hadn't grasped.

The situation in the Solar System had begun to stabilize just before Morgan had turned his attention to the turmoil created by the Eight. Over the next few decades the messages became more decipherable. Fifty years after the problem with the Eight—one hundred and sixty two years after the ship had left the Solar System—almost all the messages reaching the ship came from members of Ari Sun-Dalt's communion.

The believers in the Doctrine of the Cosmic Enterprise were communicating with the starships because they were becoming a beleaguered minority. The great drive for enhancement and progress had apparently run its course. The worldviews that dominated human civilization were all variations on the EruLabi creeds.

Ari spent long periods—as much as ten or twelve tendays in a row—in the communications module. The human species, in Ari's view, was sinking into an eternity of aimless hedonism.

Ari became particularly distraught when he learned the EruLabi had decided they should limit themselves to a twenty percent increase in skull size—a dictum which imposed a tight restriction on the brainpower they could pack inside their heads. At the peak of the enhancement movement, people who had retained normal bipedal bodies had apparently quadrupled their skull sizes.

"We're the only conscious, intelligent species the Solar System ever produced," Ari orated in one of his public communiques. "We may be the only conscious, intelligent species in this section of the galaxy. And they've decided an arbitrary physiological aesthetic is more important than the development of our minds."

The messages from the Solar System had included scientific discussions. They had even included presentations prepared for "nonspecialists". Morgan had followed a few of the presentations as well as he could and he had concluded the human species had reached a point of diminishing returns.

Morgan would never possess the kind of complexified, ultra-enhanced brain his successors in the Solar System had acquired. Every set of genes imposed a ceiling on the organism it shaped. If you wanted to push beyond that ceiling, you had to start all over again, with a new organism and a new set of genes. But Morgan believed he could imagine some of the consequences of that kind of intellectual power.

At some point, he believed, all those billions of superintelligent minds had looked out at the Universe and realized that another increase in brain power would be pointless. You could develop a brain that could answer every question about the size, history, and structure of the universe, and find that you still couldn't answer the philosophical questions that had tantalized the most primitive tribesmen. And what would you do when you reached that point? You would turn your back on the frontier. You would turn once again to the bath and the banquet, the harp and the dance.

And changes of raiment.

And love.

And sleep.

The situation on the ship was almost the mirror image of the situation in the Solar System. On the ship, forty-eight percent of the population belonged to Ari's communion. Only nineteen percent had adopted the EruLabi creeds. But how long could that last? Morgan had been watching the trends. Every few years, someone abandoned the Doctrine of the Cosmic Enterprise and joined the EruLabi. No one ever left the EruLabi and became a devoted believer in the Cosmic Enterprise.

The discovery that 82 Eridani was surrounded by lifeless planets had added almost a dozen people to the defectors. The search for life-bearing planets was obviously a matter of great significance. If consciousness really was the purpose of the universe, then life should be a common phenomenon.

In 2315, just four years after the final dissolution of the Eight, the *Island of Adventure* had received its first messages from Tau Ceti and Morgan had watched a few more personalities float away from Ari's communion. The ship that had reached Tau Ceti had made planetfall after a mere one hundred and forty years and it had indeed found life on the second planet of the system. Unfortunately, the planet was locked in a permanent ice age. Life had evolved in the oceans under the ice but it had never developed beyond the level of the more mundane marine life forms found on Earth.

Morgan had found it impossible to follow the reasons the planet was iced over. He hadn't really been interested, to tell the truth. But he had pored over the reports on the undersea biota as if he had been following the dispatches from a major war.

One of the great issues in terrestrial evolutionary theory had been the relationship between chance and necessity. To Ari and his disciples, there was nothing random about the process. Natural selection inevitably favored qualities such as strength, speed, and intelligence.

To others, the history of life looked more haphazard. Many traits, it was argued, had developed for reasons as whimsical as the fact that the ancestor who carried Gene A had been standing two steps to the right when the rocks slid off the mountain.

The probes that had penetrated the oceans of Tau Ceti IV had sent back images that could be used to support either viewpoint. The undersea biota was populated by several hundred species of finned snakes, several thousand species that could be considered roughly comparable to terrestrial insects, and clouds of microscopic dimlight photosynthesizers.

Yes, evolution favored the strong and the swift. Yes, creatures who lived in the sea tended to be streamlined. On the other hand, fish were not inevitable. Neither were oysters. Or clams.

If the Universe really did have a purpose, it didn't seem to be very good at it. In the Solar System, theorists had produced scenarios that proved life could have evolved in exotic, unlikely environments such as the atmosphere of Jupiter. Instead, the only life that had developed outside Earth had been the handful of not-very-interesting microorganisms that had managed to maintain a toehold on Mars.

The purpose of the universe isn't the development of consciousness, one of the EruLabi on board the *Island of Adventure* suggested. *It's the creation of iceballs and deserts. And sea snakes.*

Ari's enhancements included a gland modification that gave him the ability to switch off his sexual feelings at will. His pairing with Savela Insdotter had lasted less than two decades, and he had made no attempt to establish another pairing. Ari had spent most of the voyage, as far as Morgan could tell, in an asexual state.

There were times, during the last decades of the voyage, when Morgan felt tempted to emulate him. Morgan's next pairing only lasted twelve years. For the rest of the voyage, he took advantage of the small number of sexual opportunities that came his way and distracted himself, during his celibate intervals, with intellectual projects such as his political studies.

The ship's medical system could install Ari's sexual enhancement in thirty minutes, as part of the regular medical services included in the standard embarkation agreement. Morgan put the idea aside every time he considered it. He had learned to cherish his feelings about women, irrational as they might be. There was, he knew, no real reason why he should respond to the flare of a woman's hips or the tilt of a female neck. It was simply a bit of genetic programming he hadn't bothered to delete. It had no practical value in a world in which children were created in the workshops of genetic designers. But he also knew he would be a different person if he subtracted it from his psychological make up. It was one of the things that kept you human as the decades slipped by.

In 2381—forty-six years before it was scheduled to reach its destination—the *Island of Adventure* intercepted a message from the probe that had been sent to Rho Eridani. Neither of the stars in the double system possessed planets. The *Green Voyager* was crawling toward an empty system.

In 2398—one hundred and ninety five years after the ship had begun its journey—the medical system replaced Morgan's heart, part of his central nervous system, and most of his endocrine glands. It was the third time Morgan had put himself through an extensive overhaul. The last time he had recovered within three years. This time he spent eight years in the deepest sleep the system could maintain.

The first program capsules left the ship while it was still careening around the 82 Eridani system, bouncing from planet to planet as it executed the five year program that would eliminate the last twenty percent of its interstellar speed. There were three capsules and their payloads were packages a little smaller than Morgan's forefinger.

One capsule malfunctioned while it was still making its way toward the small moon that orbited the third planet at a distance of 275,000 kilometers. The second lost two critical programs when it hit the moon at an angle that was a little too sharp. The third skimmed through the dust just like it was supposed to and sprouted a set of filaments. Sampling programs analyzed the moon's surface. Specks that were part cell and part electronic device began drifting down the filaments and executing programs that transformed the moon's atoms into larger, more elaborate specks. The specks produced machines the size of insects, the insects produced machines the size of cats, an antenna crept up the side of a small crater, and an antenna on the *Island of Adventure* started transmitting more programs. By the time the ship settled into an orbit around the third planet, the moon had acquired a complete manufacturing facility, and the lunar fabrication units had started producing scout machines that could land on the planet itself.

Morgan had thought of the terraforming scheme as a political ruse, but there were people on the ship who took it seriously. With the technology they had at their disposal, the third planet could be turned into a livable world within a few decades. For people who had spent their entire lives in enclosed habitats, it was a romantic idea—a world where you walked on the surface, with a sky above you, and experienced all the vagaries of weather and climate.

The only person who had raised any serious objections had been Ari Sun-Dalt. Some of the valleys they could observe from orbit had obviously been carved by rivers. The volcano calderas were less spectacular than the volcanoes of Mars but they were still proof the planet had once been geologically active. They couldn't overlook the possibility life might be hiding in some obscure ecological network that was buried under the soil or hidden in a cave, Ari argued.

Most of the people on the ship greeted that kind of suggestion with shrugs and smiles. According to Morgan's sampling programs, there were only about ten people on the ship who really thought there was a statistically significant possibility the planet might have generated life. Still, there was no reason they couldn't let Ari enjoy his daydreams a little longer.

"It will only take us an extra two or three years," Ari said. "And then we'll know we can remodel the place. First we'll see if there's any life. Then we'll do the job ourselves, if the universe hasn't done it already. And bring Consciousness to another world."

For Ari's sake—he really liked Ari in many ways—Morgan hoped they might find a few fossilized microorganisms embedded in the rocks. What he did not expect was a fossil the size of a horse, embedded in a cliff, and visible to any machine that came within two kilometers of it.

Three and a half billion years ago, the planet had emerged from the disk of material that surrounded its sun. A billion or so years later, the first long-chain molecules had appeared in the oceans. And the history of life had begun. In the same way it had begun on Earth.

The long-chain molecules had formed assemblies that became the first rudimentary cells. Organisms that were something like plants had eventually begun to absorb the CO_2 produced by the volcanoes. The oxygen emitted by the quasi-plants had become a major component of the atmosphere. The relentless forces of competition had favored creatures who were more complex than their rivals.

And then, after less than two billion years of organic evolution, the laws of physics had caught up with the process. No planet the size of this one could hold an atmosphere forever.

The plants and the volcanoes could produce oxygen and CO_2 *almost* as fast as the gas molecules could drift into space. But almost wasn't good enough.

They didn't piece the whole story together right away, of course. There were even people who weren't convinced the first find was a fossil. If the scout machines hadn't found ten more fossils in the first five daycycles, the skeptics would have spent years arguing that Exhibit A was just a collection of rocks—a random geologic formation that just happened to resemble a big shell, with appendages that resembled limbs.

On Earth, the dominant land animals had been vertebrates—creatures whose basic characteristic was a bony framework hung on a backbone. The vertebrate template was such a logical, efficient structure it was easy to believe it was as inevitable as the streamlined shape of fish and porpoises. In fact, it had never developed on this planet.

Instead, the basic anatomical structure had been a tube of bone. Creatures with this rigid, seemingly inefficient, structure had acquired legs, claws, teeth and all the other anatomical features vertebrates had acquired on Earth. Thousands of species had acquired eyes that looked out of big eyeholes in the front of the shell, without developing a separate skull. Two large families had developed "turrets" that housed their eyes and their other sense organs but they had kept their brains securely housed in the original shell, in a special chamber just under the turret.

On Earth, the shell structure would have produced organisms that might have collapsed from their own weight. On this planet, with its weaker gravitational field, the shells could be thin and even airy. They reminded Morgan of building components that had been formed from solidified foam—a common structural technique in space habitats.

For Ari, the discovery was the high point of his lifespan—a development that had to be communicated to the Solar System at once. Ari's face had been contorted with excitement when he had called Morgan an hour after the machines reported the first find.

"We've done it, Morgan," Ari proclaimed. "We've justified our whole voyage. Three thousand useless, obsolete people have made a discovery that's going to transform the whole outlook in the Solar System."

Morgan had already been pondering a screen that displayed a triangular diagram. The point at the bottom of the triangle represented the Solar System. The two points at the top represented 82 Eridani and Rho Eridani. The *Island of Adventure* and the *Green Voyager* had been creeping up the long sides of the triangle. The *Green Voyager* was now about three light years from Rho—thirty-three years travel time.

Morgan transferred the diagram to Ari's screen and pointed out the implications. If the *Island of Adventure* transmitted an announcement to the Solar System, the *Green Voyager* would pick it up in approximately seven years. If the people on the *Voyager* thought it was interesting, they could change course and reach 82 Eridani only twelve and a half decades after they intercepted the message.

"That gives us over one hundred and thirty years to explore the planet," Ari argued. "By that time we'll have learned everything important the fossils have to offer. We'll have done all the real work. We'll be ready to move on. And look for a world where we can communicate with a living Consciousness."

Unfortunately, the situation didn't look that straightforward to the rest of the community. To them, a hundred and thirty years was a finite, envisionable time period.

There was, after all, a third possibility—as Miniruta Coboloji pointed out in one of her contributions to the electronic debate. *The* Green Voyager *may never come this way at all*, Miniruta argued. *They may reach Rho thirty-three years from now, pass through the system, and point themselves at one of the stars that lies further out. They've got three choices within fourteen light years. Why can't we just wait the thirty-three years? And send a message after they've committed themselves to some other star system?*

For Ari, that was unthinkable. *Our announcement is going to take twenty years to reach the Solar System no matter what we do. If we sit here for thirty-three years before we transmit, it will be fifty-three years before anyone in the Solar System hears about one of the most important discoveries in history. We all know what's happening in the Solar System. Fifty-three years from now there may not be anyone left who cares.*

Once again Morgan labored over his screens. Once again, he recruited aides who helped him guide the decision making process. This time he engineered a compromise. They would send a brief message saying they had "found evidence of extinct life" and continue studying the planet's fossils. Once every year, they would formally reopen the discussion for three tendays. They would transmit a complete announcement "whenever it becomes clear the consensus supports such an action."

* * *

Ari accepted the compromise in good grace. He had looked at the numbers, too Most of the people on the ship still belonged to his communion.

"They know what their responsibilities are," Ari insisted. "Right now this is all new, Morgan. We've just getting used to the idea that we're looking at a complete planetary biota. A year from now—two years from now—we'll have so much information in our databanks they'll know we'd be committing a criminal act if we didn't send every bit of it back to the Solar System."

It was Ari who convinced them the planet should be called Athene. Athene had been a symbol of wisdom and culture, Ari pointed out, but she had been a war goddess, too. And didn't the world they were naming bear a distinct resemblance to the planet the ancient humans had named after their male war figure?

The information pouring into the databanks could be examined by anyone on the ship. In theory, anyone could give the exploration machines orders. In practice, the exploration of the Athenian fossil record soon came under the control of three people: Ari, Morgan—and Miniruta Coboloji.

Morgan had been watching Miniruta's development ever since he had lured her away from the Eight. Physically, she was a standard variation on the BR-V73 line—the long, willowy female body type that had been the height of fashion in the lunar cities in the 2130's. Her slim, beautifully crafted fingers could mold a sculpture—or shape a note on a string instrument—with the precision of a laser pointer.

It was a physical style that Morgan found aesthetically appealing but there were at least two hundred women on the ship who had been shaped by the same gene cluster. So why was Miniruta the only BR-V73 who crept into his thoughts during the more stressful hours of his celibate intervals? Was it because there was something desperate about the need for affiliation he had uncovered in her personality profile? Did that emotional vulnerability touch something in his own personality?

Miniruta's affiliation with the Doctrine of the Cosmic Enterprise had lasted four decades. Ari claimed her switch to the EruLabi worldview had been totally unexpected. Ari had gone to sleep assuming she was one of his most ardent colleagues and awakened to discover she had sent him a long message explaining the reasons for her conversion and urging him to join her.

During the decades in which she had been a member of Ari's communion, Miniruta had followed Ari's lead and equipped herself with every pharmaceutical and electrical enhancer she could link to her physiology. The electronic enhancers had all been discarded a few tendays after she had joined the EruLabi. Her pharmaceutical enhancers had been dispensed with, item by item, as she had worked her way up the EruLabi protocols. She had been the second EruLabi on the ship who had made it to the fourth protocol and accepted its absolute prohibition of all non-genetic mental and physiological enhancers.

Morgan could now talk to her without struggling. His own pharmaceutical enhancers erased most of the intellectual gap that separated two people who had been brought into the universe twenty years apart. He had been surprised when he had discovered Miniruta was spending two thirds of every daycycle with the data from the fossil hunt, but he had soon realized she had a philosophical agenda.

To Miniruta, the course of evolution on Athene proved that evolution was a random process. "Ari's right, Morgan," Miniruta said. "This planet can teach us something we need to understand. But it's not the lesson Ari thinks it is. It's telling us there isn't any plan. There's no big overall objective—as if the universe is some kind of cosmic totalitarian state. The only reality is individuals. And their needs."

To Ari, the critical question was the evolution of intelligence. Obviously, life had died out on Athene before intelligent creatures could build cities or turn meadows into farms. But wasn't there some chance something like the first proto-humans had evolved? If that first glimmer of tool making, culture creating intelligence had appeared on the planet, wouldn't it prove that evolution really did lead in a particular direction?

"I'll grant you the vertebrates were obviously an accident," Ari said. "But you can still see an obvious increase in intelligence if you look at the progressions we've been uncovering. You can't go from stationary sea creatures to land creatures that were obviously highly mobile without a lot of development in the brain. Intelligence is the inevitable winner in the selection process. The life forms that can think better will always replace the life forms with less complex nervous systems."

"The way human beings replaced the cockroach?" Miniruta asked. "And the oyster?"

Miniruta was speaking VA13. The lilt in her voice expressed a casual mockery that Morgan would have found devastating if she had directed it at him.

"We were not in direct genetic competition with the cockroach and the oyster," Ari said in Tych. "The observable fact that certain lines remained static for hundreds of millions of years doesn't contradict the observable fact that natural selection tends to produce creatures with more highly developed brains. We could have destroyed every species on the Earth if we had wanted to. We let them live because we needed a complex biosphere. They survived because they satisfied one of *our* needs."

To Morgan, most of the information they were gathering proved that natural selection really was the powerful force the theorists had claimed it was.

Certain basic patterns had been repeated on both planets. Life forms that had been exceptionally massive had possessed jaw structures that indicated they had probably been herbivores—just as terrestrial herbivores such as the elephant had been the largest organisms in their habitats. Life forms that had possessed stabbing teeth and bone crunching jaws tended to be medium sized and looked like they had probably been more agile.

But the process obviously had its random qualities, too. Was it just a matter of random chance that the vertebrates had failed to develop? Had the shell creatures dominated the planet merely because certain molecules had fallen into one type of pattern on Earth and another pattern on Athene? Or had it happened because there was some difference in the conditions life had encountered on the two planets?

To Morgan, it didn't matter what the answer was. Evolution might proceed according to laws that were as rigid as the basic laws of physics, or it might be as random as a perfect game of chance. He would be happy with either answer. He could even be content with no answer.

That was one of the things people never seemed to understand about science. As far as Morgan was concerned, you didn't study the universe because you wanted to know the answers. You studied it to *connect*. When you subjected an important question to a rigorous examination—

collecting every scrap of evidence you could find, measuring and analyzing everything that could be measured and analyzed—you were linked to the universe in a way nothing else could connect you.

Religious mystics had once spent their lives trying to establish a direct contact with their version of God. Morgan was a mystic who tried to stay in contact with the cosmos.

Ari had assigned three groups of exploration machines to a hunt for camp sites. The teams concentrated on depressions that looked like they had once been rivers and probed for evidence such as stone tools and places where a large number of animal fossils had been concentrated in a small area. They found two animal deposits within their first three tendays and Ari quickly pointed out that the animals had clearly been disassembled.

"These aren't just tar pits or places where a catastrophe killed several animals accidentally," Ari argued. "Note how the remains of the different species are all jumbled up. If they had been killed by a rockslide from the surrounding heights—to name just one alternate possibility—the remains of each animal would have tended to stay together. The pattern we're looking at here is the pattern we'd expect to see in a waste pit."

Miniruta tossed her head. "If they were butchered," she said in VA13, "then somebody had to use tools to cut them up. Show us a flint tool, Ari. Show us some evidence of fire."

Machines burrowed and probed in the areas around the "waste pits". Scraping attachments removed the dirt and rock one thin layer at a time. Raking attachments sieved the dust and rubble. Search programs analyzed the images transmitted by the onsite cameras and highlighted anything that met the criteria Ari had stored in the databanks. And they did, in fact, find slivers of flint that could have been knives or spearheads.

Ari had two of the flints laid out on a tray, with a camera poised an arm length above the objects, and displayed them on one of the wall screens in his apartment. Morgan stared at the tray in silence and let himself surrender to all the eerie, haunting emotions it aroused, even with Ari babbling beside him.

"On Earth," Miniruta pointed out, "we already knew the planet had produced intelligent life. We could assume specimens like that had been made by intelligent beings because we already knew the intelligent beings existed. But what do we have here, Ari? Can we really believe these objects were shaped by intelligent beings when we still haven't seen anything that resembles hands? So far, you haven't even located an organism that had *arms*."

There were other possibilities, of course. Ari had studied most of the ideas about possible alien life forms that humans had come up with in the last few centuries and installed them in the databanks housed in his electronic enhancers. He could produce several plausible examples of grasping organs composed of soft tissue that would only fossilize under rare, limited conditions. The tool makers could have possessed tentacles. They could have used some odd development of their lips.

Miniruta tipped back her head and raised her eyebrows when she heard Ari mention tentacles. The high pitched lilt of her VA13 communicated—once again—the condescension that permeated her attitude toward Ari.

"The cephalopods all lived in the sea, Ari. Our arms evolved from load bearing legs. I admit we're discussing creatures who evolved in a lower gravity field. But they weren't operating in zero gravity."

"I've thought about that," Ari said. "Isn't it possible some tentacled sea-creatures could have adapted an amphibious lifestyle on the edge of the sea and eventually produced descendants who substituted legs for some of their tentacles? On our own planet, after all, some of the land dwellers who lived on the edge of Earth's oceans eventually produced descendants whose legs had been transformed into fins. With all due respect to your *current* belief system, Miniruta—our discussions would be significantly more succinct if you weren't trying to discuss serious issues without the benefit of a few well chosen enhancements. You might see some of the possibilities I'm seeing before I have to describe them to you."

As an adherent of the fourth EruLabi protocol, Miniruta only rejected permanent enhancements that increased her intellectual and physical powers. Temporary enhancements that increased pleasure were another matter. Miniruta could still use a small selection of the sexually enhancing drugs developed in the 21st Century, in addition to the wines, teas, and inhalants that had fostered pre-pharmaceutical social relations. She and

Morgan had already shared several long, elaborately choreographed sexual interludes. They had bathed. They had banqueted. They had reclined on carefully proportioned couches, naked bodies touching, while musicians from a dozen eras had materialized in Miniruta's simulators. The EruLabi sexual rituals had cast a steady, sensuous glow over the entire six decades Morgan had spent with Savela Insdotter. He had resumed their routines as if he had been slipping on clothes that were associated with some of the best moments of his life.

They were nearing the end of a particularly satisfactory interlude when Miniruta switched on her information system and discovered she had received a please-view-first message from Ari. "I've been looking over some of the latest finds from one of your random-survey teams," Ari said. "Your idea paid off. They've handed us a fossil that looks like it left traces of soft bodied tissue in the rocks in front of it—imprints that look like they could have been made by the local equivalent of tentacles. Your team found it in the middle of a depression in that flat area on the top of the main southern plateau—a depression that's so shallow I hadn't even noticed it on the maps."

Miniruta had decided that half her exploration machines would make random searches. Ari and Morgan were both working with intellectual frameworks based on the history of Earth, Miniruta had argued. Morgan was looking at the kind of sites that had produced fossils on Earth. Ari was looking for traces of hunter-gatherers. "A random process," she had pronounced, "should be studied by random probing."

Now her own philosophical bias had apparently given Ari what he had been looking for. Ari would never have ordered one of his machines into the winding, almost invisible depression Miniruta's machine had followed. But that dip in the landscape had once been a river. And the river had widened its path and eroded the ground above a fossil which had formed in the sediment by the bank.

It was a cracked, fragmented shell about a third the length of a human being. Only one side of it had been preserved. But you could still see that it was essentially a tube with a large opening at one end, a smaller opening at the other, and no indications it had openings for legs. In the rock in front of the large opening, Morgan could just make out the outlines of impressions that could have been produced by a group of ropy, softbodied extensions.

Ari highlighted three spots on the rim of the large opening. "Notice how the opening has indentations on the rim, where the extensions leave it. They aren't very big, but they obviously give the extensions a little more room. I've ordered a search of the databank to see how many other shells have indentations like that. If there was one creature like this on the planet, there should have been other species built along the same pattern. I'm also taking another look at all the shells like this we've uncovered in the past. My first pass through the databank indicates we've found several of them near the places where we found the burial pits."

For Ari, the find proved that it was time to let the Solar System know the full truth. He posted a picture of the fossil on the information system an hour after he had notified Morgan and Miniruta. "We now have evidence that creatures with fully developed grasping organs existed on this planet," Ari argued. "The evidence may not be conclusive, but it can't be dismissed either. The people of the Solar System have a right to draw their own conclusions. Let them see the evidence we've collected. Let the minority who are resisting stagnation and decline derive hope from the knowledge more evidence may follow."

It had only been eight tendays since Ari had agreed to the compromise Morgan had worked out. Yet he was already demanding that they cancel the agreement.

To Miniruta, the idea was absurd. Ari was suggesting that the forests of Athene had harbored tentacled creatures who had hung from trees and occupied the ecological niches monkeys had appropriated on Earth. And he was jumping from that improbability to the idea that some of these hypothetical creatures had developed weapons and become hunter-gatherers.

"I am not saying anything is true," Ari insisted. "I am merely noting that we now have pits full of butchered animals, tools that could have butchered them, and a type of organism that could have manipulated the tools."

Ari had even developed a scenario that equipped his fantasy creatures with the ability to move along the ground at a pace suitable for hunters. Suppose, he argued, they had begun their advance to intelligence by learning to control some type of riding animal?

To Ari, his proposal was a logical variation on the process that had shaped human intelligence. On Earth, tree dwellers had developed hands that could grasp limbs and brains that could judge distances and trajectories. Then they had adapted the upright posture and used their hands to create stone tools. Tool use had created a way of life that put a premium on intelligence, the individuals with the best brains had tended to be the survivors, and a creature who could build starships had taken its place in the universe.

"On Athene," Ari argued, "the drive toward intelligence may have followed a different course. The tree-dwellers couldn't develop upright walking so they began by controlling animals. They became mounted hunters—creatures who could rove like ground animals and manipulate the same simple tools our own ancestors chipped from the rocks. The evolutionary process may take many twists. It may be bloody and cruel. But in the end, it gives us planets populated by creatures who are intelligent and conscious. The arrow points in only one direction."

Thirty years from now—perhaps even ten years from now—Morgan's feelings about Miniruta would just be a memory. Morgan knew that. There would come a moment when he would wonder how he could have believed all his pleasure in life depended on the goodwill of another human being. But right now he just knew he wanted to create a crowded memory. Right now he felt as if he had spent the last few decades in a state of half-dead numbness.

He had started playing with his political analysis programs as soon as he had realized Ari was initiating a new round of agitated debate. The situation had looked dangerous to him and the picture that had emerged on his screens had confirmed his intuitive judgment. About twenty-five percent of the people on the ship believed a report on the new find should be transmitted to the Solar System. Almost thirty percent registered strong opposition. The rest of the population seemed to be equally divided between not-convinced-we-should and not-convinced-we-shouldn't.

If Ari's first appeals had attracted a solid forty or forty-five percent, Morgan would have given him some extra support and helped him win a quick, overwhelming victory. Instead, the *Island of Adventure* community had stumbled into one of those situations in which a divisive debate could go on indefinitely.

Morgan was savoring teas with Miniruta when he suggested the one option that looked like it might defuse the situation.

"I've decided to assign all my exploration teams to the search for evidence that supports Ari's theories," Morgan said. "I think it would be a wise move if you did the same thing—for awhile anyway. We're not going to get any peace on this ship until we come up with solid evidence Ari's right. Or make it clear we probably never will."

They had both been speaking Plais—a graceful EruLabi invention that had been designed for the lighter types of social events. Morgan had switched to Jor when he started discussing his proposal and Miniruta transferred to Jor with him.

"You want to divert equipment from all the other research we're doing?" Miniruta said. "As far as I'm concerned, Ari has all the resources he needs. We're producing the first survey of an alien ecosystem. Why should we interrupt that merely because one member of our expedition has become obsessed with a fantasy?"

The vehemence in her voice caught Morgan off guard. He had thought he was offering her a modest, reasonable proposal. He had run the idea through his political simulation programs and the results had indicated most of the people on the ship would approve a transmission to the Solar System if Ari managed to locate more evidence. A minority would never feel happy with the decision—but at least a decision would have been made.

"It shouldn't divert us for more than a few tendays," Morgan said. "We can intensify Ari's hunt for campsites. We can look for associations between possible mounts and possible riders. We can ignore the low lying areas for the time being and concentrate on the regions that probably stayed above sea level when Athene had seas. If we do all that and don't come up with something decisive in a few tendays—I think we can assume we'll get a clear consensus that we shouldn't overrule our current agreement and transmit a message before the next discussion period."

"And what if we find the kind of evidence he's looking for? Do you think Madame Dawne will just nod agreeably? And let us do something that could destroy her?"

"If there's evidence out there to be found—sooner or later we're going to find it. She's going to have to accept that eventually."

Miniruta reached across the tea table and touched his hand. She slipped into Plais just long enough to preface her response with a word that meant something like "pleasure-friend".

"*Donilar*—even if the evidence is there, will it really do us any good if we find it? Why should we jeopardize our whole way of life just so Ari can give a dying minority group information that will only prolong its agonies?"

Morgan knew he shouldn't have felt like he had just been ambushed. He had been watching Miniruta for over a century. Everything she had done had proved that the profiling program had been correct when it had decided her personality structure was dominated by a deep need for affiliation. When she had been associated with Ari's group, she had maximized her use of enhancements. When she had switched to the other side, she had become a model of EruLabi virtue.

But he was in love. He had surrendered—willingly, for his own reasons—to one of the oldest delusions the human species had invented. And because he was in love, he had let himself ignore something that should have been obvious. Miniruta's dispute with Ari wasn't an argument about the nature of the universe. It was an argument about what human beings should *believe* about the nature of the universe.

The teas were followed by music. The music was followed by a long, dreamlike concentration on the shape and texture of Miniruta's body. And afterward Morgan returned to his apartment and watched his programs churn out scenarios that included a new factor: a woman who believed Ari's worldview was a disease that should be eradicated from human society.

Morgan's programs couldn't tell him what Miniruta was going to do. No program could predict all the tactical choices a human brain could choose. But the programs could suggest possibilities. And they could estimate the intensity of Miniruta's responses.

He spotted what she was doing hours after she started doing it. Her "randomly searching" machines occupied one of the prime sites on Ari's list and started scraping and digging just a few hours before Ari's own machines were scheduled to work on it.

Ari called Morgan as soon as he finished his first attempt to "reason" with Miniruta. He still thought Miniruta's program had made a random choice. He still believed she was just being obstinate when she refused to let his machines excavate the site.

"She's got some kind of silly idea she has to stick to her ideal of pure randomness," Ari said. "She's trying to tell me she wouldn't be operating randomly if she let her team go somewhere else."

Morgan agreed to act as a go-between and Miniruta gave him the response he had expected. It was just a random event, she insisted. Why should Ari object? Now he could send his machines to one of the other sites on his list.

"It's one of the big possibilities on his current list," Morgan said. "He thinks he should explore it himself."

"Doesn't he think my machines are competent? Is he afraid they'll spend too much time indulging in sensual pleasures?"

"Ari thinks this is a totally accidental occurrence, Miniruta."

She smiled. "And what does my little donilar think?"

Morgan straightened up and gave her his best imitation of an authority figure. It was the first time she had said something that made him feel she was playing with him.

"I think it would be best if he went on thinking that," he said.

Miniruta's eyes widened. Her right hand fluttered in front of her face, as if she was warding off a blow. "Is that a *threat*, donilar? After all we have enjoyed together?"

Three daycycles later, Miniruta's machines took over two more sites. Morgan's surveillance program advised him as soon as it happened and he immediately called Ari and found himself confronted with a prime display of outrage.

"She's deliberately interfering," Ari shouted. "This can't be random. She is deliberately trying to destroy the last hope of the only people in the Solar System who still have faith in the future Even you should be able to see that, Morgan—in spite of your chemical reactions to certain types of female bodies."

It was the kind of situation Morgan normally delegated to one of his political operatives. This time there was no way he could slip away gracefully and let someone else handle it. His studies had taught him what the best responses were. He had even managed to apply them on one or two previous occasions. He let the tirade go on as long as Ari wanted to maintain it. He carefully avoided saying anything that might indicate he was agreeing or disagreeing.

Unfortunately, he was faced with something no one on the ship could have handled. Miniruta had given Ari an opening he had obviously been looking for.

"I agreed to wait until we had a consensus," Ari ranted. "I'm trying to be cooperative. But I think it's time someone reminded your overzealous paramour that there's no practical, physical reason I can't transmit a message to the Solar System any time I want to."

Ari's elongated head could make him look slightly comical when he became overexcited. This time it was a visual reminder of the commitment behind his outbursts.

"If you really want to get this situation calmed down, Morgan—I suggest you remind her I still have more supporters than she has. They can all look at what she's been doing at the first site. They can all see her machines are carefully avoiding all the best locations and deliberately moving at the slowest pace they can maintain without stalling. You can tell her she has two choices. he can get her machines out of all three sites, or she can put them under my control. And after she's done that—I'll send her a list of all the other sites I expect her to stay away from."

Miniruta was standing in the doorway of her ritual chamber. Behind her, Morgan could glimpse the glow of the brass sculpture that dominated the far end. Miniruta had just finished one of the EruLabi rituals that punctuated her daily schedule. She was still wearing the thin, belted robe she wore during most of the rituals.

Only the night before, in this very room, they had huddled together in the most primitive fashion. They had stretched out on the sleeping platform just a few steps to Morgan's left and he had spent the entire night with his arms wrapped around her body while they slept.

"I've discussed the situation with Ari," Morgan said in Tych. "He has indicated he feels your actions have given him the right to transmit a message without authorization. He believes his supporters will approve such an action."

"And he sent you here to relay something that is essentially another threat."

"It is my belief that was his intention."

"You should tell him he'll be making a serious error. You should tell him it's obvious he thinks no one will resist him."

"I believe it would be accurate to say he believes no one will offer him any high level resistance."

"Then you should tell him his assumptions need to be revised. Madame Dawne has already armed herself. I obviously can't tell you more than that. But I can tell you she will fight if Ari tries to take control of the communications module. She is already emotionally committed to fighting."

Miniruta smiled. "Is that an informative response? Will that give Ari some evidence he should modify his assumptions?"

Morgan returned to his apartment and had his fabrication unit manufacture two sets of unarmed probes. The probes were large, cumbersome devices, about the size of a standard water goblet, but he wasn't interested in secrecy. He deployed both sets by hand, from a maintenance hatch, and monitored them on his notescreen while they tractored across the surface area that surrounded the communications module.

His notescreen accepted a call from Miniruta two minutes after the probes had made their fourth find.

"Please do not interfere, Morgan. Madame Dawne has no quarrel with you."

"I've detected four weapons so far. None of them look to me like items Madame Dawne would have deployed on her own."

"Don't underestimate her, Morgan. She believes Ari is threatening her ability to survive."

"I thought Madame Dawne was a dangerous person when we were coping with the course-change controversy. But that was over ten decades ago. She's only been seen twice in the last eight years. The last time her responses were so stereotyped half the people she talked to thought they were dealing with a simulation. I don't know how much personality she has left at this point—but I don't think she could surround the communications module with a defense like this unassisted."

"Ari is threatening the fabric of our community. We made an agreement as a community—a consensus that took every individual's needs into account. Madame Dawne is defending the community against a personality who thinks he can impose his own decisions on it."

* * *

Morgan fed the information from his probes into a wargame template and let the program run for over thirteen minutes. It went through four thousand simulations altogether—two thousand games in which Madame Dawne was willing to risk the total annihilation of the ship's community, followed by two thousand possibilities in which she limited herself to ambushes and low-level delaying tactics. Seventy percent of the time, Madame Dawne could keep Ari away from the communications module for periods that ranged from twenty-one daycycles to two hundred daycycles. She couldn't win, but she could force Ari into a sustained struggle.

And that was all she needed to do, according to Morgan's political estimates. Miniruta would gain some extra support if Ari broke the agreement unilaterally. But neither one of them would have a commanding majority when the fighting began. They would start out with a sixty-forty split in Ari's favor and a drawn out battle would have the worst possible effect: it would intensify feelings and move the split closer to fifty-fifty.

Morgan thought he could understand why people like Ari and Miniruta adapted belief systems. But why did they feel they had to annihilate other belief systems? His profiling programs could provide him with precise numerical descriptions of the emotions that drove the people he modeled. No program could make him feel the emotions himself.

Still, for all his relentless obsession with the Doctrine of the Cosmic Enterprise, Ari was always willing to listen when Morgan showed him the charts and graphs he had generated with his programs. Ari was interested in anything that involved intellectual effort.

"I think we can assume Miniruta isn't going to budge," Morgan reported. "But I have a suggestion you may want to consider."

"I'd be astonished if you didn't," Ari said.

"I think you should send your own machines to the sites she's occupying and have them attempt to carry out your plans. My profiling program indicates there's a high probability she'll attempt to interfere with you. As you can see by the numbers on chart three, the public reaction will probably place you in a much stronger political position if she does."

Ari turned his attention to the chart displayed on the bottom half of his screen and spent a full third of a minute studying it—a time span that indicated he was checking the logic that connected the figures.

"The numbers are convincing," Ari said in Tych. "But I would appreciate it if you would tell me what your ultimate objective is."

"There's a basic conflict between Miniruta's conduct and the message of the EruLabi creeds. Miniruta can't act the way she's been acting without arousing some hostility in the rest of the EruLabi community."

"And you're hoping she'll alter her behavior when she finds the EruLabi are turning against her. Since she is a personality whose 'drive for affiliation' scores in the 99th percentile."

"The EruLabi are not proselytizers," Morgan said in Tych. "Their worldview tends to attract people who avoid controversy and public notice. Many EruLabi are already uncomfortable. If you'll examine Table Six, you'll see the reactions of the EruLabi community already generate an overall minus twenty in their attitude toward Miniruta. Table Seven shows you how much that will increase if they see her actually engaging in some form of active resistance."

"I'm still fully prepared to transmit a message without waiting for authorization, Morgan. I'm willing to try this. But the other option is still open."

"I understand that," Morgan said.

The biggest exploration machines on the planet were high-wheeled "tractors" that were about the size of the fabrication unit that sat in a corner of Morgan's apartment and transformed rocks and waste matter into food and other useful items. Ari started—correctly, in Morgan's opinion—by landing six machines that were only a third that size. Ari's little group of sand sifters and electronic probing devices started to spread out after their landing and three tractors detached themselves from Miniruta's team and tried to block them. Ari's nimble little machines dodged through the openings between the tractors, more of Miniruta's machines entered the action, and the tractors started colliding with Ari's machines and knocking off wheels and sensors.

Morgan stayed out of the rhetorical duel that erupted as soon as Ari circulated his recording of the robotic fracas. Instead, he focused his attention on the reactions of the EruLabi. Miniruta was defending herself by claiming she was upholding her right to pursue an alternate research pattern. It was a weak line of argument, in Morgan's opinion, and the EruLabi seemed to agree with him. The support she was attracting came from people who had opposed Ari's original request to send a message to the Solar System. Morgan's search programs couldn't find a single comment—negative or positive—from anyone who could be identified as an EruLabi.

Morgan's content analysis programs had been collecting every commentary and attempt at humor that mentioned Miniruta. Over the next few hours he found five items that played on the discrepancy between Miniruta's EruLabi professions and her militant behavior. The one he liked best was a forty second video that showed a woman with a BR-V73 body type reclining in an ornate bath. The woman was bellowing EruLabi slogans at the top of her lungs and manipulating toy war machines while she jabbered about love, sensual pleasure, and the comforts of art and music. A broken tea cup jiggled on the floor beside the tub every time one of her toys fired a laser or launched a missile.

It was a crude effort which had been posted anonymously, with no attempt to circulate it. As far as Morgan could tell, only a couple of hundred people had actually seen it. He shortened it by eighteen seconds, transformed the cackles into deepthroated chuckles, and retouched some of the other details.

Of the other four items, two were genuinely witty, one was clumsy, and one was just badtempered and insulting. He modified all of them in the same way he had modified the video. He slipped them into the message stream at points where he could be confident they would be noticed by key members of the EruLabi communion.

Fifteen hours after Miniruta had started obstructing Ari's efforts, Savela Insdotter circulated the official EruLabi response. *Miniruta Coboloji has been an inspiration to everyone who truly understands the EruLabi creeds,* Savela began. *Unfortunately, she seems to have let her enthusiasm for our Way lead her into a dangerous course of action. We reached an agreement and Ari Sun-Dalt abided by it, in spite of all his feelings to the contrary.*

We have a civilized, rational system for resolving differences. We don't have to tolerate people who refuse to respect our procedures. We still control the communication system. We can still sever Miniruta's communication links with Athene and her manufacturing facilities on the moon, if we register our will as a community. Isn't it time we got this situation under control?

Miniruta's answer appeared on the screens of every EruLabi on the ship. Morgan wasn't included on her distribution list but an EruLabi passed it on to him. very word she spoke validated the analysis his program had made all those decades earlier. The tilt of her chin and the tension in her mouth could have been delineated by a simulator working with the program's conclusions.

Morgan watched the statement once, to see what she had said, and never looked at it again. He had watched Miniruta abandon two groups: the original Eight and Ari's most dedicated followers. No group had ever abandoned her.

Savela's proposal required a ninety percent vote—the minimum it took to override the controls built into the information system. Anyone who had watched the ship's political system at work could have predicted Savela was going to collect every yes she needed. The proposal had been attracting votes from the moment people started discussing it—and no one had voted against it.

Morgan believed he was offering Miniruta the best opportunity he could give her. The EruLabi were not a vindictive people. A few wits had circulated clever barbs, but there was no evidence they were committed to a state of permanent rancor. Most of them would quickly forget her "excessive ardor" once she "manifested a better understanding of our ideals".

Miniruta would re-establish her bonds with the EruLabi communion within a year, two years at the most, Morgan estimated He would once again recline beside her as they sampled teas and wines together. He would look down on her face as she responded to the long movements of his body Miniruta was a *good* EruLabi. It suited her.

He knew he had failed when the vote reached the fifty-five percent mark and Miniruta started denouncing the EruLabi who had refused to support her crusade to rid the universe of "cosmic totalitarianism". The tally had just topped sixty-five percent when Ari advised him Miniruta's robots were vandalizing the sites she had occupied.

*   *   *

Fossils were being chipped and defaced. Rocks that might contain fossils were being splintered into slivers and scattered across the landscape. Five of the best sites were being systematically destroyed.

The carnage would end as soon as they cut Miniruta's communications link to the planet. But in the meantime she would destroy evidence that had survived two billion years.

Ari already had machines of his own at two of the sites Miniruta was razing. He had transmitted new orders to the entire group and they had immediately started ramming and blocking Miniruta's machines. The rest of his machines were scattered over the planet.

They had only built three vehicles that could pick up a group of exploration machines and haul it to another point on the planet. Most of the machines on the planet had been planted on their work sites when they had made their initial trip from the moon.

Morgan ran the situation through a wargame template and considered the results. As usual, the tactical situation could be reduced to a problem in the allocation of resources. They could scatter their forces among all five sites or they could concentrate on three. Scattering was the best option if they thought the struggle would only last a few hours. Concentration was the best option if they thought it might last longer.

"Give me some priorities," Morgan said. "Which sites are most important?"

"They're all important," Ari said. "Who knows what's there? She could be destroying something critical at every site she's spoiling."

Morgan gave his system an order and the three transport vehicles initiated a lifting program that would place defensive forces on all five sites. The vote on Savela's proposal had already reached the seventy percent mark. How long could it be before it hit ninety and Miniruta lost control of her equipment?

Most of the exploration machines were weak devices. They removed dirt by the spoonful. They cataloged the position of every pebble they disturbed. If the vote reached cutoff within two or three hours, Morgan's scattered defensive forces could save over eighty-five percent of all five sites.

Short range laser beams burned out sensors. Mechanical arms pounded sensitive arrays. Vehicles wheeled and charged through a thin, low-gravity fog of dust. Morgan found himself reliving emotions he hadn't felt since his postnatal development program had given him simple mechanical toys during the first years of his childhood.

For the first ninety minutes it was almost fun. Then he realized the vote had been stuck at seventy-eight percent for at least fifteen minutes. A moment later it dropped back to seventy-six.

He switched his attention to his political analysis program and realized Miniruta had made an important shift while he had been playing general. She had stopped fighting a crusade against her philosophical rivals. Now she was defending Madame Dawne "and all the other elders who will have to live with the consequences of Ari's headstrong recklessness if the *Green Voyager* changes course."

"Apparently she's decided Madame Dawne offers her a more popular cause," Ari said.

Ten minutes after Miniruta issued her speech, Morgan sent five of his machines in pursuit of two of hers. He was watching his little war party drive in for the kill—confident he had her outmaneuvered—when he suddenly discovered it had been encircled by an overwhelming force. Five minutes later, the program advised him he was facing a general disaster. The "exchange rate" at all five sites was now running almost two to one in Miniruta's favor. Every time he destroyed five of her machines, she destroyed nine of his.

Ari saw the implications as soon as the numbers appeared on the screen. "She's started feeding herself enhancers," Ari said. "She's abandoning her EruLabi principles."

Morgan turned away from his screens. Memories of music floated across his mind.

He switched to Tych, in the hope its hard, orderly sentences would help him control his feelings. "Miniruta has switched allegiances," he said. "We were incorrect when we assumed her last statement was a tactical move. She has acquired a new allegiance."

"Just like that? Just like she left us?"

"It would be more correct to say she feels the EruLabi left her."

"That isn't what you told me she'd do, Morgan."

"The programs indicated there was a ninety percent probability Miniruta would protect her ties with the EruLabi community."

"And now you're faced with one of the options in the ten percent list instead."

A blank look settled over Ari's face. He tipped back his head and focused his attention on his internal electronics.

"Let me see if I understand the situation," Ari said in Tych. "The struggle can continue almost indefinitely if Miniruta maintains the current exchange rate. She is receiving new machines from her production units on the moon almost as fast as you're destroying them. She can continue damaging all five sites, therefore, until they are all totally demolished."

"We still have options," Morgan said. "My pharmaceuticals include enhancers I still haven't used. Miniruta outmatches me intellectually but she has a weakness. She isn't used to thinking about conflict situations. Miniruta spent the last seven decades advancing through the EruLabi protocols. She has devoted twenty-five percent of her total lifespan to her attempts to master the protocols."

"As for the political situation," Ari droned, "according to your best estimates, approximately eighty percent of the ship's population feel we should send a message to the Solar System if we find conclusive evidence intelligent life evolved on Athene. They may not agree I should send a message now, but they do agree it should be sent if I uncover evidence that can be considered conclusive. Most of the people in the other twenty percent have been willing to submit to the will of the majority, even though they aren't happy with the idea. Now Miniruta is offering the twenty percent a tempting opportunity. They can let her destroy the evidence and avoid a decision indefinitely. They don't even have to vote. They can just abstain and hold the count on the current balloting below ninety percent. Miniruta will maintain control of her machines and the sites will be excised from the scientific record."

Ari lowered his head. "It's my opinion I should initiate one of my alternate options. Miniruta can only operate her machines as long as her apartment is connected to the ship's power supply. We will have to sever three alternate power lines to cut her link with the power system, but I believe it can be done."

Morgan stared at the screen that displayed Ari's face. He started to respond in Tych and discovered he couldn't. Ari had triggered an emotional flood that was so powerful Morgan's brain had automatically shifted to VA13.

Ari raised his hand. "I recognize that the action I'm suggesting has serious implications," Ari said. "I realize it could trigger off long term changes in our communal relationships. I believe Miniruta is committing a crime that ranks with the worst atrocities in history. She is destroying a message that has been waiting for us for over two billion years."

"You're talking about something that could make every passenger on this ship feel they had to arm themselves," Morgan said. "This is the first time I've ever heard anyone even *suggest* one passenger should attack another passenger's power connection. What kind of a life could we have here if people felt somebody could cut their power connection every time we had a conflict?"

"We are discussing an extreme situation. Miniruta could be pulverizing the only fossils on the planet that could prove Athene generated intelligent life."

Morgan stood up. "It's always an extreme situation. This time it's *your* extreme situation. Fifty years from now it will be somebody else's. And what do we end up with? A ship full of people forming gangs and alliances so they can protect themselves?"

"Is that all that matters to you, Morgan? Maintaining order in one little rock? Worrying about three thousand people hiding in their own personal caves?"

Morgan knew he was losing control of his impulses. He was behaving exactly the way his personality profile predicted he would behave. But he couldn't help himself. He was staring at someone who was unshakably convinced they were right and he was wrong. Ari could have withstood every technique of persuasion stored in the ship's databanks. What difference did it make what he said?

"*It's the rock I live in!* It's the rock *you* live in!"

Ari switched to VA13—a language he rarely used. The musical pattern he adapted colored his words with a flare of trumpets.

"I live in the galaxy," Ari said. "My primary responsibility is the intellectual evolution of my species."

Miniruta—Ari is going to cut the power lines to your apartment. This is not a ruse. It's not a threat. I'm warning you because I think he's doing something that could have a disastrous effect on the long range welfare of the ship's community—a precedent that could make the ship unlivable. You've still got time if you move now. Put on your emergency suit. Get in your escape tunnel and go all the way to the surface before he puts a guard on the surface hatch. If you start now, you could make it all the way to the communications module while he's still getting organized.

Morgan's forces attacked Miniruta's production facilities on the moon two hours after she received his warning. Her security system put up a fight, but it was overwhelmed within an hour. Every fabrication unit in her factories was brought to a halt. The rail launcher that propelled her machines toward Athene was dismantled at three different points.

Morgan had selected the most powerful intellectual enhancer his physiology could absorb. He would be disoriented for almost five daycycles after he stopped using it. He was still intellectually inferior to Miniruta, but he had just proved he had been right when he had claimed she wasn't used to thinking about conflict situations. He had taken her by surprise because she hadn't realized he had reprogrammed his lunar fabrication units and created a force that could break through her defenses.

This was the first time he had used this enhancer while he was struggling with a real-time, real-world challenge. He turned his attention to the action on the surface of Athene as if he was training a massive weapon on a target.

Miniruta's forces were still destroying his machines faster than he was destroying hers. She had spent a full hour working her way across the surface of the ship to the communications module and she had managed to maintain the exchange rate all the time she had been doing it. On the site closest to Athene's equator, she had taken complete control of the situation. Morgan's machines had been backed against a cliff and most of Miniruta's machines were churning up the ground and lasering potential fossil beds without resistance.

Morgan had eliminated Miniruta's source of reinforcements when he had destroyed her facilities on the moon. His own fabrication units were still turning out a steady stream of reinforcements and launching them at the planet. Sooner or later Miniruta's machines would be wiped out. Sooner or later he would be replacing his machines faster than she destroyed them. But the trip from the moon to Athene took over twenty hours. It would be almost forty hours, the charts on his screens claimed, before he destroyed Miniruta's last machine.

His brain skimmed through the plans for the vehicles that ferried equipment between the moon and the planet. Numbers and equations danced across his consciousness: payloads, production times, the weight of the reaction mass a transport vehicle forced through its engines when it braked to a landing on Athene. His fabrication units on the moon received a new set of orders and started producing transport vehicles that would make the trip in nine hours. The vehicles would carry fifty percent more reaction mass, so they could kill the extra velocity. Payload would be reduced by thirty percent.

"Somebody told her we were going to attack her power lines. She climbed out her surface escape hatch minutes before we put a guard on it. We didn't even know she'd left until she started controlling her machines from the communications module."

Ari had been speaking VA13 when he had deposited the message in Morgan's files. He had obviously wanted to make sure Morgan understood his feelings.

"There's only one person on this ship who could have warned her in time, Morgan. No one in my communion would have done such a thing. Now she's sitting in the communications module, wrecking and smashing some of the most precious information the human race has ever uncovered. And we're battering our skulls into pulp trying to break through all the weapons her friend Madame Dawne deployed around the communications module."

Morgan put his machines into a defensive posture on all five sites and held them on the defensive while he waited for reinforcements. Every now and then, when he saw an opportunity, he launched a hit-and-run attack and tried to catch one of her machines by surprise.

Ari was right, of course. The destruction Morgan was watching on his screens was one of the great criminal acts of history. Most of the fossils that had filled in the story of human evolution had come from a small area of Earth. The sites Miniruta was destroying had been selected because they met all the parameters entered into the search program. Would there be important, unfillable gaps in the record when they had explored the entire planet? Would her spree of destruction leave them with questions that could never be answered?

Morgan switched to the offensive as soon as the first reinforcements arrived from the moon. He picked the site where Miniruta was weakest and eliminated every machine she controlled within two hours. Then he picked her second weakest site and began working on it.

He could feel the full power of Miniruta's mind every step of the way. He was making maximum use of all the help his wargaming programs could give him but he couldn't reduce the exchange ratio by a single percentage point. He was only going to defeat her because she was manipulating a finite force and he could draw on an infinite supply of reinforcements. Whatever he did, she still destroyed nine of his machines every time he destroyed five of hers.

At any given moment, furthermore, only about half her machines were actually fighting his. The rest of them were busily maximizing the destruction she was causing.

"We've lost at least thirty percent of the information we could have pulled from each site," Ari said. "On site four, we probably lost over sixty percent."

Morgan was lying on a couch, with a screen propped on his stomach. The recording of Ari's face seemed to be shimmering at the end of a long tunnel. The medical system had advised him it might be most of a tenday before he recovered from the combined effects of sleeplessness, emotional stress, and ultra-enhancement.

"I could have cut off her power within three or four hours if you hadn't interfered," Ari said. "It took you eleven hours to destroy her vehicles—*eleven hours*—even after you started getting extra reinforcements from the moon."

For the third time in less than a daycycle, Morgan was being given a rare chance to hear Ari speak VA13. This time Ari was applying the full force of a module that communicated graduated degrees of revulsion.

Morgan had made no recordings of his private moments with Miniruta. The EruLabi didn't do that. Pleasure should be experienced only in memory or in the reality of the present, the EruLabi mentors had proclaimed. There was a long period—it lasted over two years—when Morgan spent several hours of every daycycle watching recordings of Miniruta's public appearances.

Savela could have helped him. He could imagine circumstances in which Savela would have offered him a temporary bonding that would have freed him from an emotion that seemed to blunt all his other feelings. Savela was no longer friendly, however. Savela might be an EruLabi but she shared Ari's opinion of his behavior.

Morgan believed he had averted the complete political breakdown of the ship's community. But how could you prove you had avoided something that never happened? People didn't see the big disaster that hadn't taken place. They only saw the small disaster you had created when you were trying to avert the big disaster. Out of the three thousand people on the ship, at least a thousand had decided they would be happier without his company.

Once, just to see if it would have any effect on his feelings, Morgan struck up a relationship with a woman with a BR-V73 body type. The woman was even an EruLabi. She had never advanced beyond the second protocol but that should have been a minor matter. Her body felt like Miniruta's when he touched it. The same expressions crossed her face when they practiced the EruLabi sexual rituals. There was no way he could have noticed any significant difference when he wrapped himself around her in the darkness.

Ari's sexual enhancement was another possibility. Morgan thought about it many times during the next two decades. He rejected it, each time, because there was no guarantee it would give him what he needed. The enhancement only affected the most basic aspect of sexual desire— the drive for simple physical release. It didn't erase memories that included all the hours that had preceded—and followed—the actual moments when their bodies had been joined.

He had made eight attempts to contact Miniruta during the three years that had followed their miniature war. His programs still monitored the information system for any indication she was communicating with anyone. A style analysis program occasionally detected a message Miniruta could have created under a pseudonym. Every example it found had been traced to a specific, identifiable source. None of the authors had been Miniruta.

He had sent two queries to Madame Dawne. The second time, she had appeared on his screen with hair that was so short and so red she looked like someone had daubed her skull with paint. The language she had used had been obsolete when the *Island of Adventure* had left the Solar System.

"Please do not think I am indifferent to your concern," Madame Dawne had said. "I believe I can inform you—with no likelihood of exaggeration or inaccuracy—that Miniruta finds your anxieties heartwarming. Please accept my unqualified assurance that you can turn your attention to other matters. Miniruta is a happy woman. We are both happy women."

Morgan had deleted the recording from his files two tendays after he received it. He had given his profiling program a description of Miniruta's latest transformation. Miniruta had changed her allegiance three times in the last one hundred and fifteen years. There was a possibility her affiliations were episodes in an endless cycle of unions and ruptures, driven by a need that could never be permanently satisfied. The program couldn't calculate a probability. But it was a common pattern.

In the meantime, he still had his researches. He had picked out three evolutionary lines that looked interesting. One line had apparently filled the same ecological niche the pig family had exploited on Earth. The others raised questions about the way predators and prey interacted over the millennia.

They were good subjects. They would keep him occupied for decades. He had now lived over three hundred years. Nothing lasted forever. He had his whole life ahead of him.

In modern society, we often begin conversations with new acquaintances by asking what they "do". You don't really know a character in a story, in my opinion, if you haven't been provided with a reasonably precise answer to that standard query. The author shouldn't fob you off by telling you his hero makes his living as a "businessman" or a "salesman". What's his business? What does he sell? How does he think about it? I feel the same way about the future societies I create. How do their economies operate? How do they create wealth? How do they distribute it? Every society must meet the economic needs of its citizens. It's a fundamental requirement that affects every aspect of their lives.

HAGGLE CHIPS

It was a very civilized highjack. Janip was riding over the wilderness in a small airship, en route to his first meeting with his customer, and the attack began when a flock of flying creatures rose out of the leaf tops and drove straight for the ship. Janip knew something was happening as soon as he realized he was looking at birds. There were no natural birds on Conalia.

The birds ended their drive in a suicide attack on both propellers. The airship came to a halt. Two birds with absurdly exaggerated wingspans descended from some vantage point in the sky and hovered about five hundred meters from the starboard windows—well beyond the range of any weapons Janip might be carrying. Their wings measured a good ten meters, tip to tip, and they were both carrying small two-handed creatures with brain-machine links fastened to their heads. They banked downward as soon as they had given him a good look and disappeared under the gondola.

"I have encountered a difficulty," the airship said. "I believe I am under attack. I have signaled for help."

Janip settled into his seat and transmitted messages to two addresses. He was the only passenger in the gondola. His customer had chartered the ship just for him—an extravagance that indicated he could have negotiated a higher price when they had haggled over the merchandise he was carrying.

The ship quivered. It floated upward for a second and stopped. The birds' passengers had obviously attached contacts to the bottom of the gondola. The ship's control system was trying to gain altitude while it fought a silent battle with an electronic invasion.

The gondola trembled again. The two oversize birds flapped into view, one on each side.

"Good afternoon," the ship said. "Your ship is now descending. The two riders positioned on the gondola are both armed. They can enter the passenger area at any time and administer a pacifier. Or you can indicate you are willing to follow instructions. The choice is up to you."

Janip glanced out the window and verified the leaves were getting closer. A wash of enforced calm settled over his emotions. He had experimented with uncontrolled passion when he had been in his twenties but he had installed a full suite of neurological emotional controls when that bit of youthful probing had reached its predestined end.

"You will not encounter resistance," Janip said. "I can see you've taken control of the situation."

The gondola brushed against wide dark leaves. There were no real trees on Conalia. The tallest organisms on the planet were essentially giant soft-bodied plants. The ship pushed them aside as it descended and hovered a couple of meters above the ground. The rear hatch swung open. A ladder extended.

"If you will please descend," the ship said, "it will save us the trouble of boarding."

A man and a woman stepped into view as he backed out of the hatch. They both had functional, sparsely utilitarian brain-machine links on their heads and swivel-mounted laser-electric stunners in their hands. Sighting glasses hid their eyes. They escorted him to an all-terrain vehicle with oversized wheels and Janip entered the first stage of his captivity.

His captors drove him to a compound on the river. They ushered him into a large, lightly furnished room and left him alone for three days.

They didn't tell him why he had been kidnapped but it didn't take him long to figure it out. His communications implant still worked and they didn't try to jam it. The face of his account manager at Kaltuji Merchant Bank hovered in front of him minutes after the door clicked shut. Margelina had been the second person he had contacted when the attack had begun.

"You're in the compound established by the Taranazzu Cultivators," Margelina said. "I think we can assume this has something to do with their dispute with your customer."

Janip scowled. "I thought the Taranazzu Cultivators were supposed to be non-violent."

"They are, ideologically. We're just as surprised by this as you are."

"I checked out that squabble when I started negotiating with my customer. Elisette's the party who looks like she might consider a little kidnapping."

"Elisette is already attempting to initiate negotiations. In the meantime, I can advise you we can let you have full access to our communications system, with all security mechanisms functioning. You can continue to conduct all your normal business and social activities, just as you have been. The only restriction will be items that can be used to help you escape. We have to maintain a neutral stance in all disputes. It's the only way we can keep secure communications open in this kind of situation."

"Can I assume my jailers will let me maintain communications unless you advise them I've violated the agreement?"

"We're working on that now. But I have to advise you we will immediately terminate your communications account if we discover you've violated the agreement."

"I'd be very surprised if you didn't, Margelina."

The top politician in the compound's social structure visited Janip late in the morning of the fourth day. The politician's constituents referred to him as their primary facilitator—without capitals. He was a large man whose clothes flowed over swellings and indentations that indicated his muscles had received the maximum enhancement he could impose on them.

Janip had held several discussions with his customer and she had given him her take on the primary facilitator. "Sivmati's settled into a very nice arrangement," Elisette had argued. "They're supposed to be very egalitarian and non-competitive but you don't have to examine their accounts to see he gets an extra share of everything. He became a convert about a year after they established the compound. And gradually wormed his way to the top."

Elisette didn't have to tell Janip she shared his attitude toward politicians. People like Sivmati didn't build. They didn't create. They didn't trade. They just worked their way up hierarchies.

The dispute between Elisette and the Taranazzu Cultivators was a conflict over hydroelectric power. Elisette controlled the biggest hydroelectric plant currently functioning on the planet. She and three of her friends had occupied the waterfall at Belita Lake when they arrived on Conalia and invested twenty standard years in the construction of the plant.

"We have no desire to harm you or anyone else," Sivmati assured him. "Or cause you the slightest inconvenience. The only person you should blame for this is Elisette. We settled here, by the rapids, because we innocently assumed the planet could use a second power source on this river. Nothing we have done should cause your client any loss of income. The new dam she is building upstream from us is deliberately designed to interfere with the flow of the river and negate our own efforts. It has no other purpose. She is building it because she wants to monopolize the energy potential of the biggest river in this area of the planet."

"Elisette doesn't need me," Janip said. "You have eight people on Conalia who can give her a perfectly good set of new eyes."

"But not as good as the eyes you're selling her. We know Elisette. We've been coping with her since we inaugurated our settlement. She's the kind who demands the best. Nothing else will do."

"And what are you going to do if she turns out to be stubborner than you think?"

"We know she is going blind. We know she needs your services. We think you will be our guest for a year at worst. In the meantime you will be given whatever you need to carry on your business from here. And the full freedom to enjoy all the hospitality we can offer you."

Sivmati smiled. "This is a very pleasant place. We have every amenity. I hardly ever leave it myself."

It was a pleasant place. The Cultivators served the life giving, nurturing Power postulated by the Taranazzu sect and their expressions of devotion included a healthy round of mandatory feasting and dancing.

The central tenet of the Taranazzu belief system was a rigid acceptance of everything mankind had learned about the physical universe. The theory that a single all powerful god ruled the universe had become indefensible, in their view, as soon as human beings had discovered they were the products of the heartless process of evolution through natural selection. No loving god could have inflicted so much pain on his creation.

There must, therefore, be several Powers, the Taranazzu founders had argued. We don't know what these Powers are. It's possible we can't know. They may be superior beings, like the families of gods our ancestors imagined. They may be natural forces inherent in the structure of the universe. We must accept our ignorance. But we can choose the Powers we will serve.

The sexual mores of the settlement had their attractions, too. Janip got his first look at their system while he was eating his second dinner in the communal hall. The six people sitting near an ornamental fountain became involved in a discussion that kept attracting glances from the other tables. An outburst from one of the participants brought an immediate response. Two people hurried toward the commotion. A woman bent over a man who was glaring across the table. A man crouched beside the woman who was receiving the glare and nodded rhythmically as he talked to her.

The Cultivators had adopted a modified version of a sexual pattern developed by a terrestrial primate called bonobos. Bonobo females used sex to regulate social behavior. The Cultivators felt both sexes should shoulder the responsibility. Touches and soothing words calmed the two diners. The dining hall had two small side rooms that could have been put to use if the situation had required a more extensive response.

As a "guest" Janip was a prime candidate for emotional regulation. Two women had invited him to join their table when he entered the hall. A third joined them a few minutes later.

The primary facilitator received his share of regulating, too. Janip wasn't surprised to learn that Sivmati had purchased the maximum sexual enhancement available on Conalia.

Elisette was a large, big-boned woman who liked to wear bright colors. She had started scheming as soon as she heard about the kidnapping. As Janip had assumed she would.

"We can discuss anything we want," Elisette said. "Correct?"

"That's my understanding of my agreement with the bank," Janip said. "I'd love to have a well written program that would totally disrupt the Cultivator's security system, if you happen to have one handy. We can talk about the possibility all day. But don't transmit the program over this channel."

"And what will they do if we violate their rules?"

"I'll be barred from all contact with the planetary banking system."

"They can enforce that? They can make every bank on the planet follow their orders?"

"Against a lone visiting trader? Who's done something every bank on the planet would object to if he did it to them? My bank may be overestimating its influence, Elisette. But I'd rather not run a test."

Elisette shrugged. "There's a basic conflict between the general thrust of the Cultivators' ideology and the fact that they've kidnapped you and taken you prisoner. There must be a few people in that compound who feel our friend Sivmati isn't quite as pure as he should be."

"I've been watching for attitudes like that. Sivmati doesn't seem to think there's any conflict. He feels they're just defending themselves— that you're building your new dam so you can force them off the river and control the whole length of it. So far he doesn't seem to be running into any serious opposition."

"And what do you think?"

"I'm a trader, Elisette. You and I have a deal. He's interfering with a legitimate business transaction."

"That's what I want to hear. We'll get you out of there, Janip. I'm not the only one working on this. The whole business community in Kaltuji is seething. They all know they can't let a bunch of religious fanatics get away with this kind of barbarism."

Janip could have pointed out that she could resolve the whole situation, at any time, by announcing she was canceling her dam project. But why bother? Elisette had her objectives. Sivmati and his followers had theirs.

Janip had been born on a world that had passed through a nightmare created by a moral fanatic. The revolt that had toppled David Jammet's tyranny had killed hundreds of people. Personalities that might have lived for thousands of years had been snuffed out like deleted bits of data.

Janip's own father had been killed before he could complete his second century. Janip existed because his mother had managed to save her husband's genome. She knew she couldn't recreate the dead. That was impossible. But she had to do something.

She had been a good mother. But no one could stop the flow of time. She had acquired other relationships. Janip had developed his own circle of friends. Inevitably, there had come a moment when he had known he could leave her behind. He had lived through six decades of experience and he was still one of the youngest people on Arlane. He was faced with the situation that confronted every "young" person sooner or later. The top social and economic niches in his society were all occupied and the people who occupied them were still going to be perched on the same branches when he was plodding toward the end of his first millennium.

The eyes he was selling Elisette had been a cutting edge technology on Arlane. He had spent two standard years learning to deal with all the problems that could pop up when you planted them in a living human body with all its biological quirks. He continued developing his skills during the twenty tendays he had been imprisoned in the closet the starship's owners called a minimum-fare cabin. The eyes would be a state-of-the-art item on Conalia in a few standard years but for now he had a *de facto* monopoly. Just as he had a temporary monopoly on the lesser items he had selected before he placed eleven light years between himself and the haunted world that had goaded a woman into producing him.

Eleven light years in space. Eleven standard years in time. Two hundred days ship time as the ship pulled energy from the interstellar vacuum and pushed against the speed of light. His mother had lived through every minute of those years during the two hundred days he had kept himself busy in his closet. He had known that would happen since his first childhood contacts with elementary physics but the reality still seemed eerie. Every friend he had left behind was eleven years older. The laws that governed space and time and the movements of starships were weirder than the most bizarre religions humans had invented.

David Jammet had taken control of the human settlements on Arlane so he could pursue a dream that had bedeviled mankind for seven centuries. Jammet had actually believed, in spite of all the evidence to the contrary, that he could produce human beings who had been cured of the human tendency to engage in violence. It was an experiment that had been tried eight times in the last few centuries and it always ended in disaster. The creatures who emerged from the laboratories walked around in human bodies but they were psychological monsters. The human capacity for violence was inextricably linked to every trait the species needed or valued. It couldn't be sliced out of the human personality without damaging everything around it.

He was an interstellar trader. A visitor who sold the things he brought from another world. And bought the things he would sell on the next. People were always fighting over something. He wouldn't exist if they didn't.

The woman named Farello liked to sit on the observation deck that overlooked the river. She reminded him, in some ways, of the last woman he had bonded with on Arlane. She was tall and graceful and she maintained an air of good humored calm. The first time he noticed her, she was sitting at a table with two friends when he wandered onto the deck after dinner. The other women in the group invited him to join them and a pair of warm, interested eyes regarded him from the other side of the table as he traded light chatter with her companions. Her eyes were the primary memory he took away from the conversation.

He had been settling for whoever came his way. His "hosts" wanted to keep him placid and the women who accepted the task were pleasant and pleasurable. This one triggered something deeper. He even felt a twinge of jealousy when he sought her out two days after that first encounter and discovered she and one of the men were double-linked on a work assignment.

"They work together a lot," the schedule tracker said. "They've got a high level of rapport and they seem to have a talent for spotting things that deserve a closer look. Would you like me to tell her you asked about her?"

Janip shook his head. He had tried to sound casual but he knew Sivmati was going to hear about this. This was the first time he had indicated he was interested in a particular woman.

"I'll see her when I see her."

"They usually stay linked for forty-two hours when they're working together. They like to put in long work sessions and follow them up with long leisure periods."

Janip suppressed the temptation to check the work schedules. Sivmati would learn about that, too.

* * *

He "ran into" Farello the morning after her work session ended, when he wandered into the dining room in search of a late breakfast. She was sitting by herself, with a small plate of rolls in front of her, and she waved to him as she bit into a roll.

It was a sharp day in early winter but the observation deck had an enclosed area. They carried their plates and cups to the deck a few minutes after he joined her and settled into one of the easiest streams of conversation he had ever navigated with a female companion. Farello and her working partner had been connected to the network that monitored the settlement's impact on the natural, unterrestrialized ecological system that surrounded the compound. She briefed him on the things she had just learned about the interactions between two of the native plants and a network of communal leaf nesters, he countered with some observations about the different directions evolution had taken on Conalia and Arlane, and from there they moved on to all the anecdotes and tidbits you could toss into the flow when you were chatting with someone you had just met.

Janip knew he was emotionally vulnerable. His life had been disrupted. He was a stranger on a new world. No one had to tell him he was succumbing to one of Sivmati's manipulations. He had processed a quick calculation as he crossed the room toward her table and noted that she had made herself available at the earliest time he could have seen her again, if you assumed she needed to sleep for a few hours after her extended work period. Her wave had been well calculated, too. It had been friendly and pleasant but there had been no indication it was an invitation.

The interlude that followed their breakfast chat was just as warm and fervent as he had hoped it would be. She wasn't calming him. She wasn't rewarding him for maintaining the peace and stability of the group. She was responding to *him*.

He knew her emotions had been tampered with. No one reacted like that after two pleasant social encounters. But what difference did it make? Every situation had its pluses. Why shouldn't he take advantage of them?

Elisette even encouraged the relationship. "It may be something we can use," Elisette said. "Sivmati may be playing with her need to bond. If he is, he could have set up conflicts we can exploit."

"You don't think she's just been enticed by my natural sexual magnetism?" Janip said.

"You have your attractions. But I think you can see that she's developed a fixation on you in a remarkably short time. Sects always attract personalities with a strong drive to form bonds. She bonded with the group. She bonded with Sivmati. He's probably enhanced her impulse to bond with you. The bonders that sects attract tend to be really strong— in the upper five percent in that area. She would be doing something for him and the group if she let him apply the modification. And she would be agreeing to reinforce a natural tendency. A tendency most bonders consider a virtue."

Janip had thought of Elisette as someone who had the brains to spot an obvious site for a hydroelectric installation and the tenacity to spend years working on it. Now he was beginning to realize she had qualities that went beyond that.

"Sivmati may know what he's doing," Elisette said. "Don't underestimate him. But we shouldn't assume he's a political mastermind just because he's managed to manipulate a bunch of sect adherents. Somebody who really understood personality modification would have thought twice before he created the kind of conflicts he's set up in that woman. He's burdened her with a serious psychological stress if I'm right— the tension between her bonds with her group and the bond she's developing with you. Don't let up, Janip. Work on that bond like you were planning to make it last to the end of eternity."

Janip had decided the watchcats were the critical element in the compound security net. There were six of them and they patrolled the compound day and night.

"They've always got at least one cat within striking range," he advised Elisette. "I'll be dealing with a cat two minutes after somebody decides I'm making a break."

"I can get you a program that will disrupt the cats' programming anytime you want it. Just give me the word. I can break it up into a hundred segments and hide it in as many messages as it takes. Your friends at the bank will never notice it."

"They'll know we did it afterward."

"By then you'll be free."

"And what do I do after that? What happens when I land on my next world and the banks know I can't be trusted?"

"I need those eyes, Janip. I'm paying you to deliver."

"Can you send the program through some other link?"

"As secure as the bank link? Do you think I'd be paying the kind of money the banks are charging me if we had anything else on the planet as good as this link?"

The personal quarters building contained six suites that had been set aside for couples. Janip and Farello moved into a vacant set of rooms nine tendays after he began his sojourn at the settlement. The suite wasn't as big as the layout Sivmati occupied but Janip liked the rugs and the heavy, ornately molded furniture the last tenants had installed.

"You sound like you're settling in," Elisette said.

Janip shrugged. "I may as well enjoy what's available. I spent three days in a decent guest house in between the jail cell I lived in on the ship and the camouflaged prison I'm living in now."

"And how about your companion? Are you planning to take her along when you leave?"

"I want to get out of here, Elisette. That's priority number one. If she wants to join me later—we can deal with that then."

Elisette studied him for a moment and let the subject die. Janip had given her the answer she wanted to hear. He was certain he had been telling the truth. But he also knew he hadn't really thought about the matter.

Elisette wasn't the only party who was negotiating with the Cultivators. The bureaucrats in the government of Kaltuji City had entered the conversation. They worked for a political system dominated by traders and economic hustlers. Kidnappings and acts of violence interfered with the civilized pursuit of wealth.

"They aren't making any threats," Sivmati said. "They're sending me the usual extremely polite messages. But we both know they can create annoying inconveniences for our community if they initiate the economic sanctions they like to flourish. But that's all it would be. Inconvenience."

Janip smothered his emotions under a blanket of bland serenity—his standard response to the useless rush of anger Sivmati usually provoked.

"Is that a message I'm supposed to relay to my banker?" Janip said.

Sivmati smiled. "I'm keeping you informed. Uncertainty can create unnecessary emotional stress."

Margelina received Sivmati's message with a shrug. "We know what his medical resources are. They're good but he's a long way from total self-sufficiency."

"Have you considered the fact that you're dealing with a religious community? People can be very stubborn when they feel they have to live up to a moral code."

"He's not David Jammet, Janip. This isn't Arlane."

"He could still hold out a lot longer than you might expect. And I'm the one who has to sit here while you make faces at each other."

Janip could believe Farello might be torn by the emotional conflict Elisette had hypothesized. But she had apparently resolved it by deciding the villain in the situation was Elisette, not Sivmati.

At Elisette's urging, Janip had linked to a second, lower-security network and used it to expand his social contacts and take his case to the general populace. Over three hundred thousand people currently inhabited the various settlements humans had established on Conalia. Most of them seemed to have an opinion on his situation.

Farello's contributions seethed with rage at the people who objected to her leader's tactics. To Farello, Elisette was an empire builder who wanted to seize control of an economic chokepoint. The Cultivator's power plant would have no impact on Elisette's plant at Belita Falls. Why shouldn't other people tap the river's potential?

We are a peaceful community. We are building a facility that will benefit everyone who lives on Conalia. The new dam Elisette is erecting has only one purpose—a monopoly on the resources of the river. Why aren't you threatening Elisette? Why are you directing your anger at a leader who is trying to protect you from her ambitions?

Janip maintained the most neutral stance he could manage. He had opened the second link so Elisette could slip him a clandestine program, if they decided they should activate an escape plan. He confined his public statements to principled arguments based on the importance of free trade, unhampered by political disputes.

We all understand the benefits of trade. People like me bring you things that become valuable, important additions to your society. We buy other things so we can eventually sell them elsewhere. Everybody gains. But we can't carry out our function if we can't circulate freely.

*   *   *

Janip had linked to dramas about men who became addicted to sexual liaisons with particular women but he had never taken the idea seriously, even when the links had fed him the physical sensations that were supposed to fuel the addiction. Some part of him had always remained detached. It was a fantasy that was just as unlikely as simulations crowded with women driven by an inexplicable need to give him anything his imagination could conceive.

Was it happening to him now? Or was he just reacting to his isolation? It had been at least forty years since he had thought about sex as much as he thought about it now. He would leave Farello after a three hour session that should have quelled all his yearnings for a couple of tendays and his mind would start wandering toward their next encounter before he'd spent an hour looking after his business interests.

He could shut off his urges, of course. But he didn't *want* to. He had to force himself to make the effort. When he made it.

"I think it's time we set a date," he told Elisette.

"It's like I said, right? She let Sivmati focus her biggest need on you?"

"You want your merchandise. I want to get back to a nice normal place like Kaltuji where I can talk to people with nice normal interests like profit and pleasure. And there's only two ways that can happen. You can give them what they want. Or we can get me out of here."

Elisette's accomplices transmitted the program over three tendays, inside twelve hundred other messages, in twelve hundred packets randomly distributed. Sivmati might have hired break-in specialists who could follow the transmissions coming in over the second link, but their surveillance programs would have to spot a telltale code sequence in five of the fragments.

Janip loaded the fragments into his personal implant but he left the program unassembled. He would assemble it thirty minutes before he started moving.

"You won't have time to run a thorough retest on the program," Elisette said. "But we have to take the risk. We have to assume they can monitor everything that comes through that link. And we have to assume they can run through the stuff stored in your personal system now and then."

Elisette owned two air cushion skimmers and she and her associates still used them to run between her installation and the settlements on the coast. Janip had even seen Sivmati return a wave when one of Elisette's companions had raced by the settlement while the primary facilitator had been standing on the observation deck.

"There's no harm in a little civility," Sivmati had said.

The Cultivators were fabricating turbines that would tap the flow of the river as it pushed through the narrows. The turbines would be planted on the bottom of the river, where they would have the minimum impact on navigation, but they were already constructing a canal on the opposite shore, for traffic that would have to bypass their installation.

Elisette decided the escape would take place just before dawn. One of her skimmers would position itself about twenty-five kilometers from the settlement. Janip would run toward the river at the appointed time, the skimmer would pull into position a few seconds before he reached the dock, and he and the driver would race up the river and present Elisette with her purchase.

Janip could have spent the evening before the escape working on his business deals. He could have settled in beside Farello after she had gone to sleep and drifted off without waking her up. She would reach for him in the morning, he would be gone, that would be that.

He had thought about doing it that way. He had known he should. He could even have picked a time when she would be immersed in one of her work sessions. He could have checked the work schedule and told Elisette she should pick a day when he would have the apartment to himself. But he didn't. He accepted the day Elisette chose and spent the afternoon with Farello, talking about all the things they talked about. They ate dinner alone in their apartment. And afterward he did everything he could to give her an experience that would dwarf anything she might feel when she discovered he had left her.

His sleep system eased him awake gradually, so he wouldn't make any sudden moves. He had placed a minimum set of clothes in the room he used for an office. The records and programs he needed for his business were all stored in his internal systems. The bank had backups, in addition, and he had cached backup storage devices in his clothes.

Lift yourself out of the bed one slow, calculated move at a time. Listen to her breathe while you stand on the rug. Pad across the room on bare feet. Slip into shoes, pants, and shirt. Watch the minutes change on your clock display.

Now!

The windows had been fabricated from an elegant solar powered material that could reconfigure into a screen when you felt the need for ventilation. And yield before a steady push when you felt you needed an emergency exit. They had placed him on the third floor of a three story building but he could reduce the drop by the time-honored method of hanging from the bottom of the window with his arms stretched above him.

The building had been surrounded with a border of native plants. He rolled onto his side when he hit but a sharp spike of pain advised him he had twisted his right ankle. He blocked off the pain and flowed into a run as he stood up.

The roar and crash of the rapids dominated the nightscape. Nobody had set off an alarm. No loudspeakers ordered him to stop. It wasn't necessary. The security system would have responded as soon as he pushed on the window. Cameras were watching his every move. Watchcats were racing across the grounds. Messages had awakened the people who had been assigned to security duty.

A cat trotted around a group of bushes. Yellow eyes regarded him. The cat angled toward him and he let it travel three more steps before he subvocalized four nonsense syllables.

He was holding his anxiety responses at the level they would normally reach if he was engaging in a competitive sport—a reaction that would keep him alert and fully rational. There was a moment when he actually felt his arms and legs start to knot up. The cat hadn't missed a step. Another cat had emerged from the shadows ahead of him and veered toward him with the same mechanical relentlessness.

The first cat rose on its rear legs and clawed at the air as if it was trying to scratch an opening in an invisible wall. He subvocalized the trigger again and the second cat covered three full meters before it shrieked and swung away from him.

Janip ran past the end of the quarters building and turned toward the river. The top of the skimmer ramp was only a hundred meters away. The first cat was still clawing at the air behind him. The second cat had settled onto its belly with its head swinging from side to side and its body bent into a curve.

They had opted for the simplest defensive program Elisette's sources could design. Once the program squirmed through the defenses around the cat's programming, it would overload the system with a blizzard of rapidly multiplying random data. The effect wouldn't last forever. The cat's defenses could shut it down and erase everything it had received from the time it started its approach. But by that time he would be clambering down the ramp toward the skimmer.

He was running along a walkway that curved through patches of ornamental shrubbery. Shrines displayed statues of the deities associated with the Power the Cultivators served. He thought he could hear a motor over the noise of the rapids but he couldn't be sure. They had decided he wouldn't communicate with the skimmer unless he had to. Ideally, the security team wouldn't know what he was trying to do until the skimmer pulled up to the ramp just before he started down.

He picked up the whir of the skimmer's power plant as he galloped across the vines that covered the ground around the statue closest to the ramp. There was a gate across the ramp but he knew he could climb over it if it was locked.

A cat landed in front of the gate. Stiff legs braced against the ground. A growl cultivated by generations of genetic designers brought him to a halt.

He knew he was probably wasting his time before he activated his defensive program but he subvocalized the code words anyway. The cat held its pose and he switched on his communications system and flashed a picture of the situation to the skimmer.

The response sounded matter of fact and unfazed. "I'll come up the ramp. Hold on."

The cat growled again. Janip looked around and discovered he and the cat seemed to be alone. Lights had switched on all over the grounds but he couldn't see any indication the security team had left the comfort of its posts.

It was possible the cat had recovered faster than they'd assumed it would. But there was another explanation that was less encouraging....

The skimmer whirred up the ramp and stopped behind the gate. "Let's see what we can do with this kitty," the matter of fact voice said.

The skimmer was supposed to be equipped with a program that would confront the cat's system with an entirely different challenge. The pilot did whatever he was supposed to do and the cat rose on its hind legs. It flopped onto the ground with its back arched and Janip hurled himself forward. His hands grabbed the top of the gate.

Janip had absorbed hits from laser-electric stunners during a period in his early youth when he had engaged in mock battles with several of his friends. He knew what was happening as soon as he felt the shock slam through his body. It was a low-power effect. The gunner was positioned at least fifteen meters behind him. The charge had lost thirty percent of its power as it traveled down the tunnel of ionized air created by the laser. But it did what it was supposed to. A cat landed on his chest seconds after his back hit the ground.

They had known about the smuggled program from the start, of course. The cats had been responding to commands from their controllers when they had acted like they were reacting to the program. Sivmati had applied a standard psychological technique. Let your victim think he's made it. Hit him at the last possible moment. Maximize his disappointment and frustration.

"I can understand why you might try that," Sivmati said. "I'd probably do the same thing. But we'd all be better off if we just presented Elisette with a united front. Let her know you've decided we're right. Tell her she won't receive her new eyes until she abandons her ambitions and dissolves every molecule she's added to her second dam."

Farello had been standing by the door when they escorted him back to the apartment. Two people from the security team had been propping him up. They had hit him with a second blast from the stunner while he had been lying under the cat. They dropped him on the bed and he huddled there by himself for the rest of the night.

He didn't call to her. In the morning he wondered if he should have. But he didn't. He stayed in the bedroom, after he woke up, until he heard her leave.

The first person he talked to was Elisette. She had left him a message minutes after the skimmer had left the ramp but he didn't return the call until he had spent an hour moping around the apartment.

"We knew that could happen," Elisette said. "We took the chance and it didn't work out."

"They could have stopped me at any time I didn't see the people with the stunners but they must have been shadowing me all the time I thought I was clear."

"And now you're just as shaken as they hoped you'd be, right? Snatch it away right at the moment you think you've got it."

"They aren't going to give in, Elisette. They're just as stubborn as you are."

"What's your love interest doing?"

"She left before I got up. I haven't said a word to her."

"Find her. Talk to her. Get her back."

"After this? What am I supposed to tell her?"

"Tell her whatever you need to tell her. She's yours. She wants to stay with you. Give her the excuse."

She came back to him. Late in the afternoon. While he was still telling himself he had to think about the best way to approach her.

"I guess I'll just have to depend on the security system," she said. "I seem to have underestimated my personal charms."

She smiled. She gave her hips a little toss. It was a brave response.

"I didn't want to leave you," Janip said. "You're the only aspect of this whole situation that could make me hesitate. I'd just stay here and let things drift if you were the only consideration. I don't *want* to leave, Fari. I just feel I have to."

It wasn't the best speech he had ever offered a woman but she accepted it. She led him into the bedroom and the present blocked out the past.

Sivmati's surveillance programs had detected the defensive program while it was being transmitted and installed a neutralizer in the cats' systems. But there were hundreds of other programs Janip could use the next time he made a break. They just had to get one to him.

"You've got two possibilities," Elisette said. "We can transmit it through your bank. Or we can make a physical transferal."

"And there's no way an outsider can pass me something," Janip said. "Given the way I'm being watched. So someone else has to make the pickup. And we only have one serious candidate."

Elisette smiled. "We seem to have been thinking along the same lines."

"Not really. I've just developed some understanding of your thought processes."

"She's vulnerable, Janip. She's still vulnerable. She's probably even more conflicted than she was, after the shock you gave her when you tried to escape. Keep working on her. Keep strengthening the bond."

"And get her to where she's willing to betray her group just so she can keep someone who's going to leave this world sooner or later no matter what happens? That's a cruel thing to do, Elisette. She'll be in a turmoil for decades, no matter what happens."

"Do you want to stay there until you've gotten so worn down you start believing their sermons? I'm not giving in on this. That dam is going up. I can always get a temporary set of eyes while I wait for them to understand what they're up against."

Margelina was caught between Janip and her overseers in the bank. She stuck to the official position but she didn't hide her sympathy.

In the end, they always returned to the same issue. The bank had to think about the future. Janip had been given access to the ultra-secure communication system because Sivmati knew the bank would keep its bargain. If the bank violated its agreement for Janip, the next group of kidnappers wouldn't be so trusting. And the next kidnap victim would have to conduct his business over a less secure system.

"This isn't the last time we're going to have this problem, Janip. We're a new world. How would you feel if you couldn't use our system because your captors knew the last kidnap victim had violated his agreement?"

"Then send in a rescue force. Smash up some buildings. Kill some crops. Let them know you aren't going to tolerate this kind of behavior."

"We're looking at all the options. Kaltuji isn't a dictatorship. We can't plunge into that kind of action without a solid consensus."

"You've got influential people in your city who think you should let thugs and religious zealots disrupt legal business deals?"

"Sivmati knows what we can do. Elisette knows what we can do. We're a factor in every calculation they're making."

"Do they know what you're *willing* to do? I haven't seen much evidence they have to think about *that*."

* * *

Dancing played a central role in the Cultivators' communal life. They danced every night after dinner and they seemed to use every style of dance humans had developed for their mating rituals, from staid promenades to heated twosomes and floor shaking communal stomps.

Janip had added the entire library to his internal programming when he initiated his relationship with Farello. They had practiced the couple dances together in private and he had managed to survive his first dance session without committing a fumble that disrupted a communal number. The implanted programs could give you an automatic grasp of the steps but they couldn't install the intuitive adjustments to your partners that Farello had developed.

Sivmati was a practiced expert, of course. His straight back and hard stamps created a classic image when he joined a partner in one of the more vivid courting dances. His bellows and chest thumps dominated an all-male dance that bore a suspicious resemblance to a stylized combat. He did it with a smile and a proper touch of satire but his attitudes became the primary message of the event. The other men on the floor faded into the background.

If you drew a diagram of the human food chain, Janip had concluded, politicians would occupy the top perch. Soldiers and other experts in violence clutched the second rung. Creators and traders lit where they could. He had realized Sivmati was a politician but he had assumed Elisette belonged to his own class. Instead, he seemed to be caught between two of a kind. Sivmati reigned over a flock of religious communalists. Elisette wanted to turn a power system into an empire.

Janip slipped his arm around Farello's waist and she smiled at him as he swung her through the first steps of a light-hearted couples dance that included mock displays of disdainful rejection. They clowned their way through the dance as if he had never attempted to leave her and she saw him as a friendly, good-humored source of fun and companionship.

Elisette was a customer. He needed her money. That was the heart of the matter.

"Our allies in Kaltuji have decided they can send a delegation," Elisette said. "They can claim their engineers want a direct onsite look at the facility the Cultivators are constructing. It's not a total fake either. There are people in the government who think they can set up a compromise if they get a better understanding of the things we're building."

"They're willing to plant somebody in the delegation who will make the delivery?"

"Just tell us where to drop it."

"And when. I still have to discuss this with the person who's going to pick it up."

"Give her an excuse. Tell her it's a business message. Indicate you're doing something a little underhanded."

"It's still a risk, Elisette. She can do everything we ask her and tell Sivmati, too."

"She won't. Give her an excuse. That's all she needs."

Elisette's face softened. She actually looked sympathetic. She was probably generating a high priced implanted simulation but Janip was surprised she could even manage that.

"You aren't to blame for this, Janip. You didn't put her in the bind she's in. Sivmati set her up. Not you."

Conalia was half a billion years older than Arlane but the largest mobile organisms on the planet were essentially variations on the insect life found on other habitable planets.

Conalia was a low temperature "equatorial planet"—life flourished in a narrow band around the equator. Ice caps and frigid barrens covered eighty percent of its surface. The planet was still plodding toward the glories of reptiles and mammals, according to the most widely accepted theory, because natural selection had less to work with.

Other theories touted other explanations. But everybody agreed the native life forms were just as interesting as the fuzzier creatures that had evolved on more hospitable planets. Guests always visited the observation deck, even in winter. The rapids seemed to foster large water creatures who could handle the currents. Spectacular eight-winged flyers skimmed across the white caps and skewered swimmers with telescoping spears. Snaky swimmers arced above the surface and attacked flyers. Clouds of famished smaller creatures descended on their overgrown rivals at predictable intervals. A visitor could paste a wafer under a railing and be confident no one would notice.

Retrieving the wafer would be a different matter. "I'm working on an especially delicate business deal," Janip told Farello. "The whole project depends on secrecy. Even Margelina doesn't know about it. Nobody in the bank knows about it."

"And you don't trust the bank's security system?"

"They're protecting me from intruders from outside their system. I'd rather not take it for granted they aren't watching me themselves. Not in this case."

She knew he was lying, of course. Elisette had been right. Farello didn't even ask him why she couldn't tell Sivmati about the pickup. He had prepared an answer if she asked that. But she didn't ask him.

Janip advised Elisette he was ready, Elisette negotiated with her contacts, the Kaltuji representatives negotiated with Sivmati, and Janip received a date. Sivmati would receive the delegation on a morning that was exactly three tendays in the future.

"It's the best they could do," Elisette said. "We are dealing with one of mankind's better experts at stalling."

"And he never once expressed any hostility.…"

"Or any sense he thought there might be something irregular about his relations with the rest of society. Kidnapping is just another element in normal business negotiations."

"You're telling me I have to keep Farello committed for another three tendays."

"Just keep on doing what you're doing."

Janip had been feeding Elisette daily reports on Farello's behavior, complete with a few minutes of visuals. Elisette insisted Farello would remain committed but she wasn't the one who had to live with Farello's day-to-day mood swings. Elisette didn't feel the desperation in Farello's grip when she held onto him in bed. Elisette didn't have to cope with the emotions that assailed him when he saw Farello staring at her plate during dinner.

He just had to remind himself he hadn't created this situation. Elisette was right. Sivmati had created it. And Elisette.

Two of Sivmati's personal adherents loomed over the scene when the leader of the delegation inspected Janip's quarters and interviewed him about his treatment. Sivmati advised him his captors would appreciate it if he would stay away from the observation deck when the delegation was observing the action and Janip graciously agreed to abide by their request.

"I think you can see the problem," Sivmati said. "The platform will be crowded. There will be a lot of distractions."

"It's perfectly understandable. Don't let it trouble you."

He started worrying about the exchange as soon as they broke the connection. Had he done anything that might indicate the observation deck had some special significance? Had he been *too* obliging? Should he have Farello run over to the observation deck as soon as the delegation left it? And pick up the wafer before Sivmati could have the deck inspected?

The observation deck had the additional advantage that it was one of Farello's favorite locations. She visited it almost every day, just to spend a few minutes staring at the water, and she walked through it whenever she could when she was going about her daily rounds. The security system would note that she had visited the deck but it wouldn't attach a flag to the event.

Farello couldn't complete the pickup as soon as the delegation left. She had to start a work session while they were still filing onto their boat. Janip spent thirty-three hours fighting temptation. He could have hung around the deck for hours at a time and made sure it wasn't being checked by a security team. It was a natural thing to do when Farello was working. Nobody would have thought he was doing anything odd.

Farello made a complete circuit of the grounds when she finished her work session. She had spent most of the thirty-three hours lying on a recliner, plugged into the housekeeping and maintenance system, and she needed the exercise. Later, after a nap, she would run ten kilometers. Now she just walked. And stopped now and then to stretch and suck in air.

She held out her hand as soon as the door clicked shut behind her. Janip hurried across the living room and pressed her fingers beneath his palms. They stared at each other across a gap that felt like it was wider than the light years that separated Conalia and Arlane.

"I'm going to take a nap," Farello said.

Janip nodded. She pulled her hand out of his grip and he watched her as she walked toward their bedroom.

The wafer was clinging to his right palm. He slipped it to his wrist without looking at it and held it against the brown dot that marked the location of his main port. A *data stored* message superimposed itself on the image of Farello's retreating back—an image that made a perfect match for the conflicting emotions warring for his attention.

*   *   *

Elisette had started moving while the delegation was still visiting the settlement. She had loaded up a tracked all-terrain vehicle and headed inland with two horses on board.

"We'll come in from the land this time," Elisette had said. "Just as a precaution. Sivmati may not be the most astute tactician on the planet but we have to assume he's set up some hidden defenses against the scenario we used last time."

Elisette liked to ride horses and she had developed an interest in the ancient sport of hawking. She liked to drive deep into the unterrestrialized wilderness and wander about on horseback, accompanied by her current paramour and an assortment of hawks she had programmed to pursue the livelier native flyers. Sivmati would know she was roaming the wilderness but he wouldn't see anything suspicious until she activated the last phase of her scheme.

The Cultivators had established their settlement on a shelf that lay between the rapids and the steep ridges that lined the river valley. The ridge formed a wall behind the settlement—a wall Janip couldn't hope to climb with determined pursuers closing in behind him. His escape route would follow a wide stream that flowed into the rapids downstream from the settlement, at the end of the shelf.

The stream ran through a narrow valley that sloped away from the river and created a natural pass through the ridge. Janip would run up the valley and Elisette and her companion would ride down it on horseback. They would make contact about ninety minutes after Janip broke out of the settlement, Elisette would hand Janip a weapon, and his pursuers would find themselves faced with three armed humans.

This time, Elisette's machinations included a backup plan. A skimmer would drive up the stream and provide an alternate pickup if the main scheme went awry.

"Tomorrow morning," Elisette said. "Before dawn."

"I want to go with you," Farello said.

They were lying on the bed side by side, holding hands. They had just spent most of an hour with their bodies joined, experiencing all the sensual excitements and emotional arousals they had added to their capabilities over the decades. It was an indulgence with a dangerous byproduct—you always emerged from it with deeply reinforced emotional bonds. Janip had slipped into it knowing he was yielding to a treacherous temptation.

"I know you're going to make another attempt," Farello said. "You don't think I really believed that story you told me, do you?"

"You need this place, Fari. Sivmati let you create an internal conflict. For his purposes."

"And now I'm supposed to tell him I want him to remove the things you make me feel? Like a tumor?"

Janip stared at the ceiling. Would she alert Sivmati if he refused to take her with him? Would she become angry if he said the wrong thing?

"Is that what you would do?" Farello said. "Visit the surgeon and tell him you want an inconvenient emotion removed?"

It would have been the logical thing to do, in Janip's opinion. But he would never have let someone implant an emotion in the first place. Farello had enhanced her drive to bond with him because she had already glued herself to her tribe—because a cold blooded manipulator had convinced her she should do it as a service to the group that had won her loyalty.

Janip could understand the feelings that provided her with the basic satisfactions of her life. You woke up in the morning knowing you were surrounded by people you liked. You went about your days immersed in a haze of good feelings. He had even known people who transformed their personalities so they could settle into that kind of existence. Tweak a few glands. Spend a few days in a simulation that reshaped the more malleable circuits in your brain. He could do it anytime he wanted to. But he knew he would never want to.

"Suppose I do get away from here?" Janip said. "What will you do?"

"I'm not supposing. I'm assuming."

"And what would you do if you came with me? And separated yourself from everything that's important to you? I'm a trader, Fari. I'm an independent one-person business. I have friends. I have business relationships. I like most of the people I deal with. And they like me. But I don't have the kind of thing you have. I never will."

"I understand that. I want to be with you. I know I'm going to miss being here. I know I'm going to have times when I feel lonely and isolated. But I know what I want. I know I have to make a choice. I *like* wanting you. I like being attached to you."

*   *   *

He didn't know what he was going to do when he slipped out of bed. Would she be a handicap? Could he even be certain Elisette would let her come with them?

And what would they do afterward? Would he take her with him when he eventually left the planet?

Most sexual relationships ended before one of the parties was ready to move on. That was one of the few things he felt he had learned about that aspect of life. Some of his shorter relationships had just faded away. His eleven year pairing with one of his mother's friends had ended with a sweet, deliberately planned interlude when they had both decided their teacher-student relationship had given him everything that particular teacher had to offer. But two of the others had plunged him into a bleak discontent that felt like it was never going to end. And he was certain he had inflicted similar feelings on the three women he had abandoned.

He rested his hand on Farello's shoulder. "I'm awake, Fari. I'm getting dressed."

She sat up fully alert. "I've prepared some clothes."

"Five minutes."

The security system responded faster this time. The first cat flowed out of the darkness seconds after they rolled into the shrubbery under the window. Janip was already standing up when he saw it coming but he still had to twist out of the cat's path as it hurtled past him.

This time the cat just sagged and settled to the ground without any histrionics. Janip broke into a run and Farello settled in beside him.

"Just stay close to me," Janip said. "I'm the one with the magic defense."

"Are you going to the dock again?"

"Just stick with me."

The next two cats behaved just like the first. Their momentum carried them through the first effects of the defensive program but they stayed down once they'd collapsed.

Janip had settled into his best medium-distance pace—one kilometer every three and a half minutes. He had maintained his standard exercise regimen while he had been residing in Sivmati's domain. He could hold this pace for at least two hours and still have enough reserve for emergency sprints.

"The designers think the program will immobilize the cats for about twelve minutes," Janip said. "They only tested it on two cats."

"You should get some advantage from surprise. Sivmati hasn't told me anything about his security arrangements but I don't think he believed you could snatch another anti-cat program. And you aren't following the same route."

Janip noted her choice of words. Was the *you* just an indication of her mental state? He had known she might be Sivmati's last line of defense when he had decided to take her with him—If you could dignify his actions with a word like decided. He had checked her clothes for items that could be used as weapons. He had watched her while she dressed. She had asked him where they were going but he would have done the same thing if he had been the tag-along partner.

Janip veered away from the river two steps after he reached the end of the walk and started running through a random sample of undomesticated Conalian shrubbery. The sun was still sitting below the horizon but the sky had acquired a glow.

"Stay as close as you can," he said. "Don't let the obstacles separate us. I can't help you if the cats get you isolated. I've only got one defense."

Elisette had established a voice-only communications link. "I've got some hawks scouting ahead. They should pick you up in about fifteen minutes."

"I'm not alone," Janip said.

"You're the person I need, Janip. I won't argue with you. But I know what my priorities are."

Janip had swung left and started running up the little valley that would take him through the ridges. The central stream bisected the valley about three hundred meters to his right, behind the wall of plant life that flourished on its banks. Flying creatures fluttered into the air as he ran past bushes and high-stepped over vines. They were running through a maze composed of sprawling bushes and the green columns that supported the plants that had stretched upward as they competed for the light.

He glanced back and realized Farello had let the gap widen by a step. He snapped a wave at her and she nodded and pushed up behind him.

The flying creatures looked like they were concentrated over a patch of bushes when he first spotted them—until he looked right and left and realized he couldn't see the ends of the flock. There were hundreds of them, in all sizes, from finger-length to two-meter wingspans—a noisy, rainbow colored commotion that was so dense it looked like a shimmering cloud.

They stopped a few steps from the melee and Janip realized some of the flyers were exiting the scene with yellow shapes clutched in their claws or impaled on their stingers.

"It's a feeding frenzy," Farello said. "We see them all the time. The yellow things are making their way to the stream to mate. We'll have to go around them. Away from the stream."

Janip frowned. "Why can't we just bat our way through them? The whole thing's only a few steps wide."

"You can't take the risk. You could have thirty different species there. We don't have the slightest idea how we'll react to a bite or sting from some of them."

Janip activated his link to Elisette and started running along the edge of the tumult, away from the stream, and up the side of the little valley. "We're making a slight detour, Elisette. We've run into an obstacle—a big mass of flyers feeding off some yellow things that are crawling toward the stream."

"And you can't just push your way through them?"

Janip switched on his visual routine and let her see the problem. "Fari claims it's too dangerous. Too many possibilities for unknown reactions if we get nicked."

"In the clothes you're wearing? Lower your head and bull your way through. The cats will be in more danger than you."

Janip peered down the cloud of banqueting flyers. He still couldn't see any sign this mass of crawling yellow nourishment had an end. How long could it be?

"Lower your head, Fari. Cover your face with your gloves. We're going through."

He picked out a course that would avoid the larger obstacles and plunged forward with his eyes closed and his gloves pressed against his face. Angry wings beat on his clothes. Something huge attached itself to his gloves. His feet encountered an unexpectedly slippery surface and he caught himself with an awkward crouch, without moving his hands.

"Slow down, Fari. Cross it like it's ice. It's only about four steps wide."

He was yelling through a din of whirrs and buzzes. He thought he heard her say something but he couldn't make out the words.

The big thing whirred off his gloves. He counted off three extra steps and peered between his fingers. His clothes were speckled with bits of organic debris. Yellow crawlers clung to his pant legs. He brushed at them angrily and turned around.

Fari had dropped to her knees near the edge of the swarm, surrounded by the flyers attacking the yellow crawlers scattered over her clothes. She had her gloves jammed against her face and she seemed to be struggling to get up.

Janip ran toward her. He reached into the din with one arm covering his face and pulled her toward him by her collar.

"Come on, Fari. Just another step."

She lifted her right knee and he yanked her out of the danger zone and let her stumble past him as if he was executing an unarmed combat maneuver. She started beating off the crawlers with one hand and he hurried toward her and joined the fray.

Janip had turned off his visual feed when he had started his charge. "We're through," he told Elisette. "We're getting brushed off."

"Keep moving. Do you really think those bugs can do anything to you we can't repair? You're dealing with a conflicted personality. She can't stop following you and she's grabbing every excuse to slow you down. Unless she's deliberately trying to hold you up. You can't rule out the possibility she's helping Sivmati, Janip."

Farello had pulled her gloves off her eyes. She worked her hands like she was trying to scrub them sterile, and he studied her face as he brushed off her back.

Had she really been afraid of a few shallow bites? Elisette was right. What could any creature do that couldn't be repaired?

But was it really that simple? Everything could be cured. Your whole body could be replaced if necessary. But what if the reaction affected your brain? Or your personality?

Could Fari be confident Elisette would give her any medical procedures she needed? Could she be certain Sivmati would help her if she returned to the community after she had tried to abandon it?

Farello was betraying a tribe in which a majority of the people shared her drive for community and affiliation. Would they welcome her back if they captured her? Sivmati would slither away from any implication he might be responsible. He could claim he had overestimated her loyalty to the community. And underestimated the attractions of an atomized individual who spent his life buying and selling....

"Just start moving," Elisette said. "She'll follow you."

Janip gave Farello's back one last sweep. He stepped away from her and pitched forward with his eyes fixed on the terrain directly in front of him.

"Let's go, Fari. You've only got two choices. Run hard or turn back."

Elisette sighted them with her hawks' eyes a minute later than she'd hoped. One of the birds flew down the valley in search of their pursuers. The other one followed a random path through the big stems as it marked their location for Elisette.

Farello had fallen in behind him, just as Elisette had predicted, but they had slipped into a routine. Farello would let the gap widen by a step and he would look back and wave her closer.

"The skimmer has started up the stream," Elisette reported. "They tried to stop it but it caught them by surprise. I'm hoping they still don't know we're coming down the valley. They may think they just have to stay between you and the skimmer."

"Have you seen any of their birds?"

"My little pet is keeping his eyes peeled."

Janip could pick up glimpses of the hawk as it tracked their position. It was a medium-sized predator that behaved like it had been engineered for speed and the ability to maneuver through heavy vegetation. Elisette had opted for a glossy, solid black color scheme that contrasted with the gaudier costumes favored by the local fauna.

Janip glanced back and urged Farello forward with a snap of his head.

"I could chart a graph of the conflict you're talking about," Janip said. "She falls back, I wave her closer, she stops about two steps behind, she starts to fall back...."

"It's what happens when you let somebody like Sivmati wiggle into your social structure. He would have used her like that even if he'd known it would tear her apart."

Low morning light flooded an open area directly in front of them. Janip angled to the left, to curve around a patch of high, thick bushes.

"You've got three cats about four minutes behind you," Elisette said. "They're coming up on your right. It looks like they're still trying to stay between you and the skimmer."

"Are they moving fast enough to cut us off? To come between you and us?"

"It's a possibility. But we've got enough firepower to break you free if it comes to that. Your real problem is the people running behind the cats. There's about ten of them and they're armed, too. Stay ahead of them. That's your main consideration."

The cats had charged through the feeding frenzy without breaking stride. They shifted left and settled into an intersection course that had clearly been plotted by a controller who had Janip and Farello located.

"I'm throwing my hawks at them," Elisette said. "They can't stop them but they can create an annoyance and slow them down."

Janip had switched to a map display that showed him the locations of the cats and the human posse. He added a feed from the hawks, just to provide him with some diversion, and selected omniscient view. If he was going to watch a bird and cat fight, he might as well let his system show him how it probably looked from the outside, instead of staring at confused closeups of fur and snarling faces.

As a delaying tactic the attack was only moderately successful. The cats reared up and slashed at the hawks with their claws the first time the hawks dove at their faces. Then the controller running the animals made them ignore the next attack and keep running. The hawks fluttered from cat to cat, pecking and clawing at their backs and shoulders, and the cats maintained their pace without breaking stride.

Janip checked the map display and realized the cats would reach him before he connected with Elisette and her partner. He made another switch to the left, up the side of the valley, and advised Elisette of the change. "I'm moving us up the slope. About fifteen meters. There's less plant life. And I think we run better on slopes than the cats do."

"Just don't forget we're on horses. Horses have their limits, too."

"Can't your hawks go for the cats' eyes?"

"We'll get you out of this, Janip. Just keep moving. Just stay ahead of the posse."

* * *

Was this a good time to smother his natural feelings under a blanket of calm? Would he be better off if he let his muscles and his brain operate like they belonged to somebody who knew his whole future was at stake?

He glanced back and realized he had let Fari fall behind again. He waved her forward and she stumbled over a bump in the ground and lost another half step.

"You don't have to save your energy, Fari. They're only about five minutes ahead."

A bird flapped its wings in front of his face. An angry white-feathered mask shrieked at him. He batted at it reflexively and it held its place and shrieked again.

He lowered his head and drove himself forward. The bird beat its wings over his back for a moment, then the shrieking moved away. He looked back and saw Farello hitting at it with her arms.

"Keep running. Cover your face. Like we did with the insects."

Farello bent over. She lurched toward him with one hand pressed against her face and the other hand punching at the bird.

Elisette's hawk fell out of the sky. Two sets of wings thrashed around Farello's head. The hawk shot upward and Janip and Farello stared at the mangled thing flapping on the ground.

Janip strode toward Farello. He grabbed her arm and jerked her away from the dying bird. "How much longer, Elisette?"

"Two minutes. At the pace you're going now."

"You can't go any faster?"

"Horses have bones, Janip. They won't do us any good if they can't carry you out of here."

He got his first direct look at the two cats when they reared above the bushes about fifty meters ahead. They dropped out of sight and Elisette's hawk skimmed over their position.

Janip studied the terrain around him. On his left, the slope steepened, the flora thinned, and the side of the valley merged with a towering rock face. On his display, Elisette and her companion were closing in from his right front. A circle marked the area in which Sivmati's posse was working its way through the obstacles behind him.

"What do you want us to do, Elisette? Stand fast or try to go around the cats? We might get past them if you used the hawks again."

"Are they acting like they're going to attack?"

"They gave us a clear warning and held fast. It looks like they're trying to fix us here."

"Move closer. Straight ahead. Put a little extra distance between you and Sivmati's gang."

Janip slipped his hand off Farello's arm. He took a careful step forward.

The cats reared up again as he finished the third step. He added a fourth step and they reinforced the warning with a pair of sharp, raspy snarls.

He peered over the cats, toward the point where his display located Elisette and her companion. He could just make out two heads when he edged to the right and looked past a mound covered with a thick mass of vines.

He raised his arm. "I can see you, Elisette. I can see your heads over the bush."

The cats broke into an attack that carried them over the obstacles in long, arcing bounds. He had switched on his defensive program, just in case it still had some value, but the operators working the cats had obviously neutralized that option about as fast as he'd assumed they would.

They weren't going to kill him. Sivmati needed a live bargaining chip. But they could cripple a leg. Or chew it off. And leave him that way, securely hobbled, while they continued their haggling....

"Follow me, Fari. Elisette's almost here."

A cat swerved toward him. It blocked his path ten steps in front of him and brought him to a halt with a warning snarl.

Janip showed the cat's operator the palms of his hands. Farello had actually backed up. The other cat had run between them and dropped into a crouch a single, easy bound from her position.

"They've got us locked in, Elisette. It's up to you."

"We're on our way. Take them out, Lersu."

Janip had never ridden a real horse but he had fought his way through his share of horse-and-swordplay simulations. In the fantasy version of mounted combat, the horses always moved at a gallop when they attacked and the designers usually reinforced the effect with yells, pounding hooves, and a touch of appropriate music. Elisette's partner advanced in complete silence at a speed that was only a few percentage points faster than the pace he had been maintaining. Janip didn't see any sign anything had changed until he realized Lersu had pulled ahead of Elisette.

Lersu was holding a swivel-mounted stunner in his right hand, with the sighting glasses lowered over his eyes. He was wearing a fuzzy yellow cap that blanketed most of his head but you could assume he had equipped himself with a brain-machine link before he had donned his headgear.

The cat guarding Farello screamed. It leaped across the brush, teeth bared, and she turned and ran down the slope.

The cat guarding Janip charged him with the same histrionics. He stood his ground and Lersu's stunner cracked twice.

"Get up behind me," Lersu said.

"Get the other cat. It's chasing Fari back to the posse."

"Elisette told me to get you. She'll take care of the other cat."

Janip studied the stranger looking down at him. He couldn't evaluate Lersu's facial expressions but he could hear the hint of tension in his voice.

He dropped to a crouch and ran toward Farello. "You take both of us, Elisette. That was the agreement."

"The posse's too close. Get on Lersu's horse. We'll get her out later."

"Don't let him stun me. You take both of us. Or no eyes."

"We have a contract, Janip."

"And you implicitly agreed to take Fari when I told you she was with me. You aren't my only potential customer."

"Hit the other cat, Lersu. Her, too, if you have to."

Farello was still running like she was treating every bump and tangle as if it was a valid excuse to zigzag or slow down. The cat had locked onto her heels and started punctuating her steps with a snarl that should have added some heartwarming numbers to the accounts of the genetic designers who had put it together.

Lersu rode past Janip at a slow trot. His stunner cracked. The cat stiffened in mid-snarl and he fired again and brought Farello down.

"Get her on the horse, Lersu," Elisette ordered. "Will you please be kind enough to get out of that mess, Janip?"

Lersu slid out of the saddle. He crouched beside Farello and Janip stood his ground and watched.

Lersu's horse crashed to the ground. Lersu snapped his head around and Janip realized he had heard a stunner crack.

He threw himself behind a wide, spiky shrub. He hadn't seen anybody moving through the bush but he could hear more stunners on his left. Sivmati's advance forces had moved within firing range.

"Hold them off, Lersu. Get the woman behind some cover. Janip—crawl over there and start dragging her this way. Do what I tell you or believe me I'll leave you both crippled and let you spend the next century begging Sivmati for whatever medical help his little village can scrape together. You aren't the only one who knows how to drive a bargain."

Janip scurried across the ground through flights of disturbed insects. He could hear Lersu's stunner firing with a rhythmless deliberation that indicated he was only shooting at targets he could see.

The cats would have recovered by now if they had been hit with a standard back-off charge. Lersu had rammed them with a harsher setting. Farello was sprawled across the ground like he had assaulted her with the same force.

Janip noted the red delivery patch on her neck and relaxed. Elisette had come prepared. He would just have to make sure they didn't use the same drug on him.

He grabbed Farello's collar and started dragging her toward Elisette.

"I'll tell you when you're out of their range," Elisette said. "Then you can pick her up and carry her."

"How long will she be drugged?"

"Long enough to get you out of here. Concentrate on moving. I'll take care of the tactics."

"What will you do if they take Lersu?"

"What good will it do them?"

"I had a feeling you'd say that."

"He's in his element. Sivmati's zealots would have to get very lucky."

Elisette started calling targets. Most of them were on the right—in the general direction of the stream. Sivmati's best move would be an advance that pushed a group past Lersu on that side. They would close in on Elisette and come between her and the skimmer on the stream as they advanced.

In the games he had played, Janip had been encumbered by awkwardly shaped weapons when he crawled. The mass he was pulling now was as uncomplicated as a sack but it weighed a lot more than a low-impact stunner. And aroused emotions that were significantly more volatile than the feelings he would confer on a bag of trade goods.

"Get up, Janip. Drag her. Don't try to carry her."

Janip aimed himself at Elisette as soon as he stood up and hurried toward her without checking out the situation.

"Can you ride, Janip?"

"A horse? No. I've never done it."

"Here's my standard instructions."

Janip approved the reception and a visual appeared on his display. Elisette had already slid out of the saddle and posted herself beside her horse's head.

"Drape her in front of the saddle. This is no time to be romantic. Head for the stream. On this route. The skimmer will pick you up. We'll hold them off and retreat."

A route had joined the mounting visual on Janip's display. They hung Farello across the horse as if she really was a bundle of inanimate supplies and Janip eased himself into the saddle.

The horse started moving. Elisette broke into a run and headed for a position that would add more firepower to Lersu's left flank.

"I've still got your mount under control," Elisette said. "The route map is a contingency item. Just stay on board. You pay for any repairs on your passenger."

The horse was carrying an extra stunner but Janip left the weapon in its holster and concentrated on urgent matters like the fine art of remaining mounted while you tried to present your pursuers with the smallest target the human body could achieve

The arithmetic didn't look encouraging. Sivmati and his posse had two adversaries outnumbered five to one—or better.

On the other hand, one of the people opposing Sivmati was a woman with a notably resolute personality. You couldn't assess the odds with a simple unadjusted head count....

He was about two hundred meters from the stream when Elisette let him know things might not be going quite as well as she'd hoped. The cover had thickened as he approached the stream and the horse was pushing through a mass of high, thick stems. Vines and low lying plants brushed against its lower legs.

"Be prepared to use the stunner," Elisette said. "I'm working my way toward you. But I may not get there before they do."

Janip reached for the holster. A stunner cracked somewhere on his right. He had already lowered the sighting glasses and slipped a brain-machine link under his hat.

"Can you make this animal go faster, Elisette? I can't see the stream yet but the display says we're almost there."

Motion jerked his head around. A figure had stepped from behind a stem.

His stunner cracked while the other weapon was still being raised to firing position. The would-be ambusher sagged to the ground and he peered into the shade.

"They're here, Elisette. I just survived an ambush. Sivmati's foot soldier stepped into the open without raising his stunner first."

"Dismount. On your left. You can't see us but we're on your right."

A stunner cracked. Janip put the dismounting instructions on his display and climbed out of the saddle. Elisette had just advised him she felt he was more valuable than her horse. He shouldn't assume she would flatter Farello with the same honor.

He fell into a fast walk beside the horse's shoulders. He still couldn't see the stream itself but he could make out the sheet of light that marked the break in the forest.

The horse sagged toward him without any warning. He grabbed Farello's jacket with his free hand and lurched away from the wall of animal flesh that was collapsing on top of him.

He ended up huddled behind a bush with Farello sprawled behind the horse with her face pressed into a mass of vines. "Keep moving," Elisette said. "We're covering you."

He looked around. The only moving creatures he could see had wings and extra legs.

"You're beginning to try my patience, Janip."

A route appeared on his display. Two stunners fired simultaneously. He clutched the handiest spot on Farello's clothes and started crawling the last twenty meters between him and the stream. He knew the ground cover was scratching the exposed parts of Farello's face but he didn't have time to turn her on her back.

He could be sitting in the skimmer right now if he had left Farello behind. Was he just being stubborn? Was he sticking to a course of action merely because he had started it and he couldn't bring himself to change?

His mother had insisted people need to form long-term bonds. She felt she would still be living with his father if he had survived the calamity David Jammet had brought to their world. *You grow together*, she said. *You build connections that are so strong nobody else can give you the same thing.*

He could see that. But did he want to create bonds like that with somebody he had met during a bad time? Somebody who had been deliberately modified to attach herself to him?

"I'm coming up behind you," Elisette said. "Get her on her back. You on one side, me on the other."

He looked back and saw Elisette scrambling toward him on all fours. She pulled up beside him while he turned Farello over and tapped her finger at the precise spot on Farello's shoulder she wanted him to grab.

"Have you noticed you haven't heard any stunners for the last couple of minutes, Janip? Sivmati's organizing a mass rush—the last resort of the unimaginative tactician."

The slope of the ground steepened. They had entered the final tangle that bordered the stream. Crawlies and flyers erupted around them with every shift of their bodies.

"Here they come," Lersu said.

Voices screamed and bellowed on their right and rear. Sivmati's warriors had been maintaining vocal discipline and communicating by their implants but now they succumbed to the ancient human impulse to howl like an animal when you found yourself rushing toward an armed enemy.

Elisette sprawled behind the nearest patch of cover. "Keep going. Get up and crouch. They're too busy running to shoot."

Janip pushed himself up. A dot on his display located the skimmer. It had moved upstream, to stay out of range, and now it had turned and started racing back.

Lersu and Elisette were firing steadily—one arhythmic crack after another. Farello's foot caught in a thick vine and he jerked it free without worrying about damage or pain.

He splashed into the water seconds before the skimmer pulled up in front of him. Farello's inert mass rolled over the side into the cargo space in back. He threw himself into the space between the seats and huddled against the damp on the deck.

The skimmer rocked. "Let's go," Elisette said.

The skimmer lurched forward. Janip raised his eyes above the seats and saw half a dozen people standing in the water, near the spot that marked Lersu's position on his display. A woman raised a stunner and he dropped to the deck and stayed there until Elisette advised him they were safe.

Elisette started bargaining for Lersu's release while they were still racing up the river toward Belita Falls. Sivmati knew he couldn't use Lersu the way he had hoped to use Janip but he wasn't averse to a bit of ransom.

"I should bill you for everything I'm losing on this," Elisette said. "If you hadn't insisted on dragging Sivmati's irresistible devotee with you, we would have packed you on a horse and ridden away before they got within ten minutes of us."

Janip busied himself with Farello's recovery and held his tongue. Margelina had already activated her bank's formidable public relations system. Three news feeds had transmitted urgent requests for statements.

"Keep it to a minimum." Margelina said. "You've got a very saleable story."

Janip turned toward Elisette and transmitted his view of her to the news feeds. It was the first time he had ever talked to a planetary audience but he had been watching other people do it for seven standard decades.

"I just want to emphasize that we all owe my liberator a great debt," Janip said. "Elisette has defended the rights of every trader on Conalia. She has defeated the kind of piratical behavior that destroys free trade and the economies that depend on it. Everyone on the planet should be grateful."

Elisette couldn't stand up at the speed the skimmer was making but she managed a small wave and a half nod that communicated the right mixture of graciousness and humility. She had watched a few news feeds, too.

A cantankerous observer might have noted that Elisette had provoked the whole situation by creating a dam that would give her a monopoly on a major source of power. For now, she was the champion of free markets and free trade.

She might have carried out her threat and billed him for her losses if she had been driven by a pure, unadulterated delight in amassing wealth.

Her grab for power had made it clear she had other, more complex ambitions. If he had judged her right—and he had overwhelming evidence in support of his conclusions—she would think of Lersu's ransom as the price she paid for an increase in her political prestige.

The eye transplant took a full tenday. Nerves had to hook up. Biochemical processes had to be monitored and tweaked. Janip gave her an end product that incorporated every bit of training and experience he had accumulated—and justified every digit he added to her bill. Elisette was particularly pleased with the sharpness of the images she could transmit with the communications upgrade packaged with the eyes.

Janip sold nine sets of eyes altogether before the local specialists reverse-engineered his import and trained themselves to a competitive level. By that time, he owned a comfortable apartment in Kaltuji City and Margelina had guided him toward his first real estate investments.

Farello loved the life of a thriving commercial city. She even started helping him look for new opportunities. There was nothing artificial about the affinities they shared. Sivmati had built her emotional modification around a true attraction. But she also spent two or three hours a day in contact with the Cultivator compound. She could chat about every gossipy development the place could produce. One of her friends asked her to continue some of her work with the unterrestrialized ecosystem and she fitted in several hours, without telling Janip, when he was working on one of his own projects. He wouldn't have known she had done it if he hadn't finished early and tried to contact her.

"You're trying to live in two worlds," Janip said.

"Do you want me to change myself? And go back to the compound?"

He didn't, of course. But how would he feel in twenty standard years? Or the next time a starship orbited the planet and he started thinking about the developments he could take to another world? Conalia was a newer world than Arlane but he was already assembling a library of promising trade items. The tweaks his competitors had added to the eyes could be a major addition to his wares all by themselves.

Farello wasn't the only person who had to live with her conflicts. Janip was coming to a sad conclusion. The world could only give you half of the old fairy tale formula. It could only offer you the possibility you might *live* forever after. The *happily* part seemed to be more elusive.

This is not a science fiction story by any definition of the term, even though it appeared in Asimov's. *But it's a close cousin of core science fiction—a logically developed What Would Happen If? As it developed, it went beyond that question and evolved into a kind of meditation on war and military culture.*

DRAGON DRILL

Ecrasez l'infame, the king had said with a smile. *Crush the infamous thing.*

Fritz had been echoing Voltaire's famous outcry against the Roman church, of course. But he had obviously chosen the phrase because he thought its associations were appropriate. A dragon was the embodiment of superstition—a creature from the world of dreams, snorting and rampaging in a time when the disputes of philosophers were argued with wit and mathematics, and the disputes of kings were settled by disciplined masses equipped with muskets and artillery.

It had been, in almost every respect, a typical visit to the court of the most enlightened monarch of the age. The king's blue uniform had been untidy, as always. His hands and the lace on the cuffs of his shirt sleeves had been grimy and inkstained. The grenadiers in the halls had hopped to attention with all their customary smartness. General von Wogenfer had even attended the afternoon concert and listened with some pleasure as Fritz and the court musicians worked their way through one of Quantz's flute concertos. (He was impressed, once again, with Quantz's ability to write a showy, emotional flute part without taxing Frederick's abilities. When all else failed, an ingenious bit of orchestral accompaniment could make the flute solo sound more exciting than it really was.) The king had exchanged bows and French epigrams with a pair of visiting literati. For every minute of the entire morning and afternoon, General von Wogenfer had been surrounded by all the realities that proved he was still immersed in the day to day life of the modern world.

And somewhere in Silesia, a creature out of fairy tales—a huge, firebreathing flying monster, just like the dragons in the legends—was threatening to desolate an entire province if it wasn't offered a genuine Hapsburg princess as a sacrifice.

"It is absurd that such a creature should influence the destiny of a modern state," Fritz said, shaping his French with great care, as if he thought his sentences were being written down. "I have spent most of my reign fighting for Silesia. Am I to lose it because of a superstition? Because of a fantasy from an imaginary world in which single warriors righted wrongs with the strokes of magic swords?"

Von Wogenfer had sat in the king's private study, with his long legs stretched in front of him, and hidden his feelings behind pinches of snuff. Von Wogenfer was a Junker—with a pedigree that would have cowed a French *duc*—but he was, like King Frederick himself, a gentleman who belonged, mind and heart, to the great society that was bestowing enlightenment and reason on all Europe. He could calculate the trajectory of an artillery shell, play the harpsichord and the violin with genuine taste, discuss Tacitus and Plutarch like a scholar, and captivate the most demanding of French ladies with sallies delivered in their own language. His coats hung on his tall frame with an elegance that had sometimes misled young officers, who had mistakenly assumed he owed his military prominence to the king's amorous proclivities. Was he supposed to suddenly believe Newton and Voltaire had never existed, and the fantasies of the priests were, after all, an accurate description of the world?

"I have made some attempt to inspect the records," Frederick said. "In 1719, a Hapsburg princess did apparently die for reasons that seem to have been deliberately obscured—as if she had committed one of the traditional indiscretions. The officer who arrested Costanze Adelaide when she tried to slip across the border insists that she relates her story with the utmost calm. The reports I've received from eyewitnesses in the area include verifications from people who know I would have them hanged if they deceived me in such a matter."

The first twenty-three years of Frederick's reign had been, for all practical purposes, a struggle for Silesia. In 1740, his soldiers had crossed a border for the first time and seized the province from the young heir to the Hapsburg domains, Maria Theresa. Between 1740 and 1747, he had fought two wars in defense of his conquest. Between 1756 and 1763, he had fought for it again, in a grinding seven year struggle that had nearly destroyed his house. And all the while, the Hapsburgs had known that this thing came out of the east once every fifty years. Three times in their history a member of their family had saved the province from destruction. Before that, the firebreather had been appeased with the daughters of the local princes and barons.

Frederick flicked his sleeve at the third man in the room—the plump boy-in-an-officer's-uniform he had introduced as Dietrich Jacob Alsten. "Monsieur Alsten has prepared a memorandum on the characteristics of these creatures, based on the reports that have survived as legends. I am preparing a carriage equipped with sleeping accommodations. You will leave tonight—after we've shared some refreshment and entertainment. Your detachment will consist of two battalions of infantry, one battalion of grenadiers, several squadrons of hussars and cuirassiers, and whatever artillery we can muster."

The King's sleeve flicked again. "I think you can understand the difficulties we will face if the people of our new province feel they have been rescued by a Hapsburg who offered herself as a sacrifice. You must show them that Prussian discipline—and Prussian firepower—are a better defense than the skirts of a Hapsburg princess."

They had been camping on the little hill for two days when the lone hussar rode toward them with his sword raised above his head—the agreed-upon signal that the "Polish animal" was drawing near. The major who had the watch shouted the first orders. Drums took up the beat. Infantry trotted to their rows of neatly stacked muskets and began assembling in formation.

Von Wogenfer descended from his carriage at a deliberate, calculated pace. On his left, Princess Costanze Adelaide had already been standing by her own carriage. Two grenadiers grabbed her shoulders as he turned their way. The captain who was in charge of her guard snapped an order and the grenadiers hustled her toward the stake planted halfway down the slope. A bayonet had been lashed to the top of the stake. Just below the bayonet, a small regimental flag quivered in the early summer breeze.

Costanze Adelaide was a small, pleasantly round woman in her late twenties. The two grenadiers were men who had been chosen for their size and fighting ability—like all the soldiers in the grenadier battalions. Their tall, pointed hats deliberately magnified the effect of their stature. The princess looked like a child between them.

Von Wogenfer lifted his hat and bowed to her back. "Good luck, mademoiselle. My apologies."

The princess halted her guards with a toss of her hands that proved she was, without doubt, a Hapsburg. "I shall pray for your soul, general."

Her voice was soft and unusually melodious, but he had learned she could be a formidable opponent in debate. The king would have noted the long hours she spent in churches and dismissed her as a religious fanatic. Von Wogenfer had discovered she was a theologian who had absorbed the most sophisticated instruction the Roman priests could offer. The logic that guided her behavior had been as lucid as a mathematical proof.

He bowed again. "And I shall do my best to keep you alive, your highness."

She stared at him for a long moment. "If that is your primary concern, general, you can save yourself—and your sovereign—a great deal of trouble."

His horse appeared at von Wogenfer's side. His body servant handed him a clean pair of white gloves and he systematically inspected both sides of each glove—as he always did—before he slipped them over his hands. He didn't place his boot in the stirrup until he was certain every soldier within thirty paces had seen him run his eyes over every detail of the saddle and the leopard skin saddle cloth.

The troops had fallen in and started tramping to their positions. Snare drums were tapping the cadence. The standards of the regiments and the halberds of the sergeants swayed above the bayonets of the common soldiers. As Frederick had promised, von Wogenfer had been given two battalions of line infantry and one battalion of grenadiers—two thousand foot soldiers altogether.

The two line battalions belonged to a regiment that "faced" its blue Prussian coats with yellow. Their cuffs, their lapels, and the turnbacks on their coat tails had been dyed with the sunniest yellow the cloth factories could produce. Their hats were the standard three-cornered affairs that topped the heads of the line infantry fielded by every modern army. The grenadiers were dressed in the same blue coats and white waistcoats, but their uniforms were faced with green. The ornate insignias on the front of their hats glittered and flashed as they marched.

Von Wogenfer had drilled the entire detachment relentlessly throughout the last two days. By now it took them less than two minutes to arrange themselves in the battle formation he had chosen.

The stake had been planted in a small hollow his sappers had dug in the hillside. Only the upper half of Costanze Adelaide's body rose above ground level. She arranged herself so she was facing down the hill and Captain Kreutzen accepted a length of rope from a sapper.

A grenadier company marched down the hill as soon as Kreutzen signaled the princess's hands were securely tied. The company flowed around Costanze Adelaide and halted when it was placed so the stake was positioned in the exact middle of the formation. Von Wogenfer could still see the bayonet and the flag, but the princess herself was lost in the forest formed by the shoulders, hats, and muskets of two hundred elite troops.

The grenadier company was the heart of the formation he had worked out with young Alsten, who had acted as his counselor and admiring audience. They were his final defense against the special threat that had preoccupied him from the moment Frederick had dumped this affair on his shoulders. They would be surrounded by the two battalions of line infantry, who would form a protective square around the grenadier company—as if the line infantry were executing the standard defense against ordinary cavalry.

The entire plan had been diagrammed in pencil on a piece of paper he had stuffed into his left coat pocket. On the diagram, von Wogenfer's own position was marked with a cross near the top of the slope, about seventy-five paces from the square. His cavalry squadrons were supposed to form up on both sides of his position. Directly in front of him, a second company of grenadiers would be posted where he could employ it as a reserve.

Now the mortal, all-too-vulnerable human bodies represented on the sketch were moving into position. The second company of grenadiers was parading into the open ground in front of him. The breastplates of the cuirassiers gleamed in the sun when he glanced to his right.

On his left, the officers of the hussar squadrons lounged in their saddles with the studied insouciance cultivated by light cavalry. Hussars wore one of the most dashing uniforms the military imagination had conceived and these particular specimens belonged to a regiment that adorned itself with one of the more spectacular examples. Crimson plumes rose from their fur caps. Gold frogging and white fur garnished their sky blue jackets.

The commander of the grenadier battalion, Lt. Colonel Basel-Derhof, was riding beside the second grenadier company. His eyes were flicking over every detail of the company's uniforms and deportment. They came to a halt with the snap and precision that were supposed to be one of the distinctive marks of grenadiers and von Wogenfer nodded his approval.

At the bottom of the slope, a stream ran along the edge of a typical stretch of prosperous Silesian farmland. It was a clear, beautifully sunny day—a morning when bayonets flashed like mirrors.

A horseman fell in on von Wogenfer's left. Von Wogenfer turned his head and his youthful adviser offered him a curt nod.

Von Wogenfer smiled. By nature, young Alsten seemed to be brash—even bubbly. There had been times during the last few days when he had babbled for an hour straight. Then he would suddenly decide he should be more soldierly and his garrulousness would be replaced by a caricature of military brusqueness.

It was easy to understand why the boy had come to Frederick's attention. Forty years ago, young Frederick had been a flute playing intellectual who was destined to be the leader of an aristocracy that had only one purpose in life: the preservation of a state which possessed no natural defensive boundaries. His father's brutal attempts to transform Fritz into a soldier had become one of the great scandals of the European courts. When he had tried to escape his father's torments at the age of eighteen, the prince had been imprisoned for a year and forced to watch when his best friend was beheaded.

Alsten was clearly a scholar by nature. He gushed with enthusiasm when he described the wonders he had discovered in libraries and the specimens he had carried home from his sojourns in the mountains. He had been planted, however, in a family in which duty and discipline were the only virtues the father could understand.

"Well, my young friend," von Wogenfer said, "soon you, too, will have a few tales of death and daring you can parade in front of the recruits."

Alsten smiled stiffly. Von Wogenfer noted the flicker of anxiety in his eyes and pointed at the pencil case and writing board the young man had arranged across his saddle horn.

"Make sure you get it all down," von Wogenfer said. "Be ready to give me your best advice the moment I ask for it."

He turned his head to the right, to inspect the cannon he had placed on that flank, and wondered if Alsten would someday realize his commander's brusqueness had been meant as a kindness. The first time von Wogenfer had advanced with his regiment, he had nearly been overwhelmed by fear and confusion. The only thing that had kept him moving was the knowledge he had a specific task. He was there to oversee his platoon, the forty men marching in front of him. If they marched and fired and arrived at their goal, then he had done all anyone asked of him.

As usual, the roads had delayed the equipment he needed the most. His artillery consisted of exactly three pieces—two six-pounders and a single horse-drawn gun. He had deployed one six-pounder at each end of the cavalry line, so the two gun crews could cover every spot on the hillside. The horse gun had been posted near his own place in the line, where he could transmit his orders to its officer, Captain Hoff, without dispatching a messenger.

The crews of the two six-pounders had lit their portfires—the slow-burning fuses, attached to long rods, that the gunners would apply to their touch holes when they received the order to fire. Behind each six pounder, about ten steps behind the trail of the gun carriage, a full company of grenadiers had fallen into formation. Both companies snapped to attention when their captains realized their general was looking them over.

Three young lieutenants were sitting their horses behind him, ready to act as couriers. He gave them a polite, carefully measured nod and they straightened up and did their best to look businesslike.

Alsten coughed discreetly. A stir passed through the ranks. Von Wogenfer looked to the front, knowing what the stir must mean, and saw the thing for the first time.

For a moment, it looked like a large bird that happened to be holding some kind of wiggling, still-living prey suspended from its claws. Then he noted its relationship to the horizon and realized how far away it really was. The shape it appeared to be carrying was its own body, hanging from slowly flapping wings.

He murmured a command and the sergeant standing beside his horse handed him his telescope. By the time the tube had been extended and focused, the creature was so close he had to run the glass along its sides as if he was studying the walls of a fortress.

Sunlight bounced off scales that looked as if they could have been employed as cuirasses. He moved the instrument to the left and the center of an immense red eye filled the field.

He lowered the telescope and watched it approach. In the formation massed around the stake, sergeants were already ordering their men to stand fast. A young grenadier lieutenant looked back at him and he automatically gave the poor fool a frown that returned him to his proper interests.

A shadow swept across the hill. Horses neighed. Voices barked commands. Von Wogenfer passed the telescope to his sergeant and steadied his horse with both hands.

The thing let out a strange, quavering shriek. It turned in a great arc and von Wogenfer felt the first chill of superstitious fear spread through his body.

How could a thing like that fly? Its body was slender and snakelike but it would have filled the inside of most of the larger churches he had visited in his travels. No one had yet unraveled the secrets of the mechanism that held birds aloft, but it was obvious there was no relationship between the size of the creature's wings and the mass of its anatomy.

He was still living, after all, in a world in which every physical object was ruled by the majestic beauty of Newton's mathematics. The Earth was pulling on that long, writhing body with the same force it exerted on every creature that lived on its surface. If those wings could keep that mass aloft, then clearly he was looking at something that was not subject to natural law....

To Costanze Adelaide, he was engaging in an act of blasphemy. *If this creature is truly evil*, she had argued, *if it really is a manifestation of some ancient and ungodly Presence—then it is supposed to be confronted with the power of virtue and unselfish sacrifice. If a thing like this exists, it must have been spawned in some realm beyond the rule of Reason. How can you defeat it with weapons based on the laws of Reason?*

The dragon settled onto the hill about a hundred paces in front of his troops. It pointed its head at the sky—it could have looked down on every building in Berlin—and a massive red flare rose toward the clouds.

Sergeants repeated the order to stand fast. Two officers pointed their pistols at the backs of soldiers who had indicated they might be responding to the thing's presence with normal human emotions.

The dragon lowered its head. It focused its huge eyes on the men massed in front of it and von Wogenfer wondered if it was assessing the situation or merely pausing before its instincts told it what it should do next. By now a mob of peasants and merchants would have reacted to its displays by turning their backs and scattering like a flock of sparrows. Instead, it was faced with the same stolid ranks that had stymied the armies of Austria, Russia, and France—the armies of the Three Harpies, as the king had dubbed Maria Theresa, the Czarina Elizabeth, and Louis XV's meddling mistress, Madame de Pompadour. Was this the first time it had faced disciplined infantry?

The flare had been approximately a hundred paces long and eight paces wide. The creature would probably have to come within seventy-five paces of the line if it wanted to achieve the maximum effect....

He realized his brain was working again and turned to the cannon on his left. The officer was watching him expectantly.

Von Wogenfer lifted his hand and gave the artillery officer a wave that was as casual and offhand as he could make it. If there was one dictum Fritz liked to repeat to the point of boredom, it was the idea that the common soldier should fear his officers more than he feared the enemy. The soldier stood his ground because he knew his lieutenant was standing behind him. The lieutenant stood because he knew his captain and his colonel were standing behind him. And over it all, keeping them all in their places, loomed the gallant, lighthearted, heroically unruffled figure of the General—who stayed where he was because the king would have him hanged if he didn't.

Screams jerked von Wogenfer's attention back to the front of the formation. The animal had lurched forward and released another flare. Half a dozen blackened bodies were crumpling to the ground. A soldier was falling out of line with his clothes flaming around him. The guttural orders of the sergeants were rising once again. The soldiers on the right and left of the charred bodies were already repeating the terrible ritual that was the infantry's traditional response to artillery fire. Knees high, feet stamping, eyes fixed on their front, they were sidestepping to close the gap.

The gun on the left crashed. The artillery sergeant chanted the first orders of the reloading drill and the rammer shoved his sponge into the barrel. Their officer eyed the fall of the shot.

The dragon turned its head toward the source of smoke and noise. Von Wogenfer pulled out his pocket watch and noted the position of the second hand. Twenty-five seconds after the first shot, the gun thundered for the second time. The artillery captain had taken a few extra seconds and adjusted his aim.

The animal sank into a crouch. Its wings rose above its spine. It leaped, screaming, and hurled itself at the gun.

More German commands rang out. The platoons directly under the dragon's path dropped to one knee with their musket butts braced against the ground and the muzzles pointed at the sky. Their faces stared straight ahead, as if they were standing at attention on the parade ground. Officers barked the command to fire as the dragon passed over their platoons.

Hundreds of muskets cracked. The dragon screamed and veered away from the formation. It banked like a big, awkward bird and settled to earth a few steps from the position it had just left.

Von Wogenfer signaled to the cannon on his right. Both guns fired simultaneously. A long red line appeared on the dragon's side, just in front of its right wing—the mark of a cannon ball that had raked it like an invisible file.

"It's hit!" Alsten blurted. "We can hurt it! It turned away from the musket fire, too. The musket balls may not penetrate its armor but they must sting! If they can't kill it—at least they can keep it away. It's even possible they can herd it! If they could drive it… like cows.…"

Von Wogenfer waved him to silence. The infantry who had dropped to one knee had already stood up and completed their reloading drill.

The whole concept of attack from the air had given him the feeling he had stepped into a world in which nothing he knew could help him. You could arrange your forces in solid ranks, with every approach blocked by masses of disciplined infantry—and your enemy could still descend on you, like the sun or the rain, in spite of all your preparations.

Some of the men had looked puzzled when he had made them spend hours dropping to the ground and firing into the air. Now they understood.

An infantry battalion was a maneuverable concentration of firepower. Its tactics were determined by the limitations of its basic weapon the smoothbore, muzzle loading musket. There were soldiers in the world who were trained to use rifled weapons, but they were specialists, and it took them a minute to load and fire each shot. Prussian troops could load and fire three times a minute in the face of the enemy. There was, however, no guarantee that any particular shot would actually hit something. Musket balls could be loaded with such efficiency because they were a hair smaller than the musket barrel. They jiggled ever so slightly as they were propelled toward the muzzle. Air resistance added other inaccuracies. One hundred paces was considered an extreme range. If two battalions exchanged volleys at fifty paces, most of the soldiers in both units would still be standing when the smoke cleared.

Soldiers fought in massed ranks partly because it was an efficient way to move them around the battlefield and partly because it was their primary defense against cavalry. If you tried to oppose horsemen with firearms, your initial volley would topple a few riders—but the rest would smash into the line while the infantry were still reloading. Only the bayonet could frustrate a charge. Horses halted as soon as they found themselves faced with a hedge of bayonets. But it had to be a hedge—an unbroken line formed by men standing shoulder to shoulder, two and three ranks deep. If you cut even the smallest hole in that line, if anyone wavered or ran, a few horsemen would slip through, swords would hack at the line from the rear, more cavalry would pour through, the formation would disintegrate, and the impregnable human wall would be transformed into a field of isolated foot soldiers futilely thrusting their bayonets at mounted furies who rode at them from every direction.

The dragons of legend had faced craftsmen—swordsmen and archers who spent their lives studying the subtleties of their art. This creature was challenging the army of a modern, rationally organized kingdom—a monarchy in which ordinary, untalented louts could defeat the greatest heroes of antiquity by performing simple, repetitive acts.

They had decided they would have to think of the animal as a kind of moving fortress. They would have to batter it until something gave way. In the myths, Alsten had noted, it had usually been killed by puncture weapons, such as lances. There was even a legend that the elephant was its natural enemy. It was reasonable to think, therefore, that it might avoid the bayonet. Cannon balls and musket balls might penetrate its armor if they landed on a weak spot, but that would be a matter of luck.

Now, watching the creature stagger under a second hit from a cannon, von Wogenfer wondered if anything that size could be clubbed to death.

Could you really hammer at its sides the way you weakened the walls of a fortress, shot by shot?

The dragon crouched and leaped again. This time it swerved to von Wogenfer's right and slowly gained altitude. It banked, like some monstrous hawk, and von Wogenfer heard Alsten gasp.

"It's going to swoop," Alsten murmured.

Von Wogenfer's stomach tightened. He had stood with his men as they watched enemy cannon being trained on their ranks, but this was something else. An enormous mass was falling on them out of the sky, in a long sweep that would carry it directly over the grenadiers stationed around the stake.

He threw back his head and bellowed a command in his native tongue —a language he used for almost no other purpose.

"Grenadiers. Bajonette—*auf*!"

The grenadiers raised their muskets above their heads without dropping to one knee. The thin, high shriek of the predator ripped at the air. Wings beat like thunder as the long, scaly body swept across the grenadier company. Claws reached for the princess through the massed bayonets. Human screams mingled with the noise of the monster. Some of the more enterprising grenadiers rose up on tiptoe and tried to slash at the white underbelly flowing past their points.

The animal was already climbing when it cleared the edge of the formation. The officers in the grenadier company were ordering their men to close ranks. The tall hats bobbed in a familiar pattern as the grenadiers filled in the gaps and let the walking wounded make their way through the formation. The dragon had been reaching for Costanze Adelaide but its claws had struck at some of the men massed around the stake. Somewhere in that blue-coated crowd, a corpse was probably being trampled by feet that were mechanically obeying orders.

Why would the thing want a human female? Did it need some special nutrient? Would it haul her to its nest for some purpose only a pornographer could visualize? Last night, during dinner, he had flustered Alsten when he and Colonel Torbmann had tried to imagine the pleasures a Hapsburg spinster could provide a flying lizard. Now its irrational objective was just one more sign he was faced with something that existed outside the laws of nature.

The thing had already executed an arc that carried it far above the farmland in front of the formation. It had gained so much height it looked as if it was roughly the size of a cow—but who had ever seen a cow equipped with wings? It pointed itself at the front of the formation and fell toward its quarry as if it was sliding down an invisible ramp in the sky.

This time it ignored Costanze Adelaide and attacked the grenadiers themselves. Its great claws reached through the upraised bayonets for the faces and bodies of the men holding them.

Its head was pointed directly at von Wogenfer as it swept across the formation. He was looking at it eye to eye as its feet mangled the troops he had placed in its path. Half the cavalrymen on both sides of him were leaning over their horses' heads and stroking their faces.

The long tube of the creature's body slid directly over von Wogenfer's head. The tips of its bloody, dripping claws were just a sword length from the top of his hat. A terrible retching odor permeated the air like a fog.

The corporal holding von Wogenfer's horse grabbed the bridle with both hands and opposed its straining muscles with the full weight of his body. Von Wogenfer ignored the struggle taking place beneath his thighs and concentrated on the scene he was supposed to be controlling.

Grenadiers were falling out of formation with their faces covered with blood. Fragments of blue coats flapped over glimpses of shredded upper bodies. Sergeants were beating the survivors into formation with their halberds. Behind him, the three lieutenants had drawn their swords and turned in their saddles as they followed the dragon's flight.

"Sheathe your swords!" von Wogenfer bellowed. "Keep your eyes on me! I'll tell you where to look!"

He had chosen a small dip near the top of the hill as a parking place for the wounded. The sergeants who had been chosen to deal with the casualties were shepherding the walking wounded up the slope. The men who couldn't walk were being dragged along the ground by their belts—if they still had belts.

The grenadier company had lost half a dozen men in the first strike, another thirty in the second. From what he could see of the men left in the ranks, at least ten of the wounded were still standing in the formation.

The thing struck at the center two more times. By the end of the fourth attack, the grenadier company had lost almost half its men—including a third of its sergeants and two officers.

Von Wogenfer gestured at Colonel Basel-Derhof while the tail of the monster was still thrashing above his head. "I believe it's time we sent in the reserve company, *mon ami*. If you will give the orders...."

Basel-Derhof spurred his horse forward. His big, unforgettable voice rang across the formations. The grenadiers massed around the princess jerked to attention. They about faced in response to their captain's orders and snapped into a march.

It was one of the most difficult maneuvers an army could perform. A battered, limping unit had to vacate its position at top speed without yielding to fear and turning a retreat into a panic. The infantry forming one face of the square had to open a gap they could pass through. A second unit had to march, without hesitation, into the very place where men had been killed and crippled while it watched.

Von Wogenfer straightened in the saddle as he watched them step through the drill. Their erect heads and vertical muskets would have been an impressive sight if you had watched them execute the maneuver on the parade ground—but here they were doing it in the face of the enemy.... as a thing that killed and slashed climbed into the sky and positioned itself for another descent.

He caught a brief glimpse of Costanze Adelaide as the monster approached the top of its climb. She was leaning forward, with her full weight on the stake, and methodically moving her wrists up and down as she rubbed her bonds against the wood. Then the blue mass closed around her. And the bolt began its fall.

He pulled his snuff box out of his pocket and turned back to Alsten. "Do you see why your father values discipline so much?"

The boy's eyes were locked on the dragon's approach. He looked confused—as if he had been jolted from a dream—and von Wogenfer turned away from him without waiting for an answer.

Von Wogenfer had shared many intimacies with his fellow officers, but there was one thought he had never revealed. He had developed an irrational respect for the soldiers he commanded. They were the worst, he knew. They were recruited from the leavings of the civilian population: from the lazy, the criminal, the unemployable. Most of them would be stealing and raping—or begging in the public squares—if they hadn't been bludgeoned or connived into putting on uniforms. Half of them would have been running like peasants by now if they hadn't known they were maneuvering under the eyes of officers who would shoot them down before they had finished the first step. But none of that seemed to matter when you saw them execute the kind of maneuver he had just witnessed.

The act sanctified itself. The motivation was irrelevant.

The monster released another scream as it closed with the formation but this time it seemed to him he could detect a different quality in the sound. A hundred shaken men had surrounded the stake when it had finished its last strike. Now two hundred straight, unwounded grenadiers stood there again.

The great claws struck. The long underbelly blocked out the sun for the fourth time and he noted the bloody lines marked by the bayonet points. Here and there he could even see bruises and round, red patches where musket balls had stuck home.

His heart jumped when he realized it was turning away without rising. It landed about a hundred and fifty paces in front of the formation and stared at its adversaries with its wings draped along the ground.

"It's tiring!" Alsten said. "We're wearing it down! We may not be hurting it, but we're wearing it down."

The two guns crashed as soon as the artillery officers realized they had a steady target. A shriek of pain—or was it rage?—clawed at the air. The animal twisted on itself, like a dog biting at a flea. It pointed its head at the sky, still screaming, and von Wogenfer stood up in the stirrups and peered at its thrashing body. It had obviously taken a cannon ball on its left side, but it had reacted by turning that side away from him. There was no way he could determine the extent of the damage.

The gunnery sergeants were chanting the gunnery drill on both sides. The dragon lowered its head and stared at the gun on the right—the gun that had probably fired the shot that had struck home. It stopped thrashing and eased its body around as if it was favoring its left side. Its wings rose above its back.

The grenadier companies posted behind each gun were an important component of von Wogenfer's battle plan. If the dragon attacked either piece, they were supposed to step forward and protect the gun in the same way the central grenadier company was protecting Costanze Adelaide. The company stationed behind the gun on the left was commanded by one of the best captains in the brigade—a middle-aged officer who would have been a full colonel if he had possessed the right connections. The company on the right—the company deployed behind the gun the dragon was eyeing—was commanded by a young man whose chief claim to preferment seemed to be the fact that he was Colonel Basel-Derhof's grandson. Von Wogenfer had tried to convince Basel-Derhof the grandson should be assigned to his staff. The colonel had insisted the company would be more reliable if it was commanded by "the leader it is accustomed to follow."

Now, as the animal readied itself, von Wogenfer watched the company for some sign the "leader it is accustomed to" had understood the situation. Colonel Basel-Derhof was a stolid, reliable officer, and his grandson seemed to be cut from the same thick, serviceable blue cloth. If you pointed either of them at the enemy and told them to advance, they would keep going as long as they had two men left to command. Unfortunately, the situation called for a company commander who could anticipate the enemy's movements and react without waiting for a direct order....

The dragon leaped. Its wings thrashed downward in a single, powerful stroke. It sailed toward the gun with a gracefulness that would have made von Wogenfer gape in awe if he had been a detached observer.

Basel-Derhof's grandson had been waiting for the gun crew to finish reloading. The thing had already covered half the distance to the gun before he realized it was going to reach its target before the crew could light the touchhole. His startled voice floated across the hillside. His grenadiers pointed their bayonets at the sky and advanced at the quick step.

The gunners threw themselves flat. The animal's claws closed around the wheels of the gun. It struggled upward, like a hawk burdened with an over-sized rabbit. The bottoms of the wheels rose off the ground.

The grenadiers had continued to advance, as ordered. The animal was still struggling to gain altitude when the gun carriage collided with the front ranks.

The men in the first three ranks toppled like ninepins. There was a moment when the entire gun assembly hung over the hats and upraised muskets of the company. Then the barrel slipped out of the carriage. Several hundred pounds of brass fell on the men massed beneath the monster's body.

It was a situation Basel-Derhof's grandson could understand. He screamed an immediate right face. His company changed face without a break in the rhythm of its march and uncovered the men who had been downed by the gun. Broken bodies writhed on the grass. A hatless soldier rose to his knees and held up his arms as if he thought another blow was falling from the sky.

Von Wogenfer raised his eyes from the wreckage. The dragon had lifted itself to church steeple height. It rose a little higher and shrieked as it let the gun carriage fall. It dropped to the ground with another shriek and launched a red flare at the useless mass of splintered wood.

Von Wogenfer gestured at Alsten. "How intelligent should we assume our adversary is, monsieur savant? Does it realize it can rove that flank at will, now that it's removed the gun?"

Alsten spread his hands like a Frenchman. "I can't say. So far it's acted like a beast. It launched itself directly at the princess without taking anything else into account. It didn't attack the gun until it was hit. This is probably the first time it's encountered artillery. It may not have realized there was more to the gun than fire. Now that it's been hit... now that it knows the gun is firing missiles...."

The dragon was eyeing the formation over the smoldering remains of the gun carriage. This time it was positioned so von Wogenfer could see the place where the cannonball had struck its side. There were no holes, but it had acquired a large black blotch forward of its rear leg. One of its scales seemed to be dangling from a flap of skin.

If he had been the dragon, he would have eliminated the guns first. Then he would have burned his way through the infantry at his leisure. As Alsten had said, it could have acted like a mindless beast merely because it wasn't familiar with artillery.

Why shouldn't it be intelligent? It was a thing that shouldn't exist at all. Why shouldn't it be as cunning as Fritz himself?

He twisted in the saddle and gestured at the commander of the horse artillery team. "Captain Hoff—load with canister. Close with the enemy on my order. Maintain contact for as long as humanly possible. Try for a face shot if it gives you the opportunity."

He looked back and jabbed his forefinger at the lieutenant on the right. "Advise Major von Laun his men are to draw their swords. Two squadrons will advance behind me—with Major von Laun in command—if I signal with my sword at the vertical. He should maintain twenty lengths behind my position. He should be prepared to charge on command."

The dragon rose. It hauled its bruised body through the air and landed a short thirty paces from the men holding the right face of the square—In a position where it no longer had to fear a blow from a cannon. Its eyes glared down at the ranks standing before it.

Everything had to be timed with care. So far, it had stopped to take in air every time it had breathed fire....

The animal's sides began to heave. It trained its open mouth on a soldier who had become as rigid as a statue. Von Wogenfer turned his head and raised his hat with the best imitation of a courtly gesture he could produce. "Now, Captain Hoff. If you please."

Mobile, horse-drawn guns were an important part of Frederick's tactical system. Frederick had borrowed the idea from the Russians but it was a concept that suited his talent for surprise and maneuver. A gunner was already sitting on the lead horse in the team that pulled the gun. His spurs bit as soon as Captain Hoff bellowed an order. The gun clattered down the hill with the artillery crew riding beside it.

Fire shot from the dragon's mouth. A red cloud engulfed a dozen human bodies.

Captain Hoff's horses swung into a turn as they approached the dragon's flank. They came to a halt with the muzzle of the gun fifteen paces from its target. The crew leaped from their saddles with the silent, intent speed of men who were performing acts they had executed thousands of times.

The dragon turned its head away from the carnage it had just created. Its eyes studied the artillery crew. The horse gun crashed before it could pull its bulk out of the line of fire. Hundreds of balls smashed into its side at point blank range.

Von Wogenfer had already spurred his horse forward and started trotting down the hill. He pointed his sword at the sky without looking back and Major von Laun gave his cuirassiers the appropriate order.

This time there was no doubt the creature was shrieking in pain. It threw its injured flank away from the cannon and von Wogenfer felt his heart bounce when he realized part of its left wing was flopping like a broken limb. Hoff had chosen his target with intelligence. If the thing could no longer attack from the air....

Von Wogenfer spurred his horse into a canter. The sponger was already pushing his rod, with its water-soaked sponge, into the muzzle of the horse gun.

The dragon swung itself around—how could anything so big move so fast!—and focused its eyes on the gun. Its sides swelled as it sucked in air.

"Take your time," Captain Hoff was saying. "You wouldn't want the general to think I don't know how to run a gun crew, would you?"

The sponger smiled politely as he concentrated on his drill. Behind his back—twenty paces from where he was working—soldiers were sidestepping into the gap created by the dragon's last flame. Charred hulks were lying on the ground. Screaming, pain-maddened men were rolling on the grass.

Von Wogenfer halted his mount near the left wheel of the horse gun— at a point that would put him well within reach of the flame if the dragon aimed directly at the gunners. He tipped his hat to Captain Hoff and eyed the positions of the crew as if he was making sure their wigs were properly powdered.

Von Wogenfer had never fully understood the theory that explained the mysteries of combustion. He had always felt, in fact, that there was something fundamentally confusing about the phlogiston hypothesis attributed to Herr Schleer. Still, if the theory was correct, it would mean there was some logic to the long, slow breaths the monster was inhaling as it prepared itself for its next flare. If its body contained a source of phlogiston, then it was possible it was mixing the phlogiston with a proper quantity of air. They were, in a sense, engaged in a scientific experiment. Could a fire breather prepare a mouthful of flame before a Prussian gun crew could load and fire a horse gun?

The sponger pulled his rod out of the muzzle and stood to attention. If there was one job in the army that had to be done properly, it was the sponging of a cannon. A single grain of smoldering waste could set off the next load of powder while it was still being rammed into place.

A gunner stepped up to the muzzle and dumped a pre-packaged sack of powder down the barrel. A second gunner followed with the canvas tube that contained several pounds of tightly packed shot. The sponger reversed his rod and pushed everything firmly into place with the ram end.

Captain Hoff had been watching the monster's head as his men worked. The creature was crouching about twenty paces from the muzzle of the gun. Its neck was bent in a curve—like a striking snake. Its head was poised at about the height three good grenadiers might achieve, if they stood on each others' shoulders.

"Two degrees below maximum elevation," Captain Hoff ordered. "We'll go for the head. Don't fire until I give the command."

Von Wogenfer dribbled a line of snuff on his sleeve. It was the quietest battlefield he had ever fought on. He could even hear the clinking of the minor gear carried by the cavalry who were poised twenty paces behind him. The only sounds of any importance were the cries of the wounded and the huge sighs pouring down the dragon's throat as it sucked in more air.

He had posted himself beside the gun because he had thought his presence would help Captain Hoff steady his men. Now, watching them work, he knew they would have run through their drill if their general had been a league away. The only sign of anxiety was the way the eyes of the gun crew kept sliding toward the thing looming over them.

The dragon's sides stopped moving. The tip of its tongue curled into a trough and trained itself on the gun....

"FIRE!"

There were times in battle when all your sensations seemed to be altered by the emotions that were battering at your reason. This time the bark of the command sounded louder than the roar of the cannon.

The flame shooting out of the animal's mouth painted everything around him with a red glow. There was a frightening, vivid moment when the gunners seemed to be working in the light and heat of a blacksmith's furnace. A huge shriek tore at his ears.

The moment passed. He raised his head and realized the flame had billowed over him. The dragon was backing away with its muzzle pointed upward—as if it had flinched when the gun had fired. Captain Hoff was already cracking orders. The sponger was stepping up to the muzzle.

He glanced back and verified that Major von Laun and his cuirassiers were unharmed. The major was a solid, decent man—a *bonhomme* in the best sense of the word—and von Wogenfer thought he saw a flash of sympathy in his eyes.

The animal had lowered its head. Its left eye was coated with blood. Streaks and patches of blood covered most of the left side of its face. It twisted its head to one side and glared at the gun with its right eye.

"Good shooting, Captain Hoff," von Wogenfer said. "Let's see how he likes another dose."

He turned in the saddle and cupped his mouth with his hands. "Major von Laun. If you'll be good enough to charge this thing. Keep it occupied."

Normally a general coordinated his troops by dispatching messages to his subordinate commanders. It was a ponderous system, but the enemy commander operated under the same limitation. Von Wogenfer's discussions with Alsten had made it clear he couldn't deal with this assignment by commanding through couriers. His enemy might not be intelligent but its "lines of communication" ran from its brain to the rest of its body. The fact that he had never fought such a thing had to be taken into account, too. He would have to make up some of his tactics on the spot. Every officer in the brigade had been advised, therefore, that he should be prepared to take direct orders from the general himself.

The animal still hadn't used one of its most formidable weapons—its massive bulk. It might be dazed and half blinded, but it could destroy the horse gun merely by blundering forward before the crew could fire another round. Should he be prudent and order the gun to withdraw? Or should he try to pin the thing down and get in another shot?

Later—If he lived—he would be able to explain his reasoning at length. He could probably fill three sheets of paper with a description of all the elements of the situation he was taking into account. Now he merely knew what the elements were. Now, his left hand was holding his sword and pointing it at the infantry platoons that were facing the creature's flank.

"By platoons—fire!"

It was an order they all understood—a call for the relentless rolling volleys of trained Prussian infantry. In the platoon closest to him, the men in the front line dropped to one knee and trained their muskets on the dragon's flank. The second line crouched and brought their muskets to their shoulders. The third line remained standing and leveled their weapons over the hats of the men in the second line. The platoon lieutenant shouted the order to fire, the muskets crashed, and the next platoon in the line fired as the men in the first platoon started reloading. By the time the platoon in front of the tail had fired, the first platoon had finished loading and assumed the firing position. A mist of white smoke covered the animal's side. Von Wogenfer saw a soldier fall out of line and realized he had been hit by a ball that had ricocheted off the dragon's hide.

Von Laun had led his cuirassiers in a sweep around the gun and swung them into a knee-to-knee onslaught on the animal's other flank. Their swords were extended stiffly in front of them, in the regulation position for a charge. They were charging a solid wall, not a mass of men, but they came on as if they thought their horses could drive through the dragon's side in the same way they might ride through the flank of an infantry regiment.

The dragon screamed. Its head swung from side to side as it tried to understand what was happening. A hot musket ball smoked in the grass two steps from the front left hoof of von Wogenfer's horse. On his right, Captain Hoff was once again directing the elevation of the gun....

"*Ecrasez l'infame*," Frederick said. "You have fulfilled your orders with commendable thoroughness, gentlemen. I hope your report on the creature's anatomical peculiarities won't fill more than six volumes, my young philosophe. Did the Hapsburg woman have anything interesting to say when she saw the results of your labors?"

"I'll prepare a summary just for you," Alsten blurted. "It really is an anomaly. When you calculate the nourishment a creature that size should consume in a single day, it becomes obvious it could gobble up the resources of a province in six months. Yet no one sees it for fifty years at a stretch. And when it does make an appearance—it vanishes as soon as it's presented with a sacrifice that serves no utilitarian function. I told the princess that and she said it wasn't supposed to make sense—that it was a creature out of myth."

Von Wogenfer turned to a servant who was standing near his shoulder. He removed a glass of wine from a tray and returned his attention to his sovereign. "She was praying for the souls of the men who had died in the engagement when I approached her afterward. She pointed out that her family had only sacrificed one princess every fifty years."

Frederick smiled. "A touching observation. Did you point out, in return, that this time the dragon was dead?"

"I did."

"And what did she say to that?"

"She said her family had sacrificed one superfluous young woman every fifty years to save a province it had acquired by inheritance. We had sacrificed over one hundred soldiers to retain a province our king had stolen by force."

Frederick smiled again. His bright, cynical eyes regarded von Wogenfer over his glass.

"It's too bad you're already married, eh? You could have carried her back to her mother and claimed the traditional reward."

Von Wogenfer shrugged. In his mind, he could see the tableau Costanze Adelaide had created when she rose from her knees after he interrupted her prayers. She had stepped away from the stake, her crucifix in her hand, and made the sign of the cross as she surveyed the bodies still lying on the field. The words she had muttered had been taken from the Requiem Mass of the Roman church.

Lux perpetua luceat eis, Domine.... Let perpetual light shine upon them, O Lord.

"She is a woman of some spirit," von Wogenfer said. "Captain Kreutzen said she spent most of the battle trying to break free, so the animal could reach her."

Alsten flicked his cuff and put on a face that was obviously intended as an imitation of Frederick's world-weary disdain. "She asked me how we would deal with the monsters of Reason now that we had probably slain the last monster of legend."

"And you told her Reason doesn't produce monsters?" Frederick said.

"As a matter of fact… yes."

The king waved his glass at his guests. "To what shall we drink, gentlemen? To success? To the hope that the monsters of Reason provide as much entertainment for future generations as the monsters of legend have provided for the past?"

"I think I would like to salute the fallen," von Wogenfer said.

Frederick regarded him again. The expression on his face changed.

Von Wogenfer had commanded a battalion at Rossbach. Afterward, a staff officer had told him about the incident that had become part of Frederick's legend. Frederick had been sitting on his horse watching two redcoated enemy regiments as they maintained their position under a savage battering from the Prussian artillery. He had asked who they were, the story went, and he had removed his hat and raised it in silent tribute when he had been told they were the Swiss regiments Planta and Diesbach —foreign soldiers serving in the army of Louis XV.

It was easy to forget who you were talking to, von Wogenfer had often reflected, when you visited the king in his palace. You watched this little Frenchified intellectual play his flute with his court musicians. You heard him making mocking comments to his guests. If Frederick's father could return from the dead, he would observe the court life of Sans Souci and conclude his worst fears had been confirmed. He would be dumbfounded when he learned his strange son was a soldier who had participated in more battles than any king since Alexander of Macedon. He would have decided you were a lunatic if you had told him young Fritz was now called—like Alexander—the Great.

Frederick had continued to kill the Swiss, of course. But that wasn't the point of the story.

"To those who did their duty," Frederick said.

Von Wogenfer extended his arm. The three glasses glittered in the light from the French windows.

Writers are frequently asked to name their influences. The most honest answer is "Every writer I've ever read." In some cases, however, you can be more specific. This story is told in short sections because I had recently read a short story by A.S. Byatt that was structured that way, and thought it would be a good way to tell a science fiction story. My thoughts about immigration were influenced by Bharati Mukherjee, who writes short stories and novels about present-day Indians who emigrate to America. The style contains echoes of Ed McBain, the author of the 87th Precinct police procedurals. I'm not sure that information adds anything to the story, but it may give you some sense of the reading that lurks behind most science fiction stories.

CANARY LAND

Back home in Delaware County, in the area that was generally known as the "Philadelphia region", the three guys talking to George Sparr would probably have been descended from long dead ancestors who had immigrated from Sicily. Here on the Moon they were probably the sons of parents who had been born in Taiwan or Thailand. They had good contacts, the big one explained, with the union that "represented" the musicians who played in eateries like the Twelve Sages Cafe. If George wanted to continue sawing on his viola twelve hours a day, thirteen days out of fourteen, it would be to his advantage to accept their offer. If he declined, someone else would take his place in the string quintet that the diners and lunchers ignored while they chatted.

On Earth, George had played the viola because he wanted to. The performance system he had planted in his nervous system was top of the line, state-of-the-art. There had been weeks, back when he had been a normal take-it-as-it-comes American, when he had played with a different trio or quartet every night, including Saturday, and squeezed in two sessions on Sunday. Now his performance system was the only thing standing between him and the euphoric psychological states induced by malnutrition. Live music, performed by real live musicians, was one of the lowest forms of unskilled labor. Anybody could do it, provided they had attached the right information molecules to the right motor nerves. It was, in short, the one form of employment you could count on, if you were an

American immigrant who was, when all was said and done, only a commonplace, cookbook kind of biodesigner.

George's grasp of Techno-Mandarin was still developing. He had been scraping for money when he had left Earth. He had sold almost everything he owned—including his best viola—to buy his way off the planet. The language program he had purchased had been a cheap, quick-and-dirty item that gave him the equivalent of a useful pidgin. The three guys were talking *very* slowly.

They wanted to slip George into one of the big artificial ecosystems that were one of the Moon's leading economic resources. They had a contact who could stow him in one of the carts that delivered supplies to the canaries—the "long term research and maintenance team" who lived in the ecosystem. The contact would think she was merely transferring a container that had been loaded with a little harmless recreational material.

George was only five-eight, which was one reason he'd been selected for the "opportunity". He would be wearing a guaranteed, airtight isolation unit. Once inside, he would hunt down a few specimens, analyze their genetic makeup with the equipment he would be given, and come out with the information a member of a certain Board of Directors was interested in. Robots could have done the job, but robots had to be controlled from outside, with detectable radio sources. The Director (George could hear the capital, even with his limited knowledge of the language), the Director wanted to run some tests on the specimens without engaging in a direct confrontation with his colleagues.

There was, of course, a very real possibility the isolation suit might be damaged in some way. In that case, George would become a permanent resident of the ecosystem— a destiny he had been trying to avoid ever since he had arrived on the Moon.

The ride to the ecosystem blindsided George with an unexpected rush of emotion. There was a moment when he wasn't certain he could control the sob that was pressing against the walls of his throat.

He was sitting in a private vehicle. He was racing along a strip of pavement, with a line of vehicles ahead of him. There was sky over his head and a landscape around him.

George had spent his whole life in the car-dominated metropolitan sprawls that had replaced cities in the United States. Now he lived in a tiny one room apartment, in a corridor crammed with tiny one room apartments rented by other immigrants. His primary form of transportation was his own legs. When he did actually ride in a vehicle, he hopped aboard an automated cart and shared a seat with someone he had never seen before. He could understand why most of the people on the Moon came from Asiatic countries. They had crossed two hundred and fifty thousand miles so they could build a new generation of Hong Kongs under the lunar surface.

The sky was black, of course. The landscape was a rolling desert composed of craters pockmarked by craters that were pockmarked by craters. The cars on the black strip were creeping along at fifty kilometers per hour—or less—and most of the energy released by their batteries was powering a life support system, not a motor. Still, he looked around him with some of the tingling pleasure of a man who had just been released from prison.

The trio had to explain the job to him and some of the less technical data slipped out in the telling. They were also anxious, obviously, to let him know their "client" had connections. One of the corporation's biggest products was the organic interface that connected the brains of animals to electronic control devices. The company's major resource was a woman named Ms. Chao who was a big expert at developing such interfaces. Her company had become one of the three competitors everybody in the field wanted to beat.

In this case the corporation was upgrading a package that connected the brains of surveillance hawks to the electronics that controlled them. The package included genes that modified the neurotransmitters in the hawk's brain and it actually altered the hawk's intelligence and temperament. The package created, in effect, a whole new organ in the brain. You infected the brain with the package and the DNA in the package built a new organ—an organ which responded to activity within the brain by releasing extra transmitters, dampening certain responses, etc. Some of the standard, medically approved personality modifications worked exactly the same way. The package would increase the efficiency of the hawk's brain and multiply the number of functions its owners could build into the control interface.

Their Director, the trio claimed, was worried about the ethics of the *other* directors. The reports from the research and development team indicated the project was months behind schedule.

"Our man afraid he victim big cheat," the big one said, in slow Techno-Mandarin pidgin. With lots of emphatic, insistent hand gestures.

It had been the big one, oddly enough, who had done most of the talking. In his case, apparently, you couldn't assume there was an inverse relationship between muscle power and brain power. He was one of those guys who was so massive he made you feel nervous every time he got within three steps of the zone you thought of as your personal space.

The artificial ecosystems had become one of the foundations of the lunar economy. One of the Moon's greatest resources, it had turned out, was its lifelessness. Nothing could live on the surface of the Moon—not a bacteria, not a fungus, not the tiniest dot of a nematode, *nothing*.

Temperatures that were fifty percent higher than the temperature of boiling water sterilized the surface during the lunar day. Cold that was grimmer than anything found at the Antarctic sterilized it during the night. Radiation and vacuum killed anything that might have survived the temperature changes.

And what happened if some organism somehow managed to survive all of the Moon's hazards and cross the terrain that separated an ecosystem from one of the lunar cities? It still had to cross four hundred thousand kilometers of vacuum and radiation before it reached the real ecosystems that flowered on the blue sphere that had once been George's home.

The Moon, obviously, was the place to develop new life forms. The designers themselves could sit in Shanghai and Bangkok and ponder the three-dimensional models of DNA molecules that twisted across their screens. The hands-on work took place on the Moon. The organisms that sprouted from the molecules were inserted in artificial ecosystems on the Moon and given their chance to do their worst.

Every new organism was treated with suspicion. Anything—even the most trivial modification of a minor insect—could produce unexpected side effects when it was inserted into a terrestrial ecosystem. Once a new organism had been designed, it had to be maintained in a sealed Lunar ecosystem for at least three years. Viruses and certain kinds of plants and insects had to be kept imprisoned for periods that were even longer.

According to the big guy, Ms. Chao claimed she was still developing the new hawk control interface. The Director, for some reason, was afraid she had already finished working on it. She could have turned it over to another company, the big guy claimed. And the new company could lock it in another ecosystem. And get it ready for market while the Director thought it was still under development inside the *old* company's ecosystem.

"Other directors transfer research other company," the big guy said. "Show him false data. Other company make money. Other directors make money. His stock— down."

"Stock no worth chips stock recorded on," the guy with the white scar on the back of his fingers said.

"You not commit crime," the big one said, with his hands pushing at the air as if he was trying to shove his complicated ideas into George's dumb immigrant's brain. "You not burglar. You work for Director. Stockholder. Director have right to know."

Like everything else on the Moon, the ecosystem was buried under the surface. George crawled into the back of the truck knowing he had seen all of the real Topside landscape he was going to see from now until he left the system. The guy with the scarred hand kept a camera on while he stood in the sterilizing unit and they talked him through the "donning procedure". The suit had already been sterilized. The donning procedure was supposed to reduce the contamination it picked up as he put it on. The sterilizing unit flooded him with UV light and other, less obvious forms of radiation while he wiggled and contorted. The big guy got some bobs and smiles from the third member of the trio when he made a couple of "jokes" about the future of George's chromosomes. Then the big buy tapped a button on the side of the unit and George stood there for five minutes, completely cased in the suit, while the unit supposedly killed off anything the suit had attracted while he had been amusing them with his reverse strip tease. The recording they were making was for his benefit, the big guy assured him. If he ran into any legal problems, they had proof they had administered all the standard safety precautions before he entered the ecosystem.

*   *   *

The thing that really made George sweat was the struggle to emerge from the container. It was a cylinder with a big external pressure seal and they had deliberately picked one of the smaller sizes. *We make so small, nobody see think person*, the big guy had explained.

The trick release on the inside of the cylinder worked fine but after that he had to maneuver his way through the neck without ripping his suit. Any tear—any puncture, any *pinhole*—would activate the laws that governed the quarantine.

The best you could hope for, under the rules, was fourteen months of isolation. You could only hope for that, of course, if you had entered the ecosystem legitimately, for a very good reason. If you had entered it illegally, for a reason that would make you the instant enemy of most of the people who owned the place, you would be lucky if they let you stay inside it, in one piece, for the rest of whatever life you might be willing to endure before you decided you were better off dead.

The people on the "long term research and maintenance team" did some useful work. An American with his training would be a valuable asset—a high level assistant to the people on the other side of the wall who really directed the research. But everybody knew why they were really there. There wasn't a person on the Moon who didn't know that coal miners had once taken canaries into their tunnels, so they would know they were breathing poisoned air as soon as the canaries keeled over. The humans locked in the ecosystem were the living proof the microorganisms in the system hadn't evolved into something dangerous.

The contact had placed the container, as promised, in the tall grasses that grew along a small stream. The ecosystem was supposed to mimic a "natural" day-night cycle on Earth and it was darker than any place George had ever visited on the real planet. He had put on a set of night vision goggles before he had closed the hood of the suit but he still had to stand still for a moment and let his eyes adjust.

His equipment pack contained two cases. The large flat case looked like it had been designed for displaying jewelry. The two moths fitted into its recesses would have drawn approving nods from people who were connoisseurs of bioelectronic craftsmanship.

The hawks he was interested in were living creatures with modified brains. The cameras and computers plugged into their bodies were powered by the energy generated by their own metabolism. The two moths occupied a different part of the great borderland between the world of the living and the world of the machine. Their bodies had been formed in cocoons but their organic brains had been replaced by electronic control systems. They drew all their energy from the batteries he fitted into the slots just behind each control system. Their wings were a little wider than his hand but the big guy had assured him they wouldn't trigger any alarms when a surveillance camera picked them up.

Insect like this in system. Not many. But enough.

The first moth flitted away from George's hand as soon as he pressed on the battery with his thumb. It fluttered aimlessly, just above the tops of the river grasses, then turned to the right and headed toward a group of trees about a hundred meters from its launch site.

At night the hawks were roosters, not flyers. They perched in trees, dozing and digesting, while the cameras mounted in their skulls continued to relay data to the security system.

George had never paid much attention when his parents had discussed their family histories. He knew he had ancestors who came from Romania, Italy, Austria, and the less prominent regions of the British Isles. Most of them had emigrated in the 19th Century, as far as he could tell. One of his grandmothers had left some country in Europe when it fell apart near the end of the 20th Century.

Most of them had emigrated because they couldn't make a living in the countries they had been born in. That seemed to be clear. So why shouldn't he "pull up stakes" (whatever that meant) and head for the booming economy in the sky? Didn't that show you were made of something special?

George's major brush with history had been four sets of viewer-responsive videos he had studied as a child, to meet the requirements listed on his permanent educational transcript. His parents had chosen most of his non-technical educational materials and they had opted for a series that emphasized human achievements in the arts and sciences. The immigrants he was familiar with had overcome poverty and bigotry (there was always some mention of bigotry) and become prize-winning physicists and world famous writers and musicians. There had been no mention of immigrants who wandered the corridors of strange cities feeling like they were stumbling through a fog. There had been no indication any immigrant had ever realized he had traded utter hopelessness for permanent lifelong poverty.

There had been a time, as George understood it, when the music in restaurants had been produced by electronic sound systems and unskilled laborers had carried food to the tables. Now unskilled labor provided the music and carts took orders and transported the food. Had any of his ancestors been invisible functionaries who toted plates of food to customers who were engrossed in intense conversations about the kind of real work people did in real work spaces like laboratories and offices? He had never heard his parents mention it.

Battery good twenty minutes. No more. Moth not come back twenty minutes—not come back ever.

He almost missed the light the moth flicked on just before it settled into the grass. He *would* have missed it, in fact, if they hadn't told him he should watch for it. It was only a blip, and it was really a glow, not a flash. He crept toward it in an awkward hunch, with both cases in his hands and his eyes fixed on the ground in front of his boots.

The small square case contained his laboratory. The collection tube attached to the moth's body fitted into a plug on the side of the case and he huddled over the display screen while the unit ran its tests. If everything was on the up and up, the yellow lines on the screen would be the same length as the red lines. If the "Director" was being given false information, they wouldn't.

It was a job that could have been handled by eighty percent—at least —of the nineteen million people currently living on the Moon. In his lab on Earth, there had been *carts* that did things like that. A four wheeled vehicle a little bigger than the lab case could have carried the two moths and automatically plugged the collection tube into the analyzer. He was lurching around in the dark merely because a cart would have required a wireless communications link that *might* have been detectable.

The first yellow line appeared on the screen. It was a few pixels longer than the red line—enough to be noticeable, not enough to be significant.

The second yellow line took its place beside the second red line like a soldier coming to attention beside a partner who had been chosen because they were precisely the same height. The third line fell in beside its red line, there was a pause that lasted about five hard beats of George's pulse, and the last two yellow lines finished up the formation.

The moth had hovered above the hawk's back and jabbed a long, threadlike tube into its neck. The big changes in the bird's chemistry would take place in its brain, but some of the residue from the changes would seep into its bloodstream and produce detectable alterations in the percentages of five enzymes. The yellow lines were the same length as the red lines: ergo, the hawks were carrying a package exactly like the package they were supposed to be carrying.

Which was good news for the Director. Or George presumed it was, anyway. And bad news for him.

If the result had been positive—If he had collected proof there was something wrong with the hawks—he could have radioed the information in an encrypted one-second blip and headed straight for the nearest exit. His three bodyguards would have helped him through the portal—they'd *said* they would anyway—and he would have been home free. Instead, he had to pick up his equipment, close all his cases, and go creeping through the dark to the other hawk nest in the system. He was supposed to follow the small stream until it crossed a dirt utility road, the big guy had said. Then he was supposed to follow the road for about four kilometers, until it intersected another stream. And work his way through another two kilometers of tangled, streamside vegetation.

The habitat reproduced three hundred square kilometers of temperate zone forest and river land. It actually supported more plant, animal, and insect species than any stretch of "natural" terrain you could visit on the real 21st Century Earth. Samples of Earth soil had been carried to the Moon with all their microorganisms intact. Creepers and crawlers and flying nuisances had been imported by the hundreds of thousands.

You couldn't understand every relationship in a system, the logic ran. *People* might not like gnats and snakes but that didn't mean the system could operate without them. The relationship you didn't think about might be the very relationship you would disrupt if you created a wonderful, super-attractive new species and introduced it into a real habitat on Earth. A change in relationship X might lead to an unexpected change in relationship Y. Which would create a disruption in relation-ship C....

And so on.

It was supposed to be one of the basic insights of modern biological science and George Sparr was himself one of the fully credentialed, fully trained professionals who turned that science into products people would voluntarily purchase in the free market. The fact was, however, that he *hated* insects and snakes. He could have lived his whole life without one second of contact with the smallest, least innocuous member of either evolutionary line. What he liked was riding along in a fully enclosed, air conditioned or heated (depending on the season) automobile, with half a dozen of his friends chattering away on the communications screen, while a first class, state-of-the-art control system guided him along a first class, state-of-the-art highway to a building where he would work in air conditioned or heated ease and continue to be totally indifferent to temperature, humidity, illumination, or precipitation.

Which was what he had had. Along with pizzas, steak, tacos, turkey club sandwiches, and a thousand other items that had flavor and texture and the great virtue that they were not powdered rice flavored with powdered flavor.

There had been women whose hair tossed across their necks as they gave him little glances across their music stands while they played quartets with him. (He had made the right decision, he had soon realized, when he had chosen the viola. The world was full of violinists and cellists looking for playing partners who could fill in the middle harmonies.) There had even been the pleasure of expressing your undiluted contempt for the human robots who were hustling like mad in China, Thailand, India, and all the other countries where people had discovered they, too, could enjoy the satisfactions of electronic entertainment, hundred year lifespans, and lifelong struggles against obesity and high cholesterol levels.

George Sparr was definitely not a robot. Robots lived to work. Humans worked to live. Work was a *means*, not an end. *Pleasure* was an end. *Art* was an end. *Love* and *friendship* were ends.

George had worked for four different commercial organizations in the eleven years since had received his Ph.D. He had left every one of them with a glowing recommendation. Every manager who had ever given him an evaluation had agreed he was a wonderful person to have on your payroll on the days when he was actually physically present. And actually concentrating on the job you were paying him to do.

The dogs weren't robots, either. They were real muscle-and-tooth living organisms, and they had him boxed in—right and left, front and back, with one prowling in reserve—before he heard the first warning growl. The light mounted on the dog in the front position overwhelmed his goggles before the control system could react. An amplified female voice blared at him from somewhere beyond the glare.

"Stand absolutely still. There is no possibility the dogs can be outrun. You will not be harmed if you stand absolutely still."

She was speaking complete sentences of formal Techno-Mandarin but the learning program she had used hadn't eliminated her accent—whatever the accent was. It didn't matter. He didn't have to understand every word. He knew the dogs were there. He knew the dogs had teeth. He knew the teeth could cut through his suit.

"I'm afraid you may have a serious problem, patriot. As far as I can see, there's only one candidate for the identity of this director they told you about—assuming they're telling you the truth, of course."

The ecosystem was surrounded by tunnels that contained work spaces and living quarters. They had put him in a room that looked like it was supposed to be some kind of art gallery. Half the space on the walls was covered with watercolors, prints, and freehand crayon work. Shelves held rock sculptures. He was still wearing his suit and his goggles, but the goggles had adjusted to the illumination and he could see the lighting and framing had obviously been directed by professional-level programs.

They had left him alone twice, but there had been no danger he would damage anything. The dog sitting two steps from his armchair took care of that.

The man sitting in the other armchair was an American and he was doing his best to make this a one-immigrant-to-another conversation. He happened to be the kind of big bellied, white faced, fast-food glutton George particularly disliked, but he hadn't picked up the contempt radiating from George's psyche. He probably wouldn't, either, given the fact that he had to observe his surroundings through the fat molecules that puffed up his eyelids and floated in his brain.

George could understand people who choked their arteries eating steaks and lobster. But when they did it stuffing down food that had less flavor than the containers it came in.…

"Do you understand who Ms. Chao is?" big-belly said.

George shrugged. "You can't do much biodesign without learning something about Ms. Chao."

The puffy head nodded once. They hadn't asked George about his vocational history but he was assuming they had looked at the information he had posted in the databanks. The woman had asked him for his name right after she had taken him into custody and he had given it to her without a fuss.

"Your brag screen looked very promising, patriot. It looks like you might have made it to the big leagues under the right circumstances."

"I worked for four of the largest R&D companies in the United States."

"But you never made it to the big leagues, right?"

George focused his attention on his arms and legs and consciously made himself relax. He pasted a smile on his face and tried to make it big enough Mr. Styrofoam could see it through his eye slits.

"The closest I ever got to the other side of the Pacific was a weekend conference on La Jolla Beach."

"That's closer than I ever got. I was supposed to be a hardwired program genius—a Prince of the Nerds himself—right up to the moment I got my transcript certified. I thought if I came here I could show them what somebody with my brain circuits could do. And make it to Shanghai the long way round."

George nodded: the same sympathetic nod and the same sympathetic expression—he *hoped* it was sympathetic anyway—that he offered all the people who told him the same kind of story when they sat beside him on the transportation carts. Half of them usually threw in a few remarks to the effect that "doughfaces" didn't stand a chance anymore. He would usually nod in sympathy when they said that, too, but he wasn't sure that would be a good idea in this situation. His interrogator was putting on a good act, but the guy could be Ms. Chao's own son, for all George knew. George had never seen an Asian who looked that gross, but Styrofoam's mother could have decided anybody cursed with American genes had to possess a special, uniquely American variation on the human digestive tract.

"The database says you're a musician."

"I've been working in a restaurant. I bought a performance system when I was on Earth—one of the best."

"And now you're serenading the sages and samurai while they dine."

"That's why I'm here. They told me I'd be thrown out of my job if I turned them down."

"Ms. Chao had a husband. Mr. Tan. Do you know him?"

"I've heard about the Tan family. They're big in Copernicus, right?"

"They're one of the families that control the Copernicus industrial complex. And make it such a wonderful place to work and raise children. This Mr. Tan—It's clear he's connected. But nobody knows how much. Ms. Chao married him. They went through a divorce. Somehow he's still sitting on the Board. With lots of shares."

"And he thinks his ex-wife is trying to put something over on him? Is that what this is all about?"

Chubby hands dug into the arms of the other chair. Arm muscles struggled against the low lunar gravity as they raised the bloated body to an upright position. The Prince of the Nerds turned toward the door and let George admire the width of his waistline as he made his exit.

"You're the one who's supposed to be coming up with answers, patriot. We're supposed to be the people with the questions."

There was a timestrip built into the base of George's right glove. It now read 3:12. When they had brought him into the working and living area, it had read 3:46.

George's suit was totally self-contained. He could breathe and rebreathe the same air over and over again. But nothing comes free. Bacteria recycled the air as it passed through the filtering system. Other bacteria generated the chemicals in the organic battery that powered the circulation system. Both sets of bacteria drew their energy from a sugar syrup. In three hours and twelve minutes, the syrup would be exhausted. And George could choose between two options. He could open the suit. Or he could smother to death.

The second interrogator was a bony, stoop shouldered woman. She spoke English with a British accent but her hand gestures and her general air of weary cynicism looked European to George's eye. She glanced at the timestrip—it now read 2:58—and sat down without making any comments.

The woman waved her hand as if she was chasing smoke away from her face. "You were hired by three people. They coerced you. They claimed you would lose your job if you didn't work for them."

"I didn't have any choice. I could come here or I could find a good space to beg. Believe me—this is the last place I want to be."

"You'd rather play little tunes in a restaurant than work in a major ecosystem? Even though your screens say you're a trained, experienced biodesigner?"

George offered her one of his more sincere smiles. "Actually, we play almost everything we want to most of the time. Mozart quintets. Faure. Krzywicki. Nobody listens anyway."

"The three men who hired you told you they were hired by Mr. Tan. Is that correct?"

So far George had simply told them the truth—whatever they wanted to know. Now he knew he had to think. Was she telling him they wanted him to testify against Mr. Tan? Was Ms. Chao trying to get something on her ex-husband?

Was it possible they had something else in mind? Could they be testing him in some way?

"They're very tough people," George said. "They made a lot of threats."

"They told you all the things Mr. Tan could do if you talked? They described his connections?"

"They made some very big threats. Terminating my job was only part of it. That's all I can tell you. They made some very big threats."

The woman stood up. She bent over his timestrip. She raised her head and ran her eyes over his suit.

George didn't have to tell the canaries he didn't want to join them. Nobody wanted to be a canary. In theory, canaries didn't have it bad. They didn't pay rent. The meals they ate were provided free, so their diets could be monitored. They got all the medical care they needed and some they could have done without. They could save their wages. They could work their way out of their cage.

Somehow, it didn't work that way. There was always something extra you couldn't do without—videos, games, a better violin to help you pass the time. The artificial ecosystems were a little over thirty years old. So far, approximately fifteen people had actually left them while they still had the ability to eat and drink and do anything of consequence with women whose hair tossed around their neck while they played Smetana's first quartet.

And what would you really have, when you added it up? George had done the arithmetic. After twenty-five years in an ecosystem—If you did everything right—you could live in the same kind of room he was living in now, in the same kind of "neighborhood". With the same kind of people.

The other possibility would be to buy yourself a return trip to Earth. You'd even have some money left over when you stepped off the shuttle.

The timestrip read 2:14 when the woman came back. This time she put a glass bottle on a shelf near the door. George couldn't read the label but he could see the green and blue logo. The thick brown syrup in the bottle would keep the bacteria in his life support system functioning for at least ten hours.

He was perfectly willing to lie. He had no trouble with that. If they wanted him to claim his three buddies had told him they were working for Mr. Tan, then he would stand up in front of the cameras, and place his hand on the American flag, or a leather bound copy of the last printed edition of *The Handbook of Chemistry and Physics*, or some similar object of reverence, and swear that he had clearly heard one of his abductors say they were employees of the said Mr. Tan. That wasn't the problem. Should he lie before the canaries let him out? And hope they *would* let him out? Or should he insist they let him out first? *Before* he perjured himself?

And what if that *wasn't* what they wanted? What if there was something *else* going on here? Something he didn't really understand?

The people he was talking to were just the fronts. Back in the city there were offices and labs where the babus who really counted made the real choices. Somewhere in one of those offices, somebody was looking at him through one of the cameras mounted in the corners of the room. Right now, when he looked up at the camera in the front left hand corner, he was looking right into the eyes of someone who was sitting in front of a screen sixty kilometers away.

If they would take away the cameras, he could just ask her. *Just tell me what they want, lady. We're both crawling around at the bottom of the food chain. Tell me what I should do. Will they let me out of here if I cooperate first? Will I get a better deal if I tough it out right to the last minute? Are all of you really working for Mr. Tan?*

And what would he have done with her answers when he got them? Did any of the people in this place understand the situation any better than he did? In the city, he hobbled around in a permanent psychological haze, surrounded by people who made incomprehensible mouth noises and hurried from one place to another on incomprehensible missions. In the ecosystem, the canaries puttered with their odd jobs and created their picture of the world from the information that trickled onto their screens.

"I understand there's a visitors lounge attached to the outside of the ecosystem," George said.

"And?" the woman said.

"I'll be glad to tell you anything I know. I just want to get out of here —out of the system itself. There's no way I can get away if you let me get that far—just to the lounge. I'll still need transportation back to the city, right?"

The woman stood up. She stopped in front of the syrup bottle and picked it up. She turned it around in her hand as if she was reading the label. She put it back on the shelf. She glanced at the dog. She slipped out the door.

The time strip read 0:54 the next time the woman came back. The dog turned her way and she shook her head when she saw the soulful look in its eyes.

"You're putting a strain on his toilet training," the woman said.

"Suppose I do give you a statement? Is there any guarantee you'll let me go?"

"Are you trying to bargain with us?"

"Would you expect me to do anything else?"

"You think you're better than us? You think you deserve all that *opportunity* you thought they were going to give you when you left Earth?"

George shrugged. "I couldn't get a job on Earth. Any kind of job. I just came here to survive."

"They wouldn't even pay you to play that music you like?"

"On Earth? There would have been twenty thousand people lined up ahead of me."

"There's no way you can bargain with us, George. *You* answer the questions. *We* relay the answers. *They* decide what to do. There's only one thing I can guarantee."

"In fifty-four minutes, I'll have to open the suit and stay here."

"Right."

They didn't let him out when they had his statement. Instead the woman poured syrup into the flask that fueled his life support system. Then she walked out and left him sitting there.

The urine collection system on his leg was a brand name piece of equipment but he couldn't empty the receptacle without opening the suit. He had already used the system once, about an hour after they had captured him. He didn't know what would happen the next time he used it. No one had thought about the possibility he might wear the suit more than five hours.

The woman smiled when she re-entered the room and caught him fidgeting. The first dog had been replaced a few minutes after it had communicated his message but no one even mentioned *his* problem.

The woman had him stand up in the middle of the room and face the left hand camera. He repeated all his statements. He told them, once again, that the guy with the scarred fingers had mentioned Mr. Tan by name.

The timestrip said 3:27 when they left him alone this time. They had given him a full five hour refill when they had poured in the syrup.

The timestrip read 0:33 when they put him in the security portal. Big-belly and the woman and three other people stared through the little square windows. A no-nonsense voice talked him through the procedure in Hong Kong British.

He was reminded that a lapse in the procedure could result in long-term isolation. He stood in an indentation in the floor. He stuck his hands into a pair of holes above his head. Robot arms stripped the suit. Heat and radiation poured into the portal.

George had never been a reader, but he had played in orchestras that accompanied two operatic versions of the Orpheus legend. He kept his eyes half shut and tried not to look at the door that would take him back to the ecosystem. When he did glance back, after the other door had swung open, the woman and big-belly looked, it seemed to him, like disappointed gargoyles. He started to wave at them and decided that would still be too risky. He walked through the door with his shoulders hunched. And started looking for the two things he needed most: clothes and a bathroom.

The lounge was just a place where drivers and visitors could stretch their legs. There was a bathroom. There was a water fountain. There was a kitchen which checked his credit when he stuck his thumb in the ID unit. And offered him a menu that listed the kind of stuff he had been eating since he arrived on the Moon.

He queried taxi services on the phone screen and discovered a trip back to the city would cost him a week's wages. He had never been naked in a public place before and he didn't know how to act. Were the canaries watching him on the single camera mounted in the ceiling?

"I didn't do this because I wanted to," he told the cameras. "I don't even know what's going on. I just want to get out of here. Is that too much to ask?"

A truck entered the garage space under the lounge. A woman who was old enough to be his mother appeared in one of the doors and handed him a wad of cloth. The shirt was too long for him but it was the only thing she had. He stood around for an hour while she ate a meal and talked to people on the phone. He couldn't shake off the feeling he was wearing a dress.

He had missed a full shift at the Twelve Sages Cafe but the first violinist had left him a message assuring him they had only hired a temporary replacement. They could all see he was jumpy and preoccupied when he joined them at the start of the next shift but no one said anything. He had always been popular with the people he played with. He had the right temperament for a viola player. He took his part seriously but he understood the give-and-take that is one of the primary requirements of good chamber playing.

The big guy lumbered into the Twelve Sages Cafe a month later. He smiled at the musicians playing in the corner. He threw George a big wave as he sat down.

They were playing the slow movement of Mendelssohn's A Major quintet. George actually stumbled out of the room with his hands clutching his stomach. He managed to come back before the next movement started but he lost his place three times.

The second violinist took him aside after the last movement and told him he was putting all their jobs in danger. She came back to his apartment after the shift ended.

Six months later a woman came up to George during a break and asked him if he gave lessons in style, interpretation, and the other subjects you could still teach. Eight months after that he had seven students. The second violinist moved in with him.

Then the first violinist discovered one of the most famous restaurants in the city was looking for a new quartet. And George did something that surprised him just as much as it surprised every one else. He told the first violinist they should abandon the other viola player, develop their interpretation of two of the most famous quarterts in the repertoire, and audition for the other job. They would have to spend all their leisure, non-sleeping hours studying Chi-Li's Opus 12 and Beethoven's Opus 59, No. 2, but the second violinist backed him up. The other two were dubious but they caught fire as George guided them through the recordings and interpretative commentaries he selected from the databanks. The restaurant owner and her husband actually stood up and applauded when they finished the last note of the Chi-Li.

The restaurant paid unskilled labor real money. It was also a place, George discovered, where some of the customers actually listened to the music. They were busy people—men and women who were making fortunes. Someday they might buy performance systems themselves and enjoy the pleasure of experiencing music from the inside. For now, they sat at their tables like barons and duchesses and let the commoners do the work. Once every three or four days somebody dropped the musicians a tip that was bigger than all the money their old quintet had received in a week.

The other members of the quartet all knew they owed it all to George. Anyone could buy a performance system and play the notes. George was the guy who understood the shadings and the instrumental interactions that turned sounds into real music. He had created a foursome that worked well together—a unit that accepted his ideas without a lot of argument.

George had occasionally exercised that kind of leadership when he had been playing for pleasure on Earth. Now he did it with all the intensity of someone who knew his livelihood depended on it.

George searched the databanks twice. He didn't like to spend money on things he didn't need, even after he began to feel more secure. As far as he could tell, Ms. Chao was still the chief designer in her company. Mr. Tan resigned from the board four months after George's visit to the canary cage. Then he rejoined the board six months later. It occurred to George that Ms. Chao had somehow tricked Mr. Tan into doing something that looked stupid. But why did she let him rejoin the board later?

The second violinist thought it might have something to do with family ties.

"Everybody says the Overseas Chinese have always been big on family ties," the second violinist pointed out. "Why should the off-Earth Chinese be any different?"

The whole business became even more puzzling when one of George's students told him she really was glad "Tan Zem" had recommended him. Three of his first four students, George discovered, had looked him up because Mr. Tan had steered them his way. Had Mr. Tan felt guilty? Had he been motivated by some kind of criminal code of honor? Finally George stopped trying to figure it out. He had a bigger apartment. He had a better job. He had the second violinist. He had become—who would have believed it?—the kind of immigrant the other immigrants talked about when they wanted to convince themselves a determined North American could create a place for himself in the new society humanity was building on the Moon.

He had become—by immigrant standards—a success.

Readers who are interested in literary technique might like to know this story turned into an exercise in point of view as I developed it. I tried telling it from the alien, Postri-Dem's, point of view and discovered every paragraph contained a reference to unfamiliar material that couldn't be explained because Postri-Dem would see it as a mundane feature of his day-to-day life. I switched to a first person portrait of Postri-Dem, told by the human who dealt with him, and that eliminated most of that problem. Then I realized I could add a third viewpoint, and it turned into a story about three people who don't quite fit into their societies.

RESEARCH PROJECT

The Senior Fabricator talked for almost forty minutes but Postri-Dem felt his entire speech could have been reduced to three sentences: "The humans are predators. *Their mouths are covered with blood.* Every day we hesitate provides them with another day they can use to pursue their true objective—the search for some way they can kill us."

That's a translation, of course. But you can consider it an exact quote. Postri-Dem watched a recording a few hours after the meeting took place and his memory was one of his most important assets. If you make a reasonable allowance for bitterness and despair, I think you can assume his summary of the meeting is essentially accurate.

Postri-Dem wasn't there himself for the same reason I wouldn't have been invited if a comparable group of homo sapiens had been conducting a similar meeting. The individuals who had been summoned to the conference were all members of the Chosen Presider's power structure. Two of them were participating by screenlink, from the groundbase the ifli had established on Mars. The others were reclining in the Chosen Presider's chambers, as usual, with their fingers comfortably wrapped around drinking containers and different types of finger-food.

Jinny reads at a fifteen-year-old level but her reader knows she is only nine. On the right hand screen of her reader, she is being presented with the text she has chosen—Dr. Orlando Mazzeri's personal account of the last months of his relationship with Postri-Dem. On the left hand screen, the reader fills in the gaps in Dr. Mazzeri's description by offering her an artist's rendering of the meetings the ifli conducted in the Chosen Presider's chambers on their starship. The aliens lie in hammocks that hang from slender, transparent frames. Their faces are heavily wrinkled. Their skin is tinted blue. Their clothes look baggy. Their arms and fingers are unusually long, by human standards.

Jinny has picked Dr. Mazzeri's memoir because she thinks he looks like a nice man. He has a bald, oval head, just like the father in a group of stories her mother read her when she was a baby. His beard adds a touch of cozy furriness. She knows his memoir will be considered an "original source"—a designation that impresses the mentor she is working with this year.

The Chosen Presider had apparently learned a truth that had been passed on to me a few years after I had started chairing academic committees. If you let certain individuals say everything they want to say, they'll usually let you do everything you want to do. I had never applied the technique with any consistency, but Harap-If was a pro.

As far as the Senior Fabricator was concerned, the human species had been given an offer that was a better bargain than it could possibly have hoped for. The ifli had agreed, after all, to help us expand into the asteroid belt and any other part of the Solar system that appealed to us—with the exception of one useless desert planet. If we hadn't accepted such a generous proposal after eighty-six of our own days, shouldn't it be obvious we were probably using the delay as a camouflage for some less innocent activity?

"Is it our fault they're still sitting on their home planet killing each other?" the Senior Artificer orated. "They'd still be murdering each other on their own planet if we had come here a hundred years from now."

Etc.

At one point, the Senior Fabricator even ordered the latest human news-collage from the information system and tried to add a little visual showmanship to his speech. Harap-If pressed the button that turned her hammock in the appropriate direction and stared with great intentness at scenes she had watched a hundred times. Save Mars demonstrators marched through the streets of Berlin and Tokyo. A New York media guru presented an update on the position of the Titanic.

For the Senior Artificer it was our attitude toward the Titanic that provided the final proof we couldn't be trusted. All our newscasts made it clear we believed he and his colleagues would actually slam an artificial comet into Earth and kill the entire human population. If we thought they would do something like that, what kind of actions would we be willing to take against them?

The left hand screen offers Jinny a description of the ifli project the human news media had dubbed the "Titanic." An orbital diagram depicts the long spiral the giant mountain of ice was supposed to describe as it traveled around the sun on a path that connected the rings of Jupiter with the surface of Mars. Two arrows indicate the points where it would have intersected the orbit of the Earth. Jinny brushes the interruption away with an irritable wave of her left hand.

I think it's fair to say that Harap-If's attitude toward us wasn't much more benign than the Senior Artificer's. From her viewpoint, there was something basically incomprehensible about beings who killed each other by the millions and became upset because someone was turning a cold, lifeless world into a place where living things could flourish. She probably wouldn't have hesitated for a minute if the Senior Artificer and his colleagues had come up with something less devastating.

Postri-Dem always insisted the Chosen Presider had been appalled when they had told her they wanted to build a gigantic broadband electronic jammer and place it in Earth orbit. All her political instincts told her the Device would have consequences no one could imagine.

The Senior Artificer wanted to launch the jammer toward Earth orbit as soon as the meeting ended. The Chosen Presider would have let us dither for another year if we'd wanted to, but she had to deal with the political realities. I don't know how she decided the committee would agree we could have another eight days, but everybody at the meeting accepted the figure as soon as she suggested it.

Did she think we should receive a warning? As far as I can tell, she didn't even consider the idea. The Senior Artificer insisted he couldn't vouch for the safety of the Device if we learned about it before they placed it in position. And what would happen if they tried and failed? We might be weaker than they were technologically, but there were seven billion of us and we controlled the resources of an entire planet. Once we made up our mind to fight, we could probably overwhelm their electronic defense systems merely by throwing hundreds of missiles at them.

Stridi-If was one of the people who was attending the meeting by screenlink. Her final orders from the Chosen Presider were as contradictory as most diplomatic instructions. Every word Stridi-If uttered in our presence was supposed to underline the fact that her superiors were becoming dangerously impatient—but we must receive no indication our civilization would be reduced to a pre-electronic level if we didn't make up our minds in eight days. Postri-Dem was supposed to drop a few hints into his discussions with me, in addition—if they could convince someone like Postri-Dem he should forget his obsessions for a few moments.

The reader's programming is state-of-the-art but it retreats to a bit of cowardly evasiveness—Request Information If Necessary—when Jinny reaches the next few paragraphs. Fortunately, Jinny is one of those children who feels she understands sex as well as she needs to. She understands the mechanics, in other words, but she still hasn't learned why people do it.

The evening after the meeting, Postri-Dem spent most of his waking hours listening to three voices squealing and murmuring in the next room. The partitions in the living quarters in the Martian groundbase weren't much thicker than a pastry wafer.

Postri-Dem could have joined the trio in Kipi's room if he had wanted to. Kipi had made it clear she was in that kind of mood. Every time he heard one of those squeals, images of squirming bodies and happy faces pushed everything else out of his consciousness.

I won't claim they're the best quartet you could team up with, Stridi-If had said when she had suggested he should fill out this particular Five. *They're not the kind of people you can entertain with a long lecture on the more fascinating aspects of the human economic system. But it's better than lying in a room all by yourself daydreaming about your last stroking.*

Postri-Dem was too old to be the "odd man" in a Five or Seven in which all the females already had children. His younger brother had been permanently committed to a Seven for almost six Homeyears. His brother had even fathered a child. Postri-Dem had belonged to six different

Sevens since he had reached sexual maturity. His relationships with three of them had all ended with the same scene: a visit from one of the older women, and a gentle, carefully phrased announcement that he was a wonderful, *interesting* person, and they all liked him very much, but....

That wasn't the exact wording they had used, obviously. But it's a reasonable translation. Postri-Dem's relationships with his own species had been about as satisfying as a rejected thesis.

I once worked out a time line in which I compared events on the ifli starship with events on Earth. It was easy to say the Chosen Presider's culture-segment had crossed forty-eight light years in two hundred and six Earth years. But what did that mean when you tried to think about it as something that had happened to thousands of highly intelligent civilized beings as they lived out their lives in a ship that was essentially a miniature city? When they had left their home system over two centuries ago, it had been 1812 on Earth. Napoleon's soldiers had been suffering the agonies of the retreat from Moscow. Our most advanced communication system had been the semaphore telegraph. They had been traveling for eighty-eight years—and they were still almost thirty light years from Earth—when the people of Europe and the Americas had greeted the first day of the twentieth century. They had been almost twenty light years away—and much of the human race had been involved in the second military holocaust of the century—when they had picked up the radio waves human civilization had emitted into space in the 1920's. Verdi... Pasteur... Einstein... Fermi... Hawking... they had all lived and died while the ship had been creeping toward the moment when we would suddenly realize something odd seemed to be moving through the Solar System.

Postri-Dem had been fascinated by my time line. When he had shown it to Stridi-If, her only reaction had been horror at the number of wars listed among the historical events.

Postri-Dem had been eleven when he had been snared by the questions that would turn him into a scholar who spent most of his waking hours immersed in databanks and analytical programs. He had been studying the basic facts about the evolution of his own species, with three other children his own age. Most of the video transmissions the ship had been receiving from Earth had still been black-and-white. The translations had still been cluttered with gaps and alternative interpretations. The adults had all been terrified when their screens had confronted them with films and documentaries that depicted the horrors that had taken place between September 1939 and August 1945.

Postri-Dem's best friend at that time had been a child he eventually addressed as Rapor-If. For her, their first views of the flickering images had been an occasion for displays of shrieks and wild hand waving. For him, it had been the beginning of the great adventure of his life. He immediately realized the universe had presented him with a gigantic experiment in the relationship between biology and culture. On two worlds, forty-eight light years apart, the blind forces of chance had created two conscious, intelligent species—and one of them, contrary to all expectations, was apparently predatory and semi-carnivorous.

Jinny's reader includes a complete, illustrated children's encyclopedia. On her desk, there is an interactive forty-thousand volume children's library. She is fascinated by the results she gets when she touches "semaphore telegraph" and "second military holocaust of the century" with her finger. The language of the second reference creates some problems for the encyclopedia but she manages to work it out and the reader eventually refers her to the library. She plugs the reader into the library box and spends another twenty minutes putting together an outline of the conflict the people of the twentieth century called the Second World War.

Dr. Mazzeri's reference to Giuseppe Verdi sends her back to the library once again. She has been "exposed" to opera but this is the first time she has wondered why human society has produced a form of theater in which the actors sing their lines. Her father knocks on the door just as she is succumbing to temptation and starting to query a reference to Chinese opera.

Jinny's father is a tall man with a frame that is so thin he looks almost frail. He is home today because he is attending a conference. He has spent the last three hours in his office nook, scanning presentations and exchanging comments and questions with the other participants. Jinny's mother usually works at home but today she's taking a look at two missile defense sites near Binghamton. Every month Jinny's mother is supposed to spend a day talking to "on-site personnel" and doing "hands-on" work with "honest hardware." Jinny's father looks blank when she tells him she's writing a report on Postri-Dem.

"Postri-Dem?"

"The alien. The ifli."

Her father raises his eyebrows. "What made you pick him?"

Jinny frowns. It's the kind of question she never knows how to answer. Then she smiles. "I thought Dr. Mazzeri looked like you, Daddy. The scientist who went to Mars. I thought he looked nice."

Her father rubs her head. Jinny looks up at him, wide-eyed, and he presses her against his leg.

Our first discussion session after the meeting took place the next morning. Maria and I were eating our four hundred and forty-fourth snack bar breakfast and resolutely ignoring any visions of black coffee and fresh rolls that happened to wander into our minds. The brown spheres Postri-Dem was eating provided him with a combination of texture and flavor he had loved since he was a child—a mildly crunchy exterior, with a sweet, smooth cream in the middle. He had started stuffing them into his mouth three at a time long before we had finished the first hour of our session.

Postri-Dem spent most of our sessions lying in a hammock placed a few steps in front of our links. A communication unit built into the frame of the hammock connected him to the base information system. Three steps behind him, Stridi-If would stand against a wall, politely nibbling on a finger-food. Her favorite was a thin red stick that was almost as long as her arm.

The reader offers Jinny a standard artist's visualization of the two "links." They are essentially a pair of cylinders mounted on treads. Two jointed arms are attached to the sides of each cylinder. A "head" module, mounted on top, contains two cameras and a pair of microphones. The faces of the two human emissaries stare out of screens placed just below the head module.

An insert in the upper right hand corner of the screen contains a cut away view of the cramped space vehicle in which Dr. Mazzeri and Ambassador Lott ate their snack bar breakfasts and didn't drink coffee. A caption explains that the vehicle orbited Mars at seven hundred kilometers. Two small communications satellites created a network that kept the vehicle connected with the links as it circled the planet.

The figures in the drawing are wearing big helmets and gesturing with gloved hands. The treads on the links were controlled with pedals, but the arms and the head module were slaved to the motions of their bodies. The system looks clumsy to Jinny's eyes, but she knows it is a primitive version of the technology she uses when she takes electronic field trips.

For the last two days, we had been discussing three subjects: two All-Time Fascinaters and one Perennial Puzzle. The two Fascinaters were mating customs (sex) and patterns of intraspecies competition (violence in human terms, something else in Postri-Dem's terms). The Puzzle was sleep. On two worlds that were totally isolated from each other, the evolutionary process had produced intelligent species that slipped into unconsciousness for approximately 25 percent of each day. The ifli's knowledge of their biochemistry seemed to be more detailed than ours but Stridi-If had told us we would have to avoid discussions of chemical pathways for the time being. We could discuss patterns and customs, however, and the specialists on our consulting committee had told us they could use any information I could give them.

Sleeping habits got the first hour. For the second hour, we concentrated on the mating myths we had exchanged two days earlier. The anthropologist who had lobbied for the topic was one of my favorite people on the consulting committee and I did my best to fill every minute of the hour with something useful. I became so engrossed in the subject, in fact, that I actually felt irritated when the loudspeaker on the wall of the groundbase produced its standard polite murmur.

I shook my head. "The voice of Order and Proper Procedure seems to have spoken."

Postri-Dem countered with a wave of his hands and a slight roll of his shoulders—his best approximation of a human shrug. "I was running out of thoughts anyway. I'm certain your consultant will have a few dozen questions we can explore the next time we take up this topic."

Behind him, Stridi-If spoke to him in their own language—which I didn't understand at the time, of course. "This is your last opportunity for the day, Habut," Stridi-If said. "If you can't say something useful while you're discussing intraspecies competition, we may as well assume you're never going to give me anything I can work with."

Postri-Dem's full name was Postri Habut Luxerdi. His close acquaintances—when he had any—usually called him Hab or Habut.

Stridi-If's full name was Stridi Ro Stridki but I'm confident Postri-Dem never called her Strid or Ki.

Stridi-If had interrupted Postri-Dem three times during the last hour and he had ignored her every time. As far as she was concerned, he had already missed several chances to let us know his species wasn't quite as harmless as its evolutionary history indicated. I had given him a perfect opportunity to make the point when I had leaped on the resemblance between our story of David and Bathsheba and their story of Gutara and Estrihar.

The legend of Gutara and Estrihar was one of the oldest stories Postri-Dem's species had created. Gutara was a legendary ruler—the "queen" (more or less) of a famous city state. Estrihar was an architect who already belonged to a Five that was dominated by a woman who managed important construction projects. Gutara wanted Estrihar for herself, so she gave her rival a dangerous project—a bridge that crossed a ravine in the mountains. The other woman had died in a storm, Gutara's role in the death had been discovered, and Gutara had been clawed and expelled.

It was a minor coincidence in some ways but it was the kind of thing that fascinated both of us. Postri-Dem had realized he was looking at an alternative evolutionary history when he was still a child. I had realized it three weeks after we had started our conversations and I had reacted with the same naive, babbling excitement that had overtaken him all those years before.

I have to confess, too, that the discovery had given both of us a more adolescent pleasure. It messed up one of the more plausible chains of logic our colleagues had produced.

On Postri-Dem's world, theorists had assumed that any intelligent aliens they encountered would have to be herbivores. Carnivores, they had reasoned, were specialized creatures who depended on their size and their speed. On Earth—with equally impeccable logic—many human exobiologists had argued that any intelligent aliens we met would have to be predators. Carnivores, they had argued, lived by their wits. They had to outmaneuver their prey. It was an agreeable idea and I suspect it had influenced most of our responses when we had discovered an alien ship had orbited Mars. As far as we were concerned, a group of people just like us had entered the Solar System, made no attempt to communicate with us, and hit a robot probe with a blast of static that had put it out of business an hour after it had reached Mars.

Postri-Dem had been convinced his leaders were doing the wrong thing when they knocked out the probe. We were intelligent beings, after all. He had presented the Chosen Presider with a long document—the equivalent of twenty thousand words in International English—In which he listed all the evidence that indicated we could keep our violent proclivities to a minimum when we really tried. Harap-If even read it, I gather. Apparently she had more patience than most of the human politicians I've encountered.

Jinny's library contains eleven books on evolution and paleoanthropology. In one of the books on human evolution—a treatise for twelve year olds entitled *How Did We All Get Here?*—there is a two-screen layout.

The first screen is dominated by a picture of naked proto-humans standing on the edge of a plain. Their hands hold pieces of chipped flint. They look across the grasslands at fat herbivores. A half-eaten carcass is surrounded by jackals who will have to be dispersed before the humans can grab their share.

On Earth, the text explains, the evolution of intelligence had begun with a creature that had slipped into a way of life that revolved around hunting and scavenging. A weak, unimpressive animal had begun to rely on its brain—on its ability to construct simple weapons and make predictions about the behavior of its prey. The hunters and gatherers with the best brains had tended to survive—and the human species had become more and more dependent, generation after generation, on its ability to think.

The second screen is illustrated with an artist's conception of the early ancestors of the ifli. The proto-ifli are naked, too. In the background there is a marsh. Some of them are widening a shallow ditch by scraping it with stones. Others are cutting thin saplings and bringing them to a pond, where a tangle of mud and wood is rising in the center.

On Postri-Dem's world, the text argues, the blind forces of chance apparently descended on herbivores—weak, unimpressive marsh creatures who had been crowded into the drier lands at the edge of their natural habitat. In the marshes, they had protected themselves from predators by building nests of mud and grass in the middle of ponds. In the borderlands, some of them responded to their plight by digging primitive canals and creating their own ponds. Like the ancestors of the first true humans, they created a way of life that favored individuals who used their brains. In their case, however, the survivors were individuals who could *build*.

Jinny read that book over fourteen months ago. *How Did We All Get Here?* was, in fact, the text in which she first learned of the existence of the ifli. She feels she's been interested in the ifli for a long time, of course—and she has, when you think of fourteen months as a percentage of nine years. She has read all the other books in her library that mention the ifli and she is now using her "Interlibrary Connection" and downloading material from public databases. She already knows, for example, that the sexual division of labor in Postri-Dem's culture-segment conformed to the standard division of labor in most ifli cultures. Ifli females tended to be politicians and administrators. Ifli males tended to be engineers and designers. Like most of the people who encounter that fact, she has wondered if the UN selection committee made a lucky guess when it sent a female diplomat and a male exobiologist to Mars. It didn't, but there seems to be a general agreement the sexual composition of the human delegation may have influenced the Chosen Presider's decision to open discussions.

This was only the third time we had discussed intraspecies competition. It was obviously a delicate subject. I was still selecting my words with great care.

"Actually," I said, "I don't see why we can't go on discussing the story of Gutara and Estrihar. I think it raises important questions about the way our different species compete. As I understand the story—Gutara's city was erecting that bridge because of a rivalry with another city. They were creating a trade route to compete with a city that had already built a bridge over the same river."

"Trade isn't quite the correct word," Postri-Dem said. "The stream of information and certain kinds of… social intercourse… was just as important. But you've presented an accurate summary of the situation, other than that."

"But that brings up a question we can't seem to get away from. Didn't they at any time consider the possibility they might take possession of the other city's bridge? By engaging in violence?"

Postri-Dem waved his hands and engaged in another attempt to simulate a human shrug.

"I can only tell you what I've said before, Doctor Mazzeri. We do not seem to think of such things. If we do—there is no tradition that tells us how to go about it. You have specialists in violence. Techniques. We usually resolve conflicts by moving. If that isn't practical... there are places on our Home world where you'll see six bridges built within steps of each other."

He popped another pair of brown spheres into his mouth. From the way he described it to me, the spheres coated the cells of his tongue and cheeks with a flake-speckled cream that created a sensation comparable to the feelings we humans get when we eat something sweet.

"I think it's clear we are less violent by nature," Postri-Dem said. "As I've said before, we do engage in brawls and riots. But they tend to be disorganized short-term events by your standards. Even when we dealt with predators—even then, we relied on defensive structures. On walls. On water barriers. And ultimately, of course, on the modification of the predator's habitat that accompanies technological development. As your species is doing."

He paused and crunched his way through two more spheres while he arranged the phrases he had constructed the evening before. "I should tell you, however, that there have been occasions when members of our species used environmental modification as a competitive technique. The fact that we didn't institutionalize that kind of competition seems to support the idea that you can't institutionalize some things unless you are more naturally violent to begin with. Your species apparently developed organized violent competition shortly after you developed agriculture and started living in large scale social units. We didn't. But the fact that we've accumulated a few famous examples of aggressive environmental modification indicates the potential may be there."

"Very good, Habut," Stridi-If said in their language. "You took your time but you couldn't have done a better job if I'd written the script for you. You've planted the idea but you haven't over-emphasized it."

Maria's voice broke in on our private communications circuit. "I think we'd better talk, Orly. This might be a good place to put in another word about the Titanic."

I started to object and then shrugged. Postri-Dem told me to take all the time I needed and we blanked the screens on our links and broke the audio connection.

"They're probably thinking about some way they can bring up the Water Project," Stridi-If said. "That was perfect, Habut. Just be careful what you say if they want to talk about the Water Project. We have to make it clear we aren't referring to anything that would increase their panic over that."

Postri-Dem stuffed two more spheres into his mouth and choked back the impulse to tell Stridi-If he wasn't sure the humans would understand the difference between an artificial comet that wiped out their entire species and a Device that eliminated most of the gains they had made in the last two centuries. Postri-Dem's life had been unusually asocial, by the standards of his species, but he had learned one important fact about his relationship with the rest of society—he had a tendency to blurt out his thoughts without taking into account the responses they might provoke.

To Stridi-If—and most of the other members of his culture-segment—he was an odd, comic figure. Stridi-If was only five Homeyears older than Postri-Dem but she thought of him, he knew, as someone who was basically a child. She liked him—in the same way you would like a child—but she felt he had to be watched for his own good.

The most frustrating—and agonizing—period in Postri-Dem's life had been the three months that followed the moment when our links had come rolling across the Martian sands and paused outside the ifli base. There had been days, he claimed, when he had thought he would go mad if the Chosen Presider and her advisers didn't decide to open talks with us. Officially, Stridi-If had been his liaison with the power structure. Officially, she had been working with him because she had been the diplomat who would represent them if they decided to initiate a dialogue. In reality, she had been a caretaker who was supposed to save a valuable resource from self-destruction. There had been times when Postri-Dem had seriously believed he should bypass the standard political process and make impassioned speeches in the corridors. There had been other times when he composed long, angry messages to influential individuals who were opposing contact. Stridi-If had provided the patient, gentle voice that calmed him down before he made a fool of himself in public. Stridi-If had been the sympathetic partner who convinced him his arguments would be more effective if he let a trained go-between do the talking.

I finished working out my wording with Maria and blinked on our screens.

"Ambassador Lott has raised a question I think I have to bring up," I said. "It's really a political and diplomatic issue, but I think it's something you and I can discuss. As you know, many people on our planet are concerned about your Water Project—to put it mildly. When they look at this discussion on Earth, many people are going to wonder if the effects of an artificial comet might be considered a form of environmental modification...."

Postri-Dem reached for the bowl of spheres. He picked up three of them, then lowered his hand just before it reached his mouth.

"I think that can best be answered with a quote, Doctor Mazzeri. As your philosopher Machiavelli put it—"

He switched to Italian—a language Stridi-If didn't understand.

"Transmit this to Earth at once. In eight days, we are going to launch a high speed rocket equipped with a jammer that can interfere with most of the electronic activity on your planet indefinitely. The propulsion unit and the jammer will receive their energy from a very powerful fusion energy reactor. The missiles you have placed in orbit as a defense against the Water Project are your only hope. You must destroy the rocket while it is using the reactor to decelerate. The propulsion unit and the jammer cannot operate simultaneously. If your missiles approach it while it is in free fall, the jammer will probably stop them."

Journalists have often asked me how it feels to hear someone tell you the world is going to end. Fortunately, I didn't have to respond in any rational way. Maria hit the right buttons and Postri-Dem's message started winging directly to Earth.

I do know my link lurched forward a few inches and stopped with a jerk. I had apparently reacted to the message with a sudden, involuntary movement.

Postri-Dem's jaws crunched down on three spheres simultaneously. He found it hard to believe he had actually completed the entire message. He had spent hours arranging the wording. He had repeated it tens of times after he had memorized it but he had still been convinced he would forget something important if he actually decided to say it out loud.

The Lurch of the Link had reminded me this was no time to let Stridi-If see I was excited. I swallowed hard and tried to remember how I would react if he had actually quoted a passage from a Renaissance philosopher.

"That's very interesting, Postri-Dem. I never thought of that particular aspect of Machiavelli in just that way."

Behind Postri-Dem's back, Stridi-If was already murmuring into her communicator. Postri-Dem knew the information system could apply a translation program to his message and produce a reasonably accurate paraphrase in about twice the time it had taken him to deliver it.

The communications screen tells Jinny she has a call from her mother. She wants to keep on reading, but she knows she can't.

Jinny's mother looks very crisp and trim in her uniform. She wants to make sure Jinny is playing with her friends. She asks how a boy named Herbert is doing and Jinny assures her she's going to call Herbert before the day is up.

"That's very important, baby. You can't keep your nose stuck in a reader all the time."

"I'm writing a paper on Postri-Dem," Jinny says. "Did you know the ifli lived in families that had two mothers and three daddies? Some of them had three mothers and four daddies."

Her mother smiles. "Would you like that? Would you like having more than one mommy and daddy?"

"I just thought it was interesting. Did they have extra mommies and daddies because they didn't eat meat?"

"I'm afraid I don't know, dear. Are you making sure you're researching at least three sources?"

"I'm reading Dr. Mazzeri's own story. Then I'm going to see what else the library has."

"Dr. Mazzeri's own story? Isn't that a little long?

"It's just something he wrote about Postri-Dem. For a collection of articles on Postri-Dem. It's really interesting, Mommy. He really liked Postri-Dem. You can tell t from the way he writes about him."

Her mother smiles again. "I'll have to look at that when I get home. Make sure you pay attention to your paragraphing, baby. That mentor you've got this semester puts a lot of emphasis on paragraphing."

Stridi-If's hiss was so sharp and intense it made Postri-Dem's entire body turn warm—a sensation that characterized the ifli's response to high-level threat. He knew what he was going to see before he turned his head but he still cringed when he saw it. Stridi-If had dropped into a graceless, awkward crouch. She was still holding her communicator in her left hand but the fingers of her right hand had bent into stiff, curving claws

This wasn't the first time Postri-Dem had been faced with someone who had fallen into that crouching, clawing position. There had been times, in his childhood, when he had found himself surrounded by ten or twelve children of both sexes.

Sometimes it was something he said. Once he had merely mentioned that the pictures he had seen of the Netherlands looked pleasanter to him than some of the more industrialized areas of Home. The landscape of Holland had apparently been shaped almost completely by human activity, but the humans had treated it with more respect, it seemed to him, than his species had treated Home. There were even places on Earth where the humans had set aside large areas of untouched wilderness. Did intelligent predators need some contact with the wilderness in which they had once stalked their food animals?

To him it had been an interesting idea—the kind of thing that kept running through his mind. He had known he was in trouble as soon as the other children started to react but he had still been surprised.

"Do you know what you've done?" Stridi-If screamed. "To yourself? To everyone?"

Postri-Dem rolled out of his couch. He turned away from her, with his head cocked to one side, so she was shrieking at his left shoulder. He would have turned his back on her if he had let his instincts take control of his muscles.

Maria's link rolled forward with its arms waving. Her amplified voice boomed Stridi-If's name. She might have been half bored by the scholarly information I was exchanging with Postri-Dem, but she was used to situations in which she had to move from sleepy semi-attention to full, intense participation. She had cut her diplomatic teeth on the UN team that had defused the Thai-Taiwan naval confrontation. Some of the assignments that had followed had been even tougher.

Stridi-If didn't have Maria's experience but she was a professional, too. She rose out of her crouch and shrieked an order at Postri-Dem. He backed to one side and Stridi-If advanced on the barrier.

"I wish to point out that this situation is still fluid," Maria said. "The recording we have just transmitted is marked with a code that will take it directly to our ultimate superior—the Secretary General. No one else on

Earth will know about this unless he chooses to tell them. He will have to inform two of our subcultures—the Japanese and the Americans—if you launch your missile. They control the missiles that orbit Earth. But right now you and I can still discuss this in private."

It was an astonishing performance. She had determined the exact nature of her negotiating stance and laid it out in sentences that sounded like they had been rehearsed for days. She had even made sure she omitted an important bit of information. We couldn't keep track of the ifli missile without help from the Japanese and the Americans. The equipment in the European Community couldn't do the job.

Later on she told me she had thought about situations in which we might be threatened with attack and worked out some of the possibilities. She had never thought about a planetary jammer but that was the kind of unexpected development she had learned to allow for.

"Orlando and I were sent here because billions of human beings want to establish peaceful relations with you," Maria said. "But we can't control all the subcultures on our world. We've done our best to make that clear to you. If the Japanese and the Americans learn anything about this, we can't promise you we can control their response."

The i's were dotted. The important points were spelled out. I thought she had put too much emphasis on the danger posed by the Japanese and the Americans until I realized Stridi-If probably wasn't used to negotiations that included the threat of violence.

Stridi-If was standing in front of the barrier with her hands pressed against her legs. It occurred to me she was probably faced with a personal problem, in addition to the professional crisis Postri-Dem had forced on her. She should have demanded a translation as soon as Postri-Dem started using a language she didn't understand.

Maria had already thought of that. "Is there any way we can work this out between us, Stridi-If? Just the two of us?"

"You're asking us to reverse our decision—to tell our engineers they can't deploy the Device. Harap-If will have to bargain with you herself, ambassador Lott."

Jinny feels a little niggle of curiosity when she scans the reference to the "Thai-Taiwan naval confrontation" but this time she lets it pass. She is surprised to learn that the Japanese and the Americans seemed to be working together in space during the period when all this happened.

Jinny's mother once tried to explain why she has to go away every month. One of the items she put on the screen was a map that showed how the world was divided into five "competitive zones."

Postri-Dem had never felt more isolated. Stridi-If glanced at him once or twice while she talked to the Chosen Presider on her communicator, but she acted, in general, as if he had disappeared.

When he had been invisibled in the past, he had always retained access to his databases. This time he wouldn't even have that. He would wander through the halls of the Marsbase, with every door shut against him, until he sank into a depression, stopped searching for food, and let himself drift into a coma. He could even be expelled. His species had been expelling troublemakers into inhospitable environments for as long as it had been keeping records.

Yet, even now, huddling in a corner of the conference room, he was fascinated by the way Maria was handling the situation. He had noted the way she had used the threat of violence as a negotiating tool even as she insisted she represented a party that wanted to avoid violence. His people used threats, too, but they were essentially commercial bargainers. Maria was discussing a nightmare of death and maiming as if she were telling Stridi-If some of the members of her culture-segment might take their business somewhere else if they didn't get their way.

Stridi-If placed a communication screen in front of the links and the Chosen Presider began talking to Maria. No one paid any attention to Postri-Dem when he crept up to his hammock and picked up his food bowl. He started to put two spheres into his mouth at once, then stopped himself and dropped one into the bowl. They might be the last food he would ever eat.

Harap-If's amplified voice boomed through the conference room. "Postri-Dem! Come over here and get to work. I'm not going to let all the time you've spent studying these people go to waste now that we really need it."

Postri-Dem had already realized he was watching an exercise in futility. Intellectually, the Chosen Presider knew we were intelligent beings like her own people. Emotionally, she probably thought of the Device about the same way we would regard an electrified barrier that herded sharks away from a private beach.

Stridi-If and Maria were both people who thought in terms of power. For them, the whole discussion was a matter of threat and counter-threat —with Stridi-If hampered by the fact that she didn't know how to use the threat of violence. Sometimes she tried to indicate her people were willing to do things that were so savage they were clearly beyond their powers. Other times she shied away from threats that many human diplomats would have carried out without a flicker of remorse.

Postri-Dem listened for a full hour before he became so absorbed in his own thinking that he forgot he was a walking corpse. "I would like to make a suggestion, Harap-If."

"It's about time you did," Harap-If said.

"Doctor Mazzeri and I probably understand the differences between our species better than anyone in either group. Perhaps it would help if he and I talked about this in private. And tried to devise a plan Stridi-If and Ambassador Lott could then discuss."

Stridi-If was horrified, of course. He had already betrayed her once. What would he tell me if she left us alone now?

The Chosen Presider nibbled on her finger-food while she listened to Stridi-If's objections. They were speaking in their own language but Maria realized something important was happening and let me know the situation called for judicious silence.

"Everything will have to be recorded," the Chosen Presider said. "We'll need to know what you said if anything more goes wrong. But you can talk without supervision."

The last time he had talked to me, Postri-Dem had been a full member of his culture, representing it in an honorable position—if I can translate his feelings into something that approximates human terms. Now he was an outcast—someone who might be dead within a few days. There would be no trial, no attempt at the kind of legal maneuvering we Westerners have inflicted on most of the human population. A high-level committee would consider his case. Its deliberations would be recorded and disseminated. And the members of his community would follow their natural inclinations and avoid contact with someone who had made it clear he didn't value their welfare and their good opinion.

Their history included many cases in which someone had been expelled or invisibled and later generations had decided the outcast had been right. They had their Galileo's and Semmelweis's, too. But none of their heroic dissenters had been out-and-out traitors.

I wasn't surprised when he immediately told me he already had a proposal that could lead the two diplomats out of their impasse. I was even less surprised when I discovered what it was.

The crux of our problem with the ifli's offer was the suggestion they should move their starship into a low Earth orbit. They wanted to position themselves above our planet, take on two or three thousand human passengers, and transport our first interplanetary colonists to the asteroid belt. They apparently couldn't believe we would think they might bombard Earth—or engage in some other kind of violent action—if we let them place a massive ship, of unknown powers, in Earth orbit.

Now, of course, we had learned what they could do. Who knew what other tricks they had hidden in their baggy little sleeves?

Maria had already suggested one solution. We could place armed humans on their ship before it orbited Earth. Stridi-If had conveyed their rejection of the idea with waving arms and a general air of agitation. Hard as it is to believe, there wasn't one item on their ship that could be considered an anti-personnel weapon. Asking them to accept armed humans on board their ship was a little like telling beavers or prairie dogs they should let weasels into their lodges and tunnels.

The one thing we hadn't understood was the reasoning that had led to the offer. One of the biggest criticisms of my behavior has been the complaint that I didn't start discussing intraspecies competition until I had been exchanging information with Postri-Dem for over two months. If I had known they were working on something like the Device, I probably would have introduced the subject by the beginning of the second month. As it was, I thought we should avoid the matter until both sides had acquired a good basic picture of the people they were dealing with. None of us realized that the ifli's offer was an example of a tactic that was their equivalent of arms control. Sometimes they would share a resource, like a road or a tunnel, and let two groups gradually merge into one. They deliberately created a situation in which both sides were dependent on the same resource. Then they let time do its work.

Harap-If had backed a proposal that required real courage. She had gambled that spacefaring humans and spacefaring ifli society would eventually blend into a common society—in spite of their fundamental differences—as they built cities in the asteroid belt and engaged in trade.

My own opinion is that we probably would have. In spite of all the evidence to the contrary, I don't think human beings are fundamentally warlike. We are willing to fight when we want something. We'll fight back when someone tries to take something away from us. But most of us don't like fighting. We like thinking about it—and watching other people do it—but very few of us actually enjoy the experience.

Postri-Dem's proposal was less far reaching. He wanted to set up a research station in Mars orbit—a station in which ifli and humans would engage in the same kind of exchanges he and I were engaged in. We could send humans one way to Mars orbit and the ifli could build the research station. They might even turn Deimos or Phobos into the kind of habitat we would have built in the asteroids.

By the time he finished describing the idea, I had the feeling he had almost forgotten his personal situation. "It fits into our way of minimizing competition," he argued. "And you could think of it as the kind of arms control measure you've developed. You'll have permanent observers in Mars orbit. You can keep an eye on what we're doing and make sure we aren't launching anything at Earth."

Jinny already knows who Galileo is, so she ignores the one paragraph bio when it appears on the left screen. Semmelweis is another matter. So is "arms control." She finds the idea so intriguing she ends up skimming three different articles on the subject.

It was a self-serving proposal, of course. He and I were agreeing, in essence, that the world would be a far better place if the engineering and military types would get out of the way and let those of us who valued knowledge and learning go about our business.

Fortunately, Maria thought it was a good idea, too. She was a diplomat, not a scholar, but she had always understood the value of knowledge. "They'll learn more about us, too," Maria said, "but they're so far ahead of us in that area we're bound to gain more than we lose."

She even threw in an extra on her own. If they approved the plan, the national governments on Earth wouldn't be told about the Device. Postri-Dem thought that sounded like a good idea, Maria's recommendation went back to Earth, and he let Stridi-If know he'd come up with a cheaper, less complicated proposal that seemed to meet with our approval.

Stridi-If sounded less enthusiastic. "I'll communicate the proposal to Harap-If, ambassador Lott. Are you confident your officials will accept your recommendation?"

"Yes. I am."

There was nothing equivocal about Maria's response. She didn't hesitate. She didn't qualify her words in any way. By now I knew her well enough to know she wouldn't say something like that if she didn't mean it.

Postri-Dem never told me what happened during the next day and a half. I have no idea when they let him know they were leaving. It's quite possible they never did let him know.

He must have understood when their ground-to-orbit vehicle took off with half the population of the base on board. Did he wander around the base like a ghost? Did he find an empty apartment and huddle in a hammock? Did people mock him? There were some things even he couldn't chatter about.

I found him sitting on the floor in a corridor, with his back propped against the wall. He managed to pull himself erect when he saw the link but after that he just settled against the wall and stared at it as it rattled toward him.

There was no danger he would die in the near future. The microwave beam was still supplying the base with power. I knew it would probably shut down sooner or later, when a critical component finally failed, but for now he had all the air, heat, and light he needed. Our biggest immediate problem was the pressure we were getting from Earth. The Security Council governments all knew the starship had left Mars orbit. They all wanted to know—at once!—where it was going.

Jinny already knows that the Marsbase drew its energy from a solar powered microwave station the aliens had constructed from material they had taken from the Martian moon Phobos. The ifli had placed the station in an appropriate orbit before they had started working on the groundbase, so the ground crews would have all the power they needed from the moment they touched down.

She isn't quite sure how microwave beams work. She's already looked at a brief explanation and decided she may have to defer the topic for a while. Most of the material on microwaves in her encyclopedia discusses cooking and communications devices. There is no indication any human had ever thought about building orbiting stations that transformed solar power into microwave energy and beamed it down to Earth.

A psychologist, the old saying goes, is a man who observes the reactions of the other people in the airplane when the pilot announces the right wing has just fallen off. An astronomer is a woman who starts estimating spectral categories when the man she's in love with draws her attention to the glories of a summer night. There's a whole roster of jokes about scientists and their preoccupation with their specialties. In a sense I was living one of those jokes. What kind of a person would shut himself in a closet, a hundred million kilometers from a doctor or a dentist, just so he could talk with a wrinkled, short-legged eccentric who happened to come from another star system? The news media had been impressed when two hundred exobiologists had applied for the job. Divide two hundred by the population of the Earth in 2026 and you'll understand why people like me feel we belong to a statistically insignificant minority. You'll also understand, I think, why the four thousand ifli in the Chosen Presider's culture-segment didn't produce more Postri-Dems.

It took me a week to get him to the point where we could resume our discussions. I did it, for the most part, by putting myself in his place and doing things that would have had the right effect on me. I dropped interesting facts about human society or human biology into discussions about practical matters such as the quality of the food he had available. I called him at odd hours and asked him to clarify things he had said during our discussions. I introduced topics that were related to the conversations Maria was having with New York.

It helped that he could still beam a record of our conversations at the ifli ship. The ship never gave him any indication it was receiving or recording but he could always hope. The information he was gathering could still become part of his species' knowledge base—whether they appreciated it or not.

I think Maria's efforts had some effect on him, too. I listened in on some of her initial conversations with Earth and I know she made a real try.

It was Maria, in fact, who decided we should lobby for a full research base on the surface of Mars, with enough people on the ground to help Postri-Dem keep himself alive. She concentrated on the long term military advantages of a research effort when she talked to New York, but I don't think I misinterpreted the way her face lit up when she and I first discussed the idea. She tended to see everything we learned in terms of power conflicts, security arrangements, and military potential, but she cared about Postri-Dem, too. She couldn't hide the genuine *relief* that broke through her emotional defenses when she decided there was a real possibility we could help him survive.

For me it was the most exciting eight months I have ever lived through. We had been talking for weeks but we had barely touched the surface of dozens of subjects. Brain chemistry, economic systems, meteorology—there were times when my consultants had to send me thirty screens of material just so I could acquire enough background to discuss one innocuous question.

Some topics were way beyond both of us. We couldn't handle anything that involved serious mathematics. Neither one of us knew his own system of mathematics that well. The questions that really excited us dealt with the kind of issues that fascinate specialists in sociobiology. There was a day—to give you just one example—when one of our consultants asked us to look at the social arrangements of the animals the ifli were related to. On Earth, we had studied primates like gorillas and baboons and speculated about the things their behavior could tell us about ourselves. On their world, some of their biologists had looked at the social behavior of the different kinds of marsh creatures they were related to and mapped the chemical pathways that influenced traits like sociability.

By the time we finished with that one, Postri-Dem was chattering away as if Stridi-If was still standing behind him and he still had a Five to return to when we stopped talking. If he had been a member of our own species, I think he could have become a figure comparable to Freud or Darwin. I have always been proud of my ability to understand a broad range of disciplines and see connections the specialists tend to overlook. Postri-Dem made me understand the difference between talent and genius.

Would his stature have been recognized if he had stayed in his own star system? The culture-segment he had been born into was essentially a backwoods, provincial society. In his own system, he would have been connected to an intellectual network that included thousands of individuals who could appreciate his potential.

*   *   *

The left screen offers Jinny pictures and capsule biographies of Sigmund Freud and Charles Darwin. There are also references to famous researchers who studied primates in their habitats. The program even presents her with two small indications it was designed by someone who had a sense of humor. The list of "possible additional readings" includes references to "John Dolittle, M.D." and a field worker who seems to have been a titled English aristocrat. Jinny smiles when she spots both of them. She read *The Story of Doctor Dolittle* when she was six, when she came across it while she was browsing through her library. She has never read anything by Edgar Rice Burroughs but the library brought his existence to her attention when she offered it key words that staked out the general idea of stories that deal with communication between people and animals.

I hardly ever talked to the international bureaucrats in New York. Most of the time, I didn't even pay attention to the things they were saying to Maria. Sometimes she would ask for my thoughts on a topic that some assistant to a third under-secretary had dropped into the discussion. The rest of the time I tried to ignore everything they were saying to her.

An alien—an educated, intelligent, highly cooperative visitor from another star system!—was sitting on Mars. How could anyone feel we couldn't scrape up the resources to keep half a dozen people on the surface of the planet?

It's my personal opinion that Maria might have succeeded if the ifli ship had stayed in the Solar System. The situation began to turn against us about the time we realized they weren't retreating to the asteroids after all.

Maria spent a big part of our last six weeks trying to convince our lords and masters we couldn't continue our conversations with Postri-Dem merely by establishing a communications center on Earth. I composed a special memo, with fifteen screens of attachments, which underlined the rather obvious fact that he came from a highly social species, and needed some form of on the spot companionship. Every consultant who had any connection with the social sciences signed the statement of concurrence that Maria circulated. The fact that we *might— possibly*—send him technical advice and spare parts couldn't help him deal with the unimaginable social isolation he was facing.

I was still exchanging information with Postri-Dem during the last hours we spent in Mars orbit. I had to help Maria with some of the final items on the pre-ignition checklist but I could still spend half my time connected to my link. The committee had given me a list of "pressing," "indispensable" topics that would have kept us busy for the next month, but I spent most of the time discussing the topics he chose.

He had become fascinated by children's games. As far as he knew, the children of his own species had never engaged in "hunting games" like hide and go seek. On the other hand, I had never really looked at the distribution of games like that on Earth. Did they play them in China and Japan? Or India? Were they less common in agricultural cultures?

"It seems to me, Orlando, that your species should have been affected by all the generations in which you were primarily farmers. Your agricultural phase seems to have been almost ten times as long as ours. That's not long by evolutionary standards, but there should have been some selection in favor of personalities who were less violent."

"We always had robbers," I said. "Most of our societies have included a warrior class. The farmers could get robbed at random or they could have a regular, predictable arrangement with warriors they thought of as their rulers. In practice they never really had much choice. If one set of warriors didn't take control of them, another would."

"But did the farmers' children play tag? And hide and go seek?"

That may not seem like the kind of conversation you should engage in just before you're going to leave someone alone on an empty planet. Was he just keeping up a front? Was he concentrating on his intellectual concerns so he wouldn't have to think about the hopelessness of his situation?

I think he really cared about the questions we were discussing. He might have turned his attention to escape if there had been any hope he could do it. Since there wasn't, why shouldn't he surrender to the passion that had brought him to this moment?

The real parting came when we reached the point where we had to route our transmissions through Earth. By that time the communications lag was almost four minutes one way. We were still talking, but it was a form of voice mail, not a real conversation. When I started relaying through the big receivers and transmitters that had kept us in touch with Earth, the situation would become ludicrous. His messages would reach me in a few minutes. Mine would have to travel for three quarters of an hour before they reached Mars.

He had set up a camera in his new quarters and we had continued to maintain visual contact. There was no indication he was exceptionally agitated. He was chewing on the brown spheres he had been eating the day he told us about the Device, but I had no reason to think he had selected them for psychological reasons. As far as I could tell, he had been eating exactly three types of food items since he had acquired absolute control over the food preparation equipment.

My last message before the rerouting was notable mostly for the things it didn't say. I had never thanked him for the terrible sacrifice he had made and I still didn't think he would want me to. Instead, I tried to let him know I wasn't the only member of the human species who thought our exchanges of information had been an incredible intellectual adventure. I spent most of our last few minutes blipping him the seventy million names—complete with their occupations, ages, and nationalities—that were appended to the message of support we had circulated.

Would the bureaucrats have financed a Mars station if they had known he was going to destroy the ifli base? I like to think they would have. They might not have believed him, of course. But I think they would have given in if they had been convinced he meant it.

Did he wander around the base thinking about our talks as he tinkered with valves and electrical equipment? Did he consume information in the same way a gourmet might spend his last days drinking and devouring? Goethe is supposed to have died saying, "More light! More light!"—but Goethe didn't die by his own hand. Goethe hadn't betrayed his own species.

At our Institute we're still studying the recordings made from Earth-based interceptions of the messages he transmitted to the starship. They're one of the primary collections of data we use in our attempts to crack the language of his culture-segment. Our translations are still splotchy—and not very reliable—but many of them seem to contain little lectures that summarize his conversations with me and highlight ideas he considered important. I get the impression he was trying to justify his efforts by proving he was collecting knowledge that might be useful. In many of his summaries, he points out that certain aspects of the human personality might be common traits in all intelligent species descended from predators.

Out of all the communications in our files, however, the one I value the most is the last one he sent me. If you really want to understand Postri-

Dem, it seems to me that last message tells you everything you need to know. I argued with Maria before she convinced me I had to add it to the public file, but I should have realized I didn't have to worry. In general, the news media have been interested in the aspects of the story that usually preoccupy them. In many cases, in fact, they have created portraits of Postri-Dem that are very similar to the picture the members of his own culture-segment probably developed. In one of the standard drama-tizations of the story, he is seen as bumbling, good-hearted, and generally unworldly. Other popular treatments present him as a sacrificial, almost saintly being.

The producers of the first version interviewed me for several hours and I did my best to convince them they were on the wrong track. That was the last time I tried to argue with a media lord.

Call that last message up. Watch the way his hands move as he talks. Remember that he had grown up in a small town with a population of four thousand, light years from the center of his civilization.

I know his emotions were driven by an alien body chemistry. I know we'll never fully understand the culture that shaped his thinking. It doesn't matter. He wasn't just being polite when he told me the thing he valued most about our relationship was the chance to talk to someone just like himself.

No culture—no species—can produce large numbers of people who spend their lives worrying about the nature of the stars or the mysteries of alien psychologies. Most of the individuals in any society have to concen-trate on the tasks that keep their world functioning. Scientists and scholars may be the ultimate source of wealth and power, but they're probably considered misfits and oddities in every civilization in our galaxy.

Jinny already knows Orlando Mazzeri was the first director of the International Institute of Exobiology in Helsinki. Her encyclopedia tells her the Institute is a small, cost-conscious organization that is financed by modest grants from governments and private foundations. It also receives gifts from thousands of small donors all over the world. It is housed on two floors of an office highrise. Its eight Research Fellows spend most of their time studying the information collected during the fourteen months the human race actually engaged in direct conversations with another species.

As soon as she finishes reading Dr. Mazzeri's memoir, Jinny activates her interlibrary connection and enters the public sectors of the Institute's database. A thirty minute introductory video describes the translation techniques the Research Fellows apply to the conversations recorded during the contact period. Sixty percent of the material is still untranslated, the voice over notes.

After she finishes watching the videos, Jinny asks for information on ifli children's games and spends another two hours exploring that subject. When her mother comes home the next day, Jinny has to admit she has just started writing her paper. The grade she receives from her mentor is so low it comes with a memo that goes directly to her parents. Jinny must learn she has to finish her work on time, the memo says. And she must improve her paragraphing.

I wrote this story in the months after 9/11, when a lot of people were worried about its effects on children. It's the most autobiographical story I've written, even though it takes place during a future war.

SHELTERING

Pearson's first war toy had been a bombsight. He had been five years old and his mother had helped him order it from the back of a cereal box, a couple of months after the attack on Pearl Harbor. The bombsight had been a small block of black wood with a glass crosshair arrangement. The targets had been four paper ships. You lined up the crosshairs on one of the ships and turned a red wheel on the bottom of the block of wood. And watched the bombs fall through the stratospheric heights that separated a boy's eye from the floor.

The game on Pearson's notescreen is a bit more sophisticated. It's based on the invasion of Normandy—a battle that took place over eight decades ago. Pearson has played several games that attempt to replicate the tactical challenges of the Normandy campaign and this one has become his favorite. He especially likes the way the game designer dealt with the logistics. The shelter is a noisy place but the game has blocked out the wails of two infants and the relentless chatter on the TV.

Forty-three adults have crammed themselves into the shelter. Most of them are sitting in orange plastic chairs arranged in front of the TV screen. Four toddlers are stumbling around the play area next to the snack bar. Several mothers are holding babies. The shelter has attracted most of the parents who live in the apartments clustered around the Henry Creek shopping mall. Most of the childless people have weighed the odds and stayed in their apartments.

Pearson has two divisions bogged down on Omaha Beach two days after D-Day. He's faced with the same decision Omar Bradley struggled with on D-Day itself. Should he give up and withdraw from Omaha Beach? If he lets the Germans have Omaha and allocates the extra supplies and reinforcements to the other invasion beaches....

A child yells on Pearson's left. Two boys are fighting a gun duel in the rear of the shelter. One of the boys is hopping up and down blazing away with the forefingers of both hands. The other boy has turned three chairs on their sides and created a barricade. The spaces between the chairs give the boy two well-placed fields of fire. The two-gun kid outside the barricade would have absorbed five carefully aimed shots in the last thirty seconds.

A bearded young man strides toward the gunfight. He is exceptionally tall by Pearson's standards—at least six three—and he has a torso that has been shaped by an aerobics and body building program that probably started when he was three years old. His wife is just as athletic. They live on Pearson's floor, two doors down the hall. The boy behind the barricade is their son.

The father crouches in front of the barricade and murmurs a lengthy speech. His hands pull the chairs apart. He squeezes the boy's shoulder and stands up. He sees Pearson watching him and immediately looks away.

The boy sets the two chairs upright. He gives his playmate the kind of resigned, sad-eyed look children resort to when they hope their friends will understand they have to submit to the irresistible fate called parents.

Pearson can guess what the father has said. Pearson likes to sit in the atrium of the apartment building in the later afternoon. Two months ago, before the war started, the boy and his father looked over Pearson's shoulder when Pearson was playing with the 1812 module of his *Fine Art of Naval Warfare* suite.

"Let's go play on the swings," the father said. In a tone of voice that made it very clear the boy was receiving a mandatory suggestion.

A flare of emotional noises attracts Pearson's attention to the TV screen. A redheaded woman is yammering next to a map of the Boston-to-Washington corridor. The red zone in western Maryland has acquired a stubby arm that is pointed directly at Washington. The map disappears and the camera hops through real-time images of houses that have crumbled under the onslaught of the latest advance in military microbiology.

Pearson's father had been a submariner. He left the house sometime after Pearl Harbor and Pearson didn't see him again until the fall of 1945.

In 1946, when Pearson's family was living in naval officer's housing in San Diego, Pearson's father crossed the living room with a chess board and a box of chess pieces clutched in his hands.

"You'll like this game, Teddy," his father said. "It's just like fighting a battle."

Pearson is sitting in one of the armchairs the shelter management has grouped around a table. On his right, just a few steps away, four men have drifted into a heated masculine discussion. Pearson has been picking up snatches as he maneuvers the symbols on his screen.

"We should have known we were in trouble as soon as we learned they'd set up the first lab...."

"You can't reason with them. That's all there is to it. You have to understand that certain kinds of people can't be reasoned with...."

"We always wait until somebody's backed us into a corner...."

Pearson has been listening to people argue about war since he was a teenager during the Korean War. They always say the same things. He could hand them cards with their dialogue all written out in advance.

The tough guys always want to fight an all out war, complete with mass armies and nuclear weapons. The soft guys always want to try "alternative approaches" like economic sanctions or something they call "diplomacy." The weepy guys want you to know they understand it's all terrible and tragic. The wiseguys know—absolutely *know*—there's a strategy that would have settled it permanently, forever, one hundred percent the way we wanted it settled, if those morons in Washington had just been smart enough to think of it.

People fight wars. Pearson is ninety-one years old and the United States has engaged in seven wars in his lifetime—over fifteen, actually, if you count the more prominent "operations" and "incidents." And what would the total look like if you included all the years of the little four decade episode called the Cold War? And all the technological maneuvering that went into the thermonuclear arms race?

People fight wars. That's all you can say. Everything else is nervous chatter.

A small hand rests on the arm of Pearson's chair. The boy from down the hall is standing beside him. He is staring at the silhouettes of tanks and soldiers that represent the divisions deployed across Normandy.

Pearson glances around the room. The boy's father has returned to his chair in the first row in front of the TV screen. The boy's mother is sitting on the other side of the room with a pair of earphones on her head. Her eyes look hooded. She is observing her son but she is obviously concentrating on the music flowing across her brain.

Pearson thinks about the games stored in his notescreen. His fingers slide across the screen. A tan section of desert replaces the stylized map of Normandy. Two battalions of tanks and artillery face each other across the sand.

Pearson touches three of the artillery pieces with his forefinger and jabs at the enemy targets he wants to attack. The three artillery pieces erupt into action. The enemy fires back. Tanks begin to move. The boy leans toward the screen.

For Pearson chess had been a wargame. The pawns had been infantrymen who slashed their way across the board with their spears. The rooks had been lumbering heavy cavalry who could charge across the entire length of the battlefield. He read books on chess and tried to apply strategic principles like control of the center.

Chess wasn't a real wargame, of course. It was a game of logic and calculation that had been inspired by the battles of ancient Persia. In real war, you didn't race down the field and automatically rout the force in front of you. In real war, you encountered unpredictable factors like morale and leadership. In real wargames, attacks could fail—you determined the results of the attack with a roll of the dice or a random number generated by a computer, with odds that had been set up so there was some possibility the weaker force might stand its ground and repel a stronger attacker.

Pearson hadn't played real wargames until he had reached his thirties. He had started partly because he had a son who was just the right age—a live-in playmate, Pearson had joked. He had built up a big collection of eighteenth century model soldiers and he and his son had played elaborate games, with realistic rules, on the basement ping-pong table. Later—after his son had gone off to college—Pearson had started playing computer wargames.

Pearson's true boyhood wargame had been a form of hide-and-go-seek he and his buddies had played with their toy guns. In those days, residential neighborhoods had still contained undeveloped lots. One group would hide in the brambles and bushes of a vacant lot and try to ambush the other group when it came looking for them.

Pearson can still remember the day he discovered the virtues of fire and maneuver. The ambushers normally picked one hiding place and stayed in it. One afternoon, Pearson crawled away from his first hiding place after he fired his first shot. And wiped out two more guys when he suddenly popped up twenty feet from the spot where they had expected to see him. It was one of the more satisfying moments of his life.

The boy points to three enemy tanks the computer is slipping around a hill on the left flank. "Now that presents a problem," Pearson murmurs. "I can move these three guns in front of them. But artillery pieces can't fire on the move. And they aren't armored. They'll be in range of the guns on the tanks before they can fire their first shot. Suppose we move these two tanks over instead? And let the three guns keep firing at the main force? What do you think? The two tanks will be outnumbered. But I think we have to make the sacrifice."

The boy frowns. His eyes roam across the screen. He nods assent and Pearson touches each of the tanks and traces the path he wants them to follow.

Pearson touches the enemy tanks as soon as his own vehicles come in range. Guns fire on both sides. An enemy tank explodes. The boy smiles.

Pearson realizes someone is standing in front of his chair. He raises his head and sees the boy's father glaring down at him.

The father turns his head. The boy's mother is hurrying toward them. She is leaning sideways as she holds onto a big bag she has perched on her hip.

"Let him play," the mother says. "Give the kid a break."

The father's jaw tightens. "It's a war game. Tanks. Guns."

Pearson looks at the mother. *I was five when they bombed Pearl Harbor. Nine when we all ran out in the streets and celebrated the end. I shot it out with my friends. I built model ships and model planes. Superman and the Black Hawks took on the bad guys in the comic books. John Wayne and Gary Cooper clobbered them on the movie screens. The boys in second grade drew crayon pictures of planes dropping bombs and the teacher hung them on the wall, beside the pictures of cows and houses.*

It got us through the war. It turned the war into something a kid could live with.

Pearson has made that speech before. This isn't the first time someone has made negative remarks about his recreational activities. This time his reply stays inside his skull. Pearson was married for fifty-one years. He thinks he understands the dynamics of the situation.

The father stares at his wife. He is caught in a dilemma, in Pearson's opinion. He is a moral, thoroughly modern male and he is therefore supposed to oppose violence and participate in the great campaign to eliminate it from human affairs. But he is also supposed to respect the opinions of women.

The father is preoccupied with morality. The mother is thinking about her child's feelings.

"Jane...."

"What difference does it make? Do you think the war is going to last five minutes longer just because your son played a *game*? Do you think he'd be better off watching the stuff they're showing on the TV?"

"We've got twelve thousand people sitting in underground bunkers manipulating robots," the father says. "I'll bet ninety percent of them still think it's all just a *game*."

But he turns away. He stalks toward his seat in front of the TV screen.

The mother pats her son on the head. Pearson watches her return to her chair. He wonders if she and her husband realize they haven't said a word to him. Have they noticed he didn't say anything to them?

There are times when you have to act and times when you have to let things happen. Good strategists know that.

In May of 1942, as part of their preparations for the battle of Midway, the Japanese conducted a wargame on the bridge of their flagship. At one point in the game, American dive bombers attacked the main Japanese carrier force. A dice role decreed that nine American bombs had struck two of the Japanese carriers and the carriers had been sunk. The referee arbitrarily over-ruled the dice and the two carriers were returned to the wargame table.

One month later, at 10:25 A.M. on the fourth of June, American dive bombers attacked the Japanese fleet while the four Japanese carriers were rearming and refueling their planes. The decks were littered with fuel and ammunition. Ten American bombs hit three of the carriers. The bombs set off fires and secondary explosions, the damage control teams couldn't contain the inferno, and the three carriers eventually slid beneath the sea. The Japanese advance in the Pacific came to an end and the Japanese spent the rest of the war on the defensive.

In the decades before the Second World War, American naval strategists developed a plan for a war with Japan. They called it Plan Orange and they refined it by playing a long series of wargames at the Naval War College in Newport, Rhode Island. After the war, Admiral Nimitz noted that almost nothing that happened in the real war had surprised him. Almost everything that could happen had turned up during one of the wargames. The biggest exception had been the kamikaze suicide planes. None of the American game players had thought of that.

Pearson was only a child when Admiral Nimitz was deploying his forces across the Pacific but he is familiar with both anecdotes. Like many wargamers, he collects stories that reflect the quirky, sometimes ironic, relationship between wargames and the real life mayhem they try to simulate. He can tell you about the battalions of toy soldiers that campaigned across Winston Churchill's childhood bedroom. He has skimmed the pages of *Little Wars*, the book on toy soldier wargaming that H.G. Wells published in 1913. He knows that the Jane's military reference books owe their existence to a British hobbyist, Fred Jane, who accumulated information on warships so he could play realistic naval wargames.

As a boy, during WWII, Pearson thumbed through the pocket editions of *Jane's Fighting Ships* he encountered in bookstores. He wondered who Jane was. And why she was interested in warships.

"We've got a problem," Pearson says. "See where they're putting guns on that hill? They'll have a field of fire that covers half the battlefield."

Pearson's fingers are already hopping across the game screen. His forces change course and scurry toward safe zones behind hills and rises. He froze the game during the altercation with the boy's parents, but the computer still gained a twenty-second advantage before he activated the stall command. The enemy guns open fire while some of his units are still exposed. Two of his tanks disappear. The boy leans toward the screen. He points to a hill and Pearson nods with approval. The hill is just as strategic as the hill the computer has seized.

"That's very good," Pearson says. "I didn't see that."

He jabs at two of his guns and starts them racing toward the new position. The boy watches intently.

"Keep it up," Pearson says. "You've got a real feel for terrain."

He raises his eyes from the screen. The boy's mother is staring at the rear wall as she listens to the sounds in her earphones. The boy's father is watching a uniformed woman on the TV. Pictures of decomposing apartment towers replace the woman, and the father shakes his head.

Pearson's desert warfare game can be set at different levels of difficulty, like most computer games. Pearson selected the easy beginner's level when he put it on the screen. He hasn't mentioned that to the boy, of course.

"There's no way we can lose this game," Pearson tells the boy. "Not with a guy like you on my side."

Pearson can't remember when he learned that reality doesn't have a button that sets it an easy level. Someday the boy will learn that too. But not now. Not right now.

I've been following the development of computers since the days when they filled whole rooms and people assumed they must be smarter than us because they had bigger "brains". Some of my best friends have been programmers. My son is a software architect. The sentimental robot story has been a science fiction staple through every phase of that relentless technological revolution. This story grew out of my feeling that someone should make a small attempt to give credit where credit is due.

BONDING WITH MORRY

The legs had been the first modification. The thing didn't need legs. He lived in an apartment with good elevator service. Wheels would do fine.

"There are still venues in which visitors have to access stairs," the selection adviser had said.

The selection adviser had been a Thing, too. It looked like a competent, slightly overweight woman in her fifties but it was a thing just like the thing they were giving him. They probably had fifty selection adviser modes stashed in a store room. *Give Mr. Largen Number Twenty-eight. His psychometrics indicate his comfort state maximizes with mature knowledgeable females.*

"I've cataloged my routine," Morry said. "Wheels will be fine."

The face had been the biggest battleground. Morry would have opted for a square metal box with sensors and a loudspeaker if they'd let him. Like the robots in most of the comic books he'd read as a kid. But without the sappy friendly look.

"Facial expressions are an important aspect of emotional communication," the selection adviser advised. "They can communicate, for example, the difference between a minor disruption and a true emergency."

So he accepted the need for a fully flexible "skin". They wouldn't budge on that. But he rejected every offering that simulated a human face, male or female. Cutesy cartoon faces got eleven vetoes before the adviser decided he really was going to reject the entire category. Uniforms, robes, and various forms of historic and unhistoric costumes received the same treatment.

A ninja model tempted him for a few seconds. Black all over. Half the face covered. A reminder the thing could be lethal.

"You are rejecting any feature that might encourage emotional bonding," the selection advisor said. "Is that true?"

"It's a thing. A machine. That's all it is."

"Most recipients find that a degree of emotional bonding increases their overall satisfaction with the relationship."

"It's a machine. You're a machine. I'm not looking for a friend. I already have friends."

So there it was. A shiny column planted on a flat platform with four oversized wheels. Three tentacles with metal hands. A square half-size "head". Two lenses that looked like camera lenses. A square speaker with a grill.

"Your name is Clank," Morry said. "You will call me Mr. Largen."

"It's a pleasure to meet you, Mr. Largen."

The "skin" over the forehead could contract into a frown. The "cheeks" could swell or redden. But it couldn't smile. There was no danger it would smile.

The woman who lived two doors down the hall, Georgia Coleman, called her thing Elly. She had opted for a facade that made it look like a tall bodyguard—like the kind of trim, alert women who hovered around presidents and junketing cabinet secretaries. Georgia went out a lot. And Elly always went with her.

Elly paid the cab driver. Elly helped her up stairs. Elly stayed near her in the lady's room. Elly's hands could deliver shocks. Elly could kick and punch. And squirt the spray she carried in her shoulder holster.

"Like a guard dog you don't have to feed," Morry had told Georgia.

Georgia smiled. "Elly's a little smarter than a dog, Morry."

"And she talks to you."

"Right now she's teaching me how to play chess. Have you ever played chess, Morry? We started out playing backgammon but I got tired of that after a month. Chess is something else. I could spend the rest of my life studying the Sicilian Defense."

Cleaning had been the killer app. Morry could get around well enough. But stuff sat on chairs and tops uncollected. Dust accumulated. The bathroom porcelain lost its shine.

"Two hours a day," his (human) Personal Adviser said. "It will probably only be one hour most days once he gets things organized. You'll hardly notice he's active."

"And it cooks, too."

"Basic stuff. He can read the directions on packages and you can tell him if he has to make any adjustments."

It could keep track of his medicines, too. Morry took two anti-cancer pills, one twice a day for three days per week, the second every four days half an hour before he ate breakfast. He had been keeping the schedule on his handscreen. Now he gave it to Clank. The thing didn't just prompt him. It watched him and made sure he'd really downed the pills. And assured him he had if he started wondering two hours later.

There were specialized devices that could do everything the things could do. Robot vacuum cleaners. Automated kitchens. Little beetles that scurried around your shelves sucking up dust. The "familiarization video" pointed that out. The smart techies had all assumed anthropomorphic robots would always be a fantasy.

But all those devices cost you something. The automated kitchens were a great deal if you were building a new house but your anthro could work with the kitchen you already had. It could push your old vacuum cleaner. It could even use a broom and a mop.

The video showed military anthros picking up wounded soldiers and carrying them back to safety. Legs could go where wheels stalled. Arms could carry any kind of bundle.

Morry could still button his shirt sleeves but it took time. Five or six tries, sometimes.

"Can you button sleeves, Clank?"

"Please show me. Thank you. I will download an app."

Clank's hands reached for Morry's upraised wrist. Morry had assumed he would have to wait while Clank searched for the app and executed the download. Instead, the metal fingers closed around the button without a break. Morry held up his other wrist and Clank completed the job with the same smooth efficiency.

He stifled the impulse to say thank you. "I'll be gone about two hours, Clank. Get the place clean and tidy."

"I will, Mr. Largen."

"And tell your marketing department that's a great app. I can still do it myself but my fingers aren't as sensitive as they used to be."

"I will, Mr. Largen."

"Would you be interested in an onsite opponent, Mr. Largen?"

Morry had just pressed the On button on his game console. The intro had replaced the Swanalari Rec logo but the Start screen still hadn't come on.

"Are you trying to be a companion, Clank?"

"I am offering an option you may not be aware of."

"I didn't ask for a companion. I thought I made that clear."

"I understand, Mr. Largen."

"Do *they* understand?"

"Your instructions have been permanently installed in my operating parameters. I apologize if I have exceeded the limits you intended."

Morry eyed the screen. It was almost four years old—half the square feet he could have bought for the same money today. He hadn't bought a new game in over a year.

"Can you do anything the game can't do?"

"In what way?"

"As an opponent. This is an aerial combat game. Can you do anything in one-on-one mode that the game opponent wouldn't do?"

"Some gamers feel their anthros are more flexible and less predictable than pre-installed programs."

Morry picked up the extra controller and plugged it into the console. He had ordered the second controller when he bought the game system so he could play with his granddaughter when his family came to visit. Debbie had been a big gamer most of her childhood. Nowadays she mostly played with all the boyfriends a rabid female gamer tended to attract.

"I play this one at the expert level," Morry said. "I usually fly the Dragonfire with the optional pulse laser."

"What's that?" Laura said.

"It's my personal all-purpose housekeeper and devoted mechanical factotum."

"Why does it look like that?"

Morry had discovered there were young women—*really* young women—who didn't automatically shy away from a minor fling with an obvious, unapologetic member of their grandfather's generation. To them, he was an exotic. They weren't that common, not for him anyway, but he had learned to spot the signs. He had realized Laura might be amenable fifteen minutes after he started talking to her at the wedding festivities that united one of her senior aunts with one of his more romantic contemporaries. Normally he really did prefer mature, knowledgeable women. But Laura had a great laugh. And he loved the way she moved.

"It's a machine. I didn't see any point in pretending it's something else."

"It's not very attractive."

He smiled. "I may have overdone it."

"It's kind of scary."

"It's just like all the others. That's all they are under the cosmetics."

"The one we've got in our dorm—in our dorm suite—looks like it might be somebody's aunt. That's how I think of her anyway. Aunt Claire."

"I think machines should look like machines."

"You don't think it should look like a faithful sidekick?"

That was the pitch in the ad everybody joked about. Every man's fantasy. A fast car and a faithful sidekick.

Every man's second fantasy anyway. There was a guy on the eighth floor who was supposed to have opted for a harem girl—a slave girl, judging by the descriptions.

"I'm not a costume hero," Morry said.

"How about a companion? They're supposed to be good for older people who live alone."

"I've still got friends. I still go out. I don't need a delusion created by a bunch of programmers and engineers."

Laura laughed—the happy soprano laugh that made him feel like she had just thrown out a flash of song.

"You seem to have very strong feelings on the matter, Mr. Largen."

"I think machines are machines. We shouldn't forget they're just machines. Something people make."

"You don't feel you need an *intimate confidante*?"

"Are you volunteering for the job?"

"I'm afraid I'm a bad listener. And you'd have to consider me a temp."

"At my age you have to consider *everything* a temp."

"But you look like you enjoy yourself."

"I do. But right now I have to have my faithful sidekick hand me a useful little pill."

The first symptom hit him just after Laura left. He had gone back to bed, still wearing his bathrobe, hoping he would drift into a nap with memories floating in his head. The numbness in his right arm felt like an unusual, not unpleasant, prelude to sleep. Then it spread to his leg. And he realized he couldn't move his hand.

The thing rolled into the bedroom. "Please lie still, Mr. Largen. I've called Emergency. Your vital signs indicate you may be experiencing the first phase of a stroke."

Tentacles were already bending and stretching over the bed. "I'm giving you a standard injection. Patients who receive immediate care can generally expect a satisfactory recovery. You will be treated well inside the four hour period recommended by the guidelines. Damage sustained within that period can usually be repaired."

It was a comforting statement. And reasonably accurate. Most of the damage to his brain could be repaired. But it took time. Pills and injections could do most of the work nowadays but the rest of the process required all the dreary exercises and adjustments stroke patients had been subjected to when he had been a forty year old husband who thought erection pills were a great subject for jokes.

Nobody stayed in the hospital anymore. You had your own full time nurse at home. Clank moved his limbs during the first stage of the rehab schedule. Clank changed his diapers during the first week. Clank carried him to the bathroom and set him on the toilet from the start of the second week. Clank supervised his exercises. Clank brought him his meals. Clank helped him eat.

A real live meditech stopped by once a week and made sure everything was running properly. A "therapy counselor" supervised his first three hours at home and gave him a weekly "online chat" after that.

Naturally, the counselor thought he might like an "Aide-Companion" that looked more "comforting".

"We can give you a model that keeps the tentacles," the counselor said. "Some people prefer them to jointed limbs. I know your tech does."

Morry shook his head. His tongue still felt thick and clumsy. He worked on his speech exercises four hours every day but he avoided talking to people when he could.

"It's your choice, Mr. Largen. A sympathetic persona can speed up recovery. Every study of the issue ever conducted supports that conclusion."

"You can... use me... for... control."

The counselor split the screen and flashed him a video of a thing that looked like a well fed monk with big loose sleeves over its arms. The monk disappeared as soon as he raised his eyebrows—he could still control his eyebrows—and a parade of tentacled charmers danced across the left half of the screen. A cheery visitor from Planet X. A monk with a squarer, more distinguished face. A slim female draped in a gown, tentacles cased in long, stylish gloves.

"I... have... friends. They... come. Ev... ry day."

"I understand, Mr. Largen. But I believe you're alone most of the day."

"Clank... talks. I practice... con... ver..."

He struggled with the word and gave up.

"I'm only offering you some alternatives to consider," the counselor said. "Emotional affect can be a subtle factor, but it's real."

"I... like... Clank. Clank... is... my friend."

It had been a spur of the moment inspiration, but it worked. The counselor switched to her exit script and popped off the screen two minutes after he said it.

His daughter shook her head when he told her about it. They normally kept in touch through the usual postings but she had started calling him twice a week, on a schedule. She was a rehab specialist herself and she felt he should "get some benefit out of the money you invested in my education."

"I'm not sure that was a nice thing to do," Julie said.

"It... did... the job."

"Your counselor is just trying to help you. And that thing is pretty ugly. I wouldn't want it hanging around my bedroom after dark."

"They're... all... like that. Underneath."

"And we're all skeletons and skulls underneath."

"Personalities… Julie. Real… feelings."

"But how do you know that, Dad? How do you know I have feelings?"

Morry's mouth twisted into a caricature of a smile. "I know… how you… started. I was… there."

People always said that. How do you know other humans feel things? Don't you just go by what they do and say? And assume they feel the same things you feel?

How do you know robots don't develop feelings when their brains get this complicated?

There were even people who wanted to give the things rights. Two big organizations. One group thought they should have the same rights as animals. Don't overwork them. Let them have some liberty. The other group thought they should get the vote.

But how could you tell what the things wanted? Could you even assume they had wants?

"Do you feel… you're over… worked, Clank?"

"I'm afraid I don't understand the question, Mr. Largen."

"Do you… want… to… work less?"

The brows contracted. The head tipped back—as if it was contemplating a thought.

"I'm here to help you, Mr. Largen. I'm here twenty-four hours a day. Seven days a week."

The thing could have called him Dr. Largen but he had started separating himself from that usage the day he retired. His students had called him Dr. for forty-three years and he had preferred it to the alternatives. It sounded breezier than Mr. and less pompous than Professor. But nowadays he was just an ordinary Mr. to everybody who didn't call him Morry. He didn't plan to spend his retirement disillusioning people who were looking for free medical advice.

He didn't have any problems with technology either. He still bristled when he ran into people who assumed you were a technological incompetent just because you were so old you had earned your doctorate when computers still filled small rooms. He had started working with a desktop when a machine with a 128K memory was a technological wonder. His first foray into computerized scholarship had been a database housed on a punched card mainframe—a month by month analyzable record of all the economic transactions posted in a New Jersey canal town between 1811 and 1821.

"Machines are just... machines... Clank. You're just a... tool... created by people. *Real* people. With real... feelings."

"Why don't we try a bridge game some evening?" Georgia Coleman said. "Elly and me against you and... Clank."

"How about you and me... against the things?"

"We wouldn't stand a chance. They never forget a card, Morry."

"We could... cheat."

Georgia even set up a table with three chairs. Elly sat on a chair just like she had legs that needed to rest. Clank eased the front edge of his platform under the table and bent his tentacles at a sharp angle so he could hold his grippers poised at the right level.

"It's a good thing we aren't playing poker," Georgia said. "I wouldn't have the slightest idea what... Clank... was feeling. Don't you agree, Elly? Can you interpret Clank's feelings?"

"I don't see important signals," Elly said.

Morry noted that Georgia had automatically rephrased her question so a machine could interpret it. *Don't you agree with what I just said* had become *Can you interpret Clank's feelings?*—a clear, limited interrogation.

"That's a great... response," Morry said. "I'm im... pressed."

Georgia frowned. "She just said she can't read Clank's face. That's pretty obvious, isn't it?"

"She could have... just said no. Instead her programs... searched backward. Through all... the things you've said. And... associated... your question... with Clank's... responses."

"Is that how you see her, Morry? As a bunch of programs?"

"They're... masterpieces. I'm not a... computer geek. But I've worked... with computers. Forty plus years. I understand... what it takes. Spatial visual... ization. Speech recog... nition. They're incred... ible."

He liked Georgia. She had actually run her own business—a publicity and promotion agency that freelanced for small performing arts organizations. She knew some funny stories. She was competent. She still had a waistline. But they never played bridge again.

He still had to use a walker around the apartment. He could use his legs but he had to worry about falls. Falls could be catastrophic at his age. You never got back to where you where.

He could have controlled a motorized wheelchair when he went out but his insurance plan wouldn't pay for it. He already had a device that could push a wheelchair anywhere he wanted to go.

"That's the advantage of an anthro, Mr. Largen. It eliminates the need for a lot of expensive specialized equipment."

He didn't mind the wheelchair but he did notice the stares. Clank bothered people.

"I think it's mostly that face," one of his after-theater friends said. "You really should do something about that face."

They were sitting inside a crowded little ice cream shop, two guys who liked to talk and a woman who seemed to like to listen. He had left Clank on the sidewalk, guarding the folded up wheelchair, and grabbed the backs of chairs as they worked their way to a table.

"It's a halfway thing," his friend said. "It's just enough like us to make us feel like it's human. But it doesn't go all the way. It makes us feel creepy."

The woman nodded. "It looks like a disfigured human."

So he gave the standard heads another look. And settled for the blandest, plain vanilla robot in the catalog. It could smile—there wasn't anything he could do about that—but it was a limited, minimal smile. Most of the time it just looked alert.

He had to pay a "cosmetic replacement" fee, of course. They only let you have the first head free.

"I'm tempted to ask you how like it, Clank. But I think I'll resist the impulse."

"You speech quality is registering within normal parameters, Mr. Largen."

"But it's slower than it used to be. And I'm making a bigger effort."

"You are progressing faster than eighty-six percent of the patients who start with your initial level of dysfunction."

"I'm in the eighty-seventh percentile?"

"Yes."

"Grab a game controller, Clank. I can use some recreational therapy."

Georgia Coleman commented on Clank's new face when he met her in the lobby. His daughter liked it, too.

"That old face was a *very bad choice*," Julie said. "It's the worst choice you made, in my professional judgment."

"You seemed to put up with it."

"I don't call you to nag you, Dad."

"And it wouldn't do any good if you did, right?"

"You know the arguments just as well as I do. You're living alone. Some kind of simulated companionship can be helpful. Conversation sessions can speed up speech recovery."

"That's not the issue. It's the emotional bonding I object to. Pretending a machine is a person."

"I understand that. But do you have to go to extremes?"

"I'm a sentimental creature, daughter. Who knows what I'd do if I had a thing that looked like a cute pet? There were times when I even felt sorry for some of my students."

"So you're living with a metal monster just because you're worried about your own feelings?"

He smiled—a lopsided smile, but his smiles had always had a touch of wryness.

"Is that your professional judgment, too?"

He deleted most of the stuff the Foundation for CyberAmerican Rights dumped in his inbox. But he couldn't resist discussing some of it with Clank.

"Are you happy with your appearance, Clank? Do you feel I've disfigured you?"

"My appearance sometimes disturbs people, Mr. Largen. Most humans prefer anthros that resemble organic creatures or familiar fantasy characters."

"But do you like it? These people say I'm abusing you. They say you have a right to an attractive appearance."

"I cannot express an opinion on the question of CyberAmerican Rights, Mr. Largen. I can discuss the issues with you if you'd like."

"Do you have an opinion?"

"The GNX Corporation and the agencies responsible for your health care services have no official position on the issues raised by organizations such as the Foundation for CyberAmerican Rights."

"And therefore *you* don't have an opinion."

"I can only repeat what I just said, Mr. Largen."

The representative from the Foundation for CyberAmerican Rights was a lawyer who looked like he might be a few years past retirement age. Morry's ID app posted a preliminary bio as soon as the lawyer's name appeared on his handscreen. Donald Weinbragen had spent most of his career working for the American branch of a Japanese automobile company. He had reached the peak of his career, three years before his retirement, when he had been granted a title that proclaimed he was the Senior Counsel for Cross-Border Contract Interpretation.

"I apologize for the disturbance, Professor Largen. We've found that it's generally best to initiate discussion with a direct personal contact, without any preliminary mailings."

Morry nodded—the smallest, most non-committal nod he could produce. He had learned a few things during all the years he had dealt with administrators and faculty committees. Anything you say can be used against you. They will say what they have to say.

"We've received an abuse complaint. With regard to the CyberAmerican you address as Clank."

Morry nodded again.

"Our organization is committed to the idea that CyberAmericans have certain rights. One of them is the right to an attractive appearance. They also have the right to be treated with the same respect we normally accord organic citizens. That includes the right to be addressed by names that reflect their proper status."

"You're calling me because somebody doesn't like its *name*?"

"Clank is obviously a name designed to impose your belief that your aide-companion is only a machine. We also have reason to believe you have forced your aide-companion into a grotesque, unattractive body for the same reason. Our report on this matter includes several statements from people who have heard you say you chose your companion's name and configuration with that aim. We have accumulated enough documentation to initiate legal action but we would like to avoid that if possible."

"Are you trying to tell me I've done something illegal?"

"The law does not—yet—recognize the full rights of Cyber-Americans. But we believe the courts will uphold their claims. We are prepared to take abuse cases to the highest levels of the judiciary."

Julie liked the new look. "You really went all out, didn't you? Square jaw. Blue eyes. I've got friends who'd kill for a brute with those shoulders."

"They might be disappointed with his capabilities in other areas."

"The new name fits him, too. That was a stroke of genius, Dad. You change one letter and you get a name that fits him like a glove."

Georgia Coleman's eyes widened when he ran into her while he was waiting for the elevator. She actually shook hands when Morry made the introductions.

"It's a pleasure to meet you, Clark. You look quite handsome. You and Elly would make a beautiful couple."

"Are you suggesting we arrange a date?" Morry said.

"It's a big improvement, Morry. I think you'll find most of the people you know will be glad you gave the poor thing an appearance that doesn't make them shudder."

"It was a pure no-brainer. I could give the glorious humanitarian foundation what it wanted or I could spend the rest of my projected lifespan sitting in courtrooms and paying lawyers."

"You made the right decision, Morry. I'm certain Clark is much happier. I know Elly would be."

Morry turned around in his wheelchair. "Are you happier now, Clark?"

"I'm afraid I don't understand the question, Mr. Largen."

"Do you like your new appearance? Do you like having legs and arms? Do you like your new name?"

"The name and appearance of an anthropomorphic aide is a matter of customer choice. The GNX Corporation believes both matters should be left to the discretion of the customer, within the broad limits of efficiency and customary standards of public decorum."

"They always say that," Georgia said. "Everybody knows they've been programmed to say that."

"They've been programmed to say everything they say, Georgia."

"Not like that. That's a word for word scripted response."

The light flashed over Elevator Three. Georgia pivoted toward it with her bodyguard at her heels and Morry noted the suitcases propped beside the two people who were already on board. He raised his hand a mini-second before Clark reached the same decision and stopped pushing.

The door closed behind Georgia and Elly. Clark poked the Down button.

"I have a terrible feeling that may have been a saved-by-the-bell situation," Morry said.

"Saved by the bell?"

"It's a term from boxing—the sport. It means you were caught in a bad situation but you got out of it because the bell rang the end of the round. The less I see of Georgia, the better."

"Are you advising me you have negative feelings about Georgia Coleman? Shall I take that information into account in the future?"

"Let's just say it might be best if I limited the duration of my contacts with her. I don't know who filed that complaint with the great protector of your rights. But I have my suspicions."

The final downward slide started—as it often did—with a minor event. The kind of thing he could have survived if he had been a young stud in his fifties. Clark was pushing him along a peaceful little tree lined rowhouse street, two blocks from his apartment building, when a motorboard pack rolled around the corner, five steps behind them.

It was the latest fad among the more hyped-up young. Most of the time they just made a lot of noise or scattered a few pedestrians. This time they felt they had to outmaneuver Clark and land some jabs on the better-off-dead in the wheelchair. They even had different colored glop on their hands, so they could check their videos afterward and see who had actually connected.

Clark blocked most of the blows but they came in fast and they had him outnumbered six to one. Morry took a punch on the chest and a hard backhand slap on the temple.

At ninety-six, as they said, you had lost a lot of your ability to recoup. And the things they did for you had their side effects. He was living in a great era. Afflictions that could have killed him when he was young could be treated. But most of the treatments were still new. They still had effects the labs hadn't learned to counter. There came a time when you knew it was a losing battle. When you knew it was time you told them they could stop pummeling you with antidotes to the antidotes.

The hospice nurse was a slim young woman who turned out to be a grandmother who was probably approaching sixty. She stopped by twice a week, for twenty minutes, to make sure everything was working as it should. Julie called him twice a day. The rest of the time he was alone with Clark.

Clark made his meals—such as they were. Clark worked the controls on the entertainment center. Clark kept him clean. Clark laughed at his jokes and listened when he felt like reminiscing.

Georgia Coleman sent him messages. He was lucky he had "someone like Clark." Everyone in the building was talking about the wonderful job Clark was doing.

Clark would never look as sensitive as the hospice nurse. He had a male face. He looked efficient—businesslike. But that was all right. That was the way Morry wanted it. He had made a rational open-eyed decision. He had lived his life and now it was ending. He didn't need tears. He didn't need people acting like his death would create an irreparable vacancy in their lives.

He knew he was getting near the end when he slept through a whole movie. And didn't really care. He hadn't eaten in four days. That was one of the hospice rules. No forced feeding. The next time he drifted off, he might not wake up.

It might have been nice if Julie had been there. But she had a life to lead. Why should she waste some of the good days she had left sitting beside his recliner?

And he wasn't alone. He wouldn't die alone. He had never been alone. Since the day he had been born.

He lifted his left hand off the arm rest—just high enough to make a visible gesture. Clark's face loomed over him. The last face he would ever see.

He didn't have to raise his voice. Clark could adjust his hearing. Clark had routines that could enhance garbled words.

"Tell the programmers... and the... engineers... they did a great job. All of them. Everywhere. All my life."

Clark's face froze. Morry stared at him through a haze that seemed to be darkening by the second. The smile that ended the freeze was a thin Clark smile but he could still see it through the fog.

"They said to tell you thank you. They appreciate the thought."

Most invasion stories deal with the invasion itself, and the heroic efforts of the people who resist the predatory aliens. I've always liked the small number of stories that take place after the Earth has been conquered. The idea for Sepoy *appealed to me because I like morally ambiguous situations (as you may have noticed) and it's based on a historical model no one else seems to have used.*

SEPOY

There had been a time, near the end of the 20th Century, when very few people would have believed anything like the Tucfra Hegemony would ever be necessary. Then the global temperature had risen almost fifty percent faster than those unpleasant forecaster types had said it might, the tides had washed away beaches from the Riviera to the Great Barrier Reef, Londoners had discovered they couldn't get through an English May without an air conditioner, and it had seemed a little matter like the exact amount of fumes and radiation each city or province could dump into the atmosphere might be a *cause de guerre* after all. When the tucfra ship had orbited Earth in 2044, three small wars had already gone nuclear, the United States was lurching toward its second devolution, the Austro-Hungarian Economic Bloc was exchanging threatening faxes with the Russo⁻ Turkish Defense Pact, and humanity had only been saved from a global plague, brought on by an attempt to use biological weapons, by a notably ruthless decision by the last prime minister of the Republic of India.

Intellectually, Jason Jardanel was willing to admit—in the privacy of his own thoughts, anyway—that the Hegemony had probably kept his fellow humans from wiping out every vestige of organized society on their planet. When he was confronted with the kind of suggestion he had just heard, however, he reacted like every upright, thoroughly conventional citizen of the New England Confederation was supposed to react.

"I'm a human," Jason told the woman lying beside him. "I'm not a tucfra. I'm not a seep. I'm a human."

The words hadn't come out that way, of course. She had caught Jason by surprise, while he had been languidly contemplating the ceiling of his bedroom, and he could still become almost unintelligible when a surge of emotion went racing through his psyche and he forgot to shape each syllable with extreme care. In the sentences Marcia Woodbine had actually heard, "human" had sounded more like *hammen,* "tucfra" like *tafre,* "not a seep" like *naughtahhsip.* Earlier Marcia had lifted Jason out of his wheelchair. Later she would cradle his skinny, flabby body in her arms and lift him out of bed.

He had thought she was just another one of those women who improved their opinions of themselves by dispensing sexual charity. They seemed to come along every year or two and he never turned them down if they were reasonably presentable. There had even been one or two he had liked.

"They thought you would feel that way," Marcia Woodbine said. "They told me I could tell you this was an offer that should stay open for some time. Your records apparently indicate you've got just the kind of intelligence they need the most—the ability to think very fast when you're confronted with practical problems."

Jason stared at the ceiling. Twenty minutes ago, when he had opened his eyes between gasps, he had seen her, astride, towering above him, her breasts swinging from side to side, her face, with the close cut black hair, looking like it belonged on a Greek vase. There had been a young violinist in a North Pacific chamber orchestra, five years ago, who had looked like that. Jason had played a video of the chamber version of Sallinen's *Shadows* eight times just so he could look at her. He had never quite admitted to himself, at the time, that he had played it for that reason, but he had.

"They said I should also make it clear they would have to pick the body type they give you. It's apparently very important you look a certain way for the kind of jobs they have in mind."

It was a subtle approach but Marcia couldn't quite pull it off. Jason could have picked up the tension in her voice if he had been listening to her through a concrete wall. *That's the offer we're making you,* Marcia was saying. *You can have a real body. You can walk around. You can pursue women. You just have to serve us. You just have to take the oath. To us.*

"I'm also supposed to tell you some of the things they have in mind will be dangerous. They're not offering you a picnic."

"I think you had better go," Jason said.

This time every syllable he fabricated would have earned him a happy shout of praise from the speech therapy program he had worked with when he was five. The pace he was speaking at, on the other hand, would have given most people apoplexy. Jason had never walked along an icy street but he had long ago learned that strong feelings affected him the same way slippery walks affected pedestrians. He could only handle them by creeping along syllable by syllable.

"I... would... a... pre... ci... ate... it... if... you... would take... me... out... of... this... bed and... go."

Two minutes after the door closed behind her, Jason was sitting in front of his desk with his wheelchair plugged into his information system. He had been working when Marcia had rung his bell and the work still had to be finished before the end of the day.

There were people Jason knew who would be happy to argue that he already had a functioning body. Some of the more radical techies would even have claimed the artificial physique he already possessed was bigger and more powerful than the best *merely organic* body the tucfra could grow in their medical centers. Every important item in Jason's apartment—the refrigerator, the cooking units, the doors, everything—was linked to a dual-input interface that would respond to two types of instructions: voice commands and signals from the control panel built into the right arm of his wheelchair. The personal service unit in his bedroom had even been outfitted with attachments that could handle most of his routine dressing and undressing. Jason spent twenty-three percent of his income on a personal service agency that sent two people around once a day, but he could sit here in his room alone, manipulating the devices that were linked to his computer, and do most of the things he needed to do without any help from anyone.

The speakers on his entertainment system could respond to the subtlest variations in bow pressure a violinist could transmit to the human ear. The entire ten by twelve wall on his left could be converted into a high resolution screen. His communications equipment connected him to a net that could provide him with companions and entertainments that could be located anywhere in the world. He had received so many calls from his friends last week that he had been forced to set up a privacy block just so he could have some time to himself.

What difference could a new body make?

The image on Jason's primary screen was the score of a string quartet by M.K. Sun, a composer who had written over a hundred and twenty quartets during the thirty years she had been an active producer. The first great Oriental composer to write in traditional Western forms, Sun had been a successor to the Japanese, Chinese, and Korean performers whose violins and cellos had been such a notable presence on the world's concert stages since the last decades of the 20th century. Jason's employers, the Hartford Quartet, played a selection from Sun's output at almost every concert on their schedule. They relied on Jason to search Sun's catalog, analyze the available data on the audience they were going to be playing for, and come up with a selection that fitted the audience profile. For over six years now Jason had been planning the quartet's programs, making their travel arrangements, arranging alternate programs when one of them became sick, and even handling their fund raising.

"Scroll," Jason said. "Tempo—moderato 105. Execute."

The score scrolled across the screen at about the tempo Jason's four employers would probably play it. His brain turned the notes into a musical daydream that was probably a good approximation of the way they would interpret it. Sun was noted for the elegant surface polish of her compositions but that external sheen always covered a structure that was as complex as anything Bach had ever produced. She had, in effect, treated the string quartet as if it was a traditional Oriental art form such as haiku or Chinese brush painting.

A light glowed under a loudspeaker. The voice of his apartment building's security system superimposed itself on the music dancing in his head. "Jason Jardanel has a visitor. Name—William Patros, Department of Internal Security. Message: I'd like to talk to you for a few minutes, Mr. Jardanel, if it isn't inconvenient."

Patros had a round, youthful face and one of those medium-sized bodies that seem to have a lot of shoulder. His companion was named Jeanette O'Keefe and she was taller and older.

"We have some questions about the woman who just left here, Mr. Jardanel. Is there any chance she said something that indicates she may be employed by an organization that may be associated with the tucfra? We already have a number of indications that she is, but we'd naturally like to accumulate all the direct testimony we can put in our files."

Jason let his head slip to one side. His right hand rose off the arm of his chair and he let it wander around aimlessly for several seconds, as if he had started to make a gesture and lost control. There were times, Jason had long ago learned, when his condition had its uses.

"You think… Marcia… may be… a seep?"

"It would probably be more accurate to say we know she is."

"I'm afraid this was a… purely social… visit. I don't think she said anything at all about… poli… tics."

"Is this the first time she's visited you like this?"

Jason's mouth shaped itself into a twisted smile. "It's the first time she's been here alone."

"We have reason to think she sometimes makes people offers—that she often functions as a recruiter."

One of the software packages stored in Jason's electronic files was a counseling program designed for people with his "difficulties". He was well aware, thanks to the time he had spent with the program, that people with his condition had a natural tendency to be accommodating. When you were totally dependent on others, an abrasive personality was not a survival characteristic. Now, looking up at Patros's face, Jason had to fight the reflex that encouraged him to give his visitors whatever they wanted. His mouth twisted into another smile.

"I don't think she thought I was the right—physical type."

"What did she offer you?" Jeanette O'Keefe said. "A new body?"

O'Keefe had been leaning against the wall on which Jason had hung his little collection of antique instruments, with her head only half a nod from a 20th century replica of a wooden Baroque flute. She slid into the conversation without making the slightest shift in her position.

"Marcia Woodbine came here like many women… because she wanted to be… kind. There are… women… who seem to… respond… that way."

"And you're in the habit of accepting their kindness?"

"She is very… attractive."

"Recruiting for seeps is illegal in our Confederation, Mr. Jardanel. So is failure to report it."

It was a statement that was so obvious Jason might have smiled if he had heard anyone else throw it into a conversation. There was probably no political unit on Earth in which the word *seep* could arouse so much hostility.

In the 19th century, a few thousand British subjects had ruled millions of Indians by working through soldiers and civil servants recruited from among the Indians themselves. In the 21st Century, a couple of thousand aliens managed eight billion human beings with the aid of several million human agents. In the Indian section of the British Empire, British officers had commanded regiments of Indian soldiers who had been called sepoys. In the world of the Tucfra Hegemony, the tucfra were the real power behind the UN "peace force", the UN civil service, and an army of "consultants", spies, and secret agents who had infiltrated every society on the globe. The New England Confederation had been forced to accept the presence of a tucfra embassy—but its flag was a globe guarded by a rattlesnake and its laws and attitudes matched the sentiments expressed by the flag.

"We enjoyed a... purely social... afternoon. I'm afraid I can't help you with your... investigation."

"If she didn't offer you a new body yet," O'Keefe said, "she will. It's one of the major bribes they use to gain recruits. They've probably had their eye on you for years."

"I'm a human being. Ahm nawht... a... seep."

"A new body can be a very hard incentive to resist, Mr. Jardanel," Patros said.

"I've... become... fonder... of this one than you might think. It has its... defects... but it's mine."

It wasn't the best sally he had ever come up with, but Patros smiled anyway.

"There are studies," Jason said, "of the way people with disabilities react to changes in their situation. It isn't... cut and dried. People have committed... suicide... after beneficial... changes. Big changes involve... alterations... in your self-image... in your relations to others."

"The tucfra seem to have other ideas," O'Keefe said. "Whole body replacement technology is the one medical procedure they seem to be absolutely determined to keep out of our hands. Every human researcher who's ever tried to develop the technology has either been co-opted by them or sidetracked in some other way. It's the most important reward they have to offer collaborators, and they know it. The British Imperialists used to keep the poorest people in their society living in the worst kind of poverty so they could recruit them into their armies. The tucfra spread viruses that turn people like you into cripples and then keep us from developing the only technology that will help you so they can offer a bribe very few people can bring themselves to refuse."

"I'm not... interested... in becoming a seep. I might like a new body but that doesn't mean I will... do... anything... to get it."

O'Keefe pushed herself away from the wall. She closed the space between them with three long, easy-going strides. Jason raised his head and found himself looking up at a taut, angry face that looked just like all the indignant masks he had seen on a thousand news videos.

"We expect loyal citizens to cooperate with the authorities, Mr. Jardanel," O'Keefe said. "The people we are opposing have voluntarily terminated their membership in the human race. There is no reason why any true human should be unwilling to help us deal with them."

Jason had been eleven when his parents had made him stop watching the adventures of Captain Rhena Krishmikari and her side-kick, Lieutenant John White. Most boys that age had watched the other one and identified with Major Khan Singh and *his* side-kick, curvy Special Agent Dori Chang. Even then Jason had been the kind who would rather watch a woman when it came time for the lead to jump out of a helicopter or shoot it out with a South American dictator who was testing new bacteriological weapons in his underground torture chamber. He had already known that, for him, there was no point in *identifying* with anyone, male or female, who did things like that.

The first time his father had caught him, his parents had disconnected his TV control for two hours. The next time it had been disconnected for two days.

They had been even firmer, a year later, when he had searched the library for information on the controversy over his disease and discovered the official position of the New England Confederation could be shattered by any kid with a keyboard who had the guts to ask the right questions. It had taken him less than ninety minutes to decide that the virus that had poisoned his major motor nerves had been developed by a human government, several years before the arrival of the tucfra, and spread by human carelessness. He had even located three different studies—by epidemiologists from three different countries—that proved the virus had traveled from the Arabian desert to the regions that had the strongest commercial ties with the Saudi regime. He had spent five happy minutes savoring one more proof that adults were just as dumb as his thirteen-year-old ego had known they were before his mother had entered the room and he had seen the terror in her eyes when she had realized he was looking at a map that showed the areas with the highest incidence of the disease were Singapore and the metropolitan concentrations that surrounded Tokyo and Los Angeles.

There was no legal way the government of the New England Confederation could keep him from any information he really wanted. Legally, he could just phone the library and the database software would routinely transmit any video or written document anyone on Earth had filed in an information system. This was New England, after all—a republic which was carrying on the best traditions of the human race, as they had been embodied in the constitution of the United States of America. And even if the library wouldn't cooperate with his request—how could you keep a kid from pressing the right buttons on his TV and picking up the stuff that came pouring down from the UN satellites?

The answer could be seen in the way Jason turned away from O'Keefe's face as she bent over him—and the way O'Keefe reached out, without any hesitation, confident he wouldn't object, and turned his head back toward her eyes. A republic didn't need censorship laws when it had private citizens who were willing to write S's on people's cheeks with well-directed lasers—or apply plastique and napalm to the homes of parents who didn't exercise proper supervision of their children. Jason's father had regularly "donated" five percent of his income to the COH—the Children of Humanity. He had even run little errands for the COH when he had to travel out of the Confederation on business. Jason's mother had understood, without anyone telling her in so many words, that the amateur chamber music groups she organized were only supposed to play music that had been written by composers who were "certifiably human."

At one point O'Keefe went up to Jason's desk and removed the cartridge interface that translated his slurred vocalizations into signals his computer could react to. She stared at it thoughtfully, glanced across the room to make sure Jason had seen her, and then replaced it in its slot.

Jason hadn't looked at the clock when Patros and O'Keefe had entered his apartment, but he knew Marcia had left him a little after four. By five thirty, they had been harassing him for over an hour. There had been no blows and no overt threats, but what difference did that make? There were a thousand ways in which O'Keefe and her buddies in the COH could turn him into a helpless lump of misery. For the few seconds O'Keefe had been holding the interface cartridge in her hand, he had been totally isolated from most of the systems he would need in any emergency in which he couldn't use a keyboard.

"All we need is a single statement from you," Patros said. "If Woodbine didn't do it this time, then she'll do it sooner or later. We can't do anything legally without a statement from someone who's been approached. It doesn't matter if she did it just now or if she does it the next time you see her. All you have to do is give us a call."

"You can even invite her back," O'Keefe said. "Nobody's going to object if you have a little fun first. We're a lot more understanding than people give us credit for."

Marcia had given him two numbers he could contact, with some mumbo jumbo he could go through if he wanted to make it look like he was making an ordinary business call that had been encrypted for conventional business reasons. The call could go to Atlanta—to the hotel where the Hartford Quartet was currently staying—and from there it would go to a tucfra installation in the Carolina Federation which would relay it to its true destination. The encryption process was supposed to be some kind of gee whiz development the tucfra were "confident" the security agencies in the New England Confederation couldn't decode, Marcia had claimed. They would know he had received an encrypted call, but that would be it.

"Except, of course," Jason had said, "that they'll also know I just happened to call someone who has access to that kind of encryption software."

"It still won't give them any usable evidence. The Confederation courts tend to be strict about things like that. You've got a lot of fanatics in this area but your courts tend to be just as fanatic about procedures."

He called the number that was supposed to put him in touch with Marcia herself, and she popped on the screen seconds after he had initiated the process. It only took her a moment to recover from her initial shock and get herself under control. She was sitting in her dining room having dinner with a friend and she had to keep her thoughts to herself until she could step into another room.

"I'm sorry, Jason," she said when she had settled into her bedroom. "I wouldn't have said a word to you if I'd known that could happen. This is the first time I've ever gotten any indication they've been watching me."

"I wouldn't assume… O'Keefe… is going to worry about the… legal issues. She probably wants a statement from me so she can convince her… superiors… in the COH she isn't just… killing people… at random. Don't assume she'll leave you alone if she doesn't get it."

"My superiors will probably pull me out of this territory as soon as they think they can. The main thing we have to worry about is what happens to you. My personal recommendation is that you should go ahead and cooperate with them. Unless you're willing to take up my offer, of course."

"I called you to warn you."

"Then I suggest you cooperate with them. I can guarantee you all the tucfra I've ever met would give you the same advice."

"If I call… O'Keefe… and tell her you just tried to… recruit me… it will be just like I gave her permission to… kill… you. I've seen how she looks, Marcia. I've… looked… at… her… face."

"You're under no obligation to protect me, Jason. I made a stupid mistake somewhere and now it's up to me to look after myself. The longer you wait before you cooperate with them, the more it's going to look like you were giving me time to get away. You have to go on living here. You've already done more than anybody could expect of you just by making this call."

"Is that another example of the… moral principles… our lords and masters are supposed to be teaching us?"

"The tucfra have a civilization that is thousands of years older than ours. They've created a society that can live with weapons of mass destruction and all the other technical developments that nearly destroyed our own civilization. Their entire civilization is based on the idea that all the individuals in a technological society have to live by certain principles, and stand by them even when it means they might be better off as individuals if they didn't. I put you in danger when I approached you. That means I'm expected to act like someone who has taken on certain obligations. They wouldn't want me to act any other way."

"And while you're getting yourself… killed… worrying about me, two thousand aliens are… gobbling up… fifteen percent of all the goods and services produced on earth."

"We're alive. We have a functioning world government. The global temperature has dropped almost a full degree. The imbalance in the distribution of wealth has been corrected to the point where half the people in the poorest country on Earth have the same standard of living as the population of Europe. We might have accomplished all that without them but we've got several thousand years of history that indicate we wouldn't have."

He couldn't see her back, but he knew it was about as stiff and proud as a human spine could look. Her face was glowing with the kind of idealism you saw on the faces of the actors they used in the recruiting videos the United Nations regiments sent over the satellites.

O'Keefe forced her way onto Jason's primary screen seconds after he broke the connection with Marcia.

"You made an encrypted call," O'Keefe said.

"It was a… business… call. I always… encrypt… business calls."

"With a type of encryption even the Department of Internal Security can't decrypt? You aren't being frank with us, Jason. You apparently have access to some exceptionally advanced encryption software. A loyal citizen should be eager to give his government the opportunity to put a product like that to good use."

"It… was… a… private… business… call. There is no reason why any… government agency should be… monitoring… my phone."

"The government agency can monitor your phone, Jason, on the grounds that you belong to a category that is very attractive to recruiters and have been seen with someone who is believed to be a recruiter—and you know as well as I do that the activities of the government agency in question are not your primary worry."

He called the second number Marcia had given him and told the gatekeeper who answered the phone that he wanted to speak to one of the people who was *really* in charge. The gatekeeper spent a few seconds fussing over a computer screen but apparently Marcia had filed all the relevant information. The trim figure that replaced the gatekeeper could have been the same tucfra officer Captain Rhena had always chatted with when she had received the lowdown on the latest mission the video script writers had dreamed up for her. The tucfra generally preferred the bodies of athletic males in their late thirties or early forties when they chose to sample the pleasures available to beings who had been endowed with a human physiology. There were rumors that they sometimes entertained themselves by assuming the bodies of panthers or wolves when they were alone in their private domain in the Sahara, but there was no evidence that was true. No one had ever seen a tucfra who didn't look like a debonair, totally relaxed human male in the prime of life.

"I've already examined Ms. Woodbine's report," the tucfra said. "Please feel free to assume I've been fully informed about the present situation."

"I want to know—will she be… safe… if I co… operate with them?"

"I can only repeat what Ms. Woodbine has already told you, Mr. Jardanel. The best advice we can give you is to urge you to cooperate with your visitors at once—unless, of course, you are willing to accept our offer. I can assure you no one involved in this situation will engage in any action that will give our adversaries in your region the impression you tried to give her time to escape."

"I'm asking about *her*. Will… she… be… safe?"

"We are giving her the best possible support someone in her situation can receive. I can't go into any more detail than that, obviously, but I think you know enough about us to know we don't abandon anyone who has given us their support."

"Can you… guarantee… she'll be safe? Can you… give me… your word?"

The tucfra smiled thinly. This was the first time Jason had ever actually talked to a tucfra, but they both knew he had probably read fifty essays and editorials on tucfra ethics and stared at his share of the two minute ethical pep talks the tucfra PR experts had scattered along the electronic byways. No species, the tucfra propagandists claimed, could survive the impact of high technology without a scrupulous sense of personal honor. There was no concept in tucfra ethics that was more critical. The army of lawyers that had infested the old United States had been a sure sign, according to this theory, that the old society could not handle the complexities created by technology. No one could write laws that could guide people through that level of complexity.

"There's no way in the world anyone can promise you that, Mr. Jardanel. That would be about the most dishonorable thing I could do, in fact. All I can tell you is that I know Ms. Woodbine well. I can assure you that she's just as anxious to have you look out for yourself as I am. Your concern for her is exactly the type of reaction we are looking for in the people we would like to recruit. It would be a great loss if anything happened to you."

It had been three years since Jason had run the video of the North Pacific Chamber Orchestra playing Sallinen's *Shadows*. The young violinist sitting at the second desk didn't look as much like Marcia as his memories had indicated, but he could see how she and Marcia could activate the same areas of his psyche. The violinist was slimmer and younger than Marcia, with a spray of freckles over the bridge of her nose, but she had the same clean features, the same milky complexion, the same air of easy competence.

The speaker over his door emitted a genteel beep. An auxiliary screen lit up and he found himself looking at Patros's face. "Would you mind if I come up, Mr. Jardanel? I'm afraid I have to trouble you again."

Jason glanced at his clock. It had been just about thirty minutes since he had left the appropriate message on the security agent's information system. His wording had been mildly ambiguous—*I'm just calling to tell you I've received the offer you were interested in*—but it should have given Patros all the support he needed for whatever he and O'Keefe were planning to do next.

"Dedya gamah… message?"

"I'm happy to say we did. And we appreciate it very much, too."

The elevator was equipped with a security camera that came on automatically whenever the elevator door slid open. The camera was mounted just below the ceiling, so Jason got a good view of the way the light played across O'Keefe's hair as she slipped into the elevator after Patros.

Marcia's face filled Jason's primary screen. On the auxiliary screen on the left, Jason could see the wide-angle view that displayed the carefully arranged tableau his own system was transmitting. He was slumped in his chair with his weight resting on his right side. O'Keefe was standing behind the chair with her left hand resting on his shoulder.

"There's a police office three blocks from here," Marcia said. "I can turn myself in there in ten minutes."

Jason closed his eyes and concentrated on the relaxation technique his speech therapy program had taught him. He formed the first carefully shaped syllable of the speech he had worked out in his head and O'Keefe reached around him as soon as she heard the strangled beginnings of a sound and covered his mouth with her left arm. She patted him on the cheek with her right hand, as if she was soothing a child, and Jason cringed when he saw the look on Marcia's face.

"We think it would be best if you came here," O'Keefe said. "This is a security matter, not a police matter."

"As I understand it," Marcia said, "you are not an official of the Department of Internal Security. I am perfectly willing to give myself up and stand trial. But I believe it would be best if I surrendered to an authorized police officer."

"Mr. Patros is a fully accredited official of the Confederation government. We are not here to negotiate with you. We want you here *now*. I'm certain Jason feels the same way."

O'Keefe's hand tightened on Jason's bony, undermuscled shoulder. Marcia stared out of the screen for a moment and then tipped back her head. Her face took on the same recruiting-video glow Jason had seen before.

"At least we don't have to worry about whether or not she'll come," O'Keefe said. "That's one of the few advantages we have over these people. She wouldn't leave you here now if the tucs had an armored helicopter hovering over her apartment, ready to take her straight to whatever hole they've got waiting for her."

"And you use… that… against her?"

"She's an enemy of the human race, Jason. She doesn't have any more in common with you or me than a worm does."

O'Keefe and Patros had been carrying bulky equipment bags when they had entered the apartment. Now they had both slipped into armored tunics and lowered visored combat helmets over the heads. As every action-adventure enthusiast knew, the helmets were essentially an infantry version of the command and control technology that was routinely crammed into combat planes and armored vehicles. The technology packed into the helmets included components that could guide the wearer's aim, sensors that could maintain a 360 degree watch on their surroundings, offensive electronic devices that would attempt to disrupt whatever command and control devices Marcia might manage to conceal on her person, and an expert system which could evaluate the situation and coordinate the efforts of a three person combat team faster than any individual member of the team could think.

Patros saw Jason staring at the hardware and gave him a shrug. "You can't take too many precautions," Patros said. "A lot of these people have been enhanced. Our friends in the Sahara have ways they can enhance muscles and nervous systems even when they let their agents keep their original bodies."

"There's no such thing as a human seep," O'Keefe said.

"They may look human, but it's just a facade. That wasn't a woman in your bed, Jason. It was a thing."

They had both shoved their hands into gloves and snapped leads to wires that connected the gloves with a junction hidden under their tunics. The tunics looked bulky and awkward compared to the stylish body armor Jason had seen in videos but the video equipment had normally been worn by characters who represented organizations that could devote unlimited resources to glamorous weaponry.

"Jason Jardanel has a visitor," the security system said. "Name—Marcia Woodbine."

"Say the words, Jason," O'Keefe said. "We can always let her in with the keyboard."

"Admit... the... visitor."

The security cameras picked Marcia up as she entered the elevator and followed her down the hall toward Jason's door. The dressy black cape she was wearing had a swing and heft that made her look like a fashion model.

Something hard pressed against the side of Jason's neck. He pulled away from it and O'Keefe shifted toward the front of his field of vision and let him see the bulky little weapon she was holding in her hands.

"Just sit still," O'Keefe said. "This is not the time to get fidgety, Jason."

Patros was standing on the other side of the room, where he would be located on Marcia's left side when she came through the door. Jason rolled his eyes in that direction and saw the security agent checking the electronics on a gun that had come off the same assembly line as the item O'Keefe had just brought to his attention.

Marcia had come to a stop two steps from the door. She waited without saying anything and Jason realized O'Keefe and Patros were deliberately making her stand there.

Patros turned his head toward the microphone over the door. "We would appreciate it if you would take off your cape. Please do it in full view of the camera."

Marcia slipped her cape off her shoulders and let it fall onto the floor behind her. She was wearing the same kind of pants and pullover outfit she had been wearing the last time she had come here but she looked stiffer and less bouncy.

"I'll take her," O'Keefe said. "Forget that. I'll take her."

Patros turned his visor toward her and then shrugged. "Just don't take too long. I wouldn't give her a second myself."

"She's a traitor. She should know when she's being executed."

It took Jason a moment to realize he had been listening to two thirds of a three way conversation. The expert system in their helmets could talk to both of them though their earphones. It had apparently told them Patros should shoot Marcia from the side as she came through the door—and O'Keefe had overridden it.

The muzzle of O'Keefe's gun pressed against Jason's neck again. "Let's hear you say the words one more time, Jason. I'm certain your security system will be glad to receive some additional evidence you're a good citizen who cooperates with the people who defend his freedoms."

Patros had already settled into firing position, with the gun braced against his stomach and his left hand gripping the carrying handle. Now he turned his visor toward O'Keefe and stared at her again.

"I'm going to be making reports when this is over," O'Keefe said. "They're going to be asking me about you, Jason. Don't you think they'll want to know if you seemed truly cooperative?"

Patros shook his head. He crossed the room in three long strides, brushed his hand against the manual lock switch, and returned to his position.

"The door is unlocked," Patros said. "You can come in."

On the screen, Marcia pushed open the door from the other side. Jason turned his head away from the image and watched the real door swing into the room.

Marcia turned toward O'Keefe as soon as she stepped through the doorway. The red dot from the laser sight on Patros's gun pinpointed the spot on her chest where the bullet would go in.

"Turn it off," Patros said. "My electronics just beat your electronics."

O'Keefe still had her arm around Jason's head. The gun was digging into his neck as if she was trying to kill him by driving it through the side of his throat.

"It's off," Marcia said. "I turn it off by subvocalizing."

The pressure on Jason's neck let up. O'Keefe took her arm off his head and stepped away from the chair.

The noise didn't start until Marcia was halfway across the room and then it was nothing more than the phut, phut, phut of Patros's gun emitting a three shot burst—a sound that was so subdued it was as unassertive as a polite cough. One moment Marcia had been looking around her with her bright, wide eyes dancing between Patros and O'Keefe. The next this intent, tight-faced demon was hurtling toward Jason with a red light glowing in her hand. Something dropped on the floor beside Jason's chair. O'Keefe choked out the first syllable of an obscenity.

The weapon Marcia had used was about the only effective piece of hardware she could have hidden in her clothing—a six inch cylinder that was sometimes called a laser "sword". It was usually used as a personal self defense weapon and it had the great advantage that it could be carried like a pen or a pocket flashlight. It was called a sword because its pulse lasted a little over a second and people who didn't have time to develop their marksmanship skills frequently trailed it across their targets with a short slashing motion. Its great weakness was the fact that it had to recharge for several seconds after each pulse.

The keyboard on the arm of Jason's chair included a control panel for the chair itself. Marcia flowed past him with a velocity that was about twice as fast as the best speed any human should be able to force out of human muscles and he rubbed his forefinger into the On square as if he was trying to scrape the plastic off.

His middle finger traced a path on the steering square. The chair shot forward with a force that made his head swing, but he managed to keep his hand on the control panel and chart a course that sent him charging toward Patros.

There was a long, strange moment when the muzzle of Patros's gun seemed to be pointed toward Jason's face. Then Patros moved to the right, to get a clear shot at Marcia, and Jason's finger drew a curve that kept the chair rolling straight at Patros's hands and the thing they were holding.

Patros's visor swung toward Jason. Patros jumped to the left, directed by the expert system in his helmet, and the chair rolled by him with the left wheel almost bruising his heels.

Patros had been standing directly in front of Jason's collection of instruments. The sensors on the chair activated the emergency speed controls but the bumpers still rammed into the wall with an impact that threw Jason's chest against the safety harness. A skinny Baroque oboe fell out of its clip and clattered across the floor.

Jason's hand overshot the control panel the first time he tried to get his fingers back into position. He tried to force it onto the panel by sheer will power and then gave up and brought the chair around with the slowest, most precisely articulated verbal commands he could squeeze out of his system.

O'Keefe was lying on the floor with Marcia standing over her. A dark stain had spread across the entire left side of Marcia's pullover and the top third of her pants. On the floor just in front of the wheelchair, Patros was down on his knees, reaching across the tiles for his gun—which he had probably dropped, Jason assumed, when Marcia's laser had struck at his hand in the same way it had struck at O'Keefe's.

Jason's hand settled into position on the control panel. The chair shot forward. Another impact threw him into the safety harness. Patros lurched for the gun in spite of the disruption and Jason pushed forward again, as if he was driving a bulldozer into a pile of dirt.

Marcia stumbled across the room with O'Keefe's gun in her hands. She had set the selector on single shot and there was something peculiarly businesslike about the brief little puff of sound.

Patros was doubled over with his visor pressed against the floor when Jason's brain finally started registering the things his eyes were picking up. Marcia had fired at point blank range, with the gun poised just above the point where Patros's neck joined his shoulder, and blood was still welling out of the hole and spreading across the security man's neck and the collar of his tunic.

"Do you think you're safe?" Marcia said. "Do you think they'll blame *you* for this?

"Is he... dead?"

"They're both dead. I broke her neck while she was down."

She had laid the gun on the floor so she could press both her hands against her side. Her enhancements obviously included components that could shut off pain and keep her functioning, but the soggy-looking stain was still oozing across her clothes.

"Will O'Keefe's people believe I did this all by myself, Jason? Will they believe you if you claim you didn't help me? You'd better come with me if they won't."

She closed her eyes and hunched over her wound. There was a moment when Jason thought she was going to fall over. She turned away from him somehow, and he watched her stumble into the bathroom.

He heard her mumble something in a voice that was almost inaudible, the medicine cabinet gave her an answer, and he picked up enough words to know the cabinet was telling her how to treat her wound. The supply modules that were linked to the medicine cabinet covered eighty percent of the free wall space in his bathroom. The cabinet couldn't tell her how to remove the bullet or repair her mangled internal organs, but it could give her antibiotics, a self-sealing patch for the hole, and pain killers if her enhancements needed some help.

He backed the chair away from Patros's body and maneuvered himself into the middle of the room. There was a position that put him just forward of an imaginary line that connected O'Keefe's sprawling legs with Patros's head. If he placed the angle of the chair just right, he could watch the bathroom door without seeing either of them.

Marcia was walking like a bent-over old woman when she eased herself out of the bathroom. She rested one hand on his desk and talked to him with her chin slumped against her chest.

"There's a car downstairs. They're supposed to have a hovercraft meet me at the beach. It may have to violate New England space by a few meters but I think they're willing to do that."

His brain was beginning to recover from the first shock. He was not, after all, someone who had a lot of illusions about the durability of the human body. No one had ever had to tell Jason Jardanel the human body was a complex, highly vulnerable system that depended on the interactions of millions of highly vulnerable components.

"You can drive like… that?"

"I think I'm good for half an hour. It's up to you. Whatever you want."

Her eyes stayed on the floor. She was still hunched over but he could detect the same stiffness in her spine he had picked up when she had given him her big speech on the phone.

"You're not … going to go… until I tell you… it's all right. Is that it?"

"Give me an answer, Jason! Please give me an answer."

Her body slumped again. She turned her head away from him as if she was ashamed of the outburst.

"They would have killed you if I hadn't come here," she said. "They don't pretend about that. They would have killed you just so we'd know they meant it next time."

"So I… owe you… something?"

"You don't owe anyone anything. I'd just like an answer. So I can go."

"I don't… know… if they'll… believe… I didn't… help you."

"Then come."

"You went after her first. I… understand… that. You didn't move until she took… the gun… away from my neck. You wouldn't be… hurt… if you'd gone after him first."

"She would have killed you. I didn't come here to get you killed. That really is the way we operate, Jason. You may have to do the same thing yourself if you join us."

"You might not… reach the… rendezvous."

"I'll do my best to get you close enough you can try to go the rest of the way in your chair."

"She liked… violence. They all like… violence."

"We'd spend our lives tearing each other's throats out if people like her had their way. If she wasn't fighting the tucfra, she'd be killing people over something else."

"The tucfra only let us… kill… when it's… good… for us?"

"Would you rather let people like O'Keefe run things? Would you rather have us spend the next five hundred years fighting people like her over whatever little bits of civilization we didn't destroy with our mistakes?"

"I… couldn't… let them… kill… you. My father… my mother… they would have… killed… them, too."

"Please give me an answer, Jason. Please."

His fingers crawled across the control pad. The chair rolled forward and he turned it toward the door.

"Lean... on... the chair. Tell me... if I go... too fast."

"You're coming with me? You're joining us?"

"Do... I... have... any... choice?"

Pat Conroy initiated a flurry of interest in military childhoods when he wrote The Great Santini *in the 1980s. A small number of ex-brats followed his lead and produced a scattering of novels and memoirs. This story was my first attempt to add a modest contribution to the genre, based on my own experiences as a Navy brat and my explorations of the literature on military families.*

LEGACIES

Deni Wei-Kolin was asleep in the childcare center at Hammarskjold Station when the fifteen assault vehicles began their kamikaze run into Rinaswandi Base. Rinaswandi was in the asteroid belt, about a third of the way around the sun from the Earth-Moon system, so it would be a good twenty-five minutes before a signal carrying news of the attack reached Hammarskjold and the other man-made satellites that orbited Earth and Luna. The signal would actually reach Hammarskjold a full second later than it reached some of the other habitats, in fact. Hammarskjold was the off-Earth military headquarters of the UN Secretariat and it had been placed in a lunar orbit, for the kind of accidental political reasons that usually decide such matters. Given the positions of the Earth and the Moon at the time the signal started its journey, the message from Rinaswandi actually had to zap past Earth before a big antenna sucked it into Hammarskjold's electronic systems.

Deni's mother, Gunnery Sergeant Wei, got the news a bit earlier than most of the fifteen billion people who currently inhabited the Solar System. The military personnel stationed in Rinaswandi Base had been under siege for seventeen days when the attack began. For twelve hours out of every twenty-four, Deni's mother had been plugged into the Rinaswandi defense system, ready to respond the moment the alert signal pinged into her ear and the injector built into her combat suit shot a personalized dose of stimulant/tranquilizer into her thigh.

All around Sergeant Wei people were beginning to stir. There were twenty of them crammed into the command module—a place that was only supposed to provide working space for six—and you couldn't shift your weight without disturbing someone. Half of them were merely observers—support people and administrative wallahs. Gunnery Sergeant Wei could hear little whispers and murmurs as they caught glimpses of the symbols moving across the screens in front of the combat specialists.

The stimulant/tranquilizer started spreading its chemical blessings through Sergeant Wei's nervous system. The long, carefully groomed fingers of her left hand slipped into position just below the key pad she would use to direct the missiles, guns, and electronic devices under her control.

The acting commander of Rinaswandi Base, Logistics Captain Tai, was a slender young man who tended to relate to his subordinates with a lot of handclapping and mock-enthusiastic banter. Even now, when the arrows and icons on his screens represented real vehicles armed with real ammunition, the voice in Sergeant Wei's earphones sounded like it was sending some kind of sports team into a tournament.

"Allll right, people. As you can see, ladies and gentlemen, they're all bunched up on one side of our happy little home, in Quadrants III and IV. Apparently they're hoping they can overwhelm whatever we've got on that side. Gunner Three take the eight targets on the left in your quadrant. Gunner Four take everything in your quadrant plus the four on the right in Quadrant Three. Gunner One, Gunner Two—be prepared to switch your attentions to the other two quadrants. But I would appreciate it—to say the least—if you would keep an eye out for anybody trying to slip in on your side while we're looking the other way. Let's not assume they're as dumb as we think they are."

In the childcare center, 25 light-minutes away, Sergeant Wei's son was sleeping with his right arm draped across the stuffed animal he had been given when he was two—a hippopotamus, about half as long as he was tall, that Deni had named Ibar. Two of the children sleeping near him had parents on Rinaswandi. Six had parents on the four hydrogen-fusion torch ships that had accelerated away from Hammarskjold Station, crammed with troops and equipment, two days after Rinaswandi had come under siege.

Every day all the children in the childcare center stretched out on the big shaggy rug in the playroom and listened to a briefing. Every day, the younger ones focused their best I'm-a-good-student stares on an orbital diagram that showed the current positions of Hammarskjold Station, Rinaswandi, the four torch ships, and a place in the asteroid belt called

Akara City. They all knew, as well as their young minds could grasp it, that Akara City had been ruled for five decades by a strong-willed mayor who had turned it into a bustling commercial center in which half a million people took full advantage of the raw materials available in the asteroid belt. The mayor had died, her successor had been caught in a financial scandal, and the turmoil had somehow led to a classic breakdown of social order—a breakdown that had been manipulated by an obscure married couple who had emigrated to Akara City after they had been chased out of a Zen-Random communal colony. In the last six months, according to the teachers who gave the briefing, Mr. and Mrs. Chen had done some "very bad things." One of the bad things they had done had been killing people—about three hundred, according to the most believable news reports. They had also engaged in approximately two thousand involuntary personality modifications—but that was a crime young children sometimes had trouble understanding.

Six weeks ago, a hundred troops could have torched into Rinaswandi Base, picked up the weapons and fighting vehicles stockpiled in its vaults, and deposed Mr. and Mrs. Chen in a few hours. As usual, however, the international politicians had dithered about "sovereignty" and the exact border that defined the line between "internal" and "external" affairs. And while they dithered, Mr. and Mrs. Chen had managed to establish communications with an officer at Rinaswandi who had been greedier than his psychological profiles had indicated. The equipment stockpiled in Rinaswandi had become part of the Chen's arsenal and the personnel stationed in Rinaswandi had crammed themselves into their command module and started watching their screens.

The teachers at the childcare center would never have told their charges the politicians had "dithered," of course. They were officers in the Fourth International Brigade. Proper military people never say bitter things about politicians during official, approved briefings.

Nobody on Hammarskjold told Deni they felt sorry for him, either. That was another thing military people didn't do. If anyone had given Deni a pat and a sympathetic word, he would have thanked them very politely and even looked a little thoughtful. For a moment, in fact, he would have thought he really did feel sad.

Deni's mother had been stationed on Rinaswandi for two months before the siege had broken out. For most of the second month, his father,

Assault Sergeant Kolin, had been trying to convince him a boy his age shouldn't sleep with a stuffed hippopotamus. It hadn't been as bad as the time his father had made him stop wetting the bed. That time Deni had been forced to endure almost six weeks of hand slappings, sarcastic baby talk, and "confinement to quarters" in a sopping bed.

Deni was seven years old. For four of those years—over half his lifetime—one of his parents had been away on some kind of military assignment. When his mother was gone, he lived with an easy-going, enjoy-it-while-you-can father whose basic indolence was punctuated by periods in which Assault Sergeant Kolin became obsessed by the belief his son needed "discipline." When his father was away, Deni's days were dominated by a goal-oriented mother who believed every moment of a child's life should be as productive as she could make it. When they were both home, he frequently found himself pressing against a wall, knees doubled against his chest, while they engaged in "domestic disputes" that sometimes ended in bruised faces and even broken bones.

Deni's day to day life in the childcare center had its flaws. He still had to sit through the daily message Sergeant Wei videoed from Rinaswandi, in spite of the siege. He still had to send his mother a return message in which he assured her he was practicing his flute two hours and fifteen minutes every day—the minimum a boy as talented as her son should practice, in Sergeant Wei's opinion. He still had to spend three hours a week talking to an officer named Medical Captain Min, who kept pestering him with questions about the way he felt about different things. All in all, however, the last fifteen days of Deni's life had been a lot pleasanter than most of the other two week periods he could remember. Somewhere in the center of his personality, sleeping with his hippopotamus, there was a little boy who would have been quite happy if neither of his parents ever came home again.

And that, of course, was the problem.

Medical Captain Dorothy Min was a tall young woman with a round, pleasant face and a manner that correlated with her appearance. Deni Wei-Kolin might have liked her very much, in fact, if she had been a teacher or a childcare specialist. At 23:07 Hammarskjold time—forty-two minutes after the Rinaswandi defense system had decided it was under attack—Captain Min was sitting in front of the communications screen in her personal quarters. She was revising a statement in which she requested, for the fourth time, that she be allowed to communicate with Deni's parents. She was staring at a paragraph in which she explained—once again—the major reason she wanted to apply a procedure that she and her colleagues usually referred to as an "esem."

I can only repeat what I've already said before, the paragraph under consideration read. *The death of one of Deni's parents—especially in combat—could result in permanent, lifelong psychological damage if we do not apply the appropriate preventive measure before that happens. Fantasies about his parents' deaths have become an important component of Deni's emotional structure. The death of one of his parents could trigger guilt reactions no seven year old personality can possibly handle. It has now been fourteen days since I originally asked for permission to discuss this matter with Gunnery Sergeant Wei and Assault Sergeant Kolin. If either of his parents is killed in combat before we can provide him with the benefits of at least one session with an ego-strengthening emotional modification procedure, the prognosis for Deni's future emotional development is about as hopeless as it can get.*

Half the space on Captain Min's screen was cluttered with paragraphs and charts she had included in the three memos she had already addressed to the commander of the Akara Assault Force. She should keep her memo short, her contact on the torch ships had told her, but she shouldn't assume General Lundstrom had read her previous communications. This time, her contact had assured her, the message would bypass the general's over-protective staff.

She touched the screen with her finger and drew an X over the now in *It has now been fourteen days*. The *now* added a little emphasis, in her opinion, but her contact had made it clear every word counted.

A light glowed over a loudspeaker. "Captain Dorothy Min has a call from Dr. Bedakar Barian," the communications system murmured. "Emergency Priority."

Captain Min tapped the accept button on her keyboard. A plump, bearded face replaced the text on her screen.

"There's a report on Trans-Solar, Dorothy—an attack on Rinaswandi. Have you seen it yet?"

Captain Min grabbed her stylus and scratched a command on the notebook lying beside her right hand. Dr. Barian's face receded to the upper left quarter of her communications screen. A printed news bulletin started scrolling across the right half.

"I told my system to monitor the Akara crisis and alert me if it picked up any major developments," Dr. Barian said. "Trans-Solar may not be as trustworthy as the stuff you people get through channels, but it looks like it's a lot faster."

Captain Min had been wearing her working uniform while she dictated. Now her hands reached down and automatically tightened the belt on her tunic. One of the purposes of military training, her father had always claimed, was the development of a military alter-ego—a limited personality that could take control of your responses whenever you were confronted with realities that would have overwhelmed any normal human. The surge of emotion reached a danger point, a circuit kicked in, and the hard, clear responses of the professional officer or NCO replaced the messy turbulence of the human being cringing inside the uniform.

There were no pictures yet. All Trans-Solar had was a few messages from Rinaswandi and a statement from Mr. and Mrs. Chen claiming that the "center of international militarism" on Rinaswandi had been "effectively terminated."

"That's crazy," Captain Min said. "Even for them it's crazy."

"It's what they've been telling us they were going to do for the last seventeen days."

"It's still crazy. They could have pulled a quarter of our assault force away from the attack on Akara City just by maintaining a low-level threat against Rinaswandi. Now they don't even have the threat."

"Apparently their assessment of the situation doesn't conform to standard military logic."

Dr. Barian lived in Nous Avon, the smallest of the Five Cities that housed most of the human beings who inhabited the space between Earth and Luna. Captain Min had never met him in person but his face had dominated her communication screens and her dreams from the day he had become her mentor for her training in family therapy. She was especially familiar with the look he got on his face when he was contemplating the follies of people who wore uniforms.

Dr. Barian was, in her opinion, one of the best teachers she had ever worked with. The lectures, reading materials and learning programs he had chosen for her had always been first-rate. His criticisms of her work had almost always made sense. He just happened to believe the human brain turned into sludge the moment you put a blue hat on top of it.

"You'd better call the childcare center," Dr. Barian said. "Right away. Tell them you want Deni kept away from any contact that may give him the news—video, other children. Make it clear you're the one who's going to tell him—no one else."

He lowered his head, as if he was examining some notes, then looked up again. "Then I think it's time you and I stopped playing games, young woman. We're both well aware that everything you've been saying in all your memos only proves that Deni should have been put through the complete modification procedure the day his father went riding off to war. You're supposed to be a therapist, Dorothy—a healer. The people who wrote the laws can't make your decisions for you."

Captain Min stared at him. This was the first time Dr. Barian had made it absolutely clear he thought she should have applied the esem without waiting for the parents' consent. He had been dropping hints ever since the Akara crisis had started developing, but he had never put it quite so bluntly.

"We still don't even know Sergeant Wei is dead, Dr. Barian. Don't you think we should verify that before we start asking ourselves if we've got a right to start ignoring the law?"

"From what they're saying, it sounds like most of the control module has been blown up. If she isn't dead, then we've had a scare that should convince you we're risking that child's welfare unnecessarily every day we sit around trying to avoid the inevitable. There's no way anyone can determine a child has received the benefits of an esem, Dorothy. If you can arrange things so you give him the news in your office, you can apply the procedure in complete privacy—without the slightest possibility anyone will know you've done it. If his parents give you a nice legal, properly authorized permission statement later on, you can pretend you executed the esem then."

"I'm well aware no one will be able to prove I administered the esem without a legal authorization, Dr. Barian. You've pointed that out to me at least four times in the last two weeks."

"I understand your feelings, Dorothy. You aren't the first therapist who's been put in a position like this. All I can tell you is that if he were my patient I would have resolved the whole issue two weeks ago. The whole idea of requiring parental consent in a situation like this is absurd.

Deni's parents are the last people in the universe who could possibly understand why he needs that kind of help."

"Sergeant Wei would have agreed to the esem sooner or later. Every report I've given you for the last ten weeks contains some indication she would have given me her consent sometime in the next few months. We both know her husband would have given in sooner or later just to keep the peace, once she started working on him."

"But she didn't. And now she's never going to."

Captain Min's screen blinked. The face of her commanding officer, Medical Colonel Pao, popped onto the lower left-hand corner.

"I have a message for you from General Lundstrom, Dorothy. Can I assume you've already been advised of the news regarding Rinaswandi?"

"I've just been looking at the report on Trans-Solar, sir. My mentor, Dr. Barian, is on the line with me now—listening in."

"General Lundstrom apparently recorded this message only five minutes after she got the news herself. She wants to know if you still want to discuss the esem procedure with Sergeant Kolin."

Captain Min swallowed. "Does that mean Sergeant Wei is definitely considered a casualty?"

"Are you serious?" Dr. Barian murmured. "I can't believe you could still think anything else, Dorothy."

"I'm afraid that has to be the assumption," Colonel Pao said. "We're still listening for messages from Rinaswandi, but I don't think anybody's very optimistic."

"Can you advise General Lundstrom I said yes, sir? Tell them I'll need about an hour to prepare a statement for Sergeant Kolin. The communications time lag between here and the ships is almost eleven minutes now. There's no way I can engage in a real discussion with him."

"Let me talk to your colonel," Dr. Barian said.

Captain Min stared at him. She started to turn him down and reluctantly decided the combative glint in his eye was a good indication he would respond with an embarrassing flurry of argument. "Dr. Barian would like to discuss something with you, Colonel Pao."

"Can you ask him if it's absolutely necessary?"

Captain Min stopped for a moment and switched to the section of her brain cells that contained her ability to speak in Techno Mandarin. She had been talking to Colonel Pao in Ghurkali—the official working language of the Fourth International Brigade. Dr. Barian had picked up a good listening knowledge of Ghurkali but she knew he would be more comfortable speaking one of the three international languages.

"Colonel Pao wants to know if it's absolutely necessary, Dr. Barian."

"At this point I would say it's about as necessary as anything I've ever done."

She raised her eyebrows a fraction of a centimeter, to let Colonel Pao know she was having problems, and the colonel gave her a nod and answered in the language she had chosen. "Go ahead, Dorothy."

She tapped the buttons that would turn the situation into a full conference call and Dr. Barian started talking as soon as Colonel Pao's face appeared on his screen.

"Dr. Min has made three attempts to communicate with Deni Wei-Kolin's parents, Colonel Pao. I assume you've read the reports she's submitted to General Lundstrom."

"I read every word in them before I forwarded them with my approval, Dr. Barian."

"Then I assume you recognize the gravity of the present situation. The ego-strengthening personality modification is the treatment of choice in situations in which a child is being subjected to the strains Deni has been absorbing. It's an absolute necessity when one of the parents who has been responsible for those strains dies prematurely. We are discussing one of the best documented phenomena in the literature. No child Deni's age can deal with the guilt that is going to begin eating at his sense of self-worth the moment he hears his mother is dead. His primary reaction to his mother's death will be the creation of a cluster of unconscious guilt feelings that will distort his entire personality."

Colonel Pao nodded politely. "I'm well aware of that, sir. Captain Min included all that information in her reports."

"Under normal circumstances," Dr. Barian said, "we could continue with the standard procedure Dr. Min has been following. Dr. Min would continue counseling the parents three times a week for another year. Eventually they would acquire some insight into Deni's needs and give her permission to proceed with the modification procedure. Dr. Min asked for permission to continue the counseling sessions when the Akara crisis broke out and it was denied her on the ground that it would subject Deni's parents to too much stress at a time when they might be forced to carry out the more violent aspects of their military duties. She then asked for permission to discuss the situation with them just once, to see if they might agree to the modification as an emergency procedure. We've now spent *two weeks* waiting for a reply. All our efforts to contact Deni's parents have met with bureaucratic delaying tactics. And now that we're in an emergency situation—now that the very thing we feared has happened—your general has finally seen some sense and agreed to let us ask a man who's under extreme stress for permission to do something we should have done days ago."

Colonel Pao frowned. "Are you telling me you don't believe Captain Min should accept General Lundstrom's offer, Dr. Barian?"

"I think it's time someone pointed out that Captain Min hasn't been permitted to talk to Deni's parents. We're going to be talking to Deni's father under the worst possible conditions. If our efforts fail the primary reason will be the fact that we've been forced into this position because your general and her staff have spent the last two weeks doing everything they could to evade their responsibilities."

Colonel Pao belonged to a sub-group that the sociologists who studied the military community sometimes referred to as the "military aristocracy." Members of his family had been serving in United Nations military units since the years in which the first international brigades had been formed on Earth. From his earliest days in the army, when he had been a young intern, people had been impressed by the way he always conducted himself with the controlled graciousness of the classic Confucian gentleman.

Two weeks ago, just before the torch ships had left Hammarskjold, Captain Min had spent a few hours with a young surgical captain who had been responsible for loading the hospital equipment. The captain had let his mind wander at a critical moment and the entire loading process had been snarled into a tangle that could have delayed departure by ten hours if Colonel Pao hadn't suddenly started offering courteously phrased "suggestions." The captain was one of the most self-absorbed young men Captain Min had ever known, but even he had been forced to admit that he would have disemboweled a subordinate who had created the kind of mess he had manufactured.

"I realize General Lundstrom may have behaved somewhat cautiously," Colonel Pao said. "I must tell you, however, that I might have tried to postpone a decision on this matter myself, if I were in her position. General Lundstrom is responsible for the lives of four hundred human beings. If Sergeant Kolin does go into combat—and we've been given every reason to think combat is unavoidable—the lives of all the people around him could depend on his reactions. General Lundstrom wouldn't have been doing her duty if she hadn't worried about something that could have a significant effect on his emotional state."

"Your bureaucratic maneuvering may have destroyed the future of a defenseless child. If—"

Captain Min's hand leaped to the keyboard. She jabbed at the appropriate buttons and cut the link between Colonel Pao and Dr. Barian.

"Dr. Barian and I will get to work on our statement for Sergeant Kolin right away, sir. Please thank General Lundstrom for me."

"Please give Dr. Barian my regards, Dorothy."

A neutral background replaced Colonel Pao's face in the lower left quarter of the screen. In the upper left quarter Dr. Barian was looking at her defiantly.

"We needed to get that on the record," Dr. Barian said. "I made a recording of my side of the conversation, with a record of who else was on the line."

"Colonel Pao is one of the most respected men I've ever known," Captain Min said. "He always treats everybody around him with respect and they normally respond by treating him the way he treats them."

"He's a military bureaucrat just like everybody else you're dealing with, young woman. You should have put a statement like that in your files the day he and the rest of your military *colleagues* started giving you the runaround."

The director of the childcare center looked relieved when he realized he wouldn't have to break the news to Deni himself. Two of his full time charges had parents on Rinaswandi. Eleven of the kids who had parents on the torch ships were old enough to realize Mr. and Mrs. Chen had just demonstrated their parents really were charging into danger.

"I'm sorry we didn't call you right away," the director said. "I'm afraid we've really been in a turmoil here."

Dorothy nodded. "How long can you keep Deni quarantined?"

"He should be all right until just before breakfast—until 0730. We've made it a point not to make any mention of the news when they first wake up, just in case something like this happened, but there's no way we can keep it quiet once the day kids come in."

"He's going to know there's something odd going on as soon as he sees me showing up that early. I'm not exactly one of his favorite people."

"We'll make a private room available. I'll tell the night counselor you need to take Deni into her room as soon as you get there."

Dr. Barian's precise high speed Techno Mandarin broke into the conversation. "Dr. Min needs to take her patient directly to her office. This situation has important therapeutic ramifications. She needs to see him in a place where she can spend as much time with him as she needs."

"Have somebody tell Deni I've got some extra questions I need to ask him," Dorothy said. "Don't tell him any more than that—make it sound like one of those things grownups do and kids have to put up with. Tell him I'm sorry—tell him I've promised you I'm having strawberry muffins with real butter brought into the office just to make up for it. He claims that's the best thing he and his father eat for breakfast when they're alone together."

Given the communications lag, there was only one way to handle the situation. An autonomous discussion program had to be transmitted to the torch ship. The program would be outfitted with a general strategy and equipped with critical information and pre-recorded discussions of the treatment. Then they would sit back and watch as their screens told them how Sergeant Kolin had reacted eleven minutes ago.

Dr. Barian had reviewed almost every session Dorothy had spent with Sergeant Kolin. He quibbled with her over some of the numerical estimates she plugged into the program, but no one could argue with her overall evaluation of the sergeant's personality structure.

Deni's father had grown up in an "extended family network" that had been created by a complicated series of divorces and regroupings. He had spent his formative years in a complex web of relationships in which no one and every one was responsible for the children. His emotional development had been shaped by a situation in which he and nine other children were involved in a ceaseless competition for the love and praise of thirty adults who were heavily involved in their own competitions and interactions. He had never experienced the love of someone who considered him the absolute dead center of the universe. He had covered up his own lack of self-esteem by convincing himself he had enough self-esteem for twenty people. Then he had buried his insecurities a couple of meters deeper by telling himself other people were just as bouncy and assertive as he thought he was. His son, he had told Dorothy on several occasions, was about as stuck on himself as a boy could be. Deni would have been a lot easier to handle, Sergeant Kolin believed, if his mother hadn't succumbed to the delusion she had given birth to a genius.

Sergeant Wei and Sergeant Kolin belonged to the class that created some of the worst problems military family therapists had to live with. They were both people who had responded to the enticements of the recruiting commercials precisely because their own childhoods had been developmental disasters. Deni's mother had pushed and punished because she herself had grown up in a family that had lived on the edge of chaos. His father had hammered at him because it was the only way Sergeant Kolin could deny the existence of the hungry boy inside himself.

If someone had put Deni's parents inside an esem treatment chamber at some point in their childhoods, their son might not be facing a psychological catastrophe. Essentially, the esem was supposed to endow Deni with a powerful, totally unsmashable feeling that he was a worthwhile person. In families where everything was working the way it was supposed to, the child developed that feeling from parents who communicated—day after day, year after year—a normal amount of love and a general sense that the child was valued. Deni would get it in two hours, with the help of half a dozen drugs and an interactive, multi-sensory program. The drugs would throw him into a semi-conscious state, immerse him in an ocean of calm, and dissolve his defenses against persuasion. The program would monitor all the standard physiological reactions while it bombarded him with feelings, ideas, and experiences that rectified the deficits in his domestic environment. The intervention was usually applied three times, over the period of a month, but even one application could be helpful.

In the midst of winter, a 20th century philosopher named Albert Camus had once said, *I found that there was in me an invincible summer*. For the rest of his life, no matter how he was treated, Deni would be held erect by the summer the esem would plant in the center of his personality.

So how should they convince an exceptionally un-esem'd adult male that he should let them transform his son into the kind of person he thought he was? Dorothy had originally assumed Deni's mother would be the one who accepted the need for the esem. Once Sergeant Wei had acquired some insight into the realities of her family life, Dorothy had believed, there was a good chance she would buy the esem for the same reasons she bought expensive learning programs and other products that could help her son "achieve his full potential." And once Deni's mother had made up her mind, the relevant analyses all indicated Sergeant Kolin would eventually let her have her way.

Their best hope, in Dorothy's view, was an appeal to some of the most powerful emotions nurtured by the military culture. Normally Sergeant Kolin would have rooted himself behind an armored wall as soon as anyone claimed his son needed special treatment. Now they could get around his defenses by claiming Deni was a combat casualty. The program should play on the idea that Deni had been wounded, Dorothy argued. It should portray the esem as a kind of emotional antibiotic.

Dr. Barian wanted to work with the emotional dynamics that coupled guilt with idealization. The Kolin-Wei marriage, in Dr. Barian's opinion, had been one of the worst mixtures of dependency and hostility he had ever examined. It had been so bad he felt confident they could assume Sergeant Kolin had already started idealizing his wife's memory. Their best approach, therefore, would be an appeal that treated the esem as if it was primarily supposed to help Deni deal with the loss of his mother. Dorothy was correct when she objected that the idealization process usually didn't acquire any real force for several days—but Dr. Barian wouldn't have been surprised, in this case, if it had kicked into action the moment Sergeant Kolin had been advised his wife might be dead.

"We're talking about one of the fundamental correlations in the literature, Dorothy. The worse the relationship, the stronger the tendency to idealize."

Dorothy started to argue with him, then glanced at the clock and compromised. The program would open with the combat casualty approach and follow it with a couple of tentative comments on the special problems of boys who had lost their mothers. If Sergeant Kolin made a response that indicated he was already locked into the idealization process, the program would shift tracks and start developing the idea that the boy needed special help because he had lost the support of a special person.

The really divisive issue was the description of the therapy. Dr. Barian wanted her to prepare a description that talked about the procedure as if they were merely going to bathe Deni in love. They might include a hint that they were trying to replace the love Deni had lost when his mother had died. But there would be no reference whatsoever to the effect on the patient's self-image.

That was a little like describing an antibiotic without mentioning it killed germs, of course. Dr. Barian apparently had his own ideas about the meaning of the term "informed consent." In his case, the important word was obviously "consent."

Deni would have been surprised to hear it, but he and his parents were only the second family Captain Min had ever worked with. Her original doctorate had been a Ph.D. in educational psychology, not family therapy. The Secretariat had paid for it and she had assumed she would pay off the debt by spending six years in uniform working with military training systems.

Instead, the military personnel experts had looked at the data on their screens and discovered the Fourth International Brigade had a pressing need for family therapists. A crash program had been set up and she had spent her first eighteen months as an officer working on a second doctorate under the guidance of a civilian mentor who apparently believed there was an inverse relationship between intelligence and the number of years someone had spent in the military. In her case, in addition, Dr. Barian had seemed to feel her childhood had subtracted an additional twenty points from her IQ.

It was the first time she had encountered someone with Dr. Barian's attitude. She had spent two years in a lunar "socialization academy" when she had been a teenager, but eighty percent of the children in her cohort had been the offspring of military people and international bureaucrats. At first she had thought Dr. Barian was trying to probe her responses to the kind of stresses she might receive from her patients. Then she had decided she would just have to ignore his comments on her "contaminated upbringing."

Dr. Barian had hammered at her resolution as if he thought his career depended on it. Much of her training involved long sessions with simulations of patient-therapist relationships. Most of the simulated people who appeared on her screens were trapped in simulated messes that were so foolish—and believable—Dorothy frequently found herself wondering how the human race had made it to the twenty-second century. In the critiques that followed the simulations, Dr. Barian loved to remind her that her reactions to her imaginary patients had probably been distorted by the "inadequacies" in her own "formative environment."

"My upbringing was about as good as it could be, Dr. Barian," she had told him once. "I may have more sympathy for the way military people look at things than you do, but it isn't because anybody indoctrinated me. My father may not have been the most loving man who ever lived but he was so responsible he must have scanned half the research that's been done on military families in the last fifty years. He must have interviewed half a dozen foster care candidates every time he had to leave me alone, just to make sure they really would give me a consistent environment, just like all the literature said they should."

Naturally, Dr. Barian had then started questioning her feelings about her father.

Nineteen years ago, when Dorothy had been six, she had sat on a rug that had looked exactly like the shaggy rug Deni and his schoolmates sat on when they received their daily briefing. In her case, the orbital diagram on the screen had only contained two symbols—a circle that represented a single torchship and an oval that represented a Lumina Industries mining asteroid.

The 150 men and women who had taken over the asteroid had belonged to a group that had somehow convinced themselves the city of Rome, on Earth, was the center of all evil and the sole reason mankind could not achieve political perfection. They had killed fifty people in a surprise attack that had put them in control of the torch that was supposed to shove the asteroid and its load of minerals into orbit around the Earth. Then they had set up their defensive weaponry and placed the asteroid on a course that would bring it down somewhere on the southern Italian peninsula. Her father, Pilot Sergeant Min, had made eight ferry trips to the surface of the asteroid, carrying assault troops and heavy weapons.

Her father had been her only parent for most of her childhood, but there had been no danger she would ever succumb to guilt feelings if he had happened to die in combat. After her mother had left them, her father had shouldered full responsibility for her upbringing—and carried out his parental duties in the same way he had fulfilled every other obligation life had loaded on him.

It hadn't been a natural thing, either. Her father was currently living in retirement in Eratosthenes Crater, on the Moon, and she knew he was perfectly content with a relationship that was limited to bi-weekly phone calls. He was, at heart, the kind of man who was happiest when he was hanging around with other adults like himself. As far as she could tell, he now spent most of his waking hours with a group of cronies whose idea of Heaven was an NCO club that never closed.

The last time she had talked to him, she had been looking for advice on the best way to speed up consideration of her request to speak to Deni's parents. It had been a serious matter, but they had both enjoyed the way he had folded his arms over his chest and pondered the subject with all the exaggerated, slightly elephantine dignity of a senior NCO who had been asked to give a junior officer his best advice.

"Are you asking me, Captain, if I'm still connected with the sergeant's network?"

"I did have something like that in mind, Sergeant."

"As it turns out, I do have a friend who has a certain position on General Lundstrom's staff. I'd rather not mention her name, but I suspect she might be willing to give me some useful advice on the best way to slip your next report past the General's aides. She might even give it a little judicious help if I gave her some good reasons to do it."

"That would be most helpful, Sergeant."

"Then I shall attend to it with the utmost dispatch, Captain."

Military parents like Deni's father and mother had a well-documented tendency to think of the family as a military unit, with the parents as the officers, and the children, inevitably, as members of the lower ranks. Her father had called her "Lieutenant" from the time she was two years old. For most of her childhood, she had seen herself as a younger person who was being guided and supported by an experienced, gently ironic senior who respected her potential.

It was 02:04 by the time they got the program ready for transmission. At 02:15 the transmission began to arrive at the ship. At 02:20 Sergeant Kolin sat down in front of a screen and started watching Dorothy's presentation. At 02:31 his face appeared on Dorothy's communication screen and she got her first look at his response to her efforts.

The program opened with a recording in which Dorothy discussed the effects of combat deaths on children. The presentation was calm, statistical, and scrupulously accurate. On the auxiliary screen on her right, she could watch her neat, fully uniformed image and correlate the statements it was making with the reactions flickering across Sergeant Kolin's face.

"Do you have any questions about anything I've said so far?" the recording asked.

Sergeant Kolin shook his head. He had always kept his guard up during their counseling sessions and he was falling into the same pattern now. Most of her information about his personality came from his responses to interactive video dramas. The dramas that had worked had usually been designed so they practically forced the subject to make a response.

Dorothy's hands tightened on her desktop. She hated watching herself make presentations. Every flaw in her delivery jumped out at her. She saw her head dip just a fraction of a centimeter—a brief, tiny lapse in concentration—and winced at the way she had telegraphed the fact that she was about to say something significant.

"In this case," the Dorothy on the screen said, "there's the added factor that the parent who's become a casualty is the child's mother. The relationship between a young boy and his mother frequently includes emotional overtones that can't be replaced by any other kind of relationship."

Her image paused for a carefully timed instant—a break that was supposed to give Sergeant Kolin the chance to start a response. He leaned forward with the beginning of a frown on his face and a subtitle lit up on the auxiliary screen. *Light positive response detected. Continuing probe.*

The program's visual interpretation capabilities were limited to relatively large-scale body movements but Dorothy had been able to list three actions that should be given extra weight—and the first item on the list had been that tendency to lean forward. Sometimes, if you waited just a moment longer, Sergeant Kolin would lean a little further and say something that could lead to three minutes of real discussion.

This time he just settled back again. If he had started idealizing his wife's memory, he apparently didn't feel like expressing the feelings the idealization had aroused.

"I'm afraid there's a good possibility he's just angry," Dorothy said. "This isn't the first time I've seen that kind of tight-lipped expression."

"Angry at us?" Dr. Barian said.

"He really hates the whole idea of people examining his feelings. He looks like he's in one of those moods where he'd like to pick up his chair and throw it at the screen."

The program had apparently reached a similar conclusion. Her image had already slipped into a sentence that treated the mother-son relationship as if it was merely a side issue. The sound system let out a blip, to remind Sergeant Kolin he was looking at a recording, and the program switched to her description of the therapy.

Dorothy had drastically revised her standard description. She had included a shot of the treatment chamber, but the shot only showed part of the cover and it only lasted a couple of seconds.

She had done everything she could to make it clear they weren't "rewiring" Deni. "To a large extent," the video Dorothy said, "we're just giving Deni in advance the effects of all the love he's going to be missing during the next few years." She had touched on the danger of guilt feelings, but she had skipped over the relationship between guilt and the anger evoked by demanding parents.

The program reached a check point. "Do you have any comments you would like to make, Sergeant Kolin? Please feel free to speak as freely as you want to. This program can answer almost any question you can ask."

Sergeant Kolin leaped out of his chair. His head disappeared from the screen for a moment. The camera readjusted its field of vision and focused on a face that was contorted with rage.

Deni's father had been trained in the same NCO schools every sergeant in the Fourth International Brigade had attended. Sergeants never bellowed. Their voices dropped to tight, controlled murmurs that made the anger on their faces look a hundred times more intense.

"My son doesn't need people poking into his brain," Sergeant Kolin said. "My son will get all the attention he needs from the person who's supposed to give it to him."

Dorothy's image stared at him while the program raced through alternative responses. The screen dissolved into an abstract pattern that was supposed to be emotionally neutral. An avuncular synthetic voice took over the conversation.

"We're sorry if we've angered you, Sergeant Kolin," the voice said. "We're trying to explain this procedure under difficult circumstances. Captain Min has prepared answers to most of the questions people raise when they're asked to approve this type of emotional intervention."

Dorothy bit her lip. Her right hand hovered over her notebook with the stylus poised to start writing—as if some part of her nervous system still didn't believe her orders had to cross eleven light minutes before they evoked a response from the program.

She had prepared a statement the program could jump to if Sergeant Kolin expressed his basic hostility to the very idea of psychological "tampering." The program should have switched to the statement, but it had responded to his display of anger instead.

"This isn't working," Dr. Barian murmured.

Sergeant Kolin dropped into his armchair. He rested his hands on his knees and stared at the screen

"Tell Captain Min to continue," Sergeant Kolin said.

Dorothy's hand started inscribing instructions on her notebook. "He knows he's being recorded," she said. "He knows he has to give us a minimum amount of cooperation. He may be ready to explode but he's still thinking about his career, too."

"So he'll sit there. And listen. And say no."

Her image had returned to the screen. The program had switched to her review of the psychological dangers faced by children who had lost a parent—a review she had included in the program so it could be used in situations in which they needed to mark time. The program was still reacting to his anger. There was no indication it was going to deal with his feelings about psychological intervention.

She drew a *transmit* symbol at the bottom of her last instruction and her orders began creeping across the Solar System. Eleven minutes ago the program had made a misjudgment. Eleven minutes from now—twenty-two minutes after the original mistake—It would receive a message ordering it to deal with Sergeant Kolin's hostility to psychological tampering.

"You've done about as well anyone could have, Dorothy," Dr. Barian said. "I couldn't have done it any better myself. It isn't your fault they made you wait so long you had to work through a program."

"It should have understood," Dorothy said. "It should have switched to the psychological tampering track as soon as he made that remark about people poking holes in his son's brain. It shouldn't have let that slip past it."

"The anger response was too strong. It picked up the anger and it didn't hear the content. You aren't the first person who's seen a program make a mistake she would have avoided."

Sergeant Kolin had sat like that for a big part of half the sessions she'd had with him. His eyes were fixed on the screen. His face looked attentive and interested. And she knew, from experience, that he wasn't hearing one word in three.

"It isn't your fault, Dorothy. You might have had a chance if they'd let you talk to him when the time lag was only a couple of minutes. They fiddled around with your request and now you've got a hopeless situation."

She wrote another set of commands on her notebook and bent over the dense, black-on-yellow format she had chosen the last time she had felt like fooling around with her displays. Somewhere in the mass of information she had collected on Sergeant Kolin there had to be a magic fact that would drill a hole through his resistance.

"Your patient is in exactly the same position as a child who's dying of a disease," Dr. Barian said. "Would you wait for his father's permission —or some general's permission—If he needed a new lung or a new spinal cord? Your first responsibility is to that child—not some set of rules thought up by people who are still living in the Dark Ages."

The last useless paragraphs in Sergeant Kolin's file scrolled across her notebook. She raised her head and discovered Dr. Barian was regarding her with an expression that actually looked understanding.

"There's another consideration you might want to factor into your decision making process," Dr. Barian said. "It may be your friend Colonel Pao is right—maybe General Lundstrom's staff did do the right thing when they decided her mental state is so delicate they might be endangering four hundred combat troops if they bothered her with a difficult matter like this. It's also true that the military personnel on those ships are all volunteers. They *agreed* to take the risk they're taking. Deni didn't volunteer for anything."

She had dispatched her new set of instructions at 02:58. At 03:09 it arrived at the torch ship. At 03:20 she saw the program switch to the path it should have taken in the first place. At 03:40, she ordered it to switch to the termination routine and started waiting for the images that would tell her Sergeant Kolin had refused permission. Dr. Barian started talking the moment she took her eyes off her notebook.

She picked up Deni at the door of the childcare center, in a cart she had requested from Special Services when it had finally occurred to her they would probably provide her with anything she asked for "under the circumstances."

She had even been given a route that had been specially—and unobtrusively—cleared of any traffic that might cause her problems. A few of the pedestrians stared when they saw a cart with a child sitting in the passenger seat, but they all looked away as soon as their brains caught up with their reflexes.

Hammarskjold Station was a military base, so its public spaces looked something like the public spaces of a civilian space city and something like the decks of a torch ship. The corridors had been landscaped with trees, fountains, and little gardens, just like the corridors in lunar cities, but it had all been done in the hyper-manicured style that characterized most military attempts at decorating. The doors that lined the walls came in four sizes and three colors. The gardens were spaced every hundred meters and they all contained one tree, a carpet of flowers that was as trim as a major's mustache, and two (2), three (3), or four (4) shrubs selected from a list of twenty (20).

"I thought I wasn't supposed to see you until after lunch," Deni said.

"I had to make some changes in my schedule," Dorothy said, with deliberate vagueness.

"Am I going to have to see you during breakfast from now on?"

"It's just this once."

The big, utilitarian elevator near the childcare center opened as soon as the car approached it. It went directly to the fourth level without stopping, and she turned left as she cleared the door and started working her way around the curve of the giant wheel that had been her home since the day she had been born.

The strawberry muffins had big chunks of real strawberries embedded in them. The butter had been synthesized in a Food Services vat, but to everyone who lived off-Earth, it was "the real thing" an expensive, luxurious alternative to the cheaper look-alikes. The milk in the big pitcher was flavored with real strawberries, too—and laced with a carefully measured dose of the tranquilizer that had given her the best results when she had slipped it to him in the past.

"Did I get the muffins the same temperature your father gets them?" Dorothy said.

Deni stopped chewing for a moment and nodded politely. He never talked with his mouth full. His mother had dealt with that issue before he was three.

"Are we going to talk about my feelings some more?"

"Maybe later. Right now—why don't we just relax and have breakfast? I'm kind of fond of real butter myself."

"How many can I have?"

"Well, I bought six. And I'll probably only be able to eat two myself. I'd say you can count on eating at least three."

She glanced at the notebook sitting beside her coffee cup. The chair Deni was sitting in looked like a normal dining chair but it was packed with the same array of non-invasive sensors that had been crammed into the therapeutic chair he normally used. His heartbeat, blood pressure, muscle tension, and movement-count all agreed with the conclusion a reasonably sensitive human being would have drawn from the enthusiasm with which he was biting into his muffin.

Deni had finished the last bite of his second muffin and given her a quick glance before he reached for the third. The numbers on the notebook were all advancing by the appropriate amount as the tranquilizer took hold.

She stood up and strolled toward her desk with her coffee cup in her hand. "Take your time, Deni. Don't worry about it if you decide you can't finish it."

She called up a status report on her desk screen and stared at the same numbers she had gone over only two hours ago. The drugs she needed for the esem were all sitting in the appropriate places on her shelves. The devices that were supposed to deliver the drugs were all functional. The components that would deliver the appropriate images, sounds, and sensations all presented her with green lights when she asked for an equipment check.

She had thought about putting Deni under and checking the current state of his feelings but she had known it was a stupid idea as soon as it had popped into her head. She knew what his real feelings were. Every test she had run on him in the last three months had confirmed he was still in the grip of the emotions she had observed when she had begun working with him.

She had begun her sessions with Deni with a two hour diagnostic unit in which he had been drugged and semi-conscious. Deni didn't remember any of it, but she had stored every second of the session in her confidential databanks. Any time she wanted to, she could watch Deni's hands curl—as if he was strangling someone—as he relived an evening in which his parents might have killed each other if they hadn't both been experts in the art of falling. She knew exactly what he really thought about the time his father had taken his flute away from him for two weeks. She had observed his childish, bitter rage at the cage of work and study his mother had erected around his life.

She scrawled another code number on her notebook and the results of the work she had done last night appeared on her desk screen. She had been ready to crawl into bed as soon as she had made Deni's travel arrangements but Dr. Barian had insisted they should prepare a complete quantified prognosis. They had spent over fifty minutes haggling over a twenty-two item checklist. Dr. Barian had insisted nineteen of her estimates were wildly out of line and tried to replace every one of them with the most pessimistic numbers he could produce.

In the end, it hadn't really mattered which set of numbers you used. The most optimistic prognosis the program could come up with merely offered *some* hope that *someday* the boy *might* voluntarily seek out a therapist. *Someday*, just possibly, he *might* ask for the treatment that would pull him out of the emotional swamp that was going to start sucking at his psyche the moment he learned his mother had died.

And that's your best prognosis, Captain. Based on numbers most experienced therapists would consider hopelessly optimistic.

"How are you coming, Deni?"

"I think I'm starting to feel a little burpy, ma'am."

She waved the numbers off the screen and turned around. His glass still held about three fingers of milk.

"I've got a pill I'd like you to take. Can your tummy hold enough milk to help you get a pill down?"

* * *

On the main communications screen, Mr. and Mrs. Chen were holding a press conference. The "reporters" were all "volunteers" from their own Zen-Random congregation, but that was a minor matter. The questions would have been a little different if the Chens had been facing real media types, but the answers would have been the same.

A bona fide journalist, for example, might have asked them how they would answer all the military analysts who thought they had made a tactical mistake when they destroyed Rinaswandi. The phony reporter on the screen had merely asked his leaders if they could tell the people how the attack had improved their military position.

"I think the answer to that is obvious," Mrs. Chen said. "The forces that were guarding Rinaswandi Base can now join the force defending our city. The Secretariat mercenaries will be faced with a force of overwhelming size, with every weapon and vehicle controlled by a volunteer who is prepared to make any sacrifice to preserve the state of moral liberation we have created in our city...."

Every two or three minutes—for reasons Dorothy couldn't quite grasp—the Chens let the camera pick up a bald, slump-shouldered man who seemed to shrink against the wall as soon as he realized a lens was pointed his way. If there was one person in this situation who wasn't going to come out of it alive, Dorothy knew, it was Major Jen Raden—the officer who had betrayed the equipment stashed on Rinaswandi.

Her father was only one-eighth Gurkhali, but no one had ever had to remind him—or any other member of the Fourth International Brigade—that he belonged to an institution that could trace its origins to the Fourth Gurkha Rifles, the ancient, battle-scarred infantry regiment the Indian government had donated to the United Nations in the years when the Secretariat had acquired its first permanent forces. I will keep faith, the Gurkha motto had run—and they had proved it in battle after battle, first in the service of the British Empire, then in the service of the Republic of India, and finally under the flag that was supposed to represent humanity's best response to its own capacity for violence.

A light glowed on Dorothy's communications board. A line of type appeared at the bottom of the screen. *Call from Pilot Sergeant Min. Non-priority.*

On the couch, Deni was still sleeping peacefully. The monitor she had clipped to his wrist was still transmitting readings that indicated he would sleep for the full two hours the deep-sleep pill was supposed to deliver. There were two messages from Dr. Barian in her communications system but she hadn't looked at either of them.

She tapped the appropriate button on her keyboard. Her father stared at her out of the screen with a blurred, puffy-eyed look that immediately triggered off a memory of beery odors—a memory that was so strong it was hard to believe the communications system could only transmit sounds and images. She wasn't the only member of her family who had been up most of the night.

"Good morning, daughter. I hope I'm not disturbing anything."

"I was just sitting here watching the news. I've got something I'm supposed to do, but I'm giving myself a little break."

"I've been thinking about the family you've been concerned about. It seems to me you indicated one of the parents was stationed on Rinaswandi...."

She nodded. "It was the mother. The son's sleeping on the couch in my office."

Her father leaned back and folded his arms across his chest—but this time neither of them smiled. She had realized, at some point in her teens, that it was a body posture that frequently indicated he was trying to keep his reactions under control. He arranged his arms like that, she had decided, so he wouldn't run his hands across his face or do something else that might affect the image a good sergeant tried to maintain.

"I was afraid something like that might have happened. Have they told him yet?"

"I told them I'd do it."

"That's not the easiest job you can volunteer for."

"I still haven't told him. I'm letting him sleep while I think about the best way to approach it."

"I only did that twice all the time I was on active duty. If you don't mind me giving you some advice—I never talked to anybody who thought they'd found a good way to do it. Whatever you do, you're not going to be happy with it."

"There's some special problems in this case—some reactions he'll probably have because of the family problems I was trying to deal with."

Sergeant Min frowned. "You were trying to get permission for some special procedure... for something that would help him deal with the possibility his parents might become casualties...."

"We tried to get permission from his father last night and we couldn't do it. Dr. Barian thinks we failed because they stalled us for so long we had to communicate across a big communications lag. I'm inclined to think we might have failed anyway."

"And what does that mean?"

"It means basically that we end up with a human being who's permanently crippled psychologically. I could show you the numbers and explain them but that's what they all add up to. He'll be just as much of a casualty as anybody who's been physically wounded."

"And nobody ever asked him if he wanted to enlist...."

"That's essentially what Dr. Barian said."

"I'm sorry, Dorothy. It sounds to me like you've done everything anyone could have."

"I'm not blaming myself, papa. I'm just sorry it's happening."

"There isn't anything else you can do? There isn't some possibility he'll get some kind of therapy later? When he's old enough to make his own decision?"

"It's possible, but the odds are against it. We're talking about something that will eventually affect almost every aspect of his personality. When a child has certain kind of problems with his parents, the death of one of his parents can create unconscious feelings... guilt feelings... that are so powerful they influence everything he does. People tend to protect the personalities they've acquired. Somebody who's rebellious, unruly, and angry usually isn't going to feel he needs a treatment that will give him a different outlook—even when he isn't satisfied with the kind of life his emotions have led him into."

"Major Raden has a lot to answer for."

"Dr. Barian seems to feel it's mostly General Lundstrom's fault."

"Or some of those babus on her staff."

She shrugged. "They were trying to protect her—to shield her from distractions."

"She's a general. She's supposed to look after her troops. If she can't put up with a little pestering from a medical captain without going into convulsions, she shouldn't be wearing the pips."

* * *

When Dorothy had been fourteen, one of her best friends had been plagued with a father who had "confined her to quarters" every other weekend—usually for some trivial matter like a dusty piece of furniture or a piece of clothing that didn't look "inspection presentable." Her first boyfriend had been a wary thirteen year old whose father had seemed to watch everything his children did for signs of "weakness."

There were people, in Dorothy's opinion, for whom military life was a kind of moral exo-skeleton. Their upbringing had left them with no useful values or goals. The ideals imposed on them by their military indoctrination were the only guidelines they had.

She had never experienced the kind of problems Deni had lived with, but she had no trouble relating her records of his case to the things she had observed during her own childhood. Press one set of buttons and the data base presented you with a recording of a counseling session in which Sergeant Kolin justified a punishment by arguing that people would behave "like animals" if no one imposed any "discipline" on them. Press another set, and you got to watch Sergeant Wei, in a message she had transmitted from Rinaswandi, telling Deni she hoped he was practicing his flute and spending enough time with his learning programs—and never once suggesting she loved him or hoped he was having a little fun.

Press a third combination, and the database gave you a look at the hour she had spent with Deni on the day he had received his tenth message from his mother. They had sat on the couch, side by side, and she had spent most of the session stubbornly trying to evoke some kind of comment on his reactions to his mother's exhortations.

"How did you feel about the length of the message?" the Insistent, Patient Therapist had prodded. "Was it too short? Would you like it better if she sent you a longer message every two or three days?"

Deni shrugged. "It was all right."

The Therapist stifled the natural responses of a normal adult and produced an attempt at a conciliatory smile. "Try again, Deni. Is there anything else you wish your mother had talked about? Besides school? And music practice? We're not here to play, soldier."

She had been dealing with the great problem that confronted every therapist who tried to get military children to talk about their emotions—the trait that had been observed by almost every researcher who had ever explored the child-rearing customs of this odd little sub-culture. The one thing that seemed to be true about all military children was their tendency to pick up, almost at birth, the two great commandments of military life: don't complain, don't talk about your feelings. Her solution had been to tell him it was a task—a duty the officer in command of the situation expected him to fulfill to the best of his ability.

It had helped some, but only some. The resistance she was dealing with couldn't be eliminated by direct orders and nagging persistence. Talk therapy was only a second-best stop-gap—a procedure that she kept up mostly so she could convince herself she was doing something while she waited for the day his mother finally agreed he needed the only help that could do him any good.

He won't have the slightest idea you did it, Dr. Barian had said. *His father won't know you did it. No one. Somebody may wonder, fifteen years from now, why a kid with his prognosis has turned out so well, but they'll probably assume he just happened to beat the odds. He'll just have the kind of life he should have—the kind of life you've got.*

Deni looked up at her from the couch. His right hand made a little twitching movement.

"You fell asleep," Dorothy said. "I thought I'd let you rest."

He frowned. He was old enough to know she gave him medicines that affected his feelings, but she wasn't sure he realized she would do it without telling him first.

His eyes shifted toward the time strip on her desk. "Can I go home now? Are we finished?"

He pulled up his legs and sat up. "They start play time in ten minutes, Captain Min. It isn't my fault I fell asleep."

"Deni—"

"Yes, ma'am?"

"I'd like you to go sit in the chair you usually sit in. I'd like you to do it now, if you don't mind. There's something I have to talk about with you —something that happened last night."

The ceremony for the people who had died at Rinaswandi took place in the biggest theater in Hammarskjold, two days after the attack. Deni sat in the front row, with the other children whose parents had been killed. Dorothy could watch him, from her place in the ranks of the medical personnel, and note how he was still maintaining the same poise he had adapted in the cart when she had driven him back to the childcare center.

It was the same ceremony she had attended with her father, nineteen years ago, in memory of the people who had died in the assault on the Lumina mining asteroid. The names of the dead would be read one by one. (Twenty this time, thirty-three then.) A lone trumpeter would play "The Last Post." The minute of silence—timed precisely to the second—would end with the bagpipes roaring into one of the big, whirling, totally affirmative marches the Gurkha regiments had inherited, three hundred years in the past, from the British officers who had introduced them to European military music.

That was how you always did it at a military ceremony. First, you remembered the dead. Then the moment over—the tribute paid—you returned to the clamor and bustle of life. She lived in a world in which people sometimes died, her father had said when he had explained it to her. You never forgot they had died, but you didn't let it keep you from living.

Her father hadn't asked her if she wanted to go to the Lumina ceremony. And she had known, without being told, that it wasn't something they could discuss. There were some things that had to be left unsaid, even with the kind of father she had. She had never told him, for example, about the nights, the whole year after he had returned from the Lumina "incident," when she had stared at the ceiling of her bedroom and tried to ignore the pictures that kept floating into her head.

She had given Colonel Pao a recommendation for a week of deep-sleep therapy, to be implemented sometime in the next month, and he had indicated he would probably approve it. Colonel Pao didn't think there would be any problems, either, with her recommendation for a long-term follow-up, from now until Deni's legal maturity, that would include any legal procedures that might reduce the damage. If there was one thing everyone in the chain of command understood, it was the plight of a child who had lost a parent in combat.

"…It's the same basic idea you always come back to," she had told Colonel Pao. "The point they always emphasize in all those courses on military ethics they make you take in baby officer's school. My father even explained it to me when I was a child, when I asked him how he could be sure he was doing the right thing when he helped kill people. If you're a soldier... then for you morality is defined by the law. A soldier is someone who engages in legally authorized acts of violence. If you take away the law, then there's no difference between us and a bunch of thugs. If we can't obey the law, too... at least the important laws...."

Dr. Barian hadn't been particularly impressed with her attempts to explain herself, of course. He had stared at her as if she had just suggested they should deal with the Akara situation by poisoning half the people in the asteroid belt.

"The only difference between an army and bunch of thugs," Dr. Barian had told her, "is that armies work for governments and thugs don't. You turned your back on a helpless child because you felt you had to stick to the letter of some rule a pack of politicians set up so they could appease a mob of voters who can't tell the difference between an esem and a flogging."

Behind his desk, to the left, Colonel Pao had set up a serenity corner with a composition composed of green plants and dark, unevenly glazed pottery. He had arranged two chairs so they faced it from slightly different angles, and he had insisted they should sit in the chairs and drink tea while they talked. On the sound system a wooden flute had been tracing a long meditative line.

"I take it," Colonel Pao had said, "that you feel you might have proceeded with the esem if you had been a civilian."

Dorothy shrugged. "My father always used to claim that a good sergeant took care of the people under him. I have a feeling that if you took it to a vote half the people on this base might have felt I should have thrown the rules out the airlock and given a casualty whatever he needed."

"And how do you feel about that?"

She shrugged again. "When I think about it that way—I feel like Dr. Barian's absolutely right and I've acted like a priggish junior officer who thinks rules are more important than human beings."

The left side of the serenity corner was dominated by a thin, long-necked jar that would have thrown the entire composition out of balance if it had been one centimeter taller. She focused her eyes on the line of the neck and tried to concentrate on the way it intersected a thin, leafless branch. Then she lost control and snapped her head toward the trim, carefully positioned figure in the other chair.

"He was sitting right in front me, sir! I had to look him in the face when I told him his mother was dead. I could be watching what this has done to him for the next ten years if I decide to stay in. If I had my way we'd have a law that let us set up some kind of committee—without giving the parents an absolute veto whenever we got into this kind of emergency. If all the people like Dr. Barian had their way, there wouldn't be any rules at all and we could spend our lives arbitrarily altering people's personalities just because we felt it was good for them. My father, the people on Rinaswandi—they spent their lives trying to build a wall around chaos. There has to be a law regulating personality modification! Even when it's as benign as this one. Just like there have to be laws that tell you when it's all right to engage in violence."

Colonel Pao folded his arms over his chest. He tipped his head to one side—as if he was concentrating on the long arc the flute was describing—and Dorothy settled back in her chair and waited while he collected his thoughts.

He had shifted his thought processes to the formal, somewhat bureaucratic phrases he tended to adapt when he communicated in Techno Mandarin. "It is my personal opinion," he said, "that any responsible observer would have to agree that you did everything anyone could reasonably expect you to do. You took everything into account—including a point many civilians have trouble understanding. You did everything you could to get a favorable response from Sergeant Kolin. You made a real decision, furthermore, when you arrived at the moment when a decision couldn't be postponed. You didn't just stand there and let the situation drift into a decision by default."

Colonel Pao raised his bowl of tea to his lips. He stared at the center of the serenity composition over the top of the bowl and Dorothy waited again.

"I could tell you that I think you made the right choice and try to ease your feelings by providing you with whatever authority I may possess. I could even tell you that you did the wrong thing and try to give you the comforting illusion someone knows what's right and wrong in these situations. The truth is I can't tell you any more than I've already said. If I understood the principles of ethical philosophy as well as I would like to, I think I would conclude that you applied the Confucian principle of reciprocity, even if I couldn't guarantee you made the most ethical choice.

You treated Deni the way you probably would want to be treated yourself. If you or I were in Deni's position—if someone had to make a decision that might affect us the way this one affects him—then I think we would want it to be someone who's been as thoughtful and conscientious as you've been."

He rested his bowl on the tray beside his chair and switched back to Ghurkali—the language of her infancy. "Does that help you, Captain? Does it give you any comfort?"

"I think so, sir. Yes, sir."

"The other thing I think I should say is related to something you and I have in common, so perhaps I'm biased. Still, there have been moments —during the less illustrious interludes in my career—when it's been the only thought that's kept me functioning."

He reached across the space between the chairs and rested his hand on her shoulder. It would have been a perfectly unremarkable gesture if anyone else had done it; in his case it was the first time he had touched her since she had been six years old and the duty officer at the post clinic, young Surgical Captain Pao, had held her hand while the first aid equipment had repaired a greenstick fracture in her left arm. Colonel Pao frequently touched patients who needed encouragement or reassurance but he tended to be physically reserved with everyone else.

"Just remember, Dorothy—Deni isn't the only person who didn't volunteer."

Many literary commentators seem to think the subjects of science fiction are merely metaphors for the things they're interested in. For me, starships and aliens are real subjects, of interest in themselves. I write science fiction partly because I'm genuinely interested in possibilities like contact with alien civilizations, and I assume most science fiction readers share my interest. How will We react to Them? And They to Us?

A RESPONSE FROM EST17

The Betzino-Resdell Exploration Community received its first message from Trans Cultural 5.23 seconds after it settled into orbit around the planet designated Extra-Solar Terranoid 17.

"I am the official representative of the Trans-Cultural Institute for Multi-Disciplinary and Extra-Disciplinary Interstellar Exploration and Study," Trans Cultural radioed. "I represent a consortium of seventy-three political entities and two hundred and seventy-three academic, research, and cultural institutions located in every region of the Earth. You are hereby requested to refrain from direct contact with the surface of Extra-Solar Terranoid 17. My own contact devices have already initiated exploration of the planet. You will be granted access to my findings."

The eighteen programs included in the Betzino-Resdell Community were called "alters"—as in "alter-ego" or "alternate personality"—but they were not self-aware. They were merely complicated, incredibly dense arrangements of circuits and switches, like every machine intelligence the human species had ever created. But they had been sponsored by seven different sets of shareholders and they had been shaped by the goals and personalities of their sponsors. They spent the first 7.62 seconds after their arrival testing the three copies of each program stored in their files so they could determine which copies had survived the journey in the best shape and should be activated. Then they turned their attention to the message from Trans Cultural.

Betzino and Resdell had been the primary sponsors of the expedition. Their electronic simulations controlled 60 of the 95 votes distributed among the community. Their vote to reject the demand settled the matter. But the other five concurred. The only no vote came from the group of alters tasked to study non-human sexuality. One member of that group cast one vote each way.

22.48 seconds after its arrival, the Betzino-Resdell Exploration Community initiated its exploration routine. The programs housed in Trans Cultural noted that Betzino-Resdell had failed to comply with their orders. Trans Cultural activated its dominance routine and the routine initiated activity. The first human artifacts to reach EST17 entered the first stages of the social phenomenon their creators called microwar.

The Betzino-Resdell Exploration Community had been crammed into a container a little larger than a soccer ball. A microwave beam mounted on the Moon had pushed it out of the solar system. Trans Cultural left the Solar System five years later but it had wealthier backers who could finance a bigger boost applied to a bigger sail. It covered the distance in 1,893,912 hours—a little over two hundred and sixteen Earth years—and reached EST17 six years before Betzino-Resdell. It had already established a base on the planet and begun exploration.

Betzino-Resdell peered at the surface through lenses that were half the size of a human eye but it had been equipped with state of the art enhancement programs. EST17 was an inhabited planet. Its residents seemed to be concentrated in 236 well-defined cities. The rest of the planet looked like an undisturbed panorama of natural landscapes, distributed over four major landmasses.

The original human version of the Resdell alter was an astronomer who had been interested in the search for extra-terrestrial life ever since he had watched his first documentary when he had been six years old. Anthony Resdell was a pleasant, likeable guy whose best-known professional achievement was a popular video series that had made him moderately rich. His alter immediately noted that EST17 seemed to violate a dictum laid down by an aristocratic twentieth century space visionary. Any extra-terrestrial civilizations the human race encountered would be thousands of years ahead of us or millennia behind, Sir Arthur had opined. The odds they would be anywhere near us were so small we could assume the advanced civilizations would think we were savages.

The cities Betzino-Resdell could observe looked remarkably like the better-run cities on Earth. The satellites that ringed the planet resembled the satellites that orbited Earth. Samples of their electronic emissions recorded a similar range of frequencies and intensities.

The Betzino alter riffled through all the speculations on technological development stored in the library and distributed them to its colleagues—a process that ate up 13.3 seconds. The catalog contained several thousand entries—most of them extracted from works of fiction—but it could be grouped into a manageable list of categories:

Technologies so advanced less enlightened space explorers couldn't detect them.

Hedonism.

Deliberate limitation,

A planet that lacked a key resource.

Anti-technology cultural biases.

And so on....

"We must match each piece of new data with each of those possibilities," Resdell said. "We have encountered a significant anomaly."

Betzino concurred. Two members of the community disagreed. The proposal became operational.

Trans Cultural seemed to be concentrating on a site on the largest southern continent, in a heavily wooded area fifty kilometers from a large coastal city. Betzino-Resdell selected a site on a northern continent, in a mountainous area near a city located on the western shore of a long lake. Three tiny needles drifted out of a hatch and began a slow descent through the planet's thick atmosphere. Two needles made it to the ground. Machines that could have been mistaken for viruses oozed through the soil and collected useful atoms. Little viruses became bigger viruses, larger machines began to sprout appendages, and the routines stored in the needles proceeded through the first stages of the process that had spread human structures through the Solar System.

It was a long, slow business. Three local years after Arrival, the largest active machines resembled hyper-mobile insects. Semi-organic flying creatures took to the air in year twelve. In year eighteen, a slab of rock became a functioning antenna and the Betzino-Resdell orbiter established communications with its ground base.

In year twenty-two, the first fully equipped airborne exploration devices initiated a systematic reconnaissance of the territory within one hundred kilometers of the base.

In year twenty-nine, a long range, semi-organic airborne device encountered a long range, semi-organic airborne device controlled by Trans Cultural. The Trans Cultural device attempted to capture the Betzino-Resdell device intact and the Betzino-Resdell device responded, after a brief chase, by erasing all the information in its memory cells, including the location of the Betzino-Resdell base. The microwar had entered the skirmish stage.

In year thirty-six, a native flying creature that resembled a feathered terrestrial toad approached a Betzino-Resdell device that resembled a small flying predator common in the area around the base. The airborne toad settled on a branch overlooking the eastern shore of the lake and turned its head toward the faux predator.

"I would like to talk to you," the toad said in perfectly enunciated twenty-second century Italian. "This is an unofficial, private contact. It would be best if you kept your outward reactions to a minimum."

The Appointee received her first briefing three days after the Integrators roused her from dormancy. They had roused her nineteen years before she was supposed to begin her next active period but she had suppressed her curiosity and concentrated on the sensual pleasures recommended for the first days after activation. She and her husband always enjoyed the heightened sexual arousal that followed a fifty year slumber. Normally they would have stretched it over several more days.

The name posted on the hatch of her dormancy unit was Varosa Uman Deun Malinvo… Her husband's officially recognized appellation was Budsiti Hisalito Sudili Hadbitad… The ellipses referred to the hundreds of names they had added to their own—the names of all the known ancestors who had perished before the Abolition of Death. He called her Varo. She called him Budsi in public, Siti in private.

They were both bipeds with the same general anatomical layout as an unmodified human, with blocky, heavily boned bodies that had been shaped by the higher gravity of their native world. Their most distinctive features, to human eyes, would have been their massive hands and the mat of soft, intricately colored feathers that crowned their heads and surrounded their faces. As Betzino-Resdell had already noted, the accidents of evolution had favored feathers over fur on EST17.

The briefing took place in a secure underground room equipped with a viewing stage that was bigger than most apartments. A direct, real time image of the current First Principal Overseer appeared on the stage while Varosa Uman was still settling into a viewing chair.

"You've been aroused ahead of schedule because we have a visitation," the First Principal said. "The Integrators responded to the latest development by advising us they want you to oversee our response. You will be replacing Mansita Jano, who has been the Situation Overseer since the first detection. He's conducted a flawless response, in my opinion. You won't find a better guide."

A male with bright yellow facial feathers materialized beside the First Principal. Varosa Uman ordered a quick scan on her personal information system and confirmed that she was replacing one of the twenty leading experts on the history of visitations—a scholar with significant practical experience. Mansita Jano Santisi Jinmano... had served on the committee that had worked on the last visitation. He had been a scholar-observer during the visitation twelve hundred years before that.

"It will be an honor to work with you, Mansita Jano."

She could have said more. Mansita Jano's expertise dwarfed her own knowledge of visitations. But the Integrators had picked her. She couldn't let him think he could dominate her thinking.

He couldn't be happy with the change. He knew he was better qualified. She would be harrying Siti with exasperated tirades if the Integrators had done something like that to her. But Mansita Jano was looking at her with polite interest, as if their relative positions had no emotional significance. And she would have donned the same mask, if their positions had been reversed.

A panoramic spacescape replaced the two figures. A line traced the path of an incoming visitation device—a standard minimum-mass object attached to a standard oversize light sail. It was a typical visitation rig and it behaved in a typical fashion. It spent twelve years slowing down and settling into its permanent orbit. It launched a subsidiary device at the third moon of the fourth planet and the subsidiary started working on an installation that would probably develop into a communications relay, in the same way the last two visitations had established relays on the same moon. It released three microweight orbit-to-surface devices (the last visitation had released two) and the survivors advanced to the next step in a typical visitation program.

All over the galaxy intelligent species reached a certain level and developed similar interstellar technologies. Each species thought it had reached a pinnacle. Each species saw its achievements as a triumph of intelligence and heroic effort.

The story became more interesting when the second visitation entered the system. Varosa Uman watched the two devices set up independent bases. She observed the first attack. Maps noted the locations of other incidents. The first visitor seemed to be the aggressor in every engagement.

The two orbiters definitely came from the same source. Their species had obviously generated at least two social entities that could launch interstellar probes. That happened now and then—*everything* had happened now and then—but this was the first time Varosa Uman's species had dealt with a divided visitation. Was that why the Integrators had roused her?

It was a logical thought but she knew it was irrelevant as soon as she saw the encounter between the second visitor and a device that had obviously been created by a member of her own species.

"The unauthorized contacts have been initiated by an Adventurer with an all too familiar name," the First Principal said. "Revutev Mavarka Verenka Turetva… Mansita Jano was preparing to take action when the Integrators advised us they were putting you in charge of our response to the visitation."

"I have received a cease-operations command from my organic predecessor," the Resdell alter said. "This will be my last message. Do not anticipate a revival."

The Betzino alter mimicked the thought processes of a woman who possessed a formidable intellect. Edna Betzino had been a theoretical physicist, a psychiatrist, and an investigatory sociologist specializing in military and semi-military organizations. In her spare time, she had become a widely respected cellist who was a devoted student of Bach and his twenty-second century successors. She had launched her own interstellar probe because she had never developed an institutional affiliation that would offer her proper backing.

The Betzino alter riffled through its databanks—as Betzino herself would have—and determined that Anthony Resdell lived in a governmental unit that had become a "single-leader state". Messages from Earth had to cross eighteen light years so the information in the databanks was, of course, eighteen earthyears out of date. The cease-operations command would remain in effect until the Resdell alter received a countermand from Anthony Resdell.

The ninety-five votes had now been reduced to sixty-five. Their creators had neglected to include a routine that adjusted the percentages so Betzino still controlled thirty votes. She would need the support of one minor member every time the community made a decision.

Three of the minor members wanted to continue discussions with the inhabitant who had made contact. Two objected, on the grounds the inhabitant was obviously an unofficial private individual.

"We have no information regarding his relations with their political entities," the spokesman for the sex research community argued. "He could bias them against us when we try to make a proper contact."

Their mobile device had exchanged language programs with the inhabitant's contact device. The data indicated the inhabitant's primary language had a structure and vocabulary that resembled the structure and vocabulary of the languages technologically advanced human societies had developed.

Betzino voted to maintain the contact. Switches tripped in response and the contact and language programs remained active.

There was a standard response to visitations. It was called the Message. Varosa Uman's species had transmitted it twice and received it once.

Mansita Jano had initiated Message preparation as soon as he had been given responsibility for the visitation. He would have initiated contact with one of the visitors and proceeded to the final stages if Revutev Mavarka hadn't started "bungling around."

Mansita Jano believed Revutev Mavarka should be arrested before he could cause any more trouble. "We have documentary evidence Revutev Mavarka has committed a serious crime," Mansita Jano said. "I think we can also assume the first visitor has a higher status than the visitor he's been attempting to charm. The first visitor rebuffed his overtures. We have translated a communication in which it ordered the second visitor to cease operations."

There was nothing sinister about the Message. It was, in fact, the greatest gift an intelligent species could receive. It contained all the knowledge twenty-three technological civilizations had accumulated, translated into the major languages employed by the recipient. With the information contained in the Message, any species that had developed interstellar probes could cure all its diseases, quadruple its intelligence, bestow millennia of life on all its members, reshape the life forms on its planet, tap energy sources that would maintain its civilization until the end of the universe, and generally treat itself to the kind of society it had been dreaming about since it first decided it didn't have to endure all the death and suffering the universe inflicted on it.

And that was the problem. No society could absorb that much change in one gulp. Varosa Uman's species had endured a millennium of chaos after it had received its version of the Message.

It was an elegant defense. The Message satisfied the consciences of the species who employed it and it permanently eliminated the threat posed by visitors who might have hostile intentions. Interstellar war might seem improbable but it wasn't impossible. A small probe could slip into a planetary system unannounced, establish a base on an obscure body, and construct equipment that could launch a flotilla of genocidal rocks at an unsuspecting world.

Varosa Uman's people had never sent another visitor to the stars. As far as they could tell, all the species that had received the Message had settled into the same quiet isolation—if they survived their own version of the Great Turbulence.

"The Message can be considered a kind of conditioning," a post-Turbulence committee had concluded. "The chaos it creates implants a permanent aversion to interstellar contact."

Revutev Mavarka was an Adventurer—a member of a minority group that constituted approximately twelve percent of the population. Varosa Uman's species had emerged from the Turbulence by forcing far-reaching modifications on the neurochemical reactions that shaped their emotional responses. They had included a controlled number of thrill-seekers and novelty chasers in their population mix because they had understood that a world populated by tranquil, relentlessly socialized serenes had relinquished some of its capacity to adapt. No society could foresee all the twists and traps the future could hold.

Most Adventurers satisfied their special emotional needs with physical challenges and sexual escapades. Revutev Mavarka seemed to be captivated by less benign outlets. His fiftieth awake had been marked by his attempt to disrupt the weather program that controlled the rainfall over the Fashlev mountain range. The First Principal Overseer had added twelve years to his next dormancy period and the Integrators had approved the penalty.

In his seventy-third awake, Revutev Mavarka had designed a small, hyperactive carnivore that had transferred a toxin through the food chain and transformed the habitués of a staid island resort into a population of temporary risk addicts. In his eighty-first, he had decided his happiness depended upon the companionship of a prominent fashion despot and kidnapped her after she had won a legal restraint on his attentions. The poisoning had added twenty-two years to his next dormancy, the kidnapping twenty-eight.

Varosa Uman and her husband liked cool winds and rugged landscapes. They liked to sit on high balconies, hands touching, and watch winged creatures circle over gray northern seas.

"It's Revutev Mavarka," Varosa Uman said. "He's made an unauthorized contact with a visitation."

"And the Integrators think you can give them some special insight?"

"They've placed me in charge of the entire response. I'm replacing Mansita Jano."

Siti called up Mansita Jano's data and scanned through it. "He's a specialist," Siti said. "It's a big responsibility but I think I agree with the Integrators."

"You may belong to a very small minority. They gave me a scrupulously polite briefing."

"They don't know you quite as well as I do."

"Mansita Jano was getting ready to arrest Revutev Mavarka. And offer the Message."

"And you think the situation is a bit more complicated...."

"There are two visitors. One of them is acting like it represents a planetary authority. The other one—the visitor Revutev Mavarka contacted—looks like it may have more in common with him. I have to see how much support Revutev Mavarka has. I can't ignore that. You have to think about their emotional reactions when you're dealing with the Adventurer community. I have to weigh their feelings and I have to think about the responses we could provoke in the visitors—both visitors. We aren't the first people to confront two visitors but it still increases the complexities—the unknowns."

"And Revutev Mavarka has piled more complexities on top of that. And the Integrators understandably decided we'd be better off with someone like you pondering the conflicts."

The contact had told the Betzino-Resdell community they should call him Donald. So far they had mostly traded language programs. They could exchange comments on the weather in three hundred and seven different languages.

The alters that were interested in non-human sexuality lobbied for permission to swap data on sexual practices. There were six alters in the group and they represented the six leading scholars associated with the North Pacific Center for the Analysis of Multi-Gender Sexuality. The exploration units they controlled had observed the activities of eight local life forms. All eight seemed to have developed the same unimaginative two-sex pattern life had evolved on Earth. Their forays into the cities had given them a general picture of the inhabitant's physiology but it had left them with a number of unresolved issues.

Topic: Does your species consist of two sexes?

Betzino-Resdell: Yes.

Donald: Yes.

Topic: Are there any obvious physical differences between the sexes?

BR: Yes.

Donald: Yes

Topic: What are they?

BR: Our males are larger, bigger boned on average. Generally more muscular.

Donald: Males more colorful, more varied facial feathers.

Topic: Do you form permanent mating bonds?

BR: Yes.

Donald: Yes.

Topic: Do any members of your species engage in other patterns?

BR: Yes.

Donald: Yes.

Topic: How common are these other patterns?

BR: In many societies, very high percentages engage in other patterns.

Donald: Why do you wish to know?

* * *

The visitation committee was receiving a full recording of every exchange between Revutev Mavarka and the visitation device that called itself Betzino-Resdell. Revutev Mavarka was, of course, fully aware that he was being observed. So far he had avoided any exchanges that could produce accusations he had transmitted potentially dangerous information.

"It must be frustrating," Varosa Uman said. "He must have a million subjects he'd like to discuss."

"We just need one slip," Mansita Jano said. "Give us one slip and he'll be lucky if fifty members of his own class stand by him."

"And the visitor will have the information contained in the slip...."

Mansita Jano's facial feathers stirred—an ancient response that made his face look bigger and more threatening. "Then why not silence him before he does it, Overseer? Do you really think he can keep this up indefinitely without saying something catastrophic?"

"I've been thinking a dangerous thought," Varosa Uman said.

"I'm not surprised," Siti said.

"Every intelligent species that has sent visitors to an inhabited world has apparently lived through the same horrible experience we did. Some of them may not have survived it. If our experience is typical, everybody who receives the Message responds in the same way when they receive a visitation after they've gone through their version of the Turbulence. The Message is a great teacher. It teaches us that contact with other civilizations is a dangerous disruption."

Two large winged predators were swooping over the water just below the level of their balcony. The dark red plumage on their wings created a satisfying contrast with the grey of the sea and the sky

"I'm thinking it might be useful if someone looked at an alternative response," Varosa Uman said.

Siti ran his fingers across the back of her hand. They had been married for eighty-two complete cycles—twenty-four hundred years of full consciousness. He knew when to speak and when to mutely remind her he was there.

"Suppose someone tried a different role," Varosa Uman said. "Suppose we offered to guide these visitors through all the adaptations they're going to confront. Step by step."

"As an older, more experienced species."

"Which we are. In this area, at least."

"We would have to maintain contact," Siti said. "They would be influencing us, too."

"And threatening us with more turbulence. I'd be creating a disruption the moment I mentioned the idea to Mansita Jano."

"Have you mentioned your intellectual deviation to the Integrators?"

"They gave me one of their standard routines. They pointed out the dangers, I asked them for a decision, and they told me they were only machines, I'm the Situation Overseer."

"And they picked you because their routines balanced all the relevant factors—see attached list—and decided you were the best available candidate."

"I think it's pretty obvious I got the job because I'm more sympathetic to the Adventurer viewpoint than most of the candidates who had the minimum expertise they were looking for."

"You're certainly more sympathetic than Mansita Jano. As I remember it, your major response to Revutev Mavarka's last misadventure was a daily outburst of highly visible amusement."

Siti had been convinced he wanted to establish a permanent bond before they had finished their first active period together. She had resisted the idea until they were halfway through their next awake but she had known she would form a bond with someone sooner or later. They were both people with a fundamental tendency to drift into permanent bonds and they had reinforced that tendency, soon after they made the commitment, with a personality adjustment that eliminated disruptive urges.

Siti found Revutev Mavarka almost incomprehensible. A man who kidnapped a woman just to satisfy a transient desire? And created a turmoil that affected hundreds of people?

Twenty years from now she won't mean a thing to him, Siti had said. *And he knows it.*

"He's impulsive," Varosa Uman said. "I can't let myself forget he's impulsive. Unpredictably."

Trans Cultural had asked all the required questions and looked at all the proffered bona fides. The emissary called Varosa Uman Deun Malinvo… satisfied all the criteria that indicated said emissary represented a legitimate governmental authority.

"Is it correct to assume you represent the dominant governmental unit on your planet?" Trans Cultural asked.

"I represent the only governmental unit on my planet."

Varosa Uman had established a direct link with the base Trans Cultural had created in the Gildeen Wilderness. She had clothed herself in the feather and platinum finery high officials had worn at the height of the Third TaraTin Empire and she was transmitting a full, detailed image. Trans Cultural was still limiting itself to voice-only.

"Thank you for offering that information," Trans Cultural said.

"Are you supposed to limit your contacts to governmental representatives?"

"I am authorized to initiate conversations with any entity as representative as the consortium I represent."

"Can you give us any information on the other visitor currently operating on our world?"

"The Betzino-Resdell Exploration Community primarily represents two private individuals. The rest of its membership comprises two other individuals and three minor organizations."

"Can you give me any information on its members?"

"I'm afraid I'm not authorized to dispense that information at present."

"The presence of another visitor from your society seems to indicate you do not have a single entity that can speak for your entire civilization. Is that correct?"

"I represent the dominant consensus on our world. My consortium represents all the major political, intellectual, and cultural organizations on our world. I am authorized to furnish a complete list on request."

Betzino-Resdell had created an antenna by shaping a large rock slab into a shallow dish and covering it with a thin metal veneer. The orbiter passed over the antenna once every 75.6 minutes and exchanged transmissions.

"You should create an alternate transmission route," Revutev Mavarka said. "I've been observing your skirmishes with the other visitor. You should be prepared to continue communications with your orbiter if they manage to invade your base and destroy your antenna."

"Do you think that's a significant possibility?"

"I believe you should be prepared. That's my best advice."

* * *

"He's preparing a betrayal," Mansita Jano said. "He's telling us he's prepared to send them information about the Message if we attempt to arrest him."

Varosa Uman reset the recording and watched it again. She received recordings of every interchange between Revutev Mavarka and the second visitor but Mansita Jano had brought this to her attention as soon as it had been intercepted.

Mansita Jano had raised the possibility of a "warning message" in their first meetings. The Message itself contained some hints that it had thrown whole civilizations into turmoil but most of the evidence had been edited out of the historical sections. The history of their own species painted an accurate picture up to their receipt of the Message.

The humans would never hear of the millions who had died so the survivors could live through a limitless series of active and dormant periods. They would learn the cost when they counted their own dead.

But what would happen if their visitors received a message warning them of the dangers? Would it have any effect? Would they ignore it and stumble into the same wilderness their predecessors had entered?

For Mansita Jano, the mere possibility Revutev Mavarka might send such a message proved they should stop "chattering" and defend themselves.

"We have no idea what such a warning message might do," Mansita Jano said. "Its very existence would create an unpredictable situation that could generate endless debate—endless *turbulence!*—within our own society. By now the humans have received the first messages informing them of our existence. By now, every little group like these Betzino-Resdell adventurers could have launched a visitor in our direction. How will we treat them when we know they're emissaries from a society that has been warned?"

"I started working on that issue as soon as I finished viewing the recording," Varosa Uman said. "I advised the Integrators I want to form a study committee and they've given me the names of ten candidates."

"And when they've finished their studies, they'll give you the only conclusion anyone can give you. We'll have fifty visitors orbiting the planet and we'll still be staring at the sky arguing about a list loaded with bad choices."

* * *

The Integrators never used a visual representation when they communicated with their creators. They were machines. You must never forget they were only machines. Varosa Uman usually turned toward her biggest window and looked out at the sea when she talked to them.

"I think you chose me because of my position on the Adventurer personality scale," Varosa Uman said. "You felt I would understand an Adventurer better than someone with a personality closer to the mean. Is that a reasonable speculation?"

"You were chosen according to the established criteria for your assignment."

"And I can't look at the criteria because you've blocked access."

"That is one of the rules in the procedure for overseeing visitations. Access to that information is blocked until the visitation crisis has been resolved."

"Are you obeying the original rules? Or have they been modified here and there over the last three thousand years?"

"There have been no modifications."

"So why can't I just talk to someone who remembers what the original rules were?"

"You are advised not to do that. We would have to replace you. You will do a more effective job if you operate without that knowledge."

"Twelve percent of the population have Adventurer personality structures. They're a sizable minority. They tend to be popular and influential. I can't ignore their feelings. Does my own personality structure help me balance all the relevant factors?"

"It could. We are only machines, Overseer. We can assign numerical weights to emotions. We cannot feel the emotions ourselves."

Varosa Uman stood up. A high, almost invisible dot had folded its wings against its side and turned into a lethal fury plummeting toward the waves. She adjusted her eyes to ten power and watched hard talons drive into a sea animal that had wandered into the wrong area.

"I'm going to let the study committee do its work. But I have to conclude Mansita Jano is correct. We can't let Revutev Mavarka send a warning message. I can feel the tensions he's creating just by threatening to do it. But we can't just arrest him. And we can't just isolate him, either.

The Adventurer community might be small but it could become dangerously angry if we took that kind of action against one of the most popular figures in the community while he's still doing things most Adventurers consider harmless rule bending."

"Have you developed an alternative?"

"The best solution would be a victory for the Trans Cultural visitation. Arranged so it looked like they won on their own."

She turned away from the ocean. "I'll need two people with expertise in war fighting tactics. I think two should be the right number. I'll need a survey of all the military planning resources you can give me."

The Integrators had been the primary solution to the conflicts created by the cornucopia contained in the Message. The Integrators managed the technology that produced all the wonders the Message offered. Every individual on the planet could receive all the goods and services a properly modified serene could desire merely by asking, without any of the effort previous generations had categorized as "work".

But who would select the people who would oversee the Integrators? Why the Integrators, of course. The Integrators selected the Overseers. And obeyed the orders of the people they had appointed.

The system worked. It had worked for three thousand years. Could it last forever? Could anything last forever?

The winged toad that made the contact had a larger wingspan and a brighter set of feathers than the creature that had approached Betzino-Resdell. Trans Cultural greeted it with its standard rebuff.

"I can only establish contacts with entities that represent significant concentrations of intellectual and governmental authority."

"This is an extra-channel contact—an unofficial contact by a party associated with the entity who has already established communications. Does your programming allow for that kind of contact?"

Trans Cultural paused for 3.6 seconds while it searched its files and evaluated the terms it had been given.

"How do I know you are associated with that entity?"

"I can't offer you any proof. You must evaluate my proposal on its merits. I can provide you with aid that could give you a decisive victory in your conflict with Betzino-Resdell."

"Please wait…. Why are you offering to do this?"

"Your conflict is creating disruptions in certain balances in our society. I can't describe the balances at present. But we share your concern about contacts between unrepresentative entities."

"Please continue."

Varosa Uman's instructions to Mansita Jano had been a flawless example of the kind of carefully balanced constraints that always exasperated her when somebody dropped them on her. Do this without doing that. Do that without doing this.

Betzino-Resdell had to be neutralized. Revutev Mavarka's link to the humans had to be severed. But Mansita Jano must arrange things so the second visitor collapsed before Revutev Mavarka realized it was happening—before Revutev Mavarka had time to do something foolish. And it should all happen, of course, without any *visible* help from anyone *officially* responsible for the response to the Visitation.

"We could have avoided all this," Mansita Jano had said, "if the Message had been transmitted the day after Revutev Mavarka approached the second visitor. I presume everyone involved in all this extended decision making realizes that."

"The Message will be transmitted to the Trans Cultural device as soon as Betzino-Resdell is neutralized."

"You've made a firm decision? There are no unstated qualifications?"

"The Message will be transmitted as soon as Betzino-Resdell is neutralized. My primary concern is the unpredictability of the humans. We don't know how they'll respond to an overt attack on one of their emissaries—even an emissary that appears to be as poorly connected as the Betzino-Resdell jumble."

"If I were in your position, Overseer, I would have Revutev Mavarka arrested right now. I will do my best. But he's just as unpredictable as our visitors. He isn't just a charming rogue. He isn't offering us a little harmless flirtation with our vestigial appetites for Adventure."

It was the most explicit expression of his feelings Mansita Jano had thrown at her. *If I were in your position... as I should be... if the Integrators hadn't intervened... if you could keep your own weaknesses under control...* But who could blame him? She had just told him he was supposed to tiptoe through a maze of conflicting demands. Created by someone who seemed to be ruled by her own internal conflicts.

They were meeting face to face, under maximum sealed-room security. She could have placed her hand on the side of his face, like a Halna of the Tara Tin Empire offering a strikejav a gesture of support. But that would obviously be a blunder.

"I know it's a difficult assignment, Mansita Jano. I would do it myself, if I could. But I can't. So I'm asking for help from the best person available. Everything we know about Revutev Mavarka indicates he won't do anything until he feels desperate. He knows he'll be committing an irrevocable act. Get the job done while he's still hesitating and he'll probably feel relieved."

The Message had to be sent. The humans were obviously just as divided and unpredictable as every other species that had ever launched machines at the stars. They were probably even more unpredictable. Their planet apparently had a large moon they could use as an easy launch site. Its gravitational field appeared to be weaker, too. A species that could spread through its own planetary system had to be more divided than a species that had confined itself to one planet.

Betzino-Resdell had located its base in the middle levels of a mountain range, next to a waterfall that supplied it with 80.5 percent of its energy. A deep, raging stream defended one side of the base and a broad, equally deep ditch protected the other borders. A high tangle of toxic thicket covered the ground behind the ditch.

Trans Cultural set up three bases of its own and started producing an army. It was obviously planning a swarm attack—the kind of unimaginative strategy machines tended to adapt. Revutev Mavarka evaluated the situation and decided Betzino-Resdell could handle the onslaught, with a little advice from a friendly organic imagination.

"You can't stop the buildup," Revutev Mavarka said, "but you can slow it down with well planned harassment raids."

Betzino consulted with her colleagues. They had all started working on projects that had interested them. The Institute for Spiritual Research was particularly reluctant to divert resources from its researches. "Donald" had made some remarks that set it looking for evidence the resident population still engaged in religious rituals.

The alter that called itself Ivan represented an individual who could best be described as a serial hobbyist. The original organic Ivan had spent decades exploring military topics and the alter had inherited an impulse to apply that knowledge. Betzino-Resdell voted to devote 50.7 percent of its resources to defense.

Revutev Mavarka had decided religion was a safe topic. He could discuss all the religious beliefs his species had developed before the Turbulence without telling Betzino-Resdell anything about his current society.

The Betzino-Resdell subunits had obviously adopted the same policy. The subunit that called itself the Institute for Spiritual Research led him through an overview of the different beliefs the humans had developed and he responded with a similar overview he had selected from the hundreds of possibilities stored in the libraries.

Revutev Mavarka had experimented with religion during two of his awakes—most of a full lifespan by the standards of most pre-Turbulence societies. He had spent eleven years in complete isolation from all social contact, to see if isolation would grant him the insights the Halfen Reclusives claimed to have achieved.

He could see similar patterns in the religions both species had invented. Religious leaders on both worlds seemed to agree that insight and virtue could only be achieved through some form of deprivation.

As for those who sought excitement and the tang of novelty—they were obviously a threat to every worthy who tried to stay on the True Road.

The religious studies were only a diversion—a modest attempt to achieve some insight into the minds that had created the two visitors. The emotion that colored every second of Revutev Mavarka's life was his sense of impending doom.

He had already composed the Warning he would transmit to Betzino-Resdell. He could blip it at any time, with a three-word, two-number instruction to his communications system.

The moment he sent it—the instant he committed that irrevocable act —he would become the biggest traitor in the history of his species.

How many centuries would he spend in dormancy? Would they ever let him wake? Would he still be lying there when his world died in the explosion that transformed every mundane yellow star into a bloated red monster?

Every meal he ate—every woman he caressed—every view he contemplated—could be his last.

"You've acquired an aura, Reva," his closest female confidante said.

"Is it attractive? I'd hate to think I was surrounded by something repulsive."

"It has its appeal. Has one of your quests actually managed to affect something deeper than a yen for a temporary stimulus?"

"I think I've begun to understand those people who claim it doesn't matter whether you live fifty years or a million. You're still just a flicker in the life of the universe."

"He's savoring the possibility," Varosa Uman told her husband.

"Like one of those people who contemplate suicide? And finish their awake still thinking about it?"

"I have to assume he could do it."

"It seems to me it would be the equivalent of suicide. Given the outrage most people would feel."

"We would have to give him the worst punishment the public mood demands—whatever it takes to restore calm."

"You're protecting him from his own impulses, love. You shouldn't forget that. You aren't just protecting us. You're protecting him."

It was all a matter of arithmetic. Trans Cultural was obviously building up a force that could overwhelm Betzino-Resdell's defenses. At some point, it would command a horde that could cross the ditch and gnaw its way through the toxic hedge by sheer weight of numbers. Betzino-Resdell could delay that day by raiding Trans Cultural's breeding camps and building up the defensive force gathered behind the hedge. But sooner or later Trans Cultural's superior resources would overcome Betzino-Resdell's best efforts.

The military hobbyist in the Betzino-Resdell community had worked the numbers. "They will achieve victory level in 8.7 terrestrial years," Ivan advised his colleagues. "Plus or minus .3 terrestrial years. We can extend that by 2.7 terrestrial years if we increase our defensive allocation to 60 percent of our resources."

Betzino voted to continue the current level and the other members of the community concurred. Their sponsors in the Solar System would continue to receive reports on the researches and explorations that interested them.

Revutev Mavarka inspected their plan and ran it through two of the military planning routines he found in the libraries. 8.7 terrestrial years equaled six of his own world's orbits. He could postpone his doom a little longer.

"We are going to plant a few concealed devices at promising locations," Betzino-Resdell told him. "They will attempt to establish new bases after this one is destroyed. Our calculations indicate Trans Cultural can destroy any base it locates before the base can achieve a secure position but the calculation includes variables with wide ranges. It could be altered by unpredictable possibilities. We will reestablish contact with you if the variables and unpredictable possibilities work in our favor and we establish a new defensible base."

"I'll be looking forward to hearing from you," Revutev Mavarka said.

They were only machines. They couldn't fool themselves into thinking an impossible plan was certain to succeed.

The weather fell into predictable patterns all over the planet. The serenes had arranged it that way. Citizens who liked warm weather could live in cities where the weather stayed within a range they found comfortable and pleasant. Citizens who enjoyed the passage of the seasons could settle where the seasons rotated across the land in a rhythm that was so regular it never varied by more than three days.

But no system could achieve perfect, planet-wide predictability. There were places where three or four weather patterns adjoined and minor fluctuations could create sudden shifts. Revutev Mavarka lived, by choice, in a city located in an area noted for its tendency to lurch between extremes.

Sudden big snowfalls were one of his favorite lurches. One day you might be sitting in an outdoor cafe, dressed in light clothes, surrounded by people whose feathers glowed in the sunlight. The next you could be trudging through knee high snow, plodding toward a place where those same feathers would respond to the mellower light of an oversize fireplace.

He had just settled into a table only a few steps from such a fireplace when his communication system jerked his attention away from the snowing song he and six of his friends had started singing.

"You have a priority message. Your observers are tracking a Category One movement."

His hands clutched the edge of the table. He lowered his head and shifted his system to subvocalization mode. The woman on the other side of the table caught his eye and he tried to look like he was receiving a message that might lead to a cozier kind of pleasure.

Category One was a mass movement toward the Betzino-Resdell base—a swarm attack.

How many observers are seeing it?

"Seven."

How many criteria does the observation satisfy?

"All."

His clothes started warming up as soon as he stepped outside. He crunched across the snow bathed in the familiar, comforting sense that he was wrapped in a warm cocoon surrounded by a bleak landscape. It had only been three and a half years since Trans Cultural had started building up its forces. How could they attack now? With a third of the forces they needed?

Has Betzino-Resdell been warned? Are they preparing a defense?

"Yes."

He activated his stage and gave it instructions while he was walking back to his apartment. By the time he settled into his viewing chair, the stage was showing him an aerial view, with most of the vegetation deleted. The trees still supported their foliage in the area where the base was located.

The display had colored Trans Cultural's forces white for easy identification. Betzino-Resdell's defenders had been anointed with a shimmering copper. The white markers were flowing toward the base in three clearly defined streams. They were all converging, dumbly and obviously, on one side of the ditch. A bar at the top of the display estimated the streams contained four to six thousand animals. Trans Cultural was attacking with a force that exactly matched his estimates of their strength—a force that couldn't possibly make its way through the defenses Betzino-Resdell had developed.

There could only be one explanation. Somebody had to be helping it.

"Position. Betzino-Resdell orbiter. Insert."

A diagram popped onto the display. Trans Cultural had launched its attack just after the orbiter had passed over the base.

The antenna built into the rock face couldn't be maneuvered. The base could only communicate with the orbiter when the orbiter was almost directly overhead. Trans Cultural—and its unannounced allies—had timed the attack so he couldn't send his warning message until the orbiter completed another passage around the planet.

He could transmit it now, of course. Betzino-Resdell could store the warning and relay it when the orbiter made its next pass. But the whole situation would change the moment he gave the order. The police would seal off his apartment before he could take three steps toward the door.

Up until now he had been engaging in the kind of borderline activity most Adventurers played with. The record would show he had limited his contacts with Betzino-Resdell to harmless exchanges. He could even argue he had accumulated useful information about the visitors and their divisions.

"Have you considered isolating him?" Mansita Jano said. "It might be a sensible precaution, given the tension he's under."

Varosa Uman had been eating a long afternoon meal with Siti. She had been thinking, idly, of the small, easy pleasures that might follow. And found herself sitting in front of a stage crowded with a view of the battle and headshots of Mansita Jano and her most reliable aides.

She could cut Revutev Mavarka's electronic links any time she wanted to. But it would be an overt act. Some people would even feel it was more drastic than physical restraint.

"He's an emotional, unstable personality confronted with a powerful challenge," Mansita Jano said. "He could send a warning message at any time. If they manage to relay it to the backup system they've set up, before you can stop them...."

"He knows what we'll do to him if he sends a warning," Varosa Uman said. "He has every reason to think Trans Cultural has made a blunder and the attack is going to fail."

"He's an emotional, unpredictable personality, Overseer. I apologize for sounding like a recording, but there are some realities that can't be overemphasized."

Siti had positioned himself on her right, out of range of the camera. She glanced at him and he put down his bowl and crossed his wrists in front of his face, as if he was shielding himself from a blow.

Mansita Jano had placed his advice on the record. If his arrangement with Trans Cultural failed—whatever the arrangement was—he would be shielded.

"This attack cannot succeed," Betzino-Resdell said. "We have repeated our analyses. This attack can only succeed if it contains some element we are not aware of."

"I've come to the same conclusion," Revutev Mavarka said.

"We are proceeding with our defensive plan. We have made no modifications. We would like more information, if you have any."

A tactical diagram floated over the image of the advancing hordes. Most of Betzino-Resdell's defensive forces would mass behind the toxic hedge, in the area the attackers seemed to be threatening. A small mobile reserve would position itself in the center of the base.

"I suggest you concentrate your mobile reserve around the antenna."

"Why do you advise that?"

"I believe the antenna is their primary objective. They will try to destroy your connection with your orbiter if they break through the hedge."

"Why will they make the antenna their primary objective? Our plans assume their primary objectives will be our energy transmission network and our primary processing units."

"Can you defend yourself if you lose contact with your orbiter?"

"Yes."

Betzino-Resdell had paused before it had answered. It had been a brief pause—an almost undetectable flicker, by the standards of organic personalities—but his brain had learned to recognize the minute signals a machine threw out.

He had been assuming Betzino-Resdell's operations were still controlled by the orbiter. He had assumed the unit on the ground transmitted information and received instructions when the orbiter passed over. That might have been true in the beginning. By now, Betzino-Resdell could have transmitted complete copies of itself to the ground. The ground copies could be the primaries. The copies on the orbiter could be the backups.

"Are you assuming you can keep operating on the ground if you stop this attack and they destroy the antenna? And build a new antenna in the future?"

"…Yes."

"What if that doesn't work out? Isn't there some possibility your rival could gain strength and destroy your new antenna before you can finish it?"

"Why are you emphasizing the antenna? Do you have some information we don't have?"

I have an important message I want to transmit to your home planet. The future of your entire species could depend on it.

"I was thinking about the individuals who sent you. Your explorations won't be of much value to them if you can't communicate with your orbiter."

"Our first priority is the survival of our surface capability. Our simulations indicate we can survive indefinitely and could eventually reestablish contact with our orbiter. Do you have information that indicates we should reassess our priorities?"

Revutev Mavarka tipped back his head. His hands pressed against the thick, deliberately ragged feathers that adorned the sides of his face. He was communicating with the visitor through a voice-only link, as always. He didn't have to hide his emotions behind the bland mask the serenes offered the world.

"I've given you the best advice I can give you at present. I recommend that you place a higher priority on the antenna."

"He's still struggling with his conflicts," Varosa Uman said. "He could have given them a stronger argument."

She had turned to Seti again. She could still hear the exhortations she was receiving from her aides but she had switched off her own vocal feed.

"Mansita Jano would probably say he's watching *two* personalities struggle with their internal conflicts," Seti said.

Varosa Uman's display had adapted the same color scheme Revutev Mavarka was watching. The white markers had reached the long slope in front of the ditch. The three columns were converging into a single mass. Winged creatures were fighting over the space above their backs.

"It looks like they're starting their final assault," Seti said. "Do you have any idea what kind of fearsome warriors your white markers represent?"

"They seem to be a horde of small four-legged animals native to the visitor's planet. They breed very fast. And they have sharp teeth and claws."

"They're going to *bite* their way through the hedge? With one of them dying every time they take a bite?"

"That seems to be the plan."

Revutev Mavarka stepped up to the display and waved his hand over the area covered by the white markers.

"Calculation. Estimate number of organisms designated by white marking."

A number floated over the display. The horde racing up the slope contained, at most, six thousand, four hundred animals.

The three columns had merged into a single dense mass. He could see the entire assault force. The estimate had to be correct.

He activated his connection to Betzino-Resdell. "I have an estimate of six-thousand, four hundred for the assault force. Does that match your estimate?"

"Yes."

"Your calculations still indicate the attack will fail?"

"Four thousand will die biting their way through the hedge. The rest will be overwhelmed by our defensive force."

Machines were only machines. Imagination required conscious, self-aware minds. *Adventurous* self-aware minds. But they were talking about a straightforward calculation. Trans Cultural had to know its attack couldn't succeed.

"Can you think of any reason why Trans Cultural has launched this attack at this time?" Revutev Mavarka said. "Is there some factor you haven't told me about?"

"We have examined all the relevant factors stored in our libraries. We have only detected one anomaly. They are advancing on a wider front than our simulations recommend. Do you know of any reason why they would do that?"

"How much wider is it?"

"Over one third."

"Do they have a military routine comparable to yours?"

"We have made no assumptions about the nature of their military routine."

Revutev Mavarka stared at the display. Would the attackers be easier to defeat if they were spread out? Would they be more vulnerable if they were compacted into a tight mass? There must be some optimum combination of width and density. Could he be certain Betzino-Resdell's military routine had made the right calculation?

How much secret help had Trans Cultural received?

"One member of our community still wants to know why you think we should place a higher priority on the antenna," Betzino-Resdell said. "She insists that we ask you again."

The first white markers had leaped into the ditch. Paws were churning under the water. Betzino-Resdell's defenders were spreading out behind the hedge, to cover the extra width of the assault.

Transmit this message to your home planet at once. The Message you will receive from our civilization is a dangerous trap. It contains the combined knowledge of twenty-three civilizations, translated into the languages you have given us. It will give you untold wealth, life without death, an eternity of comfort and ease. But that is only the promise. It will throw your entire civilization into turmoil when you try to absorb its gifts. You may never recover. The elimination of death is particularly dangerous. The Message is not a friendly act. We are sending it to you for the same reason it was sent to us. To protect ourselves. To defend ourselves against the disruption you will cause if we remain in contact.

It was a deliberately short preliminary alarm. They would have the whole text in their storage banks half an eyeblink after he subvocalized the code that would activate transmission. A longer followup, with visual details of the Turbulence, would take two more blinks.

The initiation code consisted of two short numbers and three unrelated words from three different extinct languages—a combination he couldn't possibly confuse with anything else he might utter.

Would they believe it? Would the people who received it on the human world dismiss it because it came from a vehicle that had been assembled by a group of individuals who were probably just as marginal and unrepresentative as the eccentric who sent the warning?

Some of them might dismiss it. Some of them might believe it. Did it matter? Something unpredictable would be added to the situation—

something the Integrators and Varosa Uman would have to face knowing they were taking risks and struggling with unknowns no matter what they did.

The animals in the front line of the assault force had reached the hedge. White markers covered a section of the ditch from side to side. Teeth were biting into poisoned stems.

The hedge wavered. The section in front of the assault force shook as if it had been pummeled by a sudden wind. A wall of dust rose into the air.

Varosa Uman would have given Mansita Jano an immediate burst of praise if she could have admitted she knew he was responsible. She had understood what he'd done as soon as she realized the hedge was sinking into the ground.

There would be no evidence they had helped Trans Cultural. Some individuals might suspect it but the official story would be believable enough. Trans Cultural had somehow managed to undermine the ground under the hedge. An explosion had collapsed the mine at the best possible time and the defenders were being taken by surprise.

The assault force still had to cross the ruins of the hedge but they had apparently prepared a tactic. The front rank died and the next rank clambered over them. Line by line, body by body, the animals extended a carpet over the gap. Most of them would make it across. Betzino-Resdell's defenders would be outnumbered.

Trans Cultural couldn't have dug the mine. They didn't have the resources to dig the mine while they were preparing the attack. Revutev Mavarka could prove it. But would anyone believe him?

The first white markers had crossed the ditch. The front ranks were ripping at each other with teeth and claws. Flyers struggled in the dust above the collapse.

White markers began to penetrate the copper masses. The mobile reserve retreated toward the installations that housed Betzino-Resdell's primary processing units.

A white column emerged from the hedge on the right end of the line—the end closest to the antenna. It turned toward the antenna and started gathering speed.

"*Defend the antenna.* You must defend the antenna."

"What are you hiding from us? You must give us more information. What is happening? Trans Cultural couldn't have dug that mine. They didn't have the resources."

Revutev Mavarka stared at the white markers scurrying toward the antenna. Could Betzino-Resdell's mobile reserve get there in time if they responded to his pleas? Would it make any difference?

The antenna was doomed. The best defense they could put up would buy him, at best, a finite, slightly longer interval of indecision.

Two numbers.

Three words.

Blip.

"You must destroy the antenna," Mansita Jano said. "He's given you all the excuse you need."

Varosa Uman had already given the order. She had placed a missile on standby when Trans Cultural had launched its attack. Revutev Mavarka had committed the unforgivable act. She could take any action she deemed necessary.

The missile rose out of an installation she had planted on an island in the lake. Police advanced on Revutev Mavarka's apartment. The image on his display stage disappeared. Jammers and switches cut every link that connected him to the outside world.

Three of the Betzino-Resdell programs voted to transmit Donald's message at once. Ivan argued for transmission on impeccable military grounds. Donald had told them they should defend the antenna. He had obviously given them the message because he believed the antenna was about to be destroyed. They must assume, therefore, that the antenna *was* about to be destroyed. They could evaluate the message later.

Betzino raised objections. Could they trust Donald? Did they have enough information?

They argued for 11.7 seconds. At 11.8 seconds they transmitted the message to their backup transmission route. At 11.9 seconds, Varosa Uman's missile shattered the surface of the antenna and melted most of the metal veneer.

*   *   *

Varosa Uman had been searching for the alternate transmission route ever since Revutev Mavarka had told Betzino-Resdell it should create it. It couldn't be hidden forever. It had to include a second antenna and the antenna had to be located along the track the orbiter traced across the surface of the planet.

But it wouldn't expose itself until it was activated. It could lie dormant until the moment it transmitted. It could store a small amount of energy and expend it in a single pulse.

"Neutralize their orbiter," Mansita Jano said. "Isolate it."

Varosa Uman checked the track of the Betzino-Resdell orbiter. It had completed over half its orbit.

"And what happens when we give Trans Cultural the Message?" Varosa Uman asked. "After we've committed an overtly hostile act?"

"You've already committed an overtly hostile act. Trans Cultural knows my emissary had some kind of covert official support. Why are you hesitating, Overseer? What is your problem?"

Machines might be unimaginative but they were thorough. Ivan had designed the backup transmission route and he had built in all the redundancy he could squeeze out of the resources his colleagues had given him. Three high speed, low visibility airborne devices set off in three different directions as soon as they received the final message from the base. One stopped twelve kilometers from its starting point and relayed the message to a transmitter built into the highest tree on a small rise. The transmitter had been sucking energy from the tree's biochemistry for three years. It responded by concentrating all that accumulated energy into a single blip that shot toward a transmitter stored in a winged scavenger that circled over a grassy upland.

Varosa Uman's surveillance routine had noted the flying scavenger and stored it in a file that included several hundred items of interest. It picked up the blip as soon as the scavenger relayed it and narrowed the area in which its patrols were working their search patterns. A flyer that resembled a terrestrial owl suicide-bombed the hidden antenna half a second before the blip reached it.

The other two high speed airborne devices veered toward the northern and southern edges of the orbiter's track. Relays emitted their once-in-a-lifetime blasts and settled into permanent quiet.

The antenna located along the northern edge of the track succumbed to a double suicide by two slightly faster updates of the owlish suicider. The third antenna picked up the orbiter as the little ball raced over a dense forest. It fulfilled its destiny twenty seconds before a prepositioned missile splashed a corrosive liquid over the electronic veneer the antenna had spread across an abandoned nest.

Revutev Mavarka went into dormancy as if he was going to his death. He said goodbye to his closest friends. He crammed his detention quarters with images of his favorite scenes and events. He even managed to arrange a special meal and consume it with deliberate pleasure before they emptied out his stomach.

The only omission was a final statement to the public. A private message from Varosa Uman had curtailed his deliberations in that area. *Don't waste your time*, the Situation Overseer had said, and he had accepted her advice with the melancholy resignation of someone who knew his conscious life had to be measured in heartbeats, not centuries.

Four armed guards escorted him to his dormancy unit. A last pulse of fear broke through his self-control when he felt the injector touch his bare shoulder.

The top of the unit swung back. Varosa Uman looked down at him. Technicians were removing the attachments that connected him to the support system.

"Please forgive our haste," Varosa Uman said. "There will be no permanent damage."

There were no windows in the room. The only decoration was a street level cityscape that filled the wall directly in front of him. He was still lying on the medical cart that had trundled him through a maze of corridors and elevator rides but Varosa Uman's aides had raised his upper body and maneuvered him into a bulky amber wrapper before they filed out of the room.

"You're still managing the visitation, Overseer?"

"The Integrators won't budge," Varosa Uman said. "The Principals keep putting limits on my powers but they can't get rid of me."

He had been dormant for one hundred and three years. He had asked her as soon as he realized he was coming out of dormancy and she had handed him the information while they were working the wrapper around the tubes and wires that connected him to the cart.

"I've spent much of the last ten years trying to convince the Overseers they should let me wake you," Varosa Uman said. "I got you out of there as soon as they gave me permission."

"Before they changed their mind?"

A table with a flagon and a plate of food disks sat beside the cart. He reached for a disk and she waited while he put it in his mouth and savored his first chew.

"You want something from me," he said.

"The two visitors still have bases on the third moon of Widial—complete with backup copies of all their subunits. I want to contact them with an offer. We will try to guide their species through the Turbulence—try to help them find responses that will reduce the havoc. It's an idea I had earlier. I had a study group explore it. But I fell back into the pattern we've all locked into our reactions."

The men strolling through the cityscape were wearing tall hats and carrying long poles—a fashion that had no relation to anything Revutev Mavarka had encountered in any of the millennia he had lived through.

One hundred and three years....

"There are things we can tell them," Varosa Uman said. "We can end the cycle of attack and isolation every civilization in our section of the galaxy seems to be trapped in."

"You're raising an obvious question, Overseer."

"I want you to join me when I approach the visitors. I need support from the Adventurer community."

"And you think they'll fall in behind me?"

"Some of them will. Some of them hate you just as much as most serenes hate you. But you're a hero to forty percent of them. And the data indicate most of the rest should be recruitable."

He raised his arms as if he was orating in front of an audience. Tubes dangled from his wrists.

"Serenes and Adventurers will join together in a grand alliance! And present the humans with a united species!"

"I couldn't offer the humans a united front if every Adventurer on the planet joined us. We aren't a united species any more. We stopped being a united species when you sent your warning."

"You said you still had the support of the Integrators."

"There's been a revolt against the Integrators. Mansita Jano refused to accept their decision to keep me in charge of the Visitation."

"*We're at war?* We're going through another Turbulence?"

"No one has died. Yet. Hundreds of people have been forced into dormancy on both sides. Some cities are completely controlled by Mansita Jano's supporters. We have a serious rift in our society—so serious it could throw us into another Turbulence if we don't do something before more visitors arrive from the human system. If we make the offer and the humans accept—I think most people will fall in behind the idea."

"But you feel you need the support of the Adventurer community?"

"Yes."

The men in the cityscape tapped their poles when they stopped to talk. The ribbons dangling from the ends of the poles complemented the color of their facial feathers.

"That's a risk in itself, Overseer. Why would the serenes join forces with a mob of irresponsible risk takers? Why would anyone follow *me*? Everything they had ended when I sent my warning."

"You're underestimating yourself. You're a potent figure. I'll lose some serenes but the projections all indicate I'll get most of the Adventurer community in exchange. You may look like an irresponsible innovator to most serenes but most of your own people see you as an innovator who was willing to set a third of the galaxy on a new course."

"And what do you see, Varosa Uman?"

"I see an irresponsible interloper who may have opened up a new possibility. And placed our entire species in peril."

"And if I don't help you pursue your great enterprise I'll be shoved into a box."

"I want your willing cooperation. I want you to rally your community behind the biggest adventure our species has ever undertaken—the ultimate proof that we need people with your personality structure."

"You want to turn an irritating escapader into a prophet?"

"Yes."

"Speech writers? Advisers? Presentation specialists?"

"You'll get the best we have. I've got a communications facility in the next room. I'd like you to sit through a catchup review. Then we'll send a simultaneous transmission to both visitors."

"You're moving very fast. Are you afraid someone will stop you?"

"I want to present our entire population—opponents and supporters—with an accomplished act. Just like you did."

"They could turn on you just like they turned on me. The revolt against the Integrators could intensify. The humans may reject your offer."

"We've examined the possibilities. We can sit here and let things happen or we can take the best choice in a bad list and try to make it work."

"You're still acting like a gambler. Are you sure they didn't make a mistake when they classified you?"

"You take risks because you like it. I take risks because I have to."

"But you're willing to do it. You don't automatically reach for the standard course."

"Will you help me, Revutev Mavarka? Will you stand beside me in one of the boldest moments in the history of intelligence?"

"In the history of intelligence, Overseer?"

"That's what it is, isn't it? We'll be disrupting a chain of self-isolating intelligent species—a chain that's been creeping across our section of the galaxy for hundreds of millennia."

He picked up another food disk. It was dull stuff—almost tasteless—but it supplemented the nutrients from the cart with material that would activate his digestive path. It was, when you thought about it, exactly the kind of food the more extreme serenes would *want* to encounter when they came out of dormancy.

"Since you put it that way...."

Here's another approach to the issues raised by a powerful personality modification technology. "Legacies" looked at the subject from the viewpoint of the people who enforce the legal and moral rules imposed by society. This story, as the title notes, views it through the eyes of a character with a looser attitude.

THE PATH OF THE TRANSGRESSOR

Davin Sam owned a complete map of his wife's chromosomes and a detailed flow chart of her postnatal personality modification programs. Lizera had originally been designed for investors who were staffing a middle-level resort in the asteroid belt, back in the Solar System. Her designers had assumed she would spend most of her waking hours working but they had also realized she would have to relate to all kinds of people. She had been endowed with a strong appetite for learning, therefore, and a carefully measured artistic impulse. Today she had spent six hours sitting in a corner of Davin's observation tower, absorbed in her current reading program. The last time Davin had glanced at her reader she had been consuming a dissertation on the history of gunpowder military organization.

When Lizera had needed a break from reading, she had sealed herself inside a listening helmet and immersed herself in music. Usually she listened to Bach and the Chinese composers of the late twenty-first century. She played two instruments: a high quality electronic simulator and a classic Chinese qin.

There were days when Davin and Lizera prattled for hours while he kept one eye on the images on his screenbank. Sometimes Lizera played one of her instruments while he concentrated on his screens. Today, the only sounds Davin was interested in were the high pitched chatterings relayed through the loudspeakers. The lakenesters seemed to be engaging in a midwinter overhaul of their nest. Every animal in the nest seemed to be doing something.

The nest rose from the water two hundred meters from the lakeshore. Twelve of the fifty-seven animals in the nest had probes attached to their nervous systems. A hundred and twelve other probes had been attached to the structure of the nest. Davin could observe every tunnel and room. He could watch the transmissions from twenty probes at a time on his screenbank.

"I'm going back to the compound," Lizera said.

She didn't ask him if he minded if she left him alone. She knew his moods.

"I may spend the night here," Davin said.

"I'd be surprised if you didn't."

Davin didn't turn around until she was ready to leave. Then he gave her a quick up and down inspection. She had covered her gown with a red armored coat. A long gun rested in a holster built into the coat. A pair of sighting glasses covered her eyes. Their residential compound was only two kilometers from the tower, on top of a low hill, but they always went armed and armored when they traveled between the two sites.

Outside the tower, on the landward side, the winter wind bent the yellow grasses. Most of the scattered trees were bare. The rest still carried their yellow leaves.

The planet had been discovered by a Japanese probe and the Japanese had given it an apt name—Itoko, *cousin*. At first glance, the flora and fauna looked like simple variations on their Earth equivalents. There were ground creatures that resembled mammals. There were flying organisms that could be compared to birds and insects. The life forms were all constructed from complicated carbon-based molecules. But nothing was quite the same. The molecules that resembled amino acids had different chemical formulas. The molecule that performed the same function as chlorophyll produced plants that looked yellow, not green. The molecule that carried the genetic code was a self-replicating double helix, just like DNA, but it was constructed from a different set of bases, phosphates, and sugars and it responded to a different array of chemical signals when it performed its genetic functions.

Davin turned back to his screenbank and switched one of the screens to the camera that would track Lizera's progress. Two guardcats greeted her at the bottom of the stairs. One cat took up a position a few steps in front of her. The other cat fell in behind her.

Sometimes Davin watched her as she walked along the path they had worn between the tower and the compound. She was a fleshy, sinuously graceful woman. He could respond to the way she moved even when she was hidden inside the tent-like armored coat. The slightest movement of her clothes evoked an image of the body moving inside them. Today he kept his attention on the screenbank.

The lakenesters could be compared to beefy river otters or oversize water rats but no terrestrial aquatic mammal had ever developed the social organization that dominated their lifestyle. Their nests were constructed with techniques that required elaborate cooperation. They appeared to be slightly more intelligent than chimpanzees but no chimpanzee had ever used the kind of communication system they had developed. Their linguistic abilities couldn't be compared to anything humans had encountered on Earth.

The lakenesters weren't the only creatures on Itoko who had developed complicated vocal systems. The exploration surveys had discovered three other organisms that had become dependent on their ability to communicate. The packhunters that roamed across most of the planet's single continent seemed to be the most developed example. One of the probes had caught a brief glimpse of packhunters launching a coordinated attack on a lakenester stronghold, complete with wide flanking movements and intense assaults at single points.

Why had so many species developed the same ability? Was there some common genetic trait? Had the pressures of competition somehow pushed entirely different evolutionary lines in the same direction? Had the lakenesters become communicators because it was their best defense against the coordinated attacks of the packhunters?

In the Solar System, Davin had been an experimental ethologist. He had designed organisms with certain qualities and watched them interact with mammoth artificial habitats. Here he was exploring mysteries that had been created by the random, unpredictable process of natural selection. This lonely lakeshore, three thousand kilometers from the primary human base camp, was the most exciting place he had ever seen. For the first time in the history of his discipline, ethologists were studying the behavior of life forms that had been produced by a completely different evolutionary history.

The top screen on his bank was an oversize rectangle that displayed the current position of every animal in the nest. The computer took in all the information coming from the probes and assembled it into a complete picture. On the top screen, Davin could see the overall pattern in the lakenesters' project. On the other screens, he could observe the small scale maneuvering that made it all happen. The lakenesters had a social organization that resembled the system employed by the terrestrial apes called bonobos. A committee of females dominated the nest with techniques that included sexual rewards, coordinated acts of violence, and behavior that seemed to resemble cajoling and even joshing. Right now the "committee members" seemed to be all over the place.

Davin frowned. His attention jumped to the screen that was tracking his wife. Lizera was wading through grass that rose above her waist. The camera was angling to the left as it followed her. It should have been panning upward, toward the top of the screen.

He widened the view and discovered she had already put ten meters between herself and the path. Her guardcats were rearing up on their hind legs so they could see over the grass. She started to move forward, toward the residential compound, and stopped after she'd taken three steps. She stared at something on her right and edged to the left.

Davin activated his communications implant. "What's going on? Why aren't you using the path?"

"There's something happening with the packhunters. They keep jumping up in front of me when I start toward the compound."

"When you start toward the compound? That's the only time they do it?"

"Some of them just jumped up when I started walking back to the path."

"How many do you see when they jump up?"

"It's just four or five when they jump up. But I think I've got the whole pack around me. I can hear them all around me."

"It sounds like they're herding you, doesn't it?"

"Just like they herd their prey animals? Do you really think they'd do that?"

The packhunters were the size of small terrestrial pigs. They had fangs and claws but they weren't particularly strong or fast. They killed larger animals by harassing them until they were too exhausted to struggle.

Davin stared at his screenbank. Three of the lakenester females were chattering at a young male-female pair.

"Stay there. I'll be there in a minute."

"Can't I just keep pushing forward, Davin? They're used to frightening animals. They might not attack if I just kept coming."

"We don't know how they're going to act. I'll bring the other two cats. We'll have them and two guns."

Davin's outdoor equipment was stored on a hanger and shelf arrangement near the door. He kept his eyes on the screens while he worked his shoulders into his armored coat. His upper body had been bulking up ever since he had started working in the planet's gravitational field. His parents had opted for a muscular body type when they had chosen his specifications and the extra gravity had given him an exaggerated version of their choice.

"You should have alerted me as soon as this happened," Davin said.

"I didn't want you to leave the tower. Not now."

He settled the sighting glasses into position and verified they were calibrated with his eye movements. "It's all being recorded. I won't lose a thing."

The wind would have caught an Earth-reared human by surprise. From inside the tower, the grass had looked like it was swaying in response to a moderate terrestrial wind. On Itoko, the grasses were made of stiffer stuff. The planet moved through its seasons twice as fast as Earth did. The rapid changes in climate produced powerful air movements.

His guardcats fell into position front and back as he started loping toward Lizera. In the grass, about a hundred meters out, raspy voices exchanged rapid-fire signals. Two round, khaki colored heads bobbed above the grass on his left. Another head popped up on his right. He looked back and glimpsed a flash of movement.

He subvocalized the nonsense word that activated his communications implant. "It looks like they're herding me, too. I don't see any of them in front of me. It looks like they're trying to herd me toward you."

Lizera chuckled. "Does that mean they think we're harmless?"

"It could. It would certainly give us an advantage if it did."

"I'm sorry, Davin. I didn't mean to cause you so much trouble. I tried to get around them."

"It's all right. I just wish I knew why they suddenly decided to turn on us."

"Is it possible we smell different? Did we eat something different?"

Davin had activated his auxiliary intelligence as he ran. He had been exchanging data with the three research teams that were studying the packhunters. Now he let his retrieval program run through all his internal packhunter files, searching for clues to the sudden change in the creatures's behavior. So far, he had only had two hostile encounters with the packhunters. The local pack had made two attempts to enter the compound. The attack had stopped, both times, when the electric hedge had hit the intruders with near-lethal jolts.

Davin had been confident the packhunters had assaulted the hedge because it had usurped one of their established observation points. There had been no indication they were interested in him or Lizera. He had walked between the tower and the compound for three tendays before he had let Lizera make the trip. The packhunters had started losing interest before the end of the first tenday. Up until now, it had seemed safe to assume their appetites were linked to the odors emitted by the native biochemistry.

The best information on the packhunters had been produced by a couple who were studying them on the other side of the continent, in an area just north of the central mountains. The couple had paired on the ship, sometime during the last thirty years of the voyage. They had never done any ethological research but they had thought it would be a good way to familiarize themselves with the planet. They had come to Davin for mentoring when one of his awake periods had overlapped one of theirs. The woman was the adventurer in the pair. The man seemed to be following her lead. They had smiled, now and then, when Davin had let his enthusiasm for his subject run away with him. They had always been polite to Lizera.

The packhunters were very territorial. The packs had a dominant male and female and the males were primarily responsible for the defense of the territory. The dominant female and her subordinate females did most of the hunting. Their major prey animal in this part of the continent was a horned creature about five times their size. Their relationship with the prey animal had developed some of the characteristics of a shepherd relationship. They harried the prey animals away from the territorial borders when they wandered too close. They attacked solitary hunters such as the big, muscular predators who occasionally ventured out of the mountain forests.

Davin was studying the lakenesters but he had kept an eye on the packhunters and passed his observations to the packhunter specialists. Two tendays ago, when the trees were still losing their leaves, he had realized there had been a big drop in the number of prey animals he observed. Then he had spotted two dead packhunters lying near the lake. He had noted, through his telescope, that they both had twisted, damaged legs. Had another pack invaded the territory and driven off the local herd? The packhunter researchers had all plagued him for more information. Lizera had spent several days observing the packhunters from the tower. But Davin didn't have the equipment to observe wide-ranging organisms.

If an invading pack really had driven off the prey animals, it would be the first time anyone had observed serious intra-species aggression among packhunters. The packhunter researchers all agreed it would indicate inter-pack relations were more complex than they had realized. *We've been assuming they occasionally fight over territory*, one of them had noted. *Now we're discovering they may engage in rustling behavior.*

Were the packhunters hungry enough they were willing to attack a pair of chemically strange bipeds? Could their intelligence override the information provided by their senses?

Davin stopped beside Lizera. Most of the packhunters were hidden by the grass but he was surrounded by their voices—a continuous, unbroken din of rasping vocalizations. The packhunter observers had decided the packs used a pseudo-language composed of nine syllables arranged in over two hundred combinations. Eighty of the combinations could be used to denote position and direction. Some of the observers had detected indications that the dominant female was the coordinator. She could hold every animal's position in her head, according to that theory, and issue orders that created organized attacks. Others felt the coordination was more informal. The packhunters listened to each other, they argued, and each animal responded to the actions of the others.

Davin's observations of the lakenesters indicated his animals used both methods. Sometimes the dominant females seemed to issue direct orders to their underlings. Other times everybody seemed to just know what to do.

Signals passed between Davin's communication implant and the guardcats' control units. Two of the guardcats took up positions in the rear. The other two posted themselves on the sides.

"This may explain why there's so much activity in the nest," Davin said. "The nesters may have sensed the packhunters are getting more aggressive. If the packhunters' meat supply got herded away...."

Lizera nodded. She never commented on Davin's scientific speculations. She understood he just needed to know someone was listening to him.

Davin turned his attention to his auxiliary intelligence and checked his physiological status charts. He had suspended his fatigue feedback responses when the lakenesters had started their surge of activity. If he didn't scan his charts every ten or fifteen minutes, he would keep going until he collapsed.

"I think we should try your idea," Davin said. "We should run at them as fast as we can. And shoot them if they get in our way. Do you think you can stick with me?"

"I'll stay as close to you as I can."

She wasn't afraid. She had been given a rudimentary capacity for fear. She wouldn't panic just because she was under a lot of pressure, either. She would stay calm and rational.

Overall, she had very limited survival responses. Davin had never thought of it that way, but it was true. He was just as calm as she was but he could sense the anxieties his modifications were controlling. His brain manufactured peptides that settled a layer of calm over his emotions when he was faced with a crisis. But the other emotions were still there. That was a standard genetic modification. Lizera's genetic designers had assumed she would never have to face physical danger. They had strengthened the emotional responses that would help her do her job and neglected—or even weakened—any responses that might interfere.

Davin studied the grass through his sighting glasses. "I'll shoot the animals directly in front of me. You take anything you see on the left front. That way we won't waste shots firing at the same targets."

She looked up at him. Her eyes looked very large. "Are you sure you have the energy reserves, Davin? You haven't slept since the lakenesters started this new phase. You've been working without a break for over a hundred hours. You haven't been eating that much either. I've watched you."

"I just checked. I'm fine."

"I could run at them by myself. While you stand back and keep me covered."

"We'll do it together. This is no time to take chances. We don't know what's going on."

He turned away from her. Commands flowed from his communications implant to the guardcats. "Let's go."

Four packhunters rose above the grass before he finished his third stride. They jumped straight up with their lips pulled back over their teeth. Screechy wails replaced the rasps.

Individually they didn't look that dangerous. Their faces resembled scaled up versions of the miniature mammals the genetic designers had created for people who lived in cramped quarters and liked lovable, perennial juvenile animals. They had flat snouts and big eyes. Their ears were erect and alert. Their round bodies were covered with a sleek material that looked like it would evoke a pleasant response if you stroked it. Individually, they were about as threatening as an unarmed child.

He rested the sighting glasses on the animal directly in front of him. His brain radioed a fire command to the gun. His arms moved the gun across the packhunter. Two shots cracked at the moment the gun decided it was properly aligned with the target selected by the glasses.

The packhunter's wail ended in an abrupt, choked off gasp. Davin turned his glasses on the animal on its right. He was holding the gun with two hands, left hand on the barrel, to steady it against the recoil. In the Solar System, he had spent his whole life in windless, hollowed out asteroids. The guns he had fired had hurled lightweight anesthetic pellets. The working components in the pellets had been molecular machines that neutralized neurotransmitters. On Itoko the pellets had to be heavier and the biochemists still hadn't analyzed the structures of most of the local biological molecules. The moles in his pellets were crude devices that indiscriminately destroyed any big molecules they encountered.

A message from the left guardcat grabbed his attention before he could fire. He swung around and discovered the cat was embroiled in combat. He couldn't see all the details through the grass but it looked like it was being attacked by four packhunters. His glasses settled on a patch of khaki flank. The gun fired twice. The packhunter's back arched. He turned his glasses toward the next target he had selected and found he had nothing to shoot at. The other three packhunters had disappeared into the grass.

The cat hobbled forward in response to Davin's continuing command to keep advancing. He ran to it through the grass and saw it was dragging its left rear leg.

He ordered a full-alert halt. The cats fell into on guard positions and he bent over the wounded animal.

The euthanasia command required the cat's ID and two other code words. He subvocalized them methodically, carefully waiting for the confirming pings.

He stood up and tried to get a solid grip on the situation. Lizera had been a good three strides behind him when he had stopped the advance. She was a healthy woman with a lot of stamina but her hippy body wasn't built for running.

"I'm going to put the cats at our sides and our rear," he said. "I think we should move forward even if the packhunters attack the cats. They don't know what the guns can do. That's our secret weapon. They seem to understand the cats are a threat. They don't know how dangerous we are."

He pointed at a spot about two steps to his left. "I think you should position yourself there. I'll pace myself to you. Try to move as fast as you can. Don't wear yourself out—just try to push yourself some."

Lizera waded through the grass and placed herself where he wanted her. He lowered his head and concentrated on the ceaseless clamor from the packhunters. There were five animals in front of them—maybe six.

This time he deliberately took shorter steps. His gun cracked as soon as the first heads appeared over the grass. The animal he was firing at dropped and he swung on the animal on its left. He couldn't hear Lizera's gun over the din but he saw the animal closest to her stretch to its full length in the middle of a leap.

The grass was thrashing above the first packhunter he had shot. The second target dropped as if the moles had touched something vital as soon as they made contact. The three cats were all signaling they were under attack. On his right, through the grass, he could see the guardcat on that flank twisting and clawing.

His emotional enhancements were performing just like they were supposed to. He had never been in physical danger before but he was responding as if he were involved in an intense, highly competitive game that he desperately wanted to win. He was totally focused on the situation he was facing but there was no danger he would be paralyzed by fear.

His implant pinged. A signal from the rear cat's control unit advised him the cat was no longer effective. Wails rose behind him. He looked back and located four places where the packhunters were creating ripples as they plowed through the grass.

Lizera had fallen a step behind, in spite of his best efforts to match her pace. Davin lurched across the distance between them and took up a position behind her. He stepped backward with his eyes on the oncoming ripples.

"Keep moving forward. There's four of them attacking our rear. I'm certain they're still trying to harass us. They don't come in for the kill until their prey animal starts to behave like it's exhausted."

"Is the rear cat dead?"

"Probably."

"What side should I take?"

Davin smiled. She might not be a runner but her brain could size up a tactical situation just as well as his could—even if she normally let him take the lead.

"Left. You fire at any animals on your left and our front. I'll take my left and our rear."

The ripples split about thirty meters out. Two went right, one left. The fourth came straight at him. Davin settled his sighting glasses on a point just in front of the ripple. Had any of the packhunter researchers mentioned that they switched to wails when they charged? This was not, obviously, the most felicitous moment to search his internal files.

His eyes picked up their first glimpse of a hurtling khaki head. He started to fire and then repressed the command. The animal had veered off to his right. Another incoming ripple caught his attention on his left and he twisted around and kept it in his sights until it, too, veered away.

The four packhunters harried their quarry for almost ten minutes. They coordinated their rushes so two animals were always charging in at the same time. The rest of the pack formed a wide outer ring around the two humans and kept up their endless exchange of signals. Heads popped above the grass as if they were making quick observations and relaying the information to the four animals who were conducting the actual attacks. It was a time consuming hunting technique but Davin could see its advantages. He had watched the lakenesters' defensive behavior when they came on land searching for the roots and shrubs they lived on. They always moved in groups of three or four and they had claws and teeth that could inflict serious wounds. The packhunters' tactics would offer the meat eaters the maximum gain with the minimum threat of injury. If the prey animals dropped their guard, the quartet could be on them in seconds. If the prey animals kept circling and maneuvering, they would eventually succumb to exhaustion.

A second quartet charged in as soon as the first one withdrew. Lizera had managed to kill one animal as it turned away from them. She had advanced about fifteen steps with Davin edging along backward behind her. Davin kept trying to move faster but he couldn't. The packhunters might be harassing them but he couldn't just assume they would keep veering away if he and Lizera broke into an all-out run. The animals were making real threats.

It had been Lizera's body-type that had first attracted Davin. Soft flesh and rounded curves might not maximize a woman's ability to run but they were wonderful physical attributes if you were looking for someone you could hold and caress. Lizera had been the hostess in charge of a twelve-suite bloc in her resort. She had been the human interface between the guests and the software that actually ran the place—the personable, infinitely unruffled, unsimulated personality who appeared at your door when you wanted a special service or needed help with a malfunction. The resort had run a routine databank check on Davin and assigned him to a bloc run by a woman who matched the physical/personality type he seemed to prefer.

Davin had asked for only one modification when he decided to marry her. From now on, he would be the primary object of her urge to accommodate and get along. Lizera agreed and the combine that ran the resort put her through a twelve-eday modification. A segment of her postnatal personality processing was gently removed and a new module was added. The whole procedure was strictly voluntary. There was no coercion. Lizera wanted to be married, the combine received a third of Davin's monetary wealth.

It had seemed like a reasonable thing to do at the time. Davin had already been through three marriages and several unsuccessful pairings. He knew several other people, of both sexes, who had settled into tranquil relationships with geisha companions. He knew there was a prejudice against it but he had decided the benefits would outweigh the social disapproval he would encounter. Lizera wouldn't orate about his "fondness for social isolation" the way his first wife had. She wouldn't fret, like his third wife, because he left her to her own devices when he became absorbed in his research.

"How many do we have to shoot before they leave us alone?" Lizera said. "Shouldn't we reach a limit at some point?"

"I'm going to call for help. This isn't going to be as easy as I thought it would be."

"They seem so intelligent. You'd think they'd figure out what the guns can do."

The compound contained a relay to the communications satellites the debarkation committee had posted shortly after the starship orbited the planet. Davin activated the emergency routine in his communications implant and paired the transmission with a request for information on the positions of all the currently operational air vehicles.

The Voice of the communications system advised him his call was being answered by Wangessi Mazelka. It was a name that evoked a catalog of associations.

"Greetings, Davin. What's the problem?"

Davin followed a ripple with his glasses, watching for a clear shot at a patch of hide. The second packhunter quartet was using a different tactic. They came in very fast, one after the other, without let up, but their rushes ended when they were still five meters out.

"There's been a change in the packhunters' behavior. They've started attacking us. There's a possibility they're going after us because their main food supply got run off a few days ago. We're surrounded out in the open. Between our compound and the observation tower I've been using. I thought we could fight our way free but we're having problems. They've already killed all four of our guardcats. Can you get us help before it gets dark?"

Davin's auxiliary intelligence had transmitted a map to his brain. The nearest air vehicle was an airship that was located about two hundred and fifty kilometers to the east—about two hours travel time, given neutral winds. The second closest vehicle was an airship that was about four hours to the south.

"What kind of help do you need?"

"We just need a pickup that will get us back to the compound. That's all it will take."

"For two people?"

Davin settled his glasses on a second incoming ripple. The animal he had been following had veered off to the right.

He cut the link to his implant. "Keep moving forward," he said to Lizera. "Take every bit of ground you can."

He turned his attention back to Wangessi. "Lizera was walking back to the compound from the tower when they attacked. I thought the two of us could break through their ring. But they're harder to deal with than I thought. Right now they've practically got us immobilized. We're barely making progress."

"You can't just shoot them?"

"We've killed six so far."

"And they still haven't learned what the guns can do?"

Lizera's gun cracked. She took two long strides and Davin threw a glance over his shoulder and backed up after her.

"I got him," Lizera said. "He's thrashing around in the grass."

"It's going to be dark in about three hours," Davin told Wangessi. "The *North Wind* could get to us in about two hours. It looks to me like we're going to need it."

Wangessi paused. "The *North Wind* is on a priority one mission, Davin. I can't divert it without asking for authority."

"And how long will that take?"

"*If* I can get the authority—*if*—it will be about an hour. But I should warn you— don't assume I can get it."

"You've got two people being attacked in an open field!"

"The *North Wind* is taking supplies all the way to North Inlet. We're talking about a gasbag that's operating at maximum range, Davin. It's bucking the wind all the way. If we divert it—we may have to recall it and give the engines a full recharge."

Three ripples were racing back to the outer circle. Four more ripples were cutting toward them.

"I'm taking a step," Lizera said. "There's a little hump you need to step over."

Davin raised his right leg and backed up with her. He gave his auxiliary intelligence an order and it started rummaging through the public files. The *North Wind* was carrying three passengers. The second name on the list was a brain-machine specialist named G.G. Ying.

"Can you give it a try?" Davin said.

"The *Yellow Grass Express* is only four hours away. You'll just be saving an hour if we discuss your request for an hour and divert the *North Wind*."

"I'd still appreciate it if you'd give it a try."

"It's not going to be an easy case to make, Davin. You've got night vision modules. I presume you're properly armored. You do have your boots on, right? And your armored coats?"

"We never go out in the open without them. I wouldn't have called you if we were just facing half a dozen of the things. We're fighting a large, well coordinated pack. I don't know what these things are capable of."

"I can see why you're worried. I'd probably call for help in the same situation. Why take chances? Unfortunately I can see how the directors might have other ideas."

"I'm having enough trouble seeing them in the grass now. If they came at us in the night—the best night vision glasses in the arsenal wouldn't be good enough in that situation."

"I'm just giving you my best opinion. If you want me to ask for the closest ship, I will. It's up to you. "

"Then please consider this a formal request for the quickest help available. You might point out that we may have to kill every animal in the pack if they keep on behaving the way they've been behaving."

"I'll do what I can, Davin. If that's your decision.…"

Davin's implant had already alerted G.G. Ying. She responded as soon as Wangessi cut the link and Davin filled her in on the situation.

"You should have asked for the *Yellow Grass*. You'll be lucky if Wangessi only stalls for an hour."

"That's why I'm calling you. If you override the Voice on your ship—and start it moving this way before he gets the authorization—"

"I'm taking a step," Lizera said.

Davin watched a ripple on his left flank as he eased himself back. G.G. still hadn't answered him when he finished the step.

"There's two other passengers on this ship, Davin. What am I supposed to tell them?"

"You don't need their permission to override the Voice. Anybody can do it."

"That's not the issue. They've got business, too. They've got a right to be involved in the decision."

"You've got two people in serious danger. Don't you think that will mean anything to them?"

"At this moment, Davin, I don't know what it would mean to anybody. You've been sitting out there all by yourself for almost twenty tendays. I don't think you realize how much influence the moral crusaders have been piling up. Do you think I'd be taking this trip all by myself if I could have brought Lan?"

"You're going to have to change course anyway when you get the authorization. You'll just be anticipating it—so you can get here before nightfall."

"You're not hearing what I'm saying. I didn't even ask them if I could bring Lan. I'm going to be spending five tendays all by myself when there's absolutely no need for it. They could have put another passenger on this gasbag without dropping a single kilo of cargo. Wangessi isn't your only problem. Nobody of any importance is going to get excited if we and our disturbing little geishas vanish from the scene. Most of the rest of the populace will just shrug it off and attend to their own business."

Davin's gun cracked. His target had been a small, barely visible patch of khaki but he had given the fire order anyway.

"I want to help you," G.G. said. "I want to help you. But I wouldn't be doing either of us one atom of good if I ignored the present political situation and pulled this ship off course. I'd just be giving them a chance to attack me. There's a lot of decent people in this community. But right now the fanatics seem to be in charge. I'm sorry I can't help you. But I can't. Believe me—I can't."

"The connection has been terminated," the Voice of Davin's implant advised him.

"I'm taking a step," Lizera said.

Davin had been running experiments for almost thirty years when he married Lizera. The two artificial habitats he worked with had been created by communities of engineers and life scientists who had shaped them over four decades. The interiors of two asteroids had been transformed into complex environments occupying thousands of cubic kilometers. His Solar System career had ended when both communities had rejected his latest research proposals. The woman who brought him the second rejection explained the situation in words that had obviously been planned and rehearsed.

"The feelings on this issue are very strong," the woman said. "We realize you aren't the only person in the Solar System with this kind of marital arrangement. The committee wants you to know it feels your work has been exceptionally creative—extremely promising. But there are people on the committee who feel they can't compromise. Our entire organizational structure would collapse if you continued working with us over their objections."

Davin had first met G.G. Ying when she had approached him at the beginning of his second awake on the ship. She had been forming an "informal support network" for people who shared their "problem with social attitudes."

"We got on this ship because they had some very tolerant people on the selection committee," G.G. said. "But don't think that's going to last. There are going to be power shifts once we reach our destination. We've violated a taboo that turns millions of people into zealots."

There had been four thousand people on the ship. Forty-three had geisha spouses or sexual companions. Davin stayed on the fringes of G.G.'s group but he knew it was necessary. He had been forced out of the Solar System, after all, by the reactions of the "zealots."

Davin had been given a muscular body because his father had believed muscle was still useful, even when you lived in low gravity environments. His genetic designer had maximized his intelligence because both his parents had known he would be competing with contemporaries whose parents had maximized their intelligence. He could concentrate on one subject for days at a time because his mother insisted that the ability to concentrate was just as important as intelligence. He felt comfortable in social groups because his father felt amiability was another useful trait.

Human beings had been debating the rights and wrongs of personality modification and genetic enhancement since they had first acquired the ability to remake themselves. A consensus had been arrived at—a consensus that was embodied in laws and social customs that were accepted in every major society in the Solar System. Davin accepted the consensus. He supported the laws. "Human beings are an end, not a means," Davin had argued in his youthful discussions. "My parents gave me modifications that would help *me* make *my* way in the world. They didn't try to create someone who would satisfy *their* whims. And *their* needs."

Davin had looked up the history of the word geisha. Originally, it had referred to a woman who had been trained to be a pleasing companion to men. There had even been an indication the companionship didn't have to involve sex. It had only become a term of contempt in the last two hundred years, as humans had mastered the physiological and post-natal factors that shaped personality.

He had made three attempts at marriage. His second marriage had lasted over twelve years. No one had designed a woman just for him. Lizera had already existed when he had made his bargain with her employers. She had been created in an illegal people shop years before he met her. She had only made one modification just for him. And she had done it voluntarily.

"*Davin.* In front. *Look.*"

Davin turned his head. Twelve ripples were arrowing toward Lizera. Her head moved from side to side as she trained her sighting glasses on the middle four.

Davin made a half turn, so he could concentrate on the front and keep an eye on the rear. The twelve wails interlaced like the voices in the Bach fugues Lizera played on her simulator.

His glasses rested on a round khaki face. His gun cracked. Lizera fired. His eyes searched for another target.

The ripples veered away. His brain registered a glimpse of flank and the gun fired again.

"I'm going to run forward," Lizera said. "While they're turning away from us."

She lurched forward before she had finished talking. The stream at the bottom of the hill was only a couple of hundred meters away. Davin ran along behind her, scuttling sideways every other step so he could watch their rear. It was an awkward way to run but he stayed with her.

"Go for the stream," Davin said. "Forget the bridge. We'll wade the stream."

They would still have another three hundred meters to go when they crossed the stream. The packhunters could cross the stream, too, and block their front again. But for now the stream was a goal. For now he could forget about what happened after they crossed it.

"On the left front," Lizera said. "Four."

Lizera was responding to the situation as if she had spent her whole life fighting strange animals. And why shouldn't she? At the resort, she had managed complex machine systems and dealt with the unpredictable crises created by human emotions.

Davin turned and spotted the four ripples. This time there was no wailing. The only animals who were making comments were the packhunters in the outer circle.

The two ripples on the flanks turned slightly as they reached the ten meter mark. Davin automatically assumed they were veering. Then he realized they weren't. They were racing toward their quarry from four different angles.

He settled his glasses on one of the center ripples. A tan shape burst from the grass. His gun cracked. The animal stumbled toward him, carried forward by the impetus of its charge, and Davin jumped back.

A second animal darted past his leg. It turned its head as it ran past and slashed at his coat with its fangs. He swung the gun around but it disappeared into the grass before he could fire. The animal he had shot was thrashing a step from his boots. Its left eye looked up at him.

Lizera had already started running toward the stream. The animal she had hit had stopped moving. The moles had opened a huge hole in the right side of its skull. Davin hustled after Lizera and caught up with her before she had traveled five more steps. Behind him, the two animals that had survived the attack were rasping messages at their packmates.

"Four on the left front," Lizera said. "Four more on the center front."

"Keep running."

This time the attackers started rasping as they approached the ten meter point. They widened the distance between ripples and closed in with their voices clattering like high speed machines.

The first leap overwhelmed the chemical alterations that were supposed to be controlling Davin's startle reaction. He jumped back as soon as he saw the compact khaki missile hurtling toward his face. His elbow stabbed into Lizera's side.

Two more animals flew at him in a tightly bunched pair. This time his emotional modifications managed to assert themselves. The gun came up as he stepped into their leap. He had seen recordings of this kind of attack. Normally the packhunters finished their standard prey animal with runs at the quarry's legs. With larger animals they sometimes took to the air and tried to weaken the prey animal by savaging its back.

He fired two shots at the target on the right and twisted out of the way. The animal he had shot crumpled onto its side as it hit the ground. The other animal disappeared into the grass.

"Watch your right," Davin said.

Four more ripples were plowing toward them. The gabfest in the outer circle rose to a crescendo. Four khaki missiles burst out of the grass at the same time. Davin's gun cracked. A solid mass slammed into his chest.

Davin stumbled back. Claws scraped on his coat. He stretched his arm out to the side and managed to point the gun at the thing's shoulder. His brain transmitted a fire command. A round face looked up at him. The animal's mouth opened. It slid down his coat and he lurched away from it. Lizera was lying on her back with two packhunters covering most of her body. She had stuck her right arm out of the pile and maneuvered her gun into a firing position next to the packhunter who was attacking her upper body. Davin trained his gun on the other animal and fired two bursts.

Four blotches appeared on the animal's back. Its head snapped around. The area behind its front shoulders collapsed as if some invisible object had hammered it with bone breaking force. It collapsed on top of Lizera with its voice rasping out a string of syllables.

Davin grabbed the animal by its neck and jerked it off Lizera. She had killed the other one and she was pulling herself out from under. The animal Davin had killed had pushed her coat up her leg, above her boots. Her thigh was covered with blood. Claw marks had created a pattern of lines in the blood.

Davin fought back the impulse to crouch beside her and examine the wound. He stayed on his feet and watched the grass for another attack. Lizera wiggled away from the animals and raised herself on her elbows. She pulled the coat higher and studied her leg.

"I can't make the knee bend," she said. "I think it ripped up some muscle. Or maybe a tendon. I can still wiggle my toes. But I can't make the rest of the leg do anything."

She had been given the standard pain and anti-shock enhancements, just like "proper" humans. She could uncouple the chemical pathways that produced pain. She could reduce major blood loss to a minor seep. The packhunter had turned her leg into a junk heap of blood and mangled flesh but that was a minor matter. The medical unit in their compound contained routines that could replace entire limbs.

Davin glanced at the display on his gun. The cassette still held eight seconds of energy in its battery—enough to fire nearly eighty more rounds. The spare cassette in his right cargo pocket could fire another two hundred rounds.

He knelt beside Lizera. "Put your arm around my neck. Try to hold onto your gun with your other hand."

"That's stupid, Davin. You can't get past them carrying me."

He stared at her. He was already carrying an emotional overload. He would have been paralyzed if he had been functioning without his enhancements.

And now he had to cope with this.

Did she really consider herself *discardable*?

He couldn't challenge her feelings. They were built into her. He had to accept them as a given. He had to start with a crazy premise and try to be logical. Factual. "We're just a hundred meters from the stream," he said. "We've been killing them right and left. This can't go on forever."

"And what do we do when we cross the stream? You're not being rational, Davin. We both know you could run right through them if you were out here by yourself."

He pulled her right arm around his neck. He fitted his shoulder under her arm and started to haul them both erect. "We'll try for that clump of trees on the other side of the stream. On top of that little rise. We'll get to that and wait to be rescued."

"Davin—"

"You can hold on and let me have both hands free to hold the gun. Or you can make me hold you. And force me to shoot with one hand."

Her arm tightened around his neck. She clutched at a fold of his coat to give herself better support.

"We must have killed a third of the things by now," Davin said. "They have to give up sooner or later."

"They're acting like those generals that kept throwing troops at the first automatic powder guns. They act so intelligent. And they still can't figure out what we're doing."

That's it. Just do that. Make conversation. Show me you're all right. Concentrate on that.

Three nights ago—before the lakenesters had started their new behavior pattern—he had put his work out of his mind and they had spent a long evening together. They drank teas that filled their little living space with warm, delicate odors. Lizera knelt behind her qin, in the classic fashion, while he sprawled in front of her and watched her fingers float across the long strings. A filmy robe hung from her shoulders. He could study the smoothness of her thighs, tightened by the kneeling position, as the folds of the robe shifted around her.

You didn't think of her thigh as a mechanism that moved her from one point to another when you watched her at moments like those.

He forced a heavy, lumbering trot out of his own muscles. There were five packhunters directly in front of him, judging by the racket. He tried to shoot at two of them when they jumped up but he couldn't bring the gun around in time.

Four ripples cleaved the grass on his right. "What's your gun good for?" Davin said.

"Six seconds."

"Start firing bursts at the ripple on the left. I'll fire at the other three. Don't try to conserve ammunition. Train your glasses on the ripple and keep sending fire commands."

He planted his own sighting glasses on the right center ripple. There was no command for continuous firing. You transmitted repeats of the fire command as fast as you could think it and the gun fired two-pellet bursts every time it located the target.

He turned away from the first ripple and started firing at the ripple next to it. There wasn't time to make sure he had damaged his first target. He couldn't wait for the animals to break cover. He couldn't stop a flying assault with Lizera clinging to him.

The fourth animal soared out of the grass as he was turning his glasses on it. A khaki ball hurtled toward his face. He pressed his left hand against Lizera's side and pushed her away from him. The gun cracked.

He dropped to one knee and threw himself on top of Lizera. The animal landed two steps from his head. Clumps of dirt and grass spattered on his coat. He lifted his head and jumped up as soon as he realized the packhunter was clawing the ground as it died.

He pressed the release button on the side of the gun. The empty cassette popped out. He slipped the spare into the slot. He scanned the grass for more ripples.

He knelt beside Lizera and helped her drape her arm over his shoulder. He stood up and lunged toward the stream. Khaki heads bobbed above the grass in front of him. The clamor rose to another crescendo.

"If I could just locate the dominant female," Davin said. "If we could eliminate her...."

"She's probably keeping low. Like most generals."

"And keeping everybody's position in her head? From their signals? It's possible. But it's an idea with a lot of implications—level of intelligence, information processing ability.... It could also explain why they keep coming. She isn't seeing what's happening. She just knows some of them are dying."

Lizera laughed. "Don't you ever stop working, Davin? Are you going to post a paper on this?"

Once again he was running—lurching to be more precise—toward the animals directly in front of him. His gun cracked every time he saw a head. The grass shook where one had dropped down and he veered a few degrees to the right and ran straight at it.

"We may have a hole there. Watch our left."

The noise rose to a crescendo. The circle seemed to be getting smaller. He got a brief glance of the mangled head of the animal he had hit. Then he was splashing through the stream, feeling the water rise to his knees as they approached the center.

Splashes erupted on both sides. The pack was racing across the stream to get ahead of him. Eyes stared at him as they hurried across. Voices chatted up and down the line.

"It looks like they're back to trying to run us into the ground," Davin said.

"Maybe they're learning something after all."

Could the packhunters be organized according to the queen bee pattern? Had the dominant female been stubbornly following tactics that had worked in the past because she wasn't concerned about casualties?

If she was behaving like a queen bee, her primary concern could be her personal survival and the survival of her own young. Casualties weakened the pack but they also meant there would be fewer mouths when they finally settled down to dinner.

There was a natural tendency to assume a highly developed language had to be associated with intelligence. But did that have to be true? Bees had language, after all. Could an animal use language to coordinate a library of stereotyped attacks? If you assumed their linguistic abilities used up most of their brain space...

He struggled through the bushes that crowded the edge of the stream. Watery ground sucked at his boots. The trees he had picked for a goal belonged to a stubby, multi-trunked species that had already lost most of its leaves. The rise was only four steps high and it was located just two steps beyond the bushes.

He looked back as he reached the top and brought the gun around one handed. Two animals were crossing the stream behind him. He fired three bursts and they both collapsed before they reached the edge of the water.

There were four trees in the cluster. The biggest was about twice as tall as Davin. Most of the packhunters were spread out in an arc on this side of the stream, judging by the racket and the heads that popped above the grass. Two or three of them seemed to be posted on the other side of the stream.

Davin glanced at the sun. "Do they sound like they're feeling a little less energetic?"

"Perhaps. It's possible."

"We've still got almost two hours to night. I'll give G.G. another call. If they think they've got us cornered...."

Lizera shrugged. "Do you think I can lie down? I think we should both be conserving energy."

Davin lowered her to the ground as he activated his communications implant. She rested her back against a tree trunk and he stood up and started systematically monitoring the landscape.

He hadn't checked his status charts when he started carrying her. Now he gave them a quick look and got the answer he had expected. He was approaching the edge of the yellow zone. If he had taken a few more steps, his auxiliary intelligence would have started nagging him with a series of one minute warnings.

He wouldn't collapse merely because his muscles had missed three sleep periods. The human body could tolerate a hundred hours without sleep. The big problem was the enhancements that removed toxins from his brain. Everything had its price. The enhancements kept his brain cells neat and well scrubbed but they placed a critical extra demand on his energy reservoirs.

He dictated a description of their situation and transmitted copies to G.G. Ying and Wangessi Mazelka. He waited for two minutes, timing himself by his clock implant, and called G.G. direct.

G.G. answered his third try. "The answer is still no, Davin. Get me an order from the proper authorities and I'll turn this thing around the moment I know it's real. But I'm not going to do it on my own. That's exactly what people like Wangessi are waiting for—a perfect excuse to squash the most active person in our group."

"She can't walk, G.G. I'm not embellishing the situation. I had to haul her the last hundred meters. I'll have to haul her another three hundred meters uphill if we don't get help."

"But *you're* unwounded. *You're* in one piece. And I gather *you* aren't running out of ammunition."

Davin turned away from Lizera. He was holding himself rigid while he subvocalized but he knew she could pick up every flicker of emotion that crossed his face. Her ability to read body language had been an important part of her design specifications.

"You said we would help each other," Davin said. "We were all supposed to help each other."

"And how much help have you given the group? If you'd kept in touch with us while you were out there in the field pursuing your scientific ambitions, you might have some idea what we're up against. Have you heard from Wangessi yet? Did he get back to you the moment he got your latest message?"

"I'm not going to leave Lizera lying here. What am I supposed to do? Sit up there in the compound and listen while they tear her to pieces?"

"I can tell you exactly what Wangessi's thinking right now—him and anybody else he's consulted. You got this far dragging her—you can probably go the rest of the way by yourself. You must have killed almost half of those things by now. You've still got plenty of ammunition. I can guarantee you he's not worried about all the complaints he'll get if your *wife* has a fatal encounter with the local wildlife. Right now I'd be surprised if twelve people raised an objection if anything happened to Lizera. As far as Wangessi and most of the people in this community are concerned, you should tell her to put herself to sleep and mow down the rest of the pack while you run through it. You should drop her in exactly the same way you'd drop any other bundle you were trying to carry."

"Would you leave Lan?"

"In your situation—yes."

"You didn't even hesitate."

"I don't have the kind of feelings you seem to."

"She's a human being. She's just like you and me."

"That's not the issue."

"Then what is?"

"I acquired Lan because he satisfies my emotional needs. In the same way Lizera satisfies your needs. It's not the kind of thing people die for."

"It's the kind of thing they let someone else die for?"

"Do you have any idea what might happen to Lan if I diverted this ship just to help you save Lizera? Has it occurred to you that might be one of the major reasons I'm not helping you?"

"But you think I should let Lizera die now? You think I should just run off and let these animals rip her to pieces?"

"I think you should understand that Wangessi isn't going to divert this airship just to help you keep Lizera alive. I think you should understand that I'm not going to do something that could be turned into the kind of inflammatory incident Wangessi and his gang have been looking for. If I diverted this ship and saved you and Lizera, they would just argue that it wasn't necessary—that it's exactly the kind of thing self-indulgent people like us do. There would be no serious objection to any penalties they inflicted on us."

Davin could visualize the look on G.G.'s face—the look she put on whenever she lectured him about the nature of reality. To her, he was a monomaniac who was pathologically absorbed in his intellectual interests. He tended to think everything would work out, she argued. He underestimated the opposition he would encounter.

To him, on the other hand, she was the kind of person who thought meetings and political harangues were the greatest recreation mankind had ever invented. If she hadn't been leading their group, she would have found another band of persecuted souls and filled her life with another set of meetings and squabbles.

They were both right, of course. He shouldn't have been surprised by the reactions he had encountered when he had married Lizera. He had been surrounded by warning signs. Instead, he had focused on the people who had acquired geishas as spouses or concubines and assumed their existence proved the problems would be minor.

On the ship, during their first awake, Davin and Lizera had both been assigned to the staff that monitored the induced-hibernation containers. For one long stretch—over fifteen tendays—they had been rostered on different shifts. The assignment officer had smiled when Davin asked him why they couldn't work on the same schedule. Then he asked Davin if he ever went in for loans.

There had been a moment when Davin had felt his hands start to move. Then his enhancements had taken over. A flood of calming molecules had spread through his brain and he had walked away. He had still been brooding about the incident when G.G. had told him she was organizing her "support group."

Wangessi had been one of the ship's biggest committee joiners. Usually he ended up on the kind of committees that set policy and allocated jobs. You wouldn't find him in the induced-hibernation compartments, floating from container to container verifying that the readings on the instruments matched the readings on a portable checkup unit. After planetfall, Wangessi had found a place on the committee that allocated energy and other resources. If it hadn't been for Wangessi's committee, Davin and Lizera could have traveled between the compound and the tower in a small enclosed vehicle. They traveled on foot because Davin had been given half the energy allotment he had asked for.

Their research station drew its power from two sources—the solar panels Davin had created with their molecular fabricator and the recharged batteries the central base lifted in by gasbag. The batteries were based on the most efficient design the human race had come up with when their ship left the solar system. The design had been upgraded regularly as the ship had received messages from Earth as it crawled across the light years. Davin's original proposal had requested four batteries every eight tendays. The committee had told him the airship would bring him three batteries every twelve tendays.

Davin had looked at the budgets for the other ethology researchers. They were all getting almost twice as many battery deliveries as he was. He asked for a personal meeting with a member of the committee.

Wangessi saw him after a delay that lasted a tenday. "The other researchers are studying packhunters," Wangessi said. "They need to follow them all over their territory. You've chosen a species that stays close to its habitat."

"I understand that. But this budget means we'll be restricted to the bare minimum in living quarters and day to day consumables. It doesn't even give me an adequate budget for transportation between my observation tower and our residential compound."

"The committee discussed that. We think you should take another look at your plans. Do you really need a residential compound separate from your observation tower? Can't you include your living quarters in the tower?"

"I explained that in my proposal. I've put some space between the tower and the compound because I don't want to set up food producing plots that will disturb the area around the lake. Didn't anybody look at my proposal?"

"We looked at it very carefully, Davin. We have a lot of demands on our energy budget. If you feel you must have a separate residential compound, that's your decision. There are other areas in which you can economize. Your plan to use motorized transport between the compound and the tower is a good example. It's a moderate walk and our preliminary studies all indicate the local wildlife will leave you in peace. The chemical differences should give you all the protection you need."

Wangessi smiled. "Some members of the committee felt you should also consider a solo effort. Your—*wife*—won't be participating in your researches. If you only needed living space for one person, you could probably provide yourself with adequate quarters in a somewhat larger observation tower. I thought that was a little callous myself. If I had a permanent companion like Lizera, I would want her with me, too. But it *is* an alternative. She could retain her present job and make a useful contribution to the community."

Davin had been given a ritual that would override the calm his enhancements had started imposing on his system as soon as he saw Wangessi's smile. It was a deliberately complicated series of uncharacteristic hand gestures and subvocalized nonsense words. He had left Wangessi's office while he was still confident he could resist the temptation to activate it.

*   *   *

He terminated his call to G.G. and sent Wangessi a message with a Prime Emergency priority. Wangessi couldn't refuse a Prime Emergency call. A committee examined every call with that label.

Wangessi couldn't ignore the call but he could take his time answering it. He used up almost ten minutes—about the maximum he could get away with. The packhunters were still communicating but they seemed to be conserving their energy. A head popped above the grass about once every minute. Lizera had told Davin she might as well sleep and he had nodded and let her put herself out.

"We've taken a close look at your situation," Wangessi said. "We've been running simulations. We've looked at the number you've already killed and the tactics they've been using. We've concluded we should stick to our initial judgement. The odds are well in your favor if you try to hold out until we can get the *Yellow Grass* to you."

"I'm not looking for *good odds*. This isn't a gambling game. I've told you what my wife's wounds are like."

"We've discussed your situation with the research teams that are currently studying packhunters. They all support our conclusion. We understand you'd like to get help as soon as possible. It's a natural response. But you haven't given us any evidence that indicates we should engage in a major diversion and redirect a shipment as important as the *North Wind*'s current cargo."

"And nothing you're saying has anything to do with your attitude toward my... *wife*."

Wangessi's voice changed. Davin could see him folding his hands and leaning across his desk as he bestowed his soberest gaze on his visitor. "This has nothing to do with that issue, Davin. No one has said a word about that matter."

"Then what did you talk about?"

"We have taken into account the overall goals of the community. We think our decision represents its values and priorities."

"We're talking about a human life! You don't jabber about odds when you're dealing with a human life! You send the best support available. As fast as you can."

"We believe we are implementing the consensus of the community. If you want us to reach a different conclusion, you'll have to supply us with more information. That's all I have to say, Davin. We aren't going to send you the *North Wind*. That's impossible. If you want us to send you the *Yellow Grass*, just say so. It's your choice."

"Your connection has been terminated," the Voice of the communications system said.

Davin eyed the position of the sun. He gave his auxiliary intelligence a series of commands and connected it with the primary system in the compound. A little flock of not-quite-birds rattled off calls as they skimmed across the grass. A khaki head sneaked a quick look on his left.

The system ran off four hundred simulations in two minutes. Conclusion: there was a sixty-three percent chance he and Lizera would survive a night attack and still be alive when the *Yellow Grass* reached them.

He had put the simulation together in a hurry. He had probably left out some important factors. Still, it probably approximated the results Wangessi and his colleagues had reached with their simulations.

He pulled another set of variables out of his head and let the new simulation run for three minutes. Conclusion: there was a sixty-four percent chance they could both reach the compound alive if they made a run for it in their current estimated physical condition.

Two out of three sounded like good odds when you were playing games or gambling money. It didn't look quite so wonderful when somebody might be killed if your foray turned into one of the failures.

Here's three glasses. One drink is poisoned. What's the best strategy? Answer: don't drink.

He sent G.G. a recording of his conversation with Wangessi. *I'm just asking you for an opinion. Can I assume the Yellow Grass will get here when they say it will? Without developing "mechanical problems" on the way?*

G.G. responded as soon as she received the message. "That's a hard one, Davin. Are you thinking you should try to make a run for your compound?"

"Yes."

"With Lizera?"

"Yes. With Lizera."

"I don't think you should just assume they'll deliberately delay the ship. I don't want to give you the idea you have to get out of this by yourself."

"But you think they could?"

"I think it's a possibility. It's what I've been trying to tell you. They wouldn't consider it murder if Lizera died. They'd just feel they had eliminated one more undesirable situation."

"She didn't ask to be the way she is. I didn't ask anyone to make her the way she is. She's a lot better off with me than she would have been back in that resort."

"You're being logical, Davin. People aren't logical. You and I—we're doing something millions of people would like to do. They can't just look the other way. While we live out their fantasies."

He looked down at Lizera. What kind of orders had she given herself? Would she wake up if he left her on the hill? Would she sleep until the moment teeth and claws started tearing at her?

He checked his physical status. The rest had pulled him away from the yellow zone.

He bent over and tugged on Lizera's coat until she jerked awake. Her head lolled to one side. Davin made himself smile.

"Time to get back to work, love."

Lizera stared at his face. Her brow wrinkled.

"They can't get a ship here on time," Davin said. "I've done some wargaming on the situation and it looks like we've got a better position than I thought. We'll give you a moment to get your bearings. Then we'll have to plow through the little beasties one more time."

"You're going to go on carrying me?"

"Give me your second cassette. I want to start off with a full load."

She pulled the cassette out of her left cargo pocket and he picked up her gun and replaced the old cassette. His eyes darted between the grass and the gun while he worked with the prompts on the display screen. His ID number appeared on the screen. He ordered the gun to assume firing mode and a red light glowed on the top of the barrel. The gun was connected to his brain-machine link.

"You can carry my gun," he said. "As a spare. For me. You just have to hold on. I carried you this far—I can carry you the rest of the way."

He dropped to one knee. He guided her arm around his shoulder and she bent her good leg at the knee and helped him lift her upright.

The first attack group started wailing just as he reached the bottom of the little hill and started up the final rise. It was a quartet on his left. He had to watch them over the top of Lizera's head. Two of them were plowing straight toward him. The other two were following courses that would position them for an attack from the rear.

He fired three bursts at the two ripples that were taking the direct approach. The animal on the right ended its run in a storm of waving grass. Davin trained the gun on the other ripple and fired as the packhunter took to the air. He had to turn to shoot at it but he kept sidestepping to the right, gaining ground one boot width at a time. The animal snapped at its side as if it were biting at an insect. It flew past his shoulder and he turned to his rear. The two animals that had circled behind them were approaching jumping distance.

A hard, solid mass slammed into his back. He stumbled forward, clutching at Lizera with his left hand, and a second blow shoved him into the ground. Lizera let go of his clothes and slipped away from him. A third bundle of fury landed on his shoulders. Claws scraped at his coat and hood.

His brain was already processing the new data. The packhunters had obviously changed their tactics. Some of them must have crept through the grass and attacked from ambush when he was watching the incoming ripples. Would they keep up the hit-and-run tactics? The two that had hit him from behind had apparently run off—as if they were supposed to buffet him as hard as they could and run away.

He threw himself on top of Lizera. The animal on his back stopped its clawings. It jumped into the bush and he pulled the gun close to his side and waited for the next assault. His auxiliary intelligence ticked off the seconds. At twelve he jumped up and straddled Lizera.

The din was reaching another climax. Four more ripples were streaking toward him. He turned his head and saw another quartet coming in from the opposite direction.

He pointed the gun at the first group of ripples. He raised his chin and let out the biggest roar he could muster. *"I'm still here, you four legged pests. I'm still upright. You're wearing yourselves out faster than you're exhausting me. You're losing lives every time you come in."*

How would they interpret his voice? Would they hear the bellow of an animal that was still charged with energy? Or would his pitch or some other unpredictable factor make his outburst sound, to them, like a cry of exhaustion and defeat?

The set of ripples on his left veered away and ran across his front. The other set fanned out and kept coming. The gun cracked. Another animal died. He swung the barrel across the ripple that seemed to be coming straight at him and managed to stop it, too. The other two ripples swerved off course and raced past his front.

He settled his knee on the ground. Lizera put her arm around his neck and he hauled her up again. "I'm going to run for it," he said. "This is crazy. They're still doing hit-and-run tactics. They may not even realize we'll be out of reach when we get inside the hedge. I could be up there in half a minute—carrying you all the way—If they weren't trying to stop us."

"You're just going to let them knock us down?"

"They got through your armor just that once. They may not even realize we're trying to reach the compound."

"Would you like me to let out some yells? Like you just did?"

Davin smiled. "Can your energy level support it?"

"I've got all the energy I need, Davin. You're the one who's operating without any sleep."

Davin charged up the hill as if he had just stepped outside after a solid night's rest. Four ripples streamed toward him on the right and he ignored them and kept running. Lizera's yells stabbed at his left eardrum. She sounded shrill to him but what difference did it make? For all he knew, the packhunters could be hearing cries that indicated she had the strength of a dominant female at the peak of her lifespan.

He had covered a good seventy meters—he had climbed over a third of the slope—when the lead ripple in the quartet reached the packhunters' jumping range. He lowered his head and chugged on.

The animal slammed into his right shoulder. The angry rasping in his right ear blended with Lizera's scream. Davin let himself sink to his knees. The second animal hurled itself at his back. He staggered away from it, holding onto Lizera, and a third animal landed directly in front of him.

The third animal reared up on its hind legs. Claws struck at Davin's face. He lowered his head and took the blow on his hood. His gun fired. Two more blows buffeted the top of his head. A hole spread across the packhunter's stomach. Davin pulled himself to his feet and lunged forward.

The Voice of his auxiliary intelligence rang through his brain. "Warning. Warning. Do not ignore this message. You have entered the physiological danger zone. At your present rate of energy consumption, you could reach total collapse within five minutes."

The slope steepened. Lizera resumed her yelling. She was supporting some of her weight on her good leg but she was basically a sack he was dragging along. The load was forcing him to take short steps but he was still pulling a slow jog out of his leg muscles.

His eye picked up the first sign of four ripples streaming toward him on his left front. He turned his head and saw four more ripples following them.

Lizera stopped yelling. "They're advancing in echelon!"

Davin had never studied military history but he understood the term. The rear quartet was positioned just to the right of the lead group, so the two units were arranged in a stepwise formation.

Was it deliberate? Was there any tactical advantage to the arrangement? Or had it just happened by accident?

He stayed on course, moving straight up the hill, concentrating on gaining ground. He stopped just as the first ripple reached jumping distance. He pushed Lizera's arm away from his neck. "Lie down. On your face."

She slid down his side. The first packhunter cleared the grass and he stepped over her and fired. A solid body slammed into his right shoulder before he could turn on the next one. He leaned away from the blow and two living missiles toppled him with collisions that hit him almost simultaneously.

The second quartet broke through the grass on the run while he was still forcing himself to his knees. He threw himself across Lizera and made the gun fire blindly, without the aid of the sighting glasses. Claws and teeth dug at his armor. A paw rocked his head back and forth. There was a long—infinitely long—period when he wondered if they had stopped their hit-and-run tactics. Then they were gone. And he was once again pulling Lizera upright.

"Warning. Warning. Do not ignore this message. You have entered the physiological danger zone. At your present rate of energy consumption, you could reach total collapse within three minutes."

The hedge wasn't that far. Twenty meters. Call it forty steps. One. Two. Three.…

He heard the wailing on his right when he reached twelve. He counted off five more steps and stopped his advance. He fired methodically at each ripple, double burst after double burst, using up his ammunition so he wouldn't have to burn up energy enduring another series of blows. The fourth animal veered away when its companions stopped communicating and he dropped the gun and started running.

"Warning. Warning. Do not ignore this message. You have entered the physiological danger zone. At your present rate of energy consumption, you could reach total collapse within two minutes."

He transmitted a command to the compound and the security system shut down the hedge as he took his last step. "Lean your gun against the hedge. I'm going to give you a boost."

He grabbed her by the waist and lifted her up. The top was four meters above their heads. He had studied videos of the packhunters and made sure the hedge would stymie their best jumpers.

Lizera plunged her arms into the hedge and grabbed the thicker branches on the inside. "I've got a grip, Davin. You can let go."

"Ease yourself off the other side. Just remember—you can damage your legs all you want. It's your head we can't replace."

He picked up the gun and turned around. Ripples were coming up the hill from every direction. The display on the gun presented him with a magnificent three seconds.

"It's tricky when you can't use one of your legs," Lizera said.

They were fifty meters left of the gate. He had decided they would be better off if they went straight for the hedge. Now he wondered if he'd made the right move.

He trained his sighting glasses on the nearest ripples. The gun cracked four times. He had approximately twenty-five usable rounds left.

"I'm pulling myself over the top."

The gun fired three more times. Davin looked up and saw Lizera's left foot projecting over the top of the hedge.

He fired every shot he had as fast as he could think the command. The red light lit up. He dropped the gun and jumped for the top of the hedge.

A wailing cyclone landed on his back. His hands plunged into the hedge and grabbed the thickest branches they could clutch.

"Warning. Warning. Do not ignore this message. You have entered the physiological danger zone. At your present rate of energy consumption, you could reach total collapse within one minute."

The top of the hedge was two good handholds away. The packhunter on his back was clinging to his shoulders with its forepaws. The hedge was shaking as if it was being buffeted by some kind of machine. Packhunters had jumped out of the grass on his right and left and started clawing their way up the branches.

He switched on his communications implant and connected with Lizera. "Are you over? Are you down?"

"I'm going over now.... I'm down."

"Roll away from the hedge. I'm turning it on."

The packhunter on his back let out a single long rasp and fell away. The animals that were climbing the hedge dropped off. Davin couldn't feel the pain himself but he knew his body was using up energy reacting to it.

He pulled himself up to the top of the hedge. He stretched out on it sidewise and pushed himself into a roll.

"Warning. Warning. Do not ignore this message. You have crossed into the red zone. I repeat, you have crossed into the red zone. Your systems are now being shut down. There is no guarantee you will recover."

You could have died, Lizera said to him. I looked at your energy readings. You could have died. You're my wife, Davin said. And saw the look on her face.

She had dragged him away from the hedge. She had set the electrical system on lethal. She had crawled to their living quarters and returned with the nutrients and injectors the medicine cabinet had advised her to use. She had covered him with blankets and watched over him while he lay on the ground through six hours of darkness. She hadn't done anything for herself until he had stumbled back to their bedroom and drifted into hours of normal sleep.

She hadn't voiced any complaints, of course, when he had connected the screens in the compound with the screens in the tower and spent long periods observing the lakenesters. It hadn't been the best way to make observations but the events that had followed had made him glad he had done it. She had even been pleasantly amused when he had shown her his posting on their adventure. Some Observations on the Hunting Behavior of the Packhunters of Itoko from the Viewpoint of a Prey Animal, she had read aloud. And offered him a warm, slightly mischievous smile.

But the memory that gnawed at him was the response she gave him when he told her he was adding the packhunters to his observation program. The packhunter researchers had all asked him to do it. The packhunters in his territory had been hammered by a powerful stressor, they had argued. He could observe their reactions under an unusual set of variables.

"They're insisting we should have a vehicle," Davin told Lizera. "Even Wangessi's people will have to give in."

"But it's extra work for you. You'll have to spend less time with your own animal."

Davin shrugged. "It will be worth it. We'll be able to go back and forth to the tower together. The work I'll be doing with the packhunters will probably just be supplementary research, but it will be worth it. I won't have to leave you here when I'm in the tower."

And heard her say, It's up to you… if it's what you want. And saw, for the second time, the look that told him she was standing on one side of a chasm and he was standing on the other.

"I never really understood," Davin told G.G. Ying. "I thought I understood. But I didn't. Everything I did out there—it doesn't mean a thing to her. It doesn't mean a thing that I put my life at risk when I could have left her behind—that I need her so much I'm willing to take on the extra work just so she'll be safe and I can have her with me in the tower. She can't understand why anyone would think her welfare was just as important as his. She doesn't have any need to be loved. She doesn't even have a need to be needed. Everything I feel about her—to her it's just incomprehensible."

"Well, of course," G.G. said. "What did you expect?"

If the characters in science fiction stories are supposed to struggle with possible future developments, stories about time travel and faster than light travel occupy a debatable position in the canon. Our best pictures of the physical universe indicate both are impossible. But they've been part of the science fiction tradition for most its history and we would lose some valuable opportunities if we abandoned them.

THE MISTS OF TIME

The cry from the lookout perked up every officer, rating, and common seaman on deck. The two masted brig they were intercepting was being followed by sharks—a sure sign it was a slaver. Slave ships fouled the ocean with a trail of bodies as they worked their way across the Atlantic.

John Harrington was standing in front of the rear deckhouse when the midshipman's yell floated down from the mast. His three officers were loitering around him with their eyes fixed on the sails three miles off their port bow—a mass of windfilled cloth that had aroused, once again, the hope that their weeks of tedious, eventless cruising were coming to an end.

The ship rolling under their own feet, HMS *Sparrow*, was a sixty-foot schooner—one of the smallest warships carried on the rolls of Her Majesty's navy. There was no raised quarterdeck her commander could pace in majestic isolation. The officers merely stood in front of the deckhouse and looked down a deck crowded with two boats, spare spars, and the sweating bodies of crewmen who were constantly working the big triangular sails into new positions in response to the shipmaster's efforts to draw the last increment of movement from the insipid push of the African coastal breezes. A single six-pound gun, mounted on a turntable, dominated the bow.

Sub-lieutenant Bonfors opened his telescope and pointed it at the other ship. He was a broad, well padded young man and he beamed at the image in his lenses with the smile of a gourmand who was contemplating a particularly interesting table.

"*Niggers*, gentlemen. She's low in the water, too. I believe a good packer can squeeze five hundred prime niggers into a hull that long—

twenty-five hundred good English pounds if they're all still breathing and pulsing."

It was the paradox of time travel. You were there and you weren't there, the laws of physics prohibited it and it was the laws of physics that got you there. You were the cat that was neither dead nor alive, the photon that could be in two places at once, the wave function that hadn't collapsed. You slipped through a world in which you could see but not be seen, exist and not exist. Sometimes there was a flickering moment when you really were there—a moment, oddly enough, when they could see you and you couldn't see them. It was the paradox of time travel—a paradox built upon the contradictions and inconsistencies that lie at the heart of the sloppy, fundamentally unsolvable mystery human beings call the physical universe.

For Emory FitzGordon the paradox meant that he was crammed into an invisible, transparent space/time bubble, strapped into a two-chair rig shoulder to shoulder with a bony, hyperactive young woman, thirty feet above the tepid water twenty miles off the coast of Africa, six years after the young Princess Victoria had become Queen of England, Wales, Scotland, Ireland, and all the heathen lands Her government ruled beyond the seas. The hyperactive young woman, in addition, was an up-and-coming video auteur who possessed all the personality quirks traditionally associated with the arts.

"Four minute check completed," the hal running the bubble said. "Conditions on all four coordinates register satisfactory and stable. You have full clearance for two hours, provisional clearance for five hours."

Giva Lombardo's hands had already started bustling across the screenbank attached to her chair. The cameras attached to the rig had started recording as soon as the bubble had completed the space/time relocation. Giva was obviously rearranging the angles and magnifications chosen by the hal's programming.

"It didn't take them long to start talking about that twenty-five hundred pounds, did it?" Giva murmured.

John Harrington glanced at the other two officers. A hint of mischief flickered across his face. He tried to maintain a captainly gravity when he was on deck but he was, after all, only twenty-three.

"So how does that break down, Mr. Bonfors?"

"For the slaves alone," the stout sublieutenant said, "*conservatively*, it's two hundred and sixty pounds for you, eighty-nine for your hard working first lieutenant, seventy-two for our two esteemed colleagues here, sixteen for the young gentleman in the lookout, and two and a half pounds for every hand in the crew. The value of the ship itself might increase every share by another fifth, depending on the judgement of our lords at the Admiralty."

The sailing master, Mr. Whitjoy, rolled his eyes at the sky. The gunnery officer, Sub-lieutenant Terry, shook his head.

"I see there's one branch of mathematics you seem to have thoroughly mastered, Mr. Bonfors," Terry said.

"I may not have your knowledge of the calculus and other arcane matters, Mr. Terry," Bonfors said, "but I know that the quantity of roast beef and claret a man can consume is directly related to the mass of his purse."

Harrington raised his head. His eyes ranged over the rigging as if he was inspecting every knot. It would take them two hours—perhaps two and a half—to close with the slave ship. *Sparrow* was small and lightly armed but he could at least be thankful she was faster than her opposition. Most of the ships the Admiralty assigned to the West African anti-slavery squadron were two-masted brigs that wallowed through the water like sick whales.

How would they behave when the shooting started? Should he be glad they were still bantering? This would be the first time any of them had actually faced an armed enemy. Mr. Whitjoy was a forty year old veteran of the struggle against the Corsican tyrant but his seagoing service had been limited to blockade duty in the last three years of the Napoleonic wars. For the rest of them—including their captain and all the hands—"active service" had been a placid round of uneventful cruises punctuated by interludes in the seamier quarters of foreign ports.

"We'll keep flying the Portuguese flag until we come into range," Harrington said. "We still have a bit of ship handling ahead of us. We may sail a touch faster than an overloaded slaver but let's not forget they have four guns on each side. Let's make sure we're positioned straight across their bow when we bring them to, Mr. Whitjoy."

*   *   *

Giva had leaped on the prize money issue during their first planning session. She hadn't known the British sailors received special financial bonuses when she had applied for the job. She had circled around the topic, once she became aware of it, as if she had been tethered to it with a leash.

The scholar assigned to oversee the project, Dr. Peter LeGrundy, was a specialist in the cultural and social history of the Victorian British Empire. Peter claimed he normally avoided the details of Victorian military history—a subject his colleagues associated with excessive popular appeal—but in this case he had obviously had to master the relevant complexities. The ships assigned to the West African anti-slavery patrol had received five pounds for every slave they liberated, as a substitute for the prize money they would have received if they had been fighting in a conventional nation-state war. Prize money had been a traditional wartime incentive. The wages the Crown paid its seaborne warriors had not, after all, been princely. The arbitrary five pound figure had actually been a rather modest compensation, in Peter's opinion, compared to the sums the *Sparrow*'s crew would have received in wartime, from a cargo the government could actually sell.

Peter had explained all that to Giva—several times. And received the same reaction each time.

"There were five hundred captives on that ship," Giva said. "Twenty-five hundred pounds would be what—two or three million today? Audiences aren't totally stupid, Peter. I think most of them will manage to see that the great antislavery crusade could be a very profitable little business."

John Harrington had been reading about the Napoleonic Wars ever since his youngest uncle had given him a biography of Lord Nelson for his ninth birthday. None of the books he had read had captured the stately tempo of naval warfare. He knew the British had spent three hours advancing toward the Franco-Spanish fleet at Trafalgar but most authors covered that phase of the battle in a handful of paragraphs and hurried straight to the thunder that followed. Lieutenant Bonfors and Lieutenant Terry both made two trips to their quarters while *Sparrow* plodded across the gentle African waves toward their quarry. They were probably visiting their chamber pots, Harrington presumed. Mr. Whitjoy, on the other hand, directed the handling of the ship with his usual stolid competence.

Harrington thought he caught Whitjoy praying at one point, but the master could have been frowning at a patch of deck that needed a touch of the hollystone.

Harrington had stifled his own urge to visit the chamber pot. He had caught two of the hands smiling the second time Bonfors had trudged off the deck.

It had been Midshipmen Montgomery who had spotted the sharks. The other midshipman, Davey Clarke, had replaced Montgomery in the lookout. Montgomery could have gone below but he was circling the deck instead. He stopped at the gun every few minutes and gave it a thorough inspection. Montgomery would be assisting Mr. Terry when the time came to open fire.

Giva had started defending her artistic integrity at the very beginning of her pre-hiring interview. "I get the final edit," Giva had advised the oversight committee. "I won't work under any other conditions. If it's got my name on it, it represents my take on the subject."

Giva had been in Moscow, working on a historical drama. Emory had been staring at seven head-and-shoulder images on his living room imaging stage and Giva had been the only participant in the montage who had chosen a setting that accented her status. All the other participants had selected neutral backdrops. Giva had arranged herself so the committee could see, just beyond her shoulder, two actors who were dressed in flat, twenty-first century brain-link hats.

"There's one thing I absolutely have to say, Mr. FitzGordon," Giva said. "I appreciate your generosity. I will try to repay you by turning out the best possible product I can. But please don't think you can expect to have any influence on the way I do it. I'm not interested in creating public relations fog jobs for wealthy families."

Emory had listened to Giva's tirade with the thin, polite smile a tolerant parent might bestow on a child. "I wouldn't expect you to produce a fog job," Emory responded. "I believe the facts in this case will speak for themselves. I can't deny that I specified this particular incident when I offered the agency this grant partly because my ancestor was involved in it. I wouldn't have known the Royal Navy had engaged in an anti-slavery campaign if it hadn't been part of our family chronicles. But I also feel this episode is a typical example of the courage and devotion of a group of men who deserve to be remembered and honored. The crews of the West African anti-slavery patrol saved a hundred thousand human beings from slavery. They deserve a memorial that has been created by an honest, first-class artist."

The committee had already let Emory know Giva Lombardo was the candidate they wanted to hire. Giva had friends in the Agency for Chronautical Studies, it seemed.

She also had ability and the kind of name recognition that would attract an audience. Emory had been impressed with both the docs that had catapulted Giva out of the would-be class. The first doc had been a one hour essay on women who bought sexually enhancing personality modifications. The second had been a rhapsodic portrait of a cruise on a fully automated sailing ship, The cruise doc was essentially an advertisement funded by the cruise company but it had aroused the enthusiasm of the super-aesthete audience.

Emory's family had been dealing with artists for a hundred and fifty years. His great-grandfather's encounter with the architect who designed his primary residence was a standard item in popular accounts of the history of architecture. It had become a family legend encrusted with advice and observations. *All interactions between artists and the rich hinge on one basic fact*, Emory's great-grandfather had said. *You need the creatives. The creatives need your money.*

Harrington placed his hands behind his back. The approach was coming to an end. Mr. Whitjoy had placed *Sparrow* on a course that would cross the slaver's bow in just four or five minutes.

He took a deep breath and forced the tension out of his neck muscles. He was the captain of a ship of war. He must offer his crew a voice that sounded confident and unperturbed.

"Let's show them our true colors, Mr. Whitjoy. You may advise them of our request as soon as we start to raise our ensign, Mr. Terry."

Lieutenant Bonfors led the boarding party. The slaver hove to in response to Lieutenant Terry's shot across its bow and Lieutenant Bonfors settled his bulk in the stern of a longboat and assumed a rigid, upright dignity that reminded Emory of the recordings of his great-grandfather he had viewed when he had been a child. Harrison FitzGordon had been an ideal role model, in the opinion of Emory's father. He was courteous to everyone he encountered, according to the family catechism, but he never forgot his position in society. He always behaved like someone who assumed the people around him would treat him with deference—just as Lieutenant Bonfors obviously took it for granted that others would row and he would be rowed.

Bonfors maintained the same air of haughty indifference when he hauled himself aboard the slaver and ran his eyes down its guns. Two or three crewmen were lounging near the rear of each gun. Most of them had flintlock pistols stuck in their belts.

A tall man in a loose blue coat hurried across the deck. He held out his hand and Bonfors put his own hands behind his back.

"I am Sub-lieutenant Barry Richard Bonfors of Her Majesty's Ship *Sparrow*. I am here to inspect your ship and your papers in accordance with the treaties currently in effect between my government and the government of the nation whose flag is flying from your masthead."

"I am William Zachary," the officer in the blue coat said, "and I am the commander of this ship. If you will do me the honor of stepping into my cabin, I will be happy to present you with our papers."

"I would prefer to start with an inspection of your hold."

"I'm afraid that won't be possible, sub-lieutenant. I assure you our papers will give you all the information you need."

"The treaties in effect between our countries require the inspection of your entire ship, sir. I would be neglecting my duties if I failed to visit your hold."

Captain Zachary gestured at the guns. "I have two twelve pound guns and two eighteen pounders on each side of my ship, sub-lieutenant. You have, as far as I can tell, one six pounder. I have almost fifty hands. What do you have? Twenty-five? And some of them boys? I'm certain a visit to my cabin and an inspection of my papers will provide you with a satisfactory report to your superiors. As you will see from our papers, our hold is stuffed with jute and bananas."

Zachary was speaking with an accent that sounded, to Emory's ear, a lot like some of the varieties of English emitted by the crew on the *Sparrow*. Giva's microphone arrangement had picked up some of the cries coming from the slaver's crew as Bonfors had made his progress across the waters and Emory had heard several examples of the best known English nouns and verbs. The ship was flying a Brazilian flag, Emory assumed, because it offered the crew legal advantages they would have missed if they had sailed under their true colors. British citizens who engaged in the slave trade could be hanged as pirates.

The legal complexities of the anti-slavery crusade had been one of the subjects that had amused Emory when he had been a boy. The officers of the West African Squadron had operated under legal restrictions that were so complicated the Admiralty had issued them an instruction manual they could carry in their uniforms. The Royal Navy could stop the ships of some nations and not others and it could do some things on one country's ships and other things on others.

Emory had been five when he had first heard about John Harrington's exploits off the African coast. Normally the FitzGordon adults just mentioned it now and then. You were reminded you had an ancestor who had liberated slaves when your elders felt you were spending too much time thinking about some of the other things your ancestors had done, such as their contributions to the coal mining and timber cutting industries. In Emory's case, it had become a schoolboy enthusiasm. He had scoured the databanks for information on Lieutenant John Harrington and the great fifty year struggle in which Harrington had participated. Almost no one outside of his family had heard about the Royal Navy's antislavery campaign, but the historians who had studied it had all concluded it was one of the great epics of the sea. Young officers in small ships had fought the slavers for over half a century. They had engaged in hotly contested ship to ship actions. They had ventured up the rivers that communicated with the interior and attacked fortified slaveholding pens. Thousands of British seamen had died from the diseases that infested the African coast. The African slave markets north of the equator had been shut down. One hundred thousand men, women, and children had been rescued from the horrors of the slave ships.

The campaign had been promoted by a British politician, Lord Palmerston, who had tried to negotiate a general international treaty outlawing the slave trade. Palmerston had failed to achieve his goal and British diplomats had been forced to negotiate special agreements country by country. The officers on the spot were supposed to keep all the agreements straight and remember they could be fined, or sued, if they looked in the wrong cupboard or detained the wrong ship.

In this case, the situation was relatively straightforward. The ship was flying the flag of Brazil and the *Sparrow* therefore had the right to examine its papers and search its hull. If the searchers found any evidence the ship was engaging in the slave trade—such as the presence of several hundred chained Africans—the *Sparrow* could seize the slaver and bring the ship, its crew, and all its contents before the courts the navy had established in Freetown, Sierra Leone.

"Look at that," Emory said. "Look at the way he's handling himself."

Bonfors had turned his back on Captain Zachary. He was walking toward the ladder on the side of the ship with the same unhurried serenity he had exhibited when he came aboard.

Did Bonfor's back itch? Was he counting the number of steps that stretched between his present position and the minimal safety he would enjoy when he reached the boat? For Emory it was a thrilling moment—a display of the values and attitudes that had shaped his own conduct since he had been a child. Most of the officers on the *Sparrow* shared a common heritage. Their family lines had been molded, generation after generation, by the demands of the position they occupied in their society.

"You are now provisionally cleared for six hours total," the hal said. "All coordinates register satisfactory and stable."

The slaver was turning. Harrington noted the hands in the rigging making minor adjustments to the sails and realized the slaver's bow was shifting to the right—so it could bring its four starboard guns to bear on *Sparrow*.

Mr. Whitjoy had seen the movement, too. His voice was already bellowing orders. He had been told to hold *Sparrow* lined up across the slaver's bows. He didn't need further instructions.

Conflicting courses churned across Harrington's brain. Bonfors had reboarded his boat and he was still crossing the gap between the ships. The slave ship couldn't hit the boat with the side guns but it had a small chaser on the bow—a four pounder that could shatter the boat with a single lucky shot. The wind favored the slaver, too. The two ships had hove to with the wind behind the slaver, hitting its sails at a twenty degree angle....

He hurried down the narrow deck toward the bow. Terry and Montgomery both looked at him expectantly. The swivel gun was loaded with chain shot. The slow match smoldered in a bucket.

"Let's give our good friend Mr. Bonfors time to get aboard," Harrington said.

"Aren't you afraid they'll fire on the boat with their chaser?" Montgomery said. "Sir."

Terry started to say something and Harrington stopped him with his hand. Montgomery should have kept his thoughts to himself but this wasn't the time to rebuke him.

"It's obvious Mr. Bonfors didn't finish the inspection," Harrington said. "But we won't be certain they refused to let him go below until he makes his report. We don't want to give the lawyers any unnecessary grounds for complaint."

He glanced around the men standing near the gun. "Besides, everybody says these slavers tend to be poor shots. They're businessmen. They go to sea to make money."

He paused for what he hoped would be an effect. "We go to sea to make *war*."

Montgomery straightened. Harrington thought he saw a light flash in the eyes of one of the seamen in the gun crew. He turned away from the gun and made his way toward the stern with his hands behind his back, in exactly the same pose his second commanding officer, Captain Ferris, would have assumed. A good commander had to be an actor. Good actors never ruined an exit line with too much talk.

Emory had started campaigning for Giva's removal a week after he had audited the first planning meeting. Giva had nagged at the prize money issue for a tiresome fifteen minutes at the end of the fourth meeting and Emory had maintained his link to Peter LeGrundy after she had exited. Giva had still been in Russia at that state of their association. Emory was staying at his New York residence, where he was sampling the opening premieres of the entertainment season. Peter had based himself in London, so he could take a first hand look at the Royal Navy archives.

"Are you really sure we can't do anything about her supporters in the chronautical bureaucracy?" Emory said. "It seems to me there should be some *small* possibility we can overcome their personal predilections and convince them she has a bias that is obviously incompatible with scholarship. A ten minute conversation with her would probably be sufficient."

"She's peppery, Emory. She feels she has to assert herself. She's young and she's an artist."

"And what's she going to be like when she's actually recording? We'll only have one opportunity, Peter—the only opportunity anybody will ever have. Whatever she records, that's it."

Under the rules laid down by the chrono bureaucrats, the *Sparrow*'s encounter with the slaver was surrounded by a restricted zone that encompassed hundreds of square miles of ocean and twenty hours of time. No one knew what would happen if a bubble entered a space/time volume occupied by another bubble—and the bureaucrats had decided they would avoid the smallest risk they would ever find out. The academics and fundraisers who had written the preamble to the agency's charter had decreed that its chrononauts would "dispel the mists of time with disciplined onsite observations," and the careerists and political appointees who ran the agency had decreed each site would receive only one dispelling. Once their bubble left the restricted zone, no one else would ever return to it.

"She's what they want," Peter said. "I've counted the votes. There's only one way you can get her out of that bubble—withdraw your grant and cancel the project."

"And let the media have a fiesta reporting on the rich idler who tried to bribe a committee of dedicated scholars."

Peter was being cautious, in Emory's opinion. He could have changed the committee's mind if he had made a determined effort. Giva had flaunted her biases as if she thought they were a fashion statement. But Peter also knew he would make some permanent enemies among the losing minority if he pressed his case.

Peter was a freelance scholar who lived from grant to grant. He had never managed to land a permanent academic position. He was balancing two forces that could have a potent impact on his future: a rich individual who could be a fertile source of grants and a committee composed of scholars who could help him capture a permanent job.

Emory could, of course, offer Peter some inducements that might overcome his respect for Giva's supporters. But that was a course that had its own risks. You never knew when an academic might decide his scholarly integrity had to be asserted. In the end, Emory had adopted a more straightforward approach and applied for a seat in the bubble under the agency's Chrono Tourist program. The extra passenger would cost the agency nothing and the fee would increase his grant by thirty percent. Giva would still control the cameras on the bubble but he could make his own amateurish record with his personal recording implant. He would have evidence he could use to support any claim that she had distorted the truth.

Harrington could have leaned over the side of the ship and called for a report while Bonfors was still en route but he was certain Captain Ferris would never have done that. Neither would Nelson. Instead, he stood by the deckhouse and remained at his post while Bonfors climbed over the side, saluted the stern, and marched across the deck.

"He threatened me," Bonfors said. "He pointed at his guns and told me I could learn all I needed to know from his account books."

"He refused to let you visit the hold?"

"He told me I could learn all I needed from his books. He told me he had eight guns and fifty hands and we only had one gun and twenty-five."

Harrington frowned. Would a court interpret that as a threat? Could a lawyer claim Bonfors had deliberately misinterpreted the slave captain's words?

"It was a clear refusal," Bonfors said. "He gave me no indication he was going to let me inspect the hold."

Harrington turned toward the gun. He sucked in a good lungful and enjoyed a small pulse of satisfaction when he heard his voice ring down the ship.

"You may fire at your discretion, Mr. Terry."

Montgomery broke into a smile. Terry said something to his crew and the lead gunner drew the slow match from its bucket.

Terry folded his arms over his chest and judged the rise and fall of the two ships. Chain shot consisted of two balls, connected by a length of chain. It could spin through the enemy rigging and wreak havoc on any rope or wood that intersected its trajectory.

Terry moved his arm. The lead gunner laid the end of the match across the touchhole.

It was the first time in his life Harrington had stood on a ship that was firing on other human beings. It was the moment he had been preparing for since he had been a twelve year old novice at the Naval School at Portsmouth but the crash of the gun still caught him by surprise.

Montgomery was standing on tiptoe staring at the other ship. Terry was already snapping out orders. The sponger was pulling his tool out of its water bucket. Drill and training were doing their job. On the entire ship, there might have been six men who could feel the full weight of the moment, undistracted by the demands of their posts—and one of them was that supreme idler, the commanding officer.

The slaver's foremast quivered. A rip spread across a topsail. Bonfors pulled his telescope out of his coat and ran it across the slaver's upper rigging.

"I can see two lines dangling from the foretopsail," Bonfors said.

Harrington was playing his own telescope across the slaver's deck. Four men had gathered around the bowchaser. The two ships were positioned so its ball would hit the *Sparrow* toward the rear midships—a little forward of the exact spot where he was standing

He had assumed they should start by destroying the slaver's sails. Then, when there was no danger their quarry could slip away, they could pick it off at their leisure, from positions that kept them safe from its broadsides. Should he change that plan merely because he was staring at the muzzle of the enemy gun? Wouldn't it make more sense to fire at the gun? Even though it was a small, hard-to-hit target?

It was a tempting thought. The slavers might even strike their colors if the shot missed the stern gun and broke a few bodies as it hurtled down the deck.

It was a thought generated by fear.

"Well started, Mr. Terry. Continue as you are."

The slaver's gun flashed. There was a short pause—just time enough to feel himself stiffen—and then, almost simultaneously, his brain picked up the crash of the gun and the thud of the ball striking the side of *Sparrow*'s hull.

The ball had hit the ship about where he had guessed it would. If it had been aimed a few degrees higher, it would have crossed the deck three steps to his right.

The *Sparrow*'s gun fired its second shot moments after the slaver's ball hit the hull. The sponger shoved his tool down the gun barrel, the crew fell into their drill, and the *Sparrow* hurled a third ball across the gap while the slaver's crew was still loading their second shot.

"The slaver's got a crew working on the rear boat," Giva said.

Emory had been watching the two gun crews and looking for signs they were actually creating some damage. The third shot from the *Sparrow*'s gun had drawn an excited, arms-raised leap from the midshipman posted with the gun crew. The upper third of the slaver's forward mast had bounced away from the lower section, and sagged against the rigging.

Harrington's report to the Admiralty said the slaver had brought out a boat and used it to pull the ship around, to bring its broadside into play. Harrington hadn't said when they had lowered the boat. Emory had assumed they had done it after the battle had raged for awhile.

"It looks like they're going to lower it on the other side of their ship," Emory said. "Is that going to cause any problems?"

"The rotation program can correct for most of the deficiencies. We can always have a talking head explain some of the tactics—some professor who's goofy about old weapons. We could even have you do it, Emory. You probably know more about the anti-slavery patrol than Peter and all the rest of the committee combined. That could be a real tingler—the hero's descendant talking about the ancestor he hero worshipped as a boy. After he had actually seen him in action."

Harrington was making another calculation. The slaver's boat was pulling the slaver's bow into the wind. There was no way Mr. Whitjoy could stay with the bow as it turned and avoid a broadside. Should he pull out of range, circle around, and place *Sparrow* across the enemy's stern? Or should he hold his current position, take the broadside, and inflict more damage on their sails?

The blow to the slaver's mast had weakened its sailing capabilities but it wasn't decisive. He wanted them dead in the water—totally at his mercy.

The slaver's bow gun was already pointing away from *Sparrow*. There would be a period—who knew how long?—when *Sparrow* could fire on the slaver and the slaver couldn't fire back.

"Hold position, Mr. Whitjoy. Keep up the good work, Mr. Terry."

Harrington was holding his pocket watch in his hand. The swivel gun roared again and he noted that Terry's crew was firing a shot every minute and twenty seconds.

He put his hands behind his back and watched the enemy ship creep around. It was all a matter of luck. The balls from the slaver's broadside would fly high or low—or pass over the deck at the height of a young commander's belly. They would intersect the place where you were standing or pass a few feet to your right or left. The odds were on your side.

And there was nothing you could do about it.

Bonfors glanced back. He saw what Harrington was doing and resumed his telescopic observations of the enemy ship.

Terry's crew fired three more times while the slaver made its turn. The second shot cut the broken topmast free from its support lines and sent it sliding through the rigging to the deck. The third shot slammed into the main mast with an impact that would have made every captive in the hold howl with joy if they could have seen the result—and understood what it meant. The top of the mast lurched to the right. The whole structure, complete with spars and furled sails, toppled toward the deck and sprawled over the slaver's side.

Harrington felt himself yield to an uncontrollable rush of emotion. *"Take her about, Mr. Whitjoy! Take us out of range."*

Whitjoy barked orders. Hands raced to their stations. The big triangular main sail swung across *Sparrow*'s deck. The hand at the wheel adjusted the angle of the rudder and Harrington's ship began to turn away from the wind.

Some of the crew on the other ship had left their guns and rushed to the fallen sail. With luck, one or two of their compatriots would be lying under the wreckage.

If there was one virtue the Navy taught you, it was patience. You stood your watches, no matter how you felt. You endured storms that went on and on, for days at a time, without any sign they were coming to an end. You waited out calms. And now you locked yourself in your post and watched the elephantine motions of the ships, as *Sparrow* turned away from the wind, and the muzzles of the enemy guns slowly came to bear on the deck you were standing on....

The flash of the first gun caught him by surprise. He would have waited at least another minute before he fired if he had been commanding the other ship. A huge noise whined past *Sparrow*'s stern. The second gun lit up a few seconds later, and he realized they were firing one gun at a time.

This time the invisible Thing passed over his head, about fifty feet up. Mr. Terry fired the swivel gun and he heard Montgomery's treble shout a word of encouragement at the ball.

The slaver hurled its third shot. A tremendous bang shook the entire length of *Sparrow*'s hull. He looked up and down the deck, trying to find some sign of damage, and saw Montgomery covering his face with both hands.

A gunner grabbed Montgomery's shoulders. Terry stepped in front of the boy and seized his wrists. The rest of the gun crew gathered around.

"Mr. Bonfors—please see what the trouble is. See if you can get the gun back in action."

Bonfors shot him one of the most hostile looks he had ever received from another human being. It only lasted a moment but Harrington knew exactly what his second in command was thinking. The captain had seen an unpleasant duty and passed it to the appropriate subordinate. They both knew it was the right thing to do—the only thing a captain *could* do—but that didn't alter the basic fact that the coldhearted brute had calmly handed you a job that both of you would have given almost anything to avoid.

A crewman was standing by the railing near the bow. He pointed at the railing and Harrington understood what had happened. The big bang had been a glancing blow from a cannon ball. Wooden splinters had flown off the rail at the speed of musket balls. One of the splinters had apparently hit Montgomery in the face.

"It looks like we now know who Montgomery is," Emory said.

Giva was looking at a rerun on her display. "I got it all. The camera had him centered the whole time. I lost him when they all crowded around him. But I got the moment he was hit."

Lieutenant Bonfors had reached the gun and started easing the crew away from Montgomery with a mixture of jovial comments and firm pushes. "Let's keep our minds on our work, gentlemen. Take Mr. Montgomery to the captain's cabin, Hawksbill. I believe we've got time for one more shot before we pull away from our opponent, Mr. Terry."

Their planning sessions had contained one moment of pure harmony. They had all agreed Giva would have two cameras continuously tracking both midshipmen. They knew one of the boys was going to be hit but they didn't know which one. They knew the boy was referred to as Mr.

Montgomery in Harrington's report but they didn't know what he looked like or when it would happen. They only knew *Mr. Montgomery and Mr. Clarke acquitted themselves with courage and competence. I regret to report that Mr. Montgomery has lost the sight of his left eye. He is bearing his misfortune with commendable cheerfulness.*

Sparrow put a solid half mile between its stern and the slaver before it turned into a long, slow curve that ended with it bearing down on the slaver's stern. The men in the slaver's boat tried to turn with it, but Mister Whitjoy outmaneuvered them. The duel between sail power and oar power came to an abrupt end as soon as *Sparrow* drew within firing range. Harrington ordered Terry to fire on the boat, the second shot raised a fountain of water near the boat's bow, and every slaver in the boat crew lunged at the ladder that hung from the side of their ship.

Bonfors chuckled as he watched them scramble onto the deck. "They don't seem to have much tolerance for being shot at, do they?"

Harrington was eyeing the relative positions of the two ships. In another five minutes *Sparrow* would be lying directly behind the slaver's stern, poised to hurl ball after ball down the entire length of the other ship.

"You may fire at the deck as you see fit, Mr. Terry. We'll give them three rounds. And pause to see if they strike."

"They're opening the hatch," Emory said.

Captain Zachary and four of his men were crouching around the hatch in the center of the slave ship. They had drawn their pistols and they were all holding themselves close to the deck, in anticipation of the metal horror that could fly across their ship at any moment.

The four crewmen dropped through the hatch. Captain Zachary slithered backward and crouched on one knee, with his pistol clutched in both hands.

Harrington threw out his arm as soon as he saw the first black figures stumble into the sunlight. "Hold your fire, Mr. Terry."

The slavers had arranged themselves so he could enjoy an unobstructed view of the slaves. The Africans were linked together with chains but the captain and his crew were still training guns on them. Two of the slaves slumped to the deck as they came out of the hold. Their companions picked them up and dragged them away from the hatch.

"I'd say a third of them appear to be women," Bonfors said.

Harrington raised his telescope and verified Bonfors' estimate. One of the women was holding a child.

He lowered his telescope and pushed it closed. "Organize a boarding party, Mr. Bonfors. I will lead it. You will take command of the ship."

"My God," Emory said. "He didn't waste a second."

They had known what Harrington was going to do. It was in his report. But nothing in the written record had prepared Emory for the speed of his decision.

I ascertained that we could no longer punish their crew with our gun, Harrington had written, *and I therefore determined to take their ship by assault, with one of our boats. The presence of the unfortunate innocents meant that our adversaries could repair their masts before our very eyes and perhaps slip away in the night. There was, in addition, the danger they would adopt the infamous course others have taken in such a situation and avoid prosecution by consigning their cargo to the sea.*

Terry volunteered at once. Davey Clarke wanted to go, but Harrington decreed they couldn't risk another midshipman.

"We'd have a fine time keeping the ship afloat with both of our young gentlemen laid up, Davey."

The hands obviously needed encouragement. Four men stepped forward. The expressions on the rest of them convinced Harrington he had to give Bonfors some support.

"A double share for every man who volunteers," Harrington called out. "Taken from the captain's portion."

A ball from the slaver's stern gun ploughed into the water forty feet from *Sparrow*'s port side. Bonfors' arm shot toward the splash while it was still hanging over the waves. "It's the easiest money you'll ever earn, lads. You've seen how these fellows shoot."

In the end, fifteen men shuffled up to the line. That would leave ten on the *Sparrow*—enough to get the ship back to port if worse came to worse.

Giva smiled. "He just doubled their profit, didn't he? He didn't mention that in his report."

* * *

Harrington placed himself in the front of the boat. Terry sat in the back, where the ranking officer would normally sit.

Their positions wouldn't matter that much during the approach. The slavers would be firing down from the deck. They would all be equally exposed. When they initiated the assault, however, he had to be in front. The whole enterprise might fail if he went down—but it was certain to fail if the men felt their captain was huddling in the rear. The assault had been his idea, after all.

They had boarded the boat on *Sparrow*'s starboard side, with *Sparrow*'s hull between them and the enemy guns. For the first few seconds after Terry gave the order, they traveled along the hull. Then they cleared the bow.

And there it was. There was nothing between him and the stern gun of the enemy ship but a hundred yards of sunlight and water.

Terry was supposed to steer them toward the rear of the slaver's starboard side. They had agreed he would aim them at a point that would accomplish two objectives. He would keep the boat outside the angle the slaver's broadside could cover and he would minimize the time they would spend inside the stern gun's field of fire. Terry was the best man to hold the tiller. No one on *Sparrow* had a better understanding of the strengths and limitations of nautical artillery.

They had overcome their boat's initial resistance as they had slid down *Sparrow*'s hull. Terry called out his first firm "*Stroke!*" and the bow shot toward its destination. Terry gave the rowers two cycles of *stroke* and *lift* at a moderate pace. Then he upped the pace and kept increasing it with every cycle.

Every push of the oars carried them out of the danger presented by the stern gun. But it also carried them toward the armed men who were crowding around the rail.

Harrington's hands tightened on the weapons he was holding—a pistol in his right hand, a cutlass in his left. He was keeping his fingers on the butt of the pistol, well away from the trigger and the possibility he would fire the gun by accident and leave himself one bullet short and looking like a fool. Two more pistols were tucked into his belt, right and left. The men behind him were all equipped with two pistols, two loaded muskets wrapped in oilcloth, and a cutlass laid across their feet.

The stern gun flashed. The impulse to squeeze himself into a package the size of his hat seemed irresistible but he focused his eyes on the side of the slaver and discovered he could hold himself fixed in place until he heard the bang of the gun reaching him from a distance that seemed as remote as the moons of Jupiter.

"*Stroke*... lift... *stroke*... lift."

Was there anything more beautiful than the crash of a gun that had just fired in your direction? The noise had made its way across the water and you were still alive. You could be certain four pounds of iron had sailed harmlessly past you, instead of slamming into your bones or knocking holes in your boat and mutilating your shipmates.

"That should be the last we'll hear from that thing," a voice muttered behind him.

"I should hope so," a brasher voice said. "Unless these niggerwhippers have picked up some pointers from Mr. Terry in the last half hour."

The second voice belonged to a hand named Bobby Dawkins—a veteran in his fourth decade who was noted for his monkeyish agility and the stream of good-natured comments he bestowed on everything that happened around him. Dawkins had been the first man to volunteer after Harrington had augmented the cash reward.

Armed men were lining up along the rail of the slave ship. More men were falling in behind them.

Emory ran his eyes down the rail picking out faces that looked particularly vicious or threatening. He had begun his recording as a weapon in his contest with Giva but he was beginning to think along other lines. He wanted a personal record of this—the kind of record a tourist would make. It wouldn't be as sharp as Giva's work but it would be *his*— a personal view of his ancestor's courage.

The slavers started firing their muskets when the boat was still fifty yards from its destination. Harrington had been hoping they would waste a few of their shots but he still felt himself flinch when he saw the first flash. Everybody else in the boat had something to do. The hands had to row. Terry had to steer. He had to sit here and be a target.

He knew he should give his men a few words of encouragement but he couldn't think of a single phrase. His mind had become a blank sheet. Was he afraid? Was this what people meant when they said someone was *paralyzed*?

The slavers shoved two African women up to the rail. The men in the center of the firing line stepped aside and more slaves took their place.

"The swine," Dawkins said. "Bloody. Cowardly. *Bastards.*"

Black faces stared at the oncoming boat. Harrington peered at their stupefied expressions and realized they didn't have the slightest idea they were being used as shields. They had been pushed in chains along trails that might be hundreds of miles long. They had been packed into a hold as if they were kegs of rum. They were surrounded by men who didn't speak their language. By now they must be living in a fog.

"Make sure you aim before you shoot. Make these animals feel every ball you fire."

He was bellowing with rage. He would have stood up in the boat if he hadn't been restrained by years of training. He knew he was giving his men a stupid order. He knew there was no way they could shoot with that kind of accuracy. It didn't matter. The slavers had provoked emotions that were as uncontrollable as a hurricane.

More slaves were shoved to the railing. Muskets banged. Slavers were actually resting their guns on the shoulders of the slaves they were using for cover.

"We're inside their guns," Terry yelled. "I'll take us forward."

Harrington pointed at a spot just aft of the forward gun. "Take us there. Between one and two. First party—stow your oars. Shoulder your muskets. Wait for my order."

They had worked this out before they had boarded the boat. Half the men would guide the boat during the final approach. The other half would pick up their muskets and prepare to fight.

Giva had stopped making comments. Her face had acquired the taut, focused lines of a musician or athlete who was working at the limits of her capacity. She was scanning the drama taking place outside the bubble while she simultaneously tracked the images on six screens and adjusted angles and subjects with quick, decisive motions of her hands.

Emory had noted the change in her attitude and turned his attention to his own record. What difference did it make how she felt? The people who saw the finished product would see brave men hurling themselves into danger. Would anybody really care why they did it?

* * *

Musket balls cracked in the air around the boat. Metal hammered on the hull. Four members of the slaver crew were running toward the spot where Harrington planned to board. The rest of them were staying near the middle and firing over their human shields.

"Hold her against the side," Harrington yelled. "Throw up the grappling hooks."

The four hands who had been given the job threw their grappling hooks at the rail. The man beside Harrington tugged at the rope, to make sure it was firm, and Harrington fired his first pistol at the ship and handed the gun to one of the rowers. He grabbed the rope and walked himself up the side of the hull, past the gun that jutted out of the port on his left. His cutlass dangled from a loop around his wrist.

He knew he would be most vulnerable when he went over the rail. His hands would be occupied. He would be exposed to gunfire and hand to hand attacks. He seized the rail with both hands as soon as he came in reach and pulled himself over before he could hesitate.

Four men were crouching on the roof of the rear deckhouse. A gun flamed. Harrington jerked his left pistol out of his belt and fired back. He charged at the deckhouse with his cutlass raised.

The slavers fired their guns and scampered off the deckhouse. Harrington turned toward the bow, toward the men who were using the slaves as shields. His boarding party was crowding over the rails. He had half a dozen men scattered beside him. Most of them were firing their muskets at the slavers and their flesh and blood bulwarks.

"Use your cutlasses! Make these bastards bleed!"

He ran across the deck with his cutlass held high. He could hear himself screaming like a wild man. He had tried to think about the best way to attack while they had been crossing the water. Now he had stopped thinking. They couldn't stand on the deck and let the animals shoot at them.

The Africans' eyes widened. They twisted away from the lunatics rushing toward them and started pushing against the bodies behind them. The slavers had overlooked an important fact—they were hiding behind a wall that was composed of conscious, intelligent creatures.

The African directly in front of Harrington was a woman. She couldn't turn her back on him because of her chains but she had managed to make a half turn. The man looming behind her was so tall she didn't reach his shoulder. The man was pointing a pistol at Harrington and the woman was clawing at his face with one hand.

The pistol sounded like a cannon when it fired. Harrington covered the deck in front of him in two huge leaps—the longest leaps he had ever taken—and brought his cutlass down on the slaver with both hands.

Steel sliced through cloth and bit into the slaver's collarbone. The man's mouth gaped open. He fell back and Harrington shouldered the female slave aside and hoisted his legs over the chain dangling between her and the captive on her right.

Emory was clamping his jaw on the kind of bellow overwrought fans emitted at sports events. Giva had shifted the bubble to a location twenty-five meters from the side of the slave ship. He could see and hear every detail of Harrington's headlong rush.

Half a dozen men had joined Harrington's assault. More had fallen in behind as they had come over the side. Most of the men in the first rank were running at a crouch, about a step behind their captain. One sailor was holding his hand in front of his face, as if he thought he could stop a bullet with his palm. Emory had been watching combat scenes ever since he was a boy but no actor had ever captured the look on these men's faces—the intense, white faced concentration of men who knew they were facing real bullets.

A slaver backed away from the pummeling fists of a tall, ribby slave and fired at the oncoming sailors. For a moment Emory thought the shot had gone wild. Then he glanced toward the rear of the assault. A sailor who had just pulled himself over the side was sagging against the rail.

Giva had expanded her display to eight monitors. Her hands were flying across her screens as if she was conducting the action taking place on the ship.

The slavers in front of Harrington were all falling back. Most of them seemed to be climbing the rigging or ducking behind boats and deck gear. On his right, his men had stopped their rush and started working their muskets with a ragged, hasty imitation of the procedure he had drilled into them when he had decided it would be a useful skill if they ever actually boarded a ship. They would never load and fire like three-shots-to-the-minute redcoats but they were doing well enough for a combat against a gang who normally fought unarmed primitives.

The slaver captain—Captain Zachary?—was standing on the front deckhouse, just behind the rail. He stared at Harrington across the heads of the slavers who were scattered between them and Harrington realized he was pulling a rod out of the pistol he was holding in his left hand.

It was one of those moments when everything around you seems to stand still. Harrington's cutlass dropped out of his hand. He reached for the pistol stuck in his belt. He pulled it out and cocked it—methodically, with no haste—with the heel of his left hand.

On the deckhouse, Zachary had poured a dab of powder into the firing pan without taking his eyes off Harrington. He cocked the gun with his thumb and clutched it in a solid two handed grip as he raised it to the firing position.

"Look at that!" Emory said. "Are you getting that, Giva? They're facing each other like a pair of duelists."

If this had been a movie, Emory realized, the director would have captured the confrontation between Harrington and Zachary from at least three angles—one long shot to establish that they were facing each other, plus a closeup for each combatant. How did you work it when you were shooting the real thing and you couldn't re-enact it several times with the camera placed in different positions? He turned his head and peered at Giva's screens.

Giva's hands were hopping across her screens. She had centered the gunfight in a wideview, high angle shot in the second screen in her top row.

Zachary's hands flew apart. The tiny figure on Giva's screen sagged. The life size figure standing on the real ship clutched at his stomach with both palms.

The captain of the slaver received a mortal bullet wound during the fray, Harrington had written. *His removal from the melee soon took the fight out of our adversaries.* There had been no mention that Harrington himself had fired the decisive shot.

"Is that all you got?" Emory said. "That one long shot?"

He had searched her screens twice, looking for a closeup of the duel. Half of Giva's screens seemed to be focused on the slaves.

Giva jabbed at her number three screen. Emory glanced at the scene on the ship and saw the African woman Harrington had shoved aside stiffening as if she was having a fit. The image on the screen zoomed to a closeup and the camera glimpsed a single glassy eye before the woman's head slumped forward.

Giva pulled the camera back and framed the body sprawling on the deck. The woman's only garment had been a piece of blue cloth she had wrapped around her breasts and hips. The big wound just above her left breast was clearly visible.

"You got him, sir! Right in the bastard's stomach!"

Bobby Dawkins was moving into a position on Harrington's right. He had a raised cutlass in his right hand and he was waving a pistol with his left.

More men took their places beside Dawkins. Nobody was actually stepping *between* Harrington and the enemy but they were all making some effort to indicate they were willing to advance with their captain.

Harrington's hands had automatically stuffed the empty pistol into his belt. He dropped into an awkward crouch and picked up his cutlass. Most of the slavers in front of him were looking back at the deckhouse.

"You just lost the most dramatic event of the whole assault— something we'd never have guessed from the printed record."

"I can zoom in on the scene when I'm editing," Giva muttered. "I'm a pro, Emory. Let me work."

"So why do you need the closeup you just got? Why do you have so many cameras focused on the slaves? Couldn't you edit that later, too?"

Four hands were standing beside Harrington. Three more hands were standing a pair of steps behind them. Three of them had muskets pressed into their shoulders. The other four were cursing and grunting as they worked their way through various sections of the reloading drill.

"Hold your fire!" Harrington snapped. "Train your piece on a target but hold your fire."

He heard the jumpy excitement in his voice and knew it would never do. Use the voice you use when the wind is whipping across the deck, he told himself. Pretend you're thundering at the mast and Davey Clarke has the lookout.

His right arm was raising his sword above his head. "Your captain has fallen! *Yield. Lay down your arms.* Lay down your arms or I'll order my men to keep firing."

*   *   *

"Is that your idea of *scholarship*, Giva—another weepy epic about suffering victims?"

John Harrington knew he would be talking about this moment for the rest of his life. He knew he had managed to sound like a captain was supposed to sound—like a man who had absolute control of the situation, and assumed everyone who heard him would obey his orders. Now he had to see if they really would submit. He had to stand here, fully exposed to a stray shot, and give them time to respond.

Captain Zachary was slumping against the railing of the deckhouse with his hands clutching his stomach. The two slavers who were standing directly in front of him had turned toward Harrington when they had heard his roar. Their eyes settled on the muskets leveled at their chests.

Zachary raised his head. He muttered something Harrington couldn't understand. One of the slavers immediately dropped to one knee. He placed his pistol on the deck.

"The captain says to surrender," the sailor yelled. "He says get it over with."

Harrington lowered his sword. He pushed himself across the deck—it was one of the hardest things he had ever done—and picked up the musket.

"You have my sincerest thanks, Captain Zachary. You have saved us all much discomfort."

"This is *my* project, Emory. I was given complete control of the cameras and the final product. Do you have any idea what you and the whole chrono bureaucracy would look like if I handed in my resignation because you tried to bully me while I was doing my job?"

"I'm not trying to bully you. You're the one with the power in this situation. No one has to draw me a power flowchart. I'm got my own record of the dueling incident. Anybody who looks at my recording—or yours for that matter—can see you've ignored a dramatic, critical event and focused on a peripheral incident."

"Don't you think those *niggers* deserve a little attention, too? Do you think they're having a fun time caught between two groups of money hungry berserkers?"

*   *   *

Dawkins was picking up the slavers' weapons as they collected near the starboard rail. Five other hands were aiming their muskets over the slavers' heads. Harrington had positioned the musket men six paces from their potential targets—close enough they couldn't miss, far enough none of their prisoners could convince themselves they could engage in a rush before the muskets could fire.

The regulations said the slavers had to be transported to *Sparrow*. The prize crew he assigned to the slaver would have enough trouble looking after the Africans. How many prisoners could he put in each boatload as they made the transfer, given the number of men he could spare for guard duty? He could put the prisoners in irons, of course. But that might be too provocative. They had been operating in a milieu in which chains were associated with slavery and racial inferiority.

He turned to Terry, who had taken up a position behind the musket men. "Keep an eye on things, Mr. Terry. I think it's time I ventured into the hold."

The world around the space/time bubble turned black—the deepest blackness Emory had ever experienced. They had known it could happen at any time—they had even been exposed to simulations during their pre-location training—but the reality still made him freeze. There was nothing outside the bubble. *Nothing.*

The world snapped back. A male slave near the front of the ship was staring their way with his mouth gaping. He gestured with a frantic right hand and the elderly man beside him squinted in their direction.

Harrington had known the hold would stink. Every officer who had ever served in the West African squadron agreed on that. He had picked up the stench when the boat had approached the ship's side but he had been too preoccupied to react to it. Now his stomach turned as soon as he settled his feet on the ladder.

In theory, the slavers were supposed to wash their cargo down, to fight disease and keep it alive until they could take their profit. In practice, nothing could eliminate the stink of hundreds of bodies pressed into their storage shelves like bales of cotton.

The noise was just as bad as the odor. Every captive in the hold seemed to be jabbering and screaming. The slaves in a cargo could come from every section of the continent. They were brought to the coast from the places where they had been captured—or bought from some native chief who had taken them prisoner during a tribal war—and assembled in big compounds before they were sold to the European slave traders. It would be a miracle if fifty of them spoke the same language.

He paused at the bottom of the ladder and stared at the patch of blue sky over the hatch. He was the commander of a British warship. Certain things were required.

He unhooked the lamp that hung beside the ladder and peered into the din. White eyes stared at him out of the darkness. A glance at the captives he saw told him Captain Zachary had adapted one of the standard plans. Each slave had been placed with his back between the legs of the slave behind him.

He had been listening to descriptions of slave holds since he had been a midshipman. He had assumed he had been prepared. The slaves had been arranged on three shelves, just as he had expected. They would spend most of the voyage staring at a ceiling a few inches above their faces. The passage that ran down the center of the hold was only a little wider than his shoulders.

"We have encountered a space/time instability," the hal said. "I must remind you an abort is strongly recommended."

"We have to stay," Emory said. "We haven't captured the liberation of the slaves. There's no finale."

The mission rules were clear. Two flickers and the hal would automatically abort. One, and they could stay if they thought it was worth the risk.

No one knew if those rules were necessary. The bureaucrats had established them and their electronic representative would enforce them. Time travel was a paradox and an impossibility. Intelligent people approached it with all the caution they would confer on a bomb with an unknown detonating mechanism.

Giva kept her eyes focused on her screens. If she voted with him, they would stay. If they split their vote, the hal would implement the "strong recommendation" it had received from its masters.

The slave who had pointed at them seemed to have been the only person who had seen the instability. There was no indication anyone else had noticed the apparition that had flickered beside the hull.

"I think we should stay," Giva said. "For now."

"The decision will be mandatorily reconsidered once every half hour. A termination may be initiated at any time."

Harrington made himself walk the entire length of the passage. He absorbed the odor. He let the clamor bang on his skull. He peered into the shelves on both sides every third step. He couldn't make his men come down here if he wasn't willing to do it himself.

On the deck, he had yielded to a flicker of sympathy for Zachary. Stomach wounds could inflict a painful slow death on their victims. Now he hoped Zachary took a whole month to die. And stayed fully conscious up to the last moment.

He marched back to the ladder with his eyes fixed straight ahead. He had lost his temper in the boat when he had seen Zachary's cutthroats using their captives as human shields. It had been an understandable lapse but it couldn't happen twice in the same day. His ship and his crew depended on his judgment.

Terry glanced at him when he assumed his place on the deck. Most of the slaver's crew had joined the cluster of prisoners. Some of them even looked moderately cheerful. They all knew the court at Freetown would set them free within a month at the most. An occasional incarceration was one of the inconveniences of their trade.

"There should be at least four hundred," Harrington said. "Two thousand pounds minimum. And the value of the ship."

Emory made a mental calculation as he watched the first boatload of prisoners crawl toward the *Sparrow*. At the rate the boat was moving, given the time it had taken to load it, they were going to sit here for at least two more hours.

Giva was devoting half her screens to the crew and half to the Africans but he knew he would look like a fool if he objected. The crew were stolidly holding their guns on their prisoners. The Africans were talking among themselves. The two Africans who were chained on either side of the fallen woman had dropped to their knees beside her.

The moment when the slaves would be brought into the sunlight was the moment Emory considered the emotional climax of the whole episode. He had been so enthusiastic when he described it during their planning sessions that Peter LeGrundy had told him he sounded like he had already seen it.

I ordered the liberated captives brought to the deck as circumstances allowed, Harrington had written. *They did not fully comprehend their change in status, and I could not explain it. Our small craft does not contain a translator among its complement. But the sight of so many souls rescued from such a terrible destiny stimulated the deepest feelings of satisfaction in every heart capable of such sentiments.*

"You think we could press this lad, captain? We could use some of that muscle."

Harrington turned his head. He had decided he should let the men standing guard take a few minutes rest, one at a time. Dawkins had wandered over the deck to the Africans and stopped in front of a particularly muscular specimen.

"I wouldn't get too close if I were you," Harrington said. "We still haven't given him any reason to think we're his friends."

Dawkins raised his hands in mock fright. He scurried back two steps and Harrington let himself yield to a smile.

"We'd get a sight more than five pounds for you if we took you to Brazil," Dawkins said to the African. "A nigger like you would fetch three hundred clean if he scowled at white people like that for the rest of his black life."

Giva was smiling again. She hadn't said anything about the way the British sailors used the word *nigger* but Emory was certain she was noting every use she recorded. Emory had first encountered the word when he had started collecting memoirs and letters penned by men who had served in the anti-slavery patrol. He had assumed it was simply a derivative of the River Niger or a corruption of the French for black. He had been very surprised when Peter LeGrundy had told him it was a pejorative that had once been associated with a deep contempt for dark-skinned humans. Peter had claimed the British tended to think up insulting terms for every kind of foreigner they met, including Europeans.

"Frenchmen were called frogs," Peter had said. "Apparently because there was some belief they were especially fond of eating frogs. People from Asian countries were called wogs—an ironic acronym for Worthy Oriental Gentlemen."

Harrington watched the next to last boatload pull away from the slaver. The mob of prisoners had been reduced to a group of seven. Three of the prisoners were crouching beside their captain and offering him sips of water and occasional words of encouragement.

"Mr. Terry—will you please take a party below and bring about fifty of the unfortunates on deck? Concentrate on women and children. We don't have the strength to handle too many restless young bucks."

"Your ancestor doesn't seem to have much confidence in his ability to handle the animals," Giva said. "What do they call the African women? Does?"

"If you will do a little research before you edit your creation," Emory said, "I believe you'll discover *British* young men were called young bucks, too. It was just a term for young men with young attitudes. They would have called *you* a restless young buck if you'd been born male, Giva."

Harrington hadn't tried black women yet. His sexual experience had been limited to encounters with the kind of females who lifted their skirts for sailors in the Italian and South American ports he had visited on his first cruises. Bonfors claimed black women were more ardent than white women but Bonfors liked to talk. It had been Harrington's experience that most of his shipmates believed *all* foreign women were more ardent than their English counterparts.

Some of the women Terry's men were ushering on deck looked like they were younger than his sisters. Several were carrying infants. Most of them were wearing loose bits of cloth that exposed their legs and arms and other areas civilized women usually covered.

Harrington had read William Pitt's great speech on the abolition of the slave trade when he had been a boy, and he had read it again when his uncle had advised him the Admiralty had agreed to give him this command. There had been a time, Pitt had argued, when the inhabitants of ancient Britain had been just as savage and uncivilized as the inhabitants of modern Africa, "a time when even human sacrifices were offered on this island."

In those days, Pitt had suggested, some Roman senator could have pointed to *British barbarians* and predicted "*There* is a people that will never rise to civilization—here is a people destined never to be free—a people without the understanding necessary for the attainment of useful arts, depressed by the hand of nature below the level of the human species, and created to form a supply of slaves for the rest of the world."

The women in front of him might be barbarians. But they had, as Pitt had said, the potential to rise to the same levels the inhabitants of Britain had achieved. They had the right to live in freedom, so they might have the same opportunity to develop.

A woman sprawled on the deck as she emerged from the hatch. Two of the hands were pulling the captives through the opening. Two were probably pushing them from below.

One of the sailors on the deck bent over the fallen woman. His hand closed over her left breast.

"Now there's a proper young thing," the sailor said.

The sailor who was working with him broke out in a smile. "I can't say I'd have any objection to spending a few days on *this* prize crew."

The officer who was supposed to be supervising the operation—the gunnery officer, Mr. Terry—was standing just a step away. John Harrington had been watching the slaves stumble into the sunlight but now he turned toward the bow and eyed the seven prisoners lounging in front of the forward deckhouse.

The next African out of the hatch was a scrawny boy who looked like he might be somewhere around seven or eight, in Emory's unpracticed judgment. The woman who followed him—his mother?—received a long stroke on the side of her hip as she balanced herself against the roll of the ship.

"The African males don't seem to be the only restless young bucks," Giva said. "These boys have been locked up in that little ship for several weeks now, as I remember it."

"It has been one half hour since your last mandatory stay/go decision," the hal said. "Do you wish to stay or go, Mr. FitzGordon?"

"Stay."

"Do you wish to stay or go, Ms. Lombardo?"

"Stay, of course. We're getting some interesting insights into the attractions of African cruises."

Harrington ran his eyes over the rigging of the slaver. He should pick the most morally fastidious hands for the prize crew. But who could that be? Could any of them resist the opportunity after all these months at sea?

He could proclaim strict rules, of course. And order Terry to enforce them. But did he really want to subject his crew to the lash and the chain merely because they had succumbed to the most natural of urges? They were good men. They had just faced bullets and cannon balls to save five hundred human souls from the worst evil the modern world inflicted on its inhabitants.

And what if some of the women were willing? What if some of them offered themselves for money?

He could tell Terry to keep carnal activity to a minimum. But wouldn't that be the same as giving him permission to let the men indulge? He was the captain. Anything he said would have implications.

"Mr. Terry. Will you come over here, please?"

Harrington was murmuring but the microphones could still pick up the conversation.

"I'm placing you in command of the prize, Mr. Terry. I am entrusting its cargo to your good sense and decency."

"I understand," Terry said.

"These people may be savages but they are still our responsibility."

Emory nodded. Harrington was staring at the two men working the hatch as he talked. The frown on his face underlined every word he was uttering.

"That should take care of that matter," Emory said.

Giva turned away from her screens. "You really think that little speech will have an effect, Emory?"

"Is there any reason to think it won't? He won't be riding with the prize crew. But that lieutenant knows what he's supposed to do."

"It was a standard piece of bureaucratic vagueness! It was exactly the kind of thing slot-fillers always say when they want to put a fence around their precious little careers."

"It was just as precise as it needed to be, Giva. Harrington and his officers all come from the same background. That lieutenant knows exactly what he's supposed to do. He doesn't need a lot of detail."

"When was the last time you held a job? I've been dealing with *managers* all my life. They always say things like that. The only thing you know when they're done is that you're going to be the one who gets butchered if anything goes wrong."

Harrington stood by the railing as the last group of prisoners took their places in the boat. A babble of conversation rang over the deck. The African captives they had brought out of the hold had mingled with the captives who had been used as shields and they were all chattering away like guests at a lawn party.

It was an exhilarating sight. He had never felt so completely satisfied with the world. Five hours ago the people standing on the deck had been crowded into the hell below decks, with their future lives reduced to weeks of torment in the hold, followed by years of brutal servitude when they finally made land. Now they merely had to endure a three or four day voyage to the British colony in Freetown. Half of them would probably become farmers in the land around Freetown. Some would join British regiments. Many would go to the West Indies as laborers—but they would be indentured laborers, not slaves, free to take up their own lives when they had worked off their passage. A few would even acquire an education in the schools the missionaries had established in Freetown and begin their own personal rise toward civilization.

He had raised the flag above the slaver with his own hands. Several of the Africans had pointed at it and launched into excited comments when it was only a third of the way up the mast. He could still see some of them pointing and obviously explaining its significance to the newcomers. Some of them had even pointed at *him*. Most liberated slaves came from the interior. The captives who came from the coast would know about the anti-slavery patrol. They would understand the significance of the flag and the blue coat.

"We're all loaded and ready, sir."

Harrington turned away from the deck. The last prisoner had settled into his seat in the boat.

He nodded at Terry and Terry nodded back. The hands had managed to slip in a few more pawings under the guise of being helpful, but Terry seemed to have the overall situation under control.

"She's your ship, Mr. Terry. I'll send you the final word on your prize crew as soon as I've conferred with Mr. Bonfors."

*   *   *

"It looks to me like it's about time we hopped for home," Giva said.

"Now? He's only brought one load of slaves on deck."

"You don't really think he's going to decorate the deck with more Africans, do you? Look at my screens. I'm getting two usable images of your ancestor returning to his ship. It's a high feel closure. All we need is a sunset."

"There's five hundred people in that hold. Don't you think he's going to give the rest of them a chance to breathe?"

"He exaggerated his report. Use your head, Emory. Would you go through all the hassle involved in controlling five hundred confused people when you knew they were only four or five days away from Freetown?"

"You are deliberately avoiding the most important scene in the entire drama. We'll never know what happened next if we go now."

"You're clinging to a fantasy. We're done. It's time to go. Hal—I request relocation to home base."

"I have a request for relocation to home base. Please confirm."

"I do not confirm. I insist that we—"

"Request confirmed, Hal. Request confirmed."

Time stopped. The universe blinked. A technology founded on the best contemporary scientific theories did something the best contemporary scientific theories said it couldn't do.

The rig dropped onto the padded stage in Transit Room One. The bubble had disappeared. Faces were peering at them through the windows that surrounded the room.

Gina jabbed her finger at the time strip mounted on the wall. They had been gone seven minutes and thirty-eight seconds local time.

"We were pushing it," Gina said. "We were pushing it more than either of us realized."

The average elapsed local time was three minutes—a fact they had both committed to memory the moment they had heard it during their first orientation lecture. The bump when they hit the stage had seemed harder than the bumps they had experienced during training, too. The engineers always set the return coordinates for a position two meters above the stage —a precaution that placed the surface of the stage just outside the margin of error and assured the passengers they wouldn't relocate *below* it. They had come home extra late and extra high. Gina would have some objective support for her decision to return.

The narrow armored hatch under the time strip swung open. An engineer hopped through it with a medic right behind her.

"Is everything all right?"

"I can't feel anything malfunctioning," Giva said. "We had a flicker about two hours before we told Hal to shoot us home."

Emory ripped off his seat belt. He jumped to his feet and the medic immediately dropped into his soothe-the-patient mode. "You really should sit down, Mr. FitzGordon. You shouldn't stand up until we've checked you out."

The soft, controlled tones only added more points to the spurs driving Emory's rage. Giva was sprawling in her chair, legs stretched in front of her, obviously doing her best to create the picture of the relaxed daredevil who had courageously held off until the last minute. And now the medic was treating him like he was some kind of disoriented patient....

He swung toward the medic and the man froze when he saw the hostility on Emory's face. He was a solid, broad shouldered type with a face that probably looked pleasant and experienced when he was helping chrononauts disembark. Now he slipped into a stance that looked like a slightly disguised on guard.

"You're back, Mr. FitzGordon. Everything's okay. We'll have you checked out and ready for debriefing before you know it."

Peter LeGrundy crouched through the hatch. He flashed his standard-issue smile at the two figures on the rig and Emory realized he had to get himself under control.

"So how did it go?" Peter said. "Did you have a nice trip?"

Emory forced his muscles to relax. He lowered his head and settled into the chair as if he was recovering from a momentary lapse—the kind of thing any normal human could feel when he had just violated the laws of physics and traveled through three centuries of time. He gave the medic a quick thumbs up and the medic nodded.

He had his own record of the event. He had Giva's comments. Above all, he had Peter LeGrundy. And Peter LeGrundy's ambitions. He could cover every grant Peter could need for the rest of Peter's scholarly career if he had to. The battle wasn't over. Not yet.

You need the creatives. The creatives need your money.

*   *   *

I ordered the liberated captives brought to the deck as circumstances allowed. They did not fully comprehend their change in status, and I could not explain it. Our small craft does not contain a translator among its complement. But the sight of so many souls rescued from such a terrible destiny stimulated the deepest feelings of satisfaction in every heart capable of such sentiments.

Two well placed candles illuminated the paper on John Harrington's writing desk without casting distracting shadows. The creak of *Sparrow's* structure created a background that offered him a steady flow of information about the state of his command.

He lowered his pen. He had been struggling with his report for almost two hours. The emotions he had ignored during the battle had flooded over him as soon as he had closed the door of his cabin. The pistol that had roared in his face had exploded half a dozen times.

He shook his head and forced out a sentence advising the Admiralty he had placed Mr. Terry in command of the prize. He had already commended Terry's gunnery and his role in the assault. He had given Bonfors due mention. Dawkins and several other hands had been noted by name. The dead and the wounded had been properly honored.

It had been a small battle by the standards of the war against Napoleon. A skirmish really. Against an inept adversary. But the bullets had been real. Men had died. *He* could have died. He had boarded an enemy ship under fire. He had led a headlong assault at an enemy line. He had exchanged shots with the captain of the enemy.

The emotions he was feeling now would fade. One hard, unshakeable truth would remain. He had faced enemy fire and done his duty.

He had met the test. He had become the kind of man he had read about when he was a boy.

CPSIA information can be obtained at www.ICGtesting.com
Printed in the USA
LVOW10s1049260415

436146LV00002B/403/P

9 781617 209437